DATE DUE		
JAN 0 9 1997		
FEB 1 2 1997		
MAR 2 0 '97		
FEB 26 '99		
JAN 12 '01		
MAR 05 '01		

3/01 - to med

8/96

01 ✓

Jackson

County

Library

System

HEADQUARTERS:

413 W. Main

Medford, Oregon 97501

GAYLORD M2G

A Dangerous Happiness

Hazel Hucker

St. Martin's Press   New York

A THOMAS DUNNE BOOK.
An imprint of St. Martin's Press

Library of Congress Cataloging-in-Publication Data

Hucker, Hazel.
A dangerous happiness / by Hazel Hucker.
p.   cm.
"A Thomas Dunne book."
ISBN 0-312-14307-9
I. Title.
PR6058.U27D36   1996
823'.914—dc20   96-5216   CIP

First published in Great Britain by Judy Piatkus (Publishers) Ltd

First U.S. Edition: July 1996

10   9   8   7   6   5   4   3   2   1

In loving memory of my dear son Nicholas

Chapter 1

Louise Bennett and Simon Fennell were neither married nor engaged, yet they celebrated the anniversaries of their lives together with all the sentimentality of a settled married couple: the day they met, the day they first made love, the day they moved into their little terraced house together. That is to say, Simon arranged the celebrations and Louise fell in with his arrangements, as she generally did.

The twelfth of January was the occasion of the second of these anniversaries, the day that they had discovered, to their mutual amazement and delight, a sexual compatibility that neither had found elsewhere. As she left Notting Hill Gate underground station to walk swiftly home after work on that same date five years later, Louise scarcely noticed the sharpness of the evening's developing frost, the way her travelling companions shrugged themselves deeper into their coats and scarves as they emerged into the night. She had an interior glow of her own, a glow of ambition achieved, that was warming her. Clasped in her hands were a present and a card for Simon, and in her head she was rehearsing the words with which she would tell him how tonight's would be a double celebration, anticipating too, with secret exhilaration, commemorating it later in the manner most proper to such an occasion.

She let herself into the house with her latch-key, went into the long double living room, and stopping, startled, saw Simon straighten himself from lighting the candles on the dining table to look across at her, alert, tense almost with the triumph of his surprise. In the soft light all was beautiful:

glasses glinted, a dozen red roses flaunted themselves from a white vase, the curtains were drawn, the fire flickering; the CD player sending out the gentle sounds of Mozart's flute and harp concerto. Yet as she took in the scene it struck her as almost too perfect, like a cliché seduction scene – but she'd been seduced five years ago. Simon was a reasonably domesticated man, helpful in the house and a competent cook, but it was outside his normal style to create an ambiance like this. Had someone from work telephoned and let drop her news? No, she couldn't believe it. She had only just been told and she'd not discussed it, keeping it for her lover's ears first.

Before she could speak, Simon seized her, kissed her, wished her a happy anniversary, and offered her a glass of Chablis. He said, pouring, one arm still round her: 'A special evening, darling, very special!'

'I know. And you've made the place look amazing. Here, I bought you a present.'

He took the package, but laid it unopened on the table. 'I have a present for you, too, but let's save them till later. Drinks first, then food. I'm cooking beef Stroganoff and I'm starving.'

'All right. Just let me take off my coat and get comfortable.' She took a sip from her glass, nearly choked because his arms were so tight about her, and backed away, feeling overwhelmed, unaccountably nervous.

Disposing of her coat, scarf, gloves and smart winter boots upstairs in their bedroom, she took off her office suit, swapping it for a silk blouse and the velvet pants which Simon said suited her neat bottom and long legs so well, pulled on a pair of Bruno Magli shoes with carved and gilded lowish heels, shoes which had been worth their expensive price both for their good looks and their comfort, and glanced in her dressing table mirror as she dabbed scent behind her ears. Her appearance was as Simon liked it, her dark hair smooth and gleaming, her dark eyes gleaming too, in the shadow of her lashes. Her skin was normally clear and pale – 'Sallow from London's polluted air!' Simon would say, his voice disapproving – but tonight her cheeks were flushed from frost and excitement. 'Yes,' she told that other self in the glass, 'you look sleek and sexy – and successful.'

Downstairs, she found Simon pouring himself more wine.

'My wonderful girl!' he said, lifting his glass to her and drinking. 'Listen, Louise, tonight it's a double celebration!'

'A double celebration?' she said, taken aback that he knew, disappointed that she had not been the one to tell him, yet flattered by his excitement. 'But how did you hear . . ? Who told you?'

But he was not attending, words were spilling from him: 'I heard this morning . . . I've done it, Loulou, I'm moving to a firm . . . you could say they head-hunted me . . . it's a tremendous opportunity – they've a wide variety of work – I can still hardly believe it! A top name in Hampshire, they are, Shergold & Stent.'

A sense of shock, a feeling of nausea. 'What do you mean? What are you talking about?'

'I was going to tell you before, but then I thought, No, if it doesn't come off it's a double disappointment, you and me. But it has!'

And then she heard him babbling on, felt his words flowing over her like water in a fast stream, cold water, icy water, washing away all her own triumph, drowning her dreams. Words she didn't want to hear came and went through the rushing in her ears.

It was a firm of accountants in Basingstoke, successful, expanding . . . branches in Winchester and Andover. The chance of a partnership – he'd have had years to wait in London. They could live in a village . . . an old cottage . . . relish the glories of the changing seasons . . .

Louise had always understood that Simon yearned for a rural life. He had been brought up in a country town, gone to a prep school and minor public school located in the midst of fields, gone on cross-country runs before breakfast, watching the sun rise over dewy meadows, seeing the pheasants and the partridges by the hedges and the shy deer among the trees. He had often spoken of it, lying in bed on a Sunday morning. And he'd cadged weekends with friends in the country quite shamelessly. He had come to live in London purely for the career prospects, for financial advancement. To him London had about as much appeal as a main-line station concourse: wherever he went people were strangers, foreigners travelling to some distant destination, the pavements were squalid, vehicles crawled past him in a haze of foul emissions, his clothes became dirty, and the need to be away from its people and its pollution became a craving that must be appeased. That was what he was saying now.

'. . . Just think, Louise, how it will feel to have pure air and birdsong to come home to, instead of an atmosphere filled with dust and chemicals, and all the unending unnatural roar of men and their machines. It's what I've always longed for.'

He stopped at last, breathless, awaiting her congratulations. There was silence. She was horror-struck.

'But I don't want to leave London,' she said and stopped, staring at him.

'You'll come to love Hampshire,' he said, quickly, confidently. 'You think it'll be dull, but it won't. The villages are friendly, close-knit communities; you'll find yourself involved in all sorts of activities in no time, with dozens of new friends.'

She didn't want new friends, she wanted her old friends, here, in Notting Hill. The quiet river valleys and the downs of Hampshire were nothing to her; she revelled in the hordes of people in London, in the brilliantly lit shops of Oxford Street and Bond Street and Regent Street, in the endless colour and noise and movement. She loved the blowing dusty warmth of the tubes, the friendly jolting of the red London buses, the diesel chug of the manoeuvring taxis. Above all she loved her work.

'It's an opening I can't turn down,' he added firmly. 'It's a great compliment to have been offered it. Aren't you going to congratulate me?'

'Congratulations.' Louise gave him a wan smile. 'On your achievement. If it's really what you want. You've done well.' She had to force the words from her mouth, like a guest at a dinner party compelled to praise her hostess's culinary skills while secretly looking for somewhere to spit the horrid offering.

'Thank you. Yup, I feel really good about it.'

There was a pause before she said: 'Oh, Simon, I'd be more enthusiastic if I could, but you see there's a difficulty. I was offered something today, too.'

4

'You were? What?'

'The trustees have asked me to do a series of lunchtime lectures.'

The Holbrooke Collection, where Louise worked, was famous for its mid-week lectures. Those who gave them were acknowledged experts in its paintings, its furniture, its porcelain, its treasures from the near and far East, they were men and women who had immersed themselves for years in research in their subject. Those who attended them were frequently experts themselves, liable to quiz the lecturers on abstruse points of artistic development, of history and provenance. To have been asked to contribute made Louise at once exultant and terrified.

Her success had been hard earned. She had gone straight to work from school, her A-levels in English, History of Art and Art together with a type-writing course securing her a secretarial post. Her devotion to her work together with a certain steely determination had brought swift promotion to personal assistant to the director and on to a wide range of administrative duties. It was then, in a period of bitterness over the limitations put on her career by her parents' inability to fund her through a degree course, that she had met Simon. As one who had proceeded as far as an MSc at the London School of Economics before embarking on his professional qualifications, he sympathised, but more, he sensibly suggested Birkbeck College and a History of Art degree, taken part-time. Four years of evening study and Louise found herself with a good honours degree and infinitely widened horizons. Her enthusiasm for her work at the Holbrooke Collection increasing with her scholarship, she took up detailed research into the Collection's treasures for the sheer joy of the knowledge. Today's offer from the trustees was her reward.

'Well. Well done!' Simon blinked. 'What a surprise! How much will you be paid for this?'

'They don't actually pay you a salary. You're given a small fee, an honorarium.' She named the amount.

'But that's an insult.'

'No, it isn't. Trust an accountant to think only in terms of money. It's an honour, Simon. An honour.'

'Sorry. Yes, I know it is. It's just . . . I want the best for you . . .' His voice trailed away.

There was a pause. They stood staring at each other.

'Well,' he said. 'It's great to know we're both successful. Great.'

Another pause, while they both thought how inadequate the words were.

'I'll cook dinner,' he said finally. 'We can talk while we eat. Everything's prepared, it'll only take a few minutes.' He disappeared.

Louise sat down by the fire. The cold she had ignored earlier had now reached her bones. She was not a natural optimist and her thoughts on the options available to her were full of gloom. She struggled not to dissolve into demeaning tears.

When Simon came back into the room with the food she spoke with difficulty: 'You know, we don't have to move house. Wait, see how you like the new firm. You could commute.'

'Commute to Basingstoke?' He almost dropped a dish of rice. His voice was appalled.

'Why not? You'd always get a comfortable seat on the train – you'd be going in the opposite direction from the average commuter.'

'You must be joking. That would be the worst of all possible worlds.'

'Oh no,' she said, anger rising now. 'Commuting from some hopeless little Hampshire village to the Holbrooke Collection would be far worse. Yet you'd cheerfully foist that on me!'

They were ladling food on to their plates, eyes averted one from the other. Simon stopped, dropping the spoon; his hand caught her wrist.

'No, I wouldn't. You've forgotten the most important thing. We're trying for a baby. We want to have a family – remember? And to give it a good life!' His voice had risen and taken on a scolding note; now she heard its tone alter, almost heard the mental brakes screeching as he stopped himself. 'Listen, love,' he said slowly, 'if you want to go on working for the Holbrooke people when we're first in

6

Hampshire, well, why not? Until the baby comes, that is. But by then you'd have at least six months of the lecturing under your belt, your achievements wouldn't have been wasted.'

Silence. There was a flaw in his argument, but one she dared not reveal. Simon was trying for a baby, Louise was not. Far from abandoning the contraceptive pill, she had evaded arguments by taking it each day at work with her morning coffee rather than in bed at night. She was determined to be successful at work, to enjoy a stimulating career. She refused to have it interrupted now.

It was during her childhood that she had learned to avoid unpleasant arguments by quietly going her own way. The parents of six children never have the time to check on all their doings. Her apparent submissiveness had paid off then; now, for the first time, she found herself caught in a trap of her own making. When Simon had waxed passionate on the subject of country living, she had smiled sweetly and spoken of a weekend cottage: 'Perhaps in a few years' time, when we can afford it.' When he argued equally strongly in favour of having children before they were thirty, she said reproachfully: 'But we're not married. I believe in full commitment before anyone should embark on a family.' Simon had brushed that aside: 'We'll have a big party and go to the register office when you're pregnant – I've always fancied a burgeoning bride!' She had pleaded for more time, 'Two or three years at least!', found him obdurate, and fallen silent. She was her own woman, she would control her own destiny, but there would be no rows; she had deceived him.

She forked beef Stroganoff into her mouth and studied him: a tall young man of twenty-nine, with fairish hair cut short. His high forehead from which the hair was beginning to slip away like a duvet in the night, topped a long straight nose and a firm mouth. She liked his looks and the calm, almost austere manner concealing the sensuality that entranced her. She had liked his dedication to his work and his ambition, too – until now.

'This Stroganoff is delicious,' she said politely.

'Thank you,' he said, equally formal. 'I wanted it to be good for you, for our special occasion.'

The flavour should have turned to ashes in her mouth. But

it didn't, it stayed superb. She chewed and swallowed, chewed again.

'And do I have any say in this move to Hampshire?' Her tone was ambiguous – half protest, half query.

'Of course you do,' he replied.

'And that say must be yes, mustn't it?'

'Well, no, it doesn't have to . . .' He stopped as he saw the abyss opening before him. 'That is, I mean, of course I hope it'll be yes. I want you to be pleased for me, I want us to agree . . .'

'Just tell me this, then.' She speared him with her dark eyes. 'Have you accepted the offer?'

A quick breath. 'Yes. Yes, I have.'

Anger rose up in a great swamping wave; she fought for breath, for words. 'You what? You bastard! Of all the mean under-handed . . . You went behind my back and settled everything – and then you have the nerve to tell me that I have a say in it?' She jumped up from the table with such vigour that her chair fell crashing to the floor behind her.

'You do. I could telephone them tomorrow and cancel my acceptance. *If* you feel so very strongly about it.' He leaned from his chair to pick hers up and set it on its feet, not taking his eyes from her face. 'Do you?'

'Yes, I bloody well do!' She leaned over the table towards him, her fists clenched. He sat very still. 'Oh, hell! Oh, sod you, Simon . . . I don't want you to throw up something you want so much. But why couldn't it have been in London?' She thumped the table and the wineglasses jiggled. She fell back into her chair, her voice choked with tears of fury.

'Because it isn't, that's why. Because that isn't what you want, is it?'

'No. It isn't. But I didn't know you were going to be given this offer of lectures. I thought you were on a plateau, if I can put it like that, from which you could have children, climb again afterwards. So my move would be no bomb-shell. I'm as shocked at what's happened as you.'

She grabbed a tablespoon and piled his plate with all that remained of the dishes he'd cooked. On top of it she scraped the congealing remains from her own plate. 'Eat it!' she ordered. 'You said you were hungry, so you eat the bloody lot!'

8

His eyes fell. Meekly he ate. She watched his every mouthful, watched him stuff himself to bloating point with his celebratory food.

Finished, slightly pale, he suppressed a belch and said: 'Thank you for not hurling the old gender wars at me. At least.'

'Oh,' she said, 'you took that option away from me, didn't you? Helping me at Birkbeck, taking on the housework and the cooking to give me time to study, telling me I had to fulfil my potential – all that. You've done such a lot for me, how can I blame you when you grab something for yourself?' She was to blame, not he, for letting him assume that her career would shortly be broken for child-bearing.

He took their dirty plates out to the kitchen and returned carrying a bowl of fruit lavishly topped with black and white grapes. He filled their glasses again with Beaune.

Louise watched him, her smooth face not revealing the anger that continued to seethe in lancinating passion inside her head. She wanted to rage, to scream, to throw things. She loathed the thought of leaving London; the idea of commuting on overcrowded trains horrified her. And to abandon her job for babies was worse.

Whatever happened, this house would go. She loved her house fiercely; she had chosen and fashioned it, she far more than Simon. The living room was undeniably her triumph; her eyes left Simon to caress the rich mahogany of the Victorian furniture she had rescued, stained and dusty, from tawdry junk shops advertising 'Antiques'; the long wall lined with books, many of them with handsome faded leather bindings; the Tabriz rug; the old Knole sofa piled with the silk-covered cushions that a great-aunt had given her; the modern paintings she had begun lovingly and carefully to buy from small galleries. It was a thoughtfully blended whole that she could not begin to imagine transported to a country cottage.

Simon was dangling a small bunch of black grapes in front of her. He nipped one off and leaned to push it into her mouth. Then he bent to slip off her shoes. Her heart gave a curious little jump. She had almost forgotten . . . how could she have? This was a ritual they had followed all the first

9

year of their life together, derived from the night they had
first made love. He had invited her to dinner in the cramped
garden flat he shared with a friend, the friend disappearing
elsewhere. At the end of the (delicious) meal he had knelt on
the floor and, laughing, placed tiny bunches of grapes upon
her feet, her knees, her thighs, feeding them one by one to
her and to himself, interspersing them with kisses on her
lips, and also on her feet, her knees, her thighs and further
still. Her skirt had become crushed. 'Take it off!' she had
said breathlessly. He took it off, and all else besides, from
her and from himself. They gazed at each other and were not
disappointed. 'Your breasts are perfect,' he said. 'Such a
hairy chest,' she responded blissfully, 'I love a hairy man.'
'Love me, then,' he said, and they fell into each others' arms
and on to the divan. It had been an amazing experience, a
revelation. They had never slept apart since.

Her lips were closed. He pushed the grape against them
hard. 'Eat it!' he ordered, as she had done earlier. Her lips
parted. She ate. He kissed. Another grape appeared, and
another . . . He kissed her feet. She waited, wondering. He
was kneeling now: he was wooing her. She debated whether
to kick him with her stockinged toes and decided not.

He said: 'I've something to confess to you.'

'What?'

'The cottage that Maggie and Jack took us to see when we
stayed with them the weekend before last at Abbotsbridge,
the one they had the key to, that lovely seventeenth-century
one with the view of the River Test . . .'

'Yes!' she said impatiently. She remembered it perfectly
well, a brick cottage with mullioned windows under a roof
of lichened slate. She couldn't imagine why they'd been
taken there, except she supposed it was interesting to wander
through the beamed rooms and exclaim over the old bread
oven in the wall if you liked that sort of thing. Maggie, a
plump girl who strongly resembled the rounded cottage-
women with broods of small children that you saw outside
thatched cottages in Victorian water-colours, had raved over
it. 'What about it?'

'It's on the market for not much more than we'd get for
this house – prices are lower there. I've put in an offer and I

10

heard when I got home tonight that it's been accepted.'

This time she did kick – hard.

He fell lopsidedly back on his elbows and struggled up, rubbing a funny bone. She saw the desire to slap her in return enter him and be subdued.

'Don't bloody ever do that again!' he said.

The sound of their heavy breathing filled the room.

'You said you liked it. You thought it was charming.'

'For a weekend cottage maybe. When we're wealthy.'

'It's perfect. Look at it again. Look at other houses if you like. But you won't find any better.'

She studied him, their eyes met, and instead of the normal smile or mouthed kiss of acknowledgment, the contact now was a clash, a warning of danger. Beneath his calm exterior she saw a determination to match hers. Thus far and no further, his look said. This I want and will have. She could pit her will against his and he would bend to accommodate her, but he would not break. The relationship between them would break first. And yet she knew he loved her. And in the final analysis she loved him. Damn him.

She slid her feet back into her expensive shoes; how wrong they would look in a country cottage. Unsmiling, she agreed: 'I'll look at it.'

'Thank you.' Pause. 'We could go at the weekend.'

She felt terrible; she needed a drink. She picked up her glass and drained it.

He stood up to follow suit. 'We need another bottle,' he said, and went to find it.

When he returned she saw he looked unusually pale. His hand shook as he poured. He sank on to his knees beside her again and put his arms round her. 'I didn't expect it to be like this,' he said, his voice sad. 'I thought it was going to be all lovely and loving.'

'I know.' Her hand stroked his hair.

Obliquely he said as if quoting: 'We do not wish to acknowledge our friends in the fullness of their worth.'

'Not when it clashes with realising our own.'

'Men are more ruthless at using people . . . and some people are user-friendly.'

'Yes,' she said with sardonic resignation. 'That'll be me.'

'But I do recognise your worth.' He fished in his trouser pocket. 'And I have a present to show you how much.' He put a tiny cube of a parcel into her hand. 'This . . . it was all going to be part of our lovely evening. I want to rescue that.'

Louise eased off a square of gold paper and opened the box inside to reveal a ring. 'Oh!' she said. 'God, it's beautiful.'

Simon picked it out. 'Our life together is going to change. Fundamentally. Loulou, I . . . I want it to start out in the best way . . . with full commitment – all that.' He mocked himself. 'Look, I'm even on my knees. Will you marry me?'

She felt a stab of irritation at the tactlessness of his timing. But through all her rage over this evening's revelations she had never thought of leaving him; he was the only man she had ever met with whom she could contemplate spending all the days of her life. She wanted that ring, not because she was mad about the old-fashioned institution of marriage whose decline her mother so bemoaned, but because it would signify their bond.

She blew out a long cool breath and gave him a sweet smile. 'How could I resist that? Yes, all right, put it on my finger.' She kissed him, watched him ease the ring on to her hand, reached for a grape, popped it between his lips. 'Darling Simon.'

'Mm.'

'I've only got a tie for you.'

'Symbolic. I'm going to be tied to you.'

They were silent while she turned her hand this way and that admiringly. Its worth shone in blue and green flashes of light.

She asked: 'How did you know which one to buy?'

'You had a friend who got married recently. Josie. You said that her ring was perfect, except that you would prefer an emerald flanked by two diamonds, not a sapphire. I remembered.'

He cared, he had recognised her worth. But in the back of her mind there still lurked the thought that she was being manipulated.

Chapter 2

Brozie Hamilton was the first person in the village to meet Charley.

It was a typical English mid-winter morning, cold, grey and intermittently drizzling. Brozie was trudging home from the post office stores when a sporty red car, make unknown, skidded its way round the muddy bends of Rectory Lane, hit a great puddle and deluged her with water. It was the last straw in an intolerable morning of endlessly pricking straws. She gasped, glared at the dripping foul hem of her coat and her soaked shopping basket, and then let fly full-throatedly at the car's receding rear, using words, as she later confided to a friend, that she didn't like to know she knew. Running out of these, she ended weakly, breathlessly: 'You . . . you horrible thoughtless man! You careless oaf!'

The car stopped in a screech of brakes and shot backwards as fast as it had come, braking just in front of her. The car door jerked opened, a man emerged from the front seat, banged the door to, and advanced upon her. He was young and very large. Brozie stepped back nervously.

'Help!' he said, surveying her. 'Did I do all that?'

She nodded, reddening at the remembrance of her abusive yells.

'Oh dear. One inundated lady. Very sorry. Very very sorry. I didn't see that damned pond until I shot into it.' His voice was deep, assured and cheerful. He pulled a red spotted handkerchief from a trouser pocket and began to mop at her coat. 'The car was in racing mode, as usual,' he threw out.

'Quite disgraceful. I'll kick the brute!' And straightening, he aimed a sturdy shoe at a rear wheel arch.

Her heart still pumping from the irritation and shock, Brozie managed a half-smile and watched him turn his attention to her shopping.

'Only surface damage,' he said, dabbing at a packet of tea.

He must have been all of six foot three tall, and broad in proportion, or more than proportion, she thought, as she observed the bulging outline of his stomach above a constricted waistband. A great bear of a man, his height in his torso rather than his legs. A bear comfortably clad in a dilapidated Barbour jacket over a vast woolly brown pullover and brown corduroy trousers. His hair was brown and bearlike also, a thick short pelt.

'How far to your house?'

'Oh, a couple of hundred yards or so.'

'Get in,' he commanded, holding open the passenger door.

'No, no, it's perfectly all right,' she protested.

'In!' he said.

Brozie hesitated, warnings against trusting strangers jostling in her mind, pitting their weight of good sense against the lure of a lift and the relief to her arms from carrying the heavy basket. He looked all right, this man; his clothes and his voice spoke of the sort of person you could trust; he was standing there patiently waiting for her as though somehow he understood. Her boots were squelching, her feet cold. She capitulated, stooped and wriggled into the car.

She found herself sitting surprisingly near to the ground, in a car of a totally different configuration from any she had known in all her fifty-two years.

'What sort of car is this?' she asked, as the engine started into a deep snarl.

Grey-green eyes looked down at her in amazement. 'It's a Porsche.'

She began to smile. This was something new and exciting. The hedges blurred as the car powered forward, the smell of leather entranced her, the sight of the rector's jaw dropping as they passed him in the road made her bubble with amusement. In the sky the clouds parted and the low winter sun glowed

14

across the Hampshire landscape, shining along the curves of the lane, sparkling from the raindrops in the black hedgerows. The man took his hand from the wheel to gesture at the prospect before them, the oaks and sycamores standing in their bare winter beauty against the brightening sky, the ploughed fields and meadows that ran down to the river, the low hills that rolled away in blue-grey waves like a gentle sea.

'Outstanding natural beauty, that's what the pundits call it. Tremendous, isn't it?'

'Yes,' she said, enraptured herself by a fresh vision of the familiar land, 'yes, it is.' And the day that had broken so bleak and grey took on an unexpected loveliness.

When Brozie stopped him in front of her house, the last in the village, one that stood apart from the others as if in pique, he gave it an assessing stare through the car window.

'Well,' he said with a bluntness that somehow wasn't unkind, 'no outstanding natural beauty there.'

She looked at its uncompromising Victorian facade of lurid red brick and yellow diapering, and said: 'No. It's horrid. But it's cool in summer and warm in winter.' She'd been telling herself that for nearly twenty years; it didn't change the ugliness that daily offended her.

'Paint over those bricks,' he told her, 'and you'd eradicate the look of municipal lavatories. And with a honeysuckle over that nasty porch you'd have an entirely different place.'

She shook her head. 'Nice thought, but too expensive.' And she gave a long, painful, involuntary sigh at the thought of her husband's horror.

'If you think it's awful,' the man asked, 'why d'you live in it?'

'Not my choice,' Brozie said. 'My husband bought it when he married his first wife more than than thirty years ago.'

'Oh. Did she die or were they divorced?'

'She died. Multiple sclerosis.'

'And you stepped into her ghostly shoes and ghastly house. Not much fun for a bride.' His voice was matter of fact, but through its words she felt the unspoken sympathy.

'I wasn't that sort of a bride.' She snorted faintly at the memory.

Brozie had been lanky and dowdy, then as now. Her hair was mousy, her eyes a curious pale blue-green speckled like a blackbird's egg with darker spots, her skin sallow. She had never caught male eyes. After first her mother and then her father had died from long debilitating illnessess through which Brozie nursed them, she had found herself alone, on the wrong side of thirty, untrained for any reasonably remunerative job and with an income that would sustain life but little more. Shortly after her father became ill he had taken on a partner in the antiques and furniture restoration firm he ran in Winchester. When this middle-aged widower showed an interest in her, she thanked the Lord for his mercies, polished up her culinary skills, boned up on Victorian watercolours, his particular interest, and, after a courtship even she with her low expectations had found prosaic, married him and took on his house in Abbotsbridge.

Now she was an integral part of the village scene, a stalwart in the church flower-arranging team, and, until recently, organiser of the local flower show. A women given to self-deprecation, bird-lore and black gumboots, she had not been disconcerted to find that her husband had married her solely for the business; she had never expected more. She led her own life and refrained from complaint.

She was about to step out of the car when the man beside her remarked with an air of satisfaction: 'I shall be a neighbour of yours shortly.'

'Really?'

'Yes, I've always planned to live in this village. I'm taking over The Old Barn.'

For a moment she couldn't think where he meant, and then she remembered the converted eighteenth-century manor barn just off the road on the far side of the village. Its hump of rotting thatch had been an eyesore for years until a smart young architect working with a local builder had transformed the building into an eclectic mixture of the ancient and modern. This, while deplored by the establishment side of the community, did display a certain chic in the sweep of its long-paned window from beneath the re-thatched roof to the ground, and the jacuzzi that bubbled in the bathroom under the vast dark beams. 'Vulgar!' had pronounced Brozie's husband. 'But fun,' said Brozie.

She asked the young man whether he had a wife and family, because the Old Barn had four bedrooms. No, he said, but he did have a fabulous girl-friend who spent most weekends with him. Together, he boasted, they would transform the place, particularly the garden. And he drew a word-picture of how they would change the bramble and thistle-filled paddock that surrounded the barn into a show place, speaking of wide lawns and brick paths, of lavender and old roses, of sweet-smelling herbs and flowering trees. They would have an Open Day with Teas in the summer. He had an instinct for words that illuminated his ideas, and Brozie was happily involved in planning with him the bulbs he would plant for next spring, snowdrops and crocuses and great clumps of narcissus, 'Oh, and fritillaries too, under the trees!' when, beyond them, the front door opened. In the rigid box of the porch an elderly man appeared. He was short and stocky, with grey hair and a grey skin. He wore grey clothes, too, a cardigan hanging limp from his hunched shoulders.

'What's going on?' he wanted to know as he advanced down the path towards the car. 'Why are you sitting in that car, Brozie? What's the problem?' A sharp Adam's apple darted up and down his crepey throat as if it would slice through it.

Brozie and the man both got out of the car. 'My husband,' Brozie said to him in flat tones, 'Hubert Hamilton. I can't introduce you, I don't know your name.'

'I'm Charley,' the young man said, smiling with wide, full lips. 'Charley St George.' He stepped forward and held out his hand to Hubert Hamilton, who ignored it.

'What are you doing with my wife? What are you hanging around here for?' The Adam's apple bobbed and lunged.

'He gave me a lift home,' Brozie intervened hastily. 'It was very kind of him.'

'Why? What d'you need a lift home for? You always walk. Being nosy, is he? Trying to see what sort of folk we are? What we've got? You're a fool, Brozie. Trust anyone. Only fools do that these days. Send him away.' He turned abruptly and made his way back indoors. From inside the house his voice came again, harsh and stiff. 'I've not had my mid-morning drink yet. Get a move on, woman.'

Brozie hesitated, looking at Charley, feeling humiliated, buttoning down her anger, hating her husband, the house, even her clothes, so dull against the big cheerful man and his flamboyant car. 'I'm sorry,' she said.

'Is he sick?' Charley asked with blunt good humour. 'Or is he sick in the head?'

'He's sick . . .' she said and stopped. Hubert had never been an easy man; the years of cancer had made him additionally irritable.

Charley stood with his hand on the car door handle, looking at her. 'I see,' he said. He lifted an eyebrow quizzically. 'Brozie. Brozie? That right? What sort of a name is that?'

'My father wanted a son to call Ambrose after his own father. I got lumbered with Ambrosine, but I couldn't pronounce it, and Brozie I've been ever since.'

He chuckled. 'It's a good name. Original. It suits you.'

Brozie stooped to collect her shopping from the car. 'I must go,' she said. Then she noticed sodden mud on its carpet. 'Oh dear,' she said apologetically, 'I'm so sorry, just look what my mucky old boots have done. I need new ones – these leak.'

Charley said: 'Hey, well, come with me. I'm going to the fishing tackle shop in Stockbridge right now.'

She stared, sure that he must be mad. Perfect strangers did not offer to take you shopping. She stood very straight, thinking how kind he was, what fun it would be to go in that exciting car again, what a break from the grey routine of her life, and yet at the same time knowing that she shouldn't accept, knowing how shocked her husband would be, how horrified and enraged by her step out of the ordinary. His vision of life rejected strangers, especially the young, particularly when they drove fast cars; it eliminated the acceptance of favours, it loathed her doing anything he had not himself decreed.

There are moments of decision that can change life's course. Many are made after days of concentrated deliberations. Other turning points pass unrecognised, innocent-seeming as a still pool in a stream. Yet beneath the surface are unseen currents, waiting to whirl their victims to a wholly different destiny. In a rare flicker of defiance against her husband, Brozie again accepted the offer of a lift, and, by doing so, without knowledge or intention, changed her life.

'All right,' she heard herself say. 'Thanks. I'll just put my shopping in the kitchen.'

Feeling almost disembodied, a spectator of her own actions, she left her basket on the kitchen table, walked into the sitting room to inform Hubert where she was going and shut the door on his protests. He could make his own coffee for once. She was struck with amazement at herself. Was this really her? Racing along the lanes in the car, catching glimpses of snowdrops in the hedgerows, seeing the flash of a green woodpecker as it crossed their path, Brozie felt euphoric. It was a wonderful day, a day like the first day of spring.

In the shop the elderly man who served her knew Charley and spoke to him by name. Brozie asked for plain black gumboots, the kind she'd always had, but Charley rejected them.

'Green wellies go with your green coat, much smarter.'

Hubert disliked green wellies; they were symbols of the wealthy, the privileged. They matched her coat exactly. She bought them.

Charley had wandered off and was trying on fishing hats. They perched on top of his massive head, ludicrously too small. He pulled faces at himself in the shop looking-glass, clowning.

'Nobody makes anything for someone of my size,' he observed. 'I'm treated as a rare species.' He stopped clowning and looked at Brozie. 'Easier for you, you've got a neat head.' He rummaged among a pile of tweed hats on the counter. 'This one is absolutely you, look!' He tossed it over, a Harris tweed with a green band.

Brozie caught it, laughing, and put it on, mocking herself in the glass as he had done. It was old-fashioned, a caricature of country wear, and yet in an extraordinary way she saw that the hat did suit her. It sat well on her greying head, giving her almost an aristocratic look, oddly rakish, the look of an eccentric dowager. Still smiling, she studied her image more closely. 'It's rather fun,' she said.

19

'Tremendous!' Charley said. 'I knew it would be.'

The elderly assistant nodded in solemn agreement. 'He's right.'

'I'll have it,' Brozie said, feeling quite mad now and not caring. She paid for the boots and the hat and put them on with a flourish. She was reluctant to part with her friendly old gumboots, but, 'Bin job!' said Charley, and out they went.

The assistant was producing boxes of clay pigeons and cartons of cartridges and putting them on the counter.

'Right,' Charley said. He opened up his Barbour and from a gamekeeper's pocket inside he tugged the biggest wad of notes Brozie had ever seen, peeling off two notes.

'Never understand why you don't use cards like everybody else,' the assistant said, counting out change.

Charley looked rueful. 'I used to, but I was always punishing the plastic, dealing it blow after blow, sending bank managers and financiers reeling. Now I pay in folding notes and eliminate the protest movements. Safer. If it isn't in my pocket, I can't spend it.'

Brozie thought him eccentric but sensible. Even Hubert would approve his care with money.

As they drove off back to Abbotsbridge she struggled to guess what sort of work Charley might do. His clothes suggested a farmer, an agricultural engineer or a vet. But the Porsche and his casual attitude to time seemed to exclude them. She couldn't work him out. She asked him.

'Me? I'm an entrepreneur . . . a businessman, if you like.'

'What sort of business?'

'More than one. Publishing. Icarus Publishing is my firm. We do one stop book services for authors – a really up-to-the-minute development. They pay, we publish as they want it. Local history, poetry, fiction, health books, whatever. We've been in business two years and it's really growing amazingly.' A pause while he exchanged rude gestures with an aggressive lorry driver on a roundabout, then he continued with a wide and somehow ingenuous smile: 'But I'm also a property developer. I've bought some office buildings in Southampton and a couple of warehouses, too, and they're being redeveloped.' He began to describe the office complex to be, light, air-conditioned, spacious, specifically designed for the latest in computers and office technology. He spoke in lyrical terms of ergonometric seating and modular furniture – his designer girlfriend would handle that, of course, and everything would be in sleek flowing lines. A large paw left the wheel to gesticulate. 'This side of my life is a sideline as yet, but I've plans for it to grow, big plans. Prices are low now, I'm getting in at the bottom of the market and I'll see a big return.'

'It sounds exciting.'

'You can say that again. I'm always working, I love it. Weekends I help my girlfriend with her interior design work; we look at places together and I can come up with as many schemes as she can. I'm an ideas man, always have been. When I left school I started off studying architecture, because I love buildings, houses, interiors, all that. I did all right there, too, but I was always wanting to break free and do my own thing, work for myself. Now I'm able to do just that, and it's great.'

'I envy you,' Brozie heard herself say, and it was true. He had opened up a view of untrammelled horizons, of a busy and fascinating life to be built through his own endeavours. She saw him racing along the roads of Hampshire in his scarlet car, going from one stimulating business meeting to another, perhaps running up to London to talk to authors, famous authors maybe, then studying architects' plans for his buildings, talking to foremen on hard hat sites and giving his instructions. And, in addition, he would be living in that amusing barn conversion, creating with his girlfriend the beautiful garden he'd described to her – *and* going shooting as well.

She felt breathless and exhilarated by his enthusiasm and his ideas, by a life so totally different from her own. How wonderful, she thought, to be young and energetic and free, like him. He had transformed her morning. She remembered the awfulness of its start, her head thick and aching after a night of Hubert tossing and groaning beside her, and how she had first broken a favourite milk jug, an old blue and white jug she'd inherited from her grandmother, and then how she had swept up the pieces and gone regretfully to put

21

them in the dustbin to find her little friend the robin lying dead on the doorstep, his spindly legs sticking up in the air. Her neighbour's cat must have caught him at last and left him there. She had shed a few tears of sorrow that he would no longer tap on her window for attention or come to her steps for his crumbs, and swept him up too. A walk to the post-office stores in the damp grey morning, no fresh fruit in the place, no cheeses but plastic Cheddar or Edam, nothing to tempt Hubert, her spirits as bleak as the day . . . and then had come the walk back and Charley St George in his car. And with Charley the morning had changed She looked at the big rumpled man beside her and felt a sense of well-being warm her, an inward certainty that the world could be a happy, an exciting place, after all, that something good was round the corner.

The car sped down the lane into Abbotsbridge, but as her house came into sight Brozie's mental barometer swooped from high to stormy low and her stomach began suffering anticipatory butterflies at the thought of Hubert's reaction to her jaunt in the Porsche and her extravagances.

As if he knew her mind, Charley asked abruptly: 'What's the matter with your husband then? Why's he snarl at you like a pit bull terrier?'

'He's ill. He has to take drugs, horrid little tablets that make him feel nauseated and low all the time.'

'Is it cancer?'

'Yes,' she said dully, 'it's cancer.'

She remembered back over five years how Hubert had railed at fate when the diagnosis was made, how he'd swung erratically in mood from the certainty that he'd die in agony in only a few weeks, to the wild optimism that a good day would engender: 'Doctors know all about it nowadays, they can operate, give you new wonder drugs, chemotherapy, all that – plenty of people live on for years and years, no re-occurrences – you'll see!' Now there were just the endless days, months, years, of dragging ill-health, and the stealthy, creeping but inexorable progress of the disease, sometimes held at bay for a few months by a new set of pills, but always there, always seeking to claw its evil way into new areas.

'He doesn't have any pain,' she told Charley, 'but he's retired from work and he's bored as well as feeling awful. He's not a man to do nothing and like it. He never had any hobbies, never had any interests outside work. Except politics, but he's not up to attending meetings. All he can do is shout at politicians on the television.'

'Sounds absolutely bloody,' Charley said with feeling. 'But he shouldn't take it out on you.'

'He hardly knows he's doing it,' Brozie said unconvincingly. Then she added in a gust of fury: 'But I'd like to take it out on the doctors and the drugs manufacturers. Damn them! Damn them! They give statistics to the papers to tell the world of their astounding success in extending the lives of cancer sufferers, but they don't tell you the down side – the lack of any quality to those lives, the sickness, the failure of energy, the fear of death lurking just out of sight.'

'I reckon there's not much of quality to your life, either,' Charley commented, drawing the car up outside her gate and switching off the engine. 'Not from my glimpse of it. When do you have any fun?'

She sidestepped the question. 'It was fun being with you this morning, riding in your car and buying my new hat. I'm very grateful.'

'Christ, big deal!' He looked across her towards the house. 'And you won't have any more fun today, not by the look of your husband there. He's signalling at you from the window – see?'

Hubert was mouthing through the panes like the gargoyles on the church roof. When he saw no reaction from Brozie, he disappeared from the window to bob out under the porch, shouting and beckoning.

'The rector's wife wanted to speak to you on the telephone. I had to tell her I didn't know where you were, that you'd gone off with some fellow in a flashy car. Go and ring her back – it might be urgent.'

Brozie extricated herself from the car. 'I know what it's about,' she said, 'and it isn't.'

Balked by this response, he informed her that her hat and her boots looked silly. 'And tell that young man to move on. I don't want that car outside my house, thank you very much.'

He turned and stomped back inside.

Charley was out of the car now, standing staring after Hubert Hamilton with a long cool look.

'Well,' he said, and then stopped and for a moment did not speak. Then he started again. 'I wouldn't say I was a man for euthanasia. But if I were in your shoes, I'd bop him on the head. That's what I'd do, just bop him on the head. Kinder all round.'

Chapter 3

Louise and Simon were silent most of the way as they drove down the M3 to Hampshire three days later, Louise restlessly shifting in her seat, her mind restless and shifting too. Was it mean of her to want Simon to be the one to commute? His was the career that would support them if she did stop work to have children, he was the larger earner of the two. Or was it Simon who was the mean one, devious and hypocritical, ensuring that her career remained the lesser by loading pressures on her? She reproached herself for her suspicions, reminded herself of his shining record so far, but the thoughts refused to go.

Shaking her head as if to clear it, she turned at last to speak to him: 'Are you sure Maggie and Jack really wanted us to come for lunch? I feel it's imposing on them, so soon after we spent the weekend there.'

Simon was sure. 'I said that myself to Jack on the phone; three lively small boys to cope with and them so recently bereaved, we'd just call in for tea – but he said Maggie would be furious if we didn't come for the whole day. In fact, he made a special point of it. Made me hang on while he pulled the kitchen door to so Maggie couldn't hear. He's worried about her – she's still very down over little Felicity. Six months it is now, she ought to be recovering, but Jack says she swings between bouts of hysterical rage and weeping and a kind of dull resignation when she'll hardly speak to him or the boys. But with visitors she makes an effort and pulls herself together. She can even enjoy herself. Jack wants her encouraged to be positive, to look forward, not back.'

Louise considered. 'I thought she was surprisingly normal over our weekend there. Subdued, but that was only to be expected.'

'Maggie's fond of you. I'd have thought you were too different to hit it off as you do, but she seems to find the differences stimulating. Jack says she's thrilled that we're going – that we're considering living near them. It's about the only thing she's shown enthusiasm about since . . . it happened. She needs a close female confidant.'

Louise shied mentally. The ties of her affection for Simon were pulling her slowly, inexorably, it seemed, to Hampshire, and here were more ties: Maggie's needs. Pity for Maggie in her grief was no compelling reason for such a move . . . and yet she would hate to disappoint her. They were good friends, as Simon had said, unexpectedly good friends. Jack had been a schoolfriend of Simon's; Louise had been surprised to discover in his wife an old acquaintance, a schoolfriend of her next oldest sister. Maggie was domesticated, revelling in cake-making for the WI sales, in rearing runner beans and rabbits, and, above all, in rearing her children. She was secretary to the pre-school playgroup that operated in the village hall, a keen member of the village horticultural society, where she won prizes for her vegetables, and a flower lady at the church. In none of these activities could Louise ever imagine herself becoming even remotely interested, let alone entangled. So why, she wondered as the car turned on to the A303, and deeper into the country, were they such friends?

They shared a sense of humour, that was a strong bond. She enjoyed Maggie's tales of the politics of playgroup and horticultural society, and of the village social hierarchy, so oddly inbred and inward-looking. She recalled, with an interior laugh, her story of how some ferocious female had arrived unannounced at the playgroup, intent on putting the villagers to rights. 'You know the sort, social services or whatever, all theory and no sense. Well . . . We introduce the four year olds to the idea of books and reading, so they feel comfortable with school and what's going to happen there. We read them stories and teach them the old nursery rhyme games and they learn to recognise their names in writing,

Darren or Tom, Kylie or Katie – useful, and they love it. Ms Bossy-Boots is horrified. Early learning? She's busily telling us that we mustn't impose our middle-class values on the village children when Arabella Manningford arrives. She's from the Manor, rich, four children, full of wit, no side. She listens for a few seconds, one eyebrow lifted, then draws a deep breath and tells this female she's shocked to find such a narrow outlook in one who should be of liberal views.

'"Classism," she says, "sheer classism. You hate the working classes, don't you? You want to keep them in their place, in case they challenge yours. That's why you refuse them access to any other culture, middle-class or otherwise. Heaven forbid we should have Hindu or Moslem workers here – the poor souls would have to keep total silence about their most cherished beliefs!" Ms Bossy-Boots tries to tell us she's never had a racist thought in her life, but Arabella sweeps on in that upper-class voice of hers, not affected, just English at its immaculate best, winding her up, muddling her, saying she's the epitome of Victorianism, scolding her for the snobbery, sexism and racism of that era until she flees in terror, convinced that Arabella is about to denounce her to her fellow toilers as an enemy of the multi-cultural and uni-sexual society. Arabella escorts her from the hall and comes back dusting off her hands, grinning when she finds us groaning with the pain of laughter suppressed too long. "Such an affected cow," she says, "but I milked her a bit, didn't I?"'

Louise had enjoyed that story and others of life in a Hampshire village. And she enjoyed the occasional after-noon antique furniture hunting with Maggie. The superb pieces owned by the Holbrooke Collection were very differ-ent from the comfortable country furniture the Eastons sought for their rambling eighteenth-century cottage, but, as Maggie pointed out, Louise was a damn' sight more know-ledgable than anyone else they knew, and she had a good eye for a bargain.

The car slowed, turning into a narrow lane running down-hill between ivy-covered banks. A sign announced the approaching village of Abbotsbridge. Louise jumped with disgust as a black and white bird shot up from a furry corpse squashed on the road surface: the brute had been eating it – ugh, how revolting! The bird darted off over the hedge and Simon said:

'A magpie – aren't they handsome birds? Always seem to be magpies by that oak!' as if he were pointing out some special sight to a tourist. In the same vein he added: 'Ah, there's the manor – Abbotsbridge House. The Manningfords have been there for hundreds of years, you know.'

It occurred to Louise that a sentimental view of history was one of the reasons the country and country villages lured him: some lore about the closeness of rural communities, a search for continuity and eternal verities, some ancient tug. He was hooked on the past. Louise found history interesting too but not, she told herself, to the extent of wanting to seek out the inconveniences of other ages.

Abbotsbridge House was a Palladian building, symmetrical, three-storeyed, immaculate, set at the end of a great avenue of lime trees. It was lavishly praised in all the local guide books. She knew what Simon would say next – and he did. He always did as they passed this point.

'It must be one of the most handsome manor houses in Hampshire, or in England come to that. And that's a particularly fine old avenue of trees. It was pollarded for gunstocks during the Civil War, you know.'

Most of the trees didn't look old enough for that.

'Mm,' she said. 'Fascinating.' As she looked a shaft of sunlight descended from between two clouds to wink at her from the gilded weather-cock on the lead cupola of the gatehouse roof. She nearly winked back. The house was wonderful, but it was nothing to do with her.

Next they passed the rectory, four-square, Georgian and brick. Beyond it was the squat shape of the mediaeval church, its open-mouthed gargoyles waiting to vomit rainwater from the roof as they had done for centuries, the knapped flints of its walls gleaming like metal, the churchyard crammed with leaning and lichened tombstones and presided over by three great yews. As they passed, the church clock struck the hour from the low tower. It made Louise almost irritable that she liked it so much.

The lane widened into the village street, with a scattering

of thatched cottages among its more modern houses, a post-office stores in one half of a long low building labelled Ye Olde Forge, and beyond it a whitewashed inn, The Bull, its sign a snorting animal in full charge.

'Good pub,' Simon mentioned. 'Serves good meals as well as Real Ale. The landlord's popular, I'm told.'

'So what?' Louise snapped. 'Stop behaving like some unctuous estate agent, Simon, for Christ's sake. I can discover these things for myself. If I'm interested, that is.'

He stood on the brakes, skidding the car to a stop. 'Well, sod you!'

Her head jerked forward, slammed back again against the head-rest. 'And sod you, too. Stop force-feeding me!'

'I'll say what I want. But if you're going to be like this I'll turn the car round and we'll go straight back home.'

'You couldn't be so rude. Maggie and Jack are expecting us.'

'I'll apologise for you. Tell them you're in a foul mood and not fit to be seen.'

They stared in front of themselves at the village street, breathing heavily. Behind them a horn sounded, making them jump.

Simon made a gesture, let in the clutch and the car moved on.

A hundred yards later they muttered in unison: 'Sorry!'

Jack must have been on the watch for the front door was flung open almost before they were out of the car and he advanced down the path, solid, ruddy, tweed-clad, reliable, looking more like a farmer than the successful solicitor he in fact was.

'Lovely to see you – what a relief you're here in good time! Mm . . . Louise!' A brisk hug. 'How are you, Simon? Sorry to rush you, but you have to view the cottage straight away. The Maddens have an unexpected lunch engagement – inconsiderate brutes – but it's people they probably won't see for years once they've moved and it's twenty miles away so could you get a move on!' He finished, breathless, gave Louise another hug and then a little push. 'We'll have drinks waiting when you come back.'

The cottage was set behind generous billowing hedges of yew, hedges of positively fleshy proportions that from the front half-hid what once must have been a farmhouse. Privacy, that's something, Louise thought as she waited for a response to Simon's knock on an aged door that was thick and gnarled and faintly worm-eaten, and she sighed.

The Maddens were a tall couple of about their own age, he wearing a smooth grey suit, she a loose knitted dress which did not quite conceal the middle-months of her pregnancy. They shook hands and the woman – 'Susie, please!' – observing that they would rather look over the house on their own, discreetly removed herself and her husband to the sitting-room.

Louise and Simon wandered over a house in which little had changed over the centuries. It had been constructed around the time of the Restoration, and the heavy beams across the low-ceilinged rooms, the oak lintels of the doors, the inglenook, the bread oven, were all as they had always been. Even the scents of woodsmoke and potpourri seemed the accretions of more than three hundred years. Only the Maddens' flower-bestrewed furnishings and prints were new. They walked round without speaking, Simon ostentatiously tactful in his silence, Louise struggling to take in essential details while deep in internal battles.

After a while they let themselves out into the garden, through the stable door which was the kitchen entrance, walking slowly over a damp lawn towards the beech hedge boundary, still russet brown with leaves. Beyond it were meadows, ploughed land and woods, rising gently to the low hills. Here Simon abandoned tactfulness to enthuse over the way the silver line of the River Test appeared and disappeared behind clumps of alders and willows, exclaiming at the deer he spied by a distant copse.

'And the silence! Listen to the silence!' he said.

The silence of the countryside was a mixture of tiny sounds: a background rustle different from London's dull roar because the sounds could be separated. Louise heard woodpigeon's coos, currents of air whispering among the leaves of the hedge, the faint shouts of village children down by the river.

'Not silent at all,' she said, and walked on.

'Peaceful,' he said. 'Wonderfully peaceful.' And he continued to speak with persistent ecstacy about the fields and hills surrounding them, perhaps with a touch of aggression towards Louise who was not displaying a similar delight.

'Lovely,' she said at length. 'It is lovely.' And she recognised that it was special.

Yet she was not at ease. To her the country was inimical, alarming; its open spaces and its woods were threatening in their lack of people, hazardous places where the wild threatened. Louise's distaste had been formed by a crowded childhood passed in London, in Belsize Park, and by remembered stories of children like Hansel and Gretel, lost in the forest; by tales of the Wild Woods, of wolves and foxes, stoats and weasels, evil in the dark. On a rare visit to a small friend in the country she'd heard a rabbit screaming in the night, sounds that haunted her for days, knowing death had stopped the screams. When her father and mother had taken their family on country trips, she had refused to explore out of eyesight of them. She needed to know where they were, as unable to establish herself in these surroundings of woods or hills as a country child set loose in an unknown city. Such excursions unnerved her: to pick blackberries or climb trees held no lures, she knew the brambles would scratch her limbs and tear her clothes, she knew she would fall from the branches – and so it happened. Transporting two adults and six children anywhere, along with feeding them, was a logistical problem of considerable dimensions for a family with but one car. When Louise urged Hampstead Heath or Richmond Park or the zoo, her parents agreed with relief that these were simpler alternatives. The true countryside stayed remote and hostile.

As she grew older she realised that her fears were illogical; the wild animals of today's woods turned out to be small creatures, not dangerous at all. She transferred her dislike to mud, cowpats and mosquitoes, subjects on which she could be amusing. But when she read that seventeenth- and eighteenth century travellers feared the hills and mountains, and on the Grand Tour were likely to pull down the blinds of their coaches to avoid seeing the horrors of the high Alps,

31

she understood their feelings exactly. But she hated to admit to them.

When they went back indoors the Maddens were pouring them drinks in the sitting room. Louise found herself by the window, talking to Susie over a glass of wine, while the men stood warming their backsides at the log fire, drinking whisky and discussing the possibility of Simon getting a rod on the Test.

Susie told Louise about the post-office stores: 'The stock's reasonably fresh and *he's* all right, but watch out for Nancy Chubb's tongue . . .' about the mobile library: 'Mostly romantic muck or standard stuff you're bound to have read, but it's something in an emergency!' and had moved on to the Manningfords at the manor, 'She'll probably want to involve you in worthy causes but don't unless you really want . . .' when abruptly she stopped to say: 'I'm boring you? Putting you off?'

'No,' Louise said uncomfortably. 'No, it's just . . . all so new and unexpected . . .'

'You're not convinced, are you?' Susie said, meeting the problem head-on. 'Even your back was unconvinced, walking down the garden. Is it this house or the whole thought of the move?'

'The cottage is enchanting,' Louise acknowledged, surprising herself with the truth she'd been trying not to admit. 'No, it's the move.'

'Don't want to move at all? Rather be elsewhere?'

'Don't want to move.'

'Then why are you?'

Louise explained, ending: 'I love my job, you see, I don't want to give it up, to have my mind stagnate. But commuting? It would be two to three hours a day out of my life.'

'Quite a few people do it from round here. And from further afield. Better a husband in Basingstoke than in Peru!'

'Peru?'

'That's where mine's accepted a post.'

'Peru! Unbelievable. What's he do?'

'He's a civil engineer. He's going to build spectacular roads and bridges there, that's what he reckons. A chance in a million, he says.'

32

'And you? What do you do?'

'I'm a teacher. Till the end of term I'm head of science in a local comprehensive. Not the most wonderful thing in the world, not with all the recent curriculum changes and pressures on teachers, but I enjoy it.'

'But you're pregnant.'

'Yes. And I'd planned to have a short time off before the birth, my statutory few months afterwards, then to go back to work, with the help of a trained nanny. Peter wasn't happy. He believes children need their mothers full-time, at least in the pre-school years. Then he came up with this job. He swore it was a coincidence. I blew my top anyway. But when I'd come down from the ceiling I realised it was compromise time. So . . . I give up work and concentrate on babies – I couldn't work in Peru, anyway, I don't speak Spanish – Peter does a maximum of five years out of England, and then it's Susie-back-to-work time.'

'I don't believe I could be that unselfish,' Louise said. 'Not South America. Not that big a gap.'

'You don't know what you can do until you have to. And in the end I expect to have children and a career both. I've never wanted to be the sterile career woman, I think that's rather sad. Besides, when all's ended, which would one prefer to have over one's grave – "A dearly loved wife and mother" or "She was a conscientious teacher"?'

'Mm. So in comparison with you I've got it made.'

'Something like that.'

Thoughtfully: 'I don't believe our relationship, Simon's and mine, could stand Peru.'

'Then you have to look very hard at that relationship. Or at yourselves.' Susie picked up a small brass can and watered the plants on her windowsill. 'And if you should want to renege on your offer, let us know soon, please. We need to have the sale organised by Easter.' She put the watering can down and turned her head. 'But it's a good house, this. No hidden problems. And it has a good feeling to it. I shall miss it.'

Chapter 4

Simon wanted to know Louise's views immediately they were out of earshot of Walnut Tree Cottage – was it all right, could he instruct solicitors straight away or did she want to compare it with other houses? Louise refused to respond; in a strange form of ferocious good temper she almost ran back up the village street to Maggie and Jack's cottage, hopping and dancing over the muddy puddles, refusing to allow Simon the serious talk he craved, teasing him with an imitation of estate agent's hyperbole.

'Oh, the cottage is absolutely charming. The rural ambiance captured incarnate. Impossible to imagine a place more wholly conducive to the fullest enjoyment of the special tranquillity and repose of the countryside, so suitable for the upbringing of balanced and stable children. The view – the low hills, the river, the timelessness of it all – it takes the breath away!'

'Oh, shut up!' he said. 'That's not me.'

'And the sunshine!' She closed her eyes to the misty sun and twirled round in front of him, opened them and staggered, seeing floating spots of blue and orange and black. 'Genuine Hampshire sunshine, unpolluted by the chemical smog of London town, unsullied by the dust and detritus of a hundred thousand factories!' She waved a hand in the air. 'Touch it, it's real!'

'Shut up or I'll smack you!'

'You wouldn't dare!'

But she shut up when she saw Maggie and Jack at the door to welcome them. Maggie's eyes were red, the lids swollen, and her skin was white and blotchy. She had powdered her face and put on eye make-up, but it sat uneasily on the damp skin, a sad clown's unconvincing disguise.

The two men appeared oblivious to her appearance, either through embarrassment or lack of perception. They went to deal with drinks and were immediately talking house prices and changes in the interest rates.

Louise hugged Maggie, aware of bow-taut tension in the plump body, and handed her a bunch of flowers retrieved from the car. 'How are you, love? You don't look so good today.'

'Lovely flowers. Thanks. No, I don't, do I? But leave it out. It's just . . . It's six months today. It shouldn't make any difference, should it?' Bitterly. 'One month, six months, one year, sixty years . . . So what? Felicity's gone.'

'Oh, Maggie . . .'

'No. No sympathy. That brings a gush of self-pity. Like Pavlov's dogs watering at the mouth, give me the right signals and I water at the eyes. Endlessly.' She lifted a hand to push impatiently at straggling tails of blonde hair. 'Come on, we'll go by the fire and get Jack to give us strong drink. Just let me find a vase for your flowers . . .' Her hand flew to cover her mouth. 'Flowers! Christ, I was supposed to do the church flowers this week and I clean forgot. Shot away, that's what I am. Totally shot away.'

'Can you do them now?'

'I suppose I'll have to,' she said distractedly. 'Let me think . . . There's beef roasting in the Aga and roast potatoes – they'll look after themselves. Yes, I'll have to fly down there or chaos and ructions and upbraidings and God wot not will ensue tomorrow – you just can't imagine! Dead flowers in stinking stale water don't add to the charm of the Sunday service. And the village prides itself on its flowers.'

She thrust Louise's flowers into a jug, scrabbled in a kitchen drawer for secateurs, disappeared outside, reappeared, said: 'Come with me, won't you? Great, we'll let the men and the boys know . . .' put her hand on the sitting-room door and opened it on what was apparently a young war.

The sitting-room was low ceilinged, hot, untidy and noisy.

The three small boys, all with flaxen heads and limbs of astonishing substance and shining good health, were rushing to and fro making machine-gun noises and shouting at the top of stunningly well-developed lungs. Jack and Simon, who had seized the two wing chairs and were sprawled in them with their legs stuck out, were also shouting in a necessary effort to make themselves heard. Under Jack's chair a black tom cat cowered, its ears back.

The smallest boy emerged from the mêlée to stand back and shriek, 'Pow, bang, thud! You're dead, Hugh!' before firing his fingers and hurling himself upon his oldest brother, pushing him, tripping, over Simon's legs, to fall in a heap by the hearth.

Hugh demonstrated how far from dead he was by rising in fury and clouting four-year-old Toby in the stomach, the nearest part of his anatomy, winding him. Toby gasped, doubled up and began to retch. His brothers retreated backwards, as cats from spilt milk, Maggie clutched Toby in maternal solicitude and Louise silently prayed he wouldn't throw up over her feet, stepping aside hastily.

There was stillness and silence broken by the sound of the boy's heaving. When he stopped Maggie looked down at him, her face tight.

'All right now?'

'Yes.' He took a tentative breath, paused to judge its effect, then burst out: 'Hugh's horrid! He hit me!'

Maggie let go of him, solicitude vanishing with recovery. 'You are horrid! You hit Hugh! And don't you ever, ever, ever let me hear you playing nasty games of dead. Dead isn't a game, do you hear me? Never, never, ever!'

There was more than anger in her voice; there was a rising note of hysteria Louise did not like.

'Steady,' Jack said.

'I'm perfectly steady, thank you. Hugh, it is bad to hit anyone where you hit Toby. Tummies are special places, you treat them gently. Don't ever do that again. Now say sorry – both of you!'

The two boys stared at each other, at their feet, finally at their mother. At the sight of her implacable face they mumbled a reluctant: 'Sorry!'

'Good. Now, both of you, and Eddie too, you can tidy up those toys and put them away.'

Toby stumped round to pick up bricks and cars and stood on the tail of the black cat. It yowled, spat and fled.

'I didn't mean it!' Toby shrieked.

Maggie stood silently counting. Then she told the two men where she and Louise were going, informed them they could keep an eye on the boys, caught Louise by the arm and tugged her from the house, swirling a black poncho over her head as she went.

'God, aren't they awful?' she said outside, patting down the poncho.

'It's not normally like this when we come,' Louise said, trying to sound reassuring while feeling unnerved herself.

'No,' Maggie agreed. 'No, it's not. But I'm in a state today. And that's when all hell breaks loose. It worries the boys, you see, makes them jumpy and then aggressive.' She sighed and made an odd resigned gesture with the flowers and blossoming twigs she was clutching. 'I started a period an hour ago,' she added. 'That just topped the lot.'

'I get PMT occasionally,' Louise remarked with sympathy, but a sideways look from Maggie made her feel she had missed a point somewhere.

Maggie started to speak, checked herself, then set off at a brisk pace, chattering inconsequentially about the church and its ancient charms – a Tudor pulpit with linenfold panels, a six-hundred year-old font with a carved wooden cover of the sixteenth century, and a handsome roof with most of its original beams – and, oh, the endless chompings of the woodworm that infested them all and the headaches that gave to the rector, who, she said, was a love. 'Head in the clouds but feet firmly fixed on the earth. Sounds contradictory, but it isn't. You'll see.'

As they panted round the steep rise to the church they saw a scarlet Porsche, parked by the lych-gate.

'Visitors,' Maggie remarked pleasedly. 'Wealthy, by the look of it. Hope they put plenty in the church box.'

Stepping down into the church was like walking into a forgotten world for Louise: its echoing dim spaces, its rounded pillars pushing up the great weight of the wooden

37

roof, its smell of damp and candlewax and centuries of ecclesiastical dust, all smote her with childhood memories and beliefs she had long since pushed away as irrelevant. There was a scent, too, faint but alluring, of flowers, and there were voices. She traced these to the top of the nave, to where a woman was, by the tilt of her head and the quick touches of her hands, putting the final touches to a flower arrangement on a wrought iron stand by the chancel steps and a man, a very large man, was leaning against the pulpit and watching her.

'Brozie!' Maggie's voice was high with embarrassment. 'Brozie, you shouldn't have bothered, really. Did you think I'd forgotten? Well, I had, but not entirely, as you can see. But it was sweet of you to step into the breach you thought you saw.'

'No problem at all, my dear. Thought you might have difficulties . . . those boys of yours – measles, mumps, bumped heads – one never knows what they'll have next! I'm happy to help.'

Brozie sounded almost as embarrassed as Maggie was by her act of helpfulness. She was an unusual-looking woman whom Louise found it impossible to place; the mixture of the old-fashioned school-teacher clothes with the dowager's hat and the buckled green boots making her at once odd and somehow endearing.

'It's amazing,' the big man said comfortably, his long back still propped by the pulpit, 'how many people there are in this village willing to do these chores. And create something of beauty out of them, too.' His eyes appraised the gold and green of the arrangement. 'Winter jasmine and mahonia – terrific, isn't it?'

Brozie introduced him as Charley St George, who was about to move into The Old Barn, Maggie introduced Louise to them both as a future owner of Walnut Tree Cottage, and then Brozie and Maggie disappeared into the vestry.

Charley had an easy manner. He levered himself off the pulpit's panelling and stretched. 'Do you know this church? No? Lots of things here worth a minute or two of anybody's time. But first I'll show you something you wouldn't look to find. Graffiti.'

Louise imagined ballpoint pen and *Tracy 4 Wayne*. 'No thanks!'

'These are different,' he assured her. 'You'll like these.' He led her to the choir stalls and pointed: 'Look, centuries old graffiti! They did things properly in those days.'

Deep in the gleaming oak where hymnbooks and psalters rested the names were carved. *Robert Swynton, Singinge Manne, 1588*, and *Jhon Walters, 1592, sate here*, Louise read, followed by others over a period of two decades. She ran her fingers across the indentations, fascinated and moved by the antique lettering and the efforts the carvers had made.

'How many dull sermons did it take to complete the work?' Charley wanted to know. 'And 1588, that's the year of the Armada – perhaps only a few weeks after finishing that one Robert went off to fight.'

'Yes,' Louise said, awed. 'Perhaps he did. But I bet he came back; his sort would. Four centuries ago. Thank you for showing me.'

They strolled back down into the nave. 'So you're going to move to Walnut Tree Cottage, are you? Gorgeous place. I looked at it myself – couldn't afford it, but I never can resist the chance of a good nose around. It's got some amazing nooks and crannies, and the roof timbers are superb – old ship's timbers, did you know?'

Louise shook her head.

'Hard as iron from all their weathering. Little chance of woodworm there, not like the church. Look.' He drew her a few steps sideways and pointed upwards. 'There, to your left. See it?'

Above a carved boss Louise saw a scattering of black holes in a great beam that curved up into the roof. She nodded.

'Death watch!' Charley said with a sort of ghoulish triumph. 'Those rabbit warrens are made by the death watch beetle. Cost a bomb to eradicate him. Brozie introduced me to the rector the other day, he's got a committee working to raise money – co-opted me on to it, the pair of them did. You should join it too, seeing you're interested in old places. What sort of a job do you do?'

Louise told him, adding firmly: 'But I shall be travelling

up to London every day, so I can't think of joining committees.'

Charley tossed the excuse aside as irrelevant. 'Commuting's a rest period, just sitting in a train, reading or chatting! I did it for a year, it was fine. You have to catch an early train to avoid standing, but that has its own pay-off – your partner or whatever has to do all the morning chores! Besides,' he returned firmly to his point, 'with a job like yours, with a knowledge of old things and administration, you'd be invaluable!'

'No!' she protested. 'No, I don't know how I'm going to plan my life yet!' And then, at his reproachful look, she felt guilty. Louise often felt guilty in church, something to do with her sins of omission and selfishness and the 'Thou God seest me' that had hung in fading pokerwork at the top of the stairs in her childhood home. Her father had told her that God was everywhere, but she felt His eyes burning with special intensity when she was in His own house. Odd, she thought, how incomplete her unbelief became at such times. Perhaps it was because the fabric of the church was full of the simple beliefs and the earnest thoughts of those who had prayed in it over many centuries, and it was this goodness, soaked into the very stones, that she could sense, this that made her feel unworthy. Her thoughts returned again to her dilemma and now her mind was filled with Simon's hurt eyes, with Maggie's need of her, and even with this man Charley who urged involvement in what she had always considered other people's problems, and she knew they were spinning a web around her, a web woven of affection and expectations that it would be selfish to break. Inexorably they were forcing her. And yet . . . 'I don't want it!' she said aloud. 'I don't want it. I've other things to do.'

'All right,' Charley said equably. 'I'm probably going too fast. That's me all over. I have an idea and it's reality in my mind immediately, never mind any difficulties. You've your move to grapple with. I'll come back to you when you're settled.'

Maggie passed them, displaying a delicate arrangement of blossoming twigs. 'Brozie helped me. Aren't they lovely? I'll put them by the font to lighten that dark corner as you come into the church.' She placed them and returned to take Louise's arm. 'Now we must run or lunch will be vilely late and the boys will play up.'

Charley called: 'Brozie!' in a booming voice that echoed round the roof and remarked that she had better get back quickly too: 'Or Hubert the horrible husband will be another one playing up.'

Maggie blinked. 'You've met old Mr Hamilton, then?'

'Old?' he grunted with a gesture of disgust. 'Past his sell-by date, he is. Should be binned.'

A snort of amusement came from Maggie. 'And Brozie? How d'you come to know Brozie?'

'Ah,' he said with a sidelong look. 'I picked her up.'

'Picked her up?' Maggie repeated with relish.

'Of course. What else could I do? There she was, wet and forlorn by the side of the road . . .'

Brozie appeared beside them. 'And just what are you talking about?'

'You,' Charley acknowledged. 'When I met you.'

'Wet and forlorn? I should think I was. He soaked me,' she told Maggie and Louise with auntish fondness, 'soaked me with that wicked car of his, racing through the puddles. And now he tells me he's making up for it by acting as my chauffeur. So come on, lad, let's go!'

'Well,' said Maggie, watching them go with interest. 'How very odd. One might be worried – the picking up by a stranger, I mean. But him, Charley, he does seem nice, doesn't he? Fun. What she needs. You haven't met her husband, Louise, but if you had, you'd see. Exactly. He never drives her anywhere if he can help it, never does anything.'

They closed the great wooden door of the church behind them with a clang as they left and immediately they were free of its shelter a breeze whisked round the church to ruffle Louise's hair. She put up a hand to smooth it and Maggie let out a yell.

'A ring! Look at that! An engagement ring – and you never said anything. Why not? When did this happen?'

'Three days ago.'

'Well, congratulations!' They passed out through the lych-gate and she looked at Louise, her face animated. 'So what's the plan? Church or register office? Does Simon carry you over the threshold of Walnut Tree Cottage as the start of your great new life here?'

Louise shrugged. 'I don't know. Nothing's planned yet. Not on the marriage, not on the move. Or not by me, anyway.'

Maggie looked blank. 'Sorry, I'm not with you.'

'We've things to work out between us. Simon's got plans, lots. Start new career-enhancing job, marry, move to the country, have children – that's what he's inked in on his life's diary for this year and next. But me? My priority is fulfilment in my career, which is London-based – but Simon doesn't believe career women can be wholly fulfilled. Oh, he doesn't go around saying so directly. Oh no, he talks about the importance of intelligent people reproducing their genes, and how stable loving couples should rear the next generation. Young couples, naturally. Old motherhood is poor motherhood. Dear God. I just loathe the idea of being pregnant.'

Maggie kicked a stone along the lane. 'I love it,' she murmured fervently. 'I love it, I love it, I love it!'

'Yuk. How could you?'

'How can you ask, coming from a family like yours, with a mother like yours?' She turned to look at Louise, her deep blue eyes full of reproach. Maggie had first met her as the friend of Louise's next oldest sister; like many of her sisters' friends, Maggie, worried and dejected as her parents fought their way to divorce, had found refuge in their house, lolling on the untidy sofas watching television and eating crisps, or chatting in the cluttered bedrooms that were full of pets and discarded clothing and cheap make-up. 'Six children. She must have loved it, too.'

'She did. She wallowed in motherhood – like a sow in a mucky sty.'

'Come on,' Maggie protested, 'your house may have been untidy but it wasn't dirty. It was lived-in – all lovely and lived-in and relaxed.'

'It was overcrowded and stifling,' Louise said, her face austere. 'We all had to share bedrooms – except Austin, of course. There was no peace, no privacy, no room to keep my books properly or my clothes. I shared with Katie and she

42

always had cages of hamsters or gerbils where I wanted to put a bookcase. And they smelt. And she used to take them out and let them run anywhere. On *her* bed was bad enough, but on *my* bed – ugh! And once one of the hamsters peed on the pages of a book I'd borrowed from a teacher. I didn't know where to put myself when I took it back to her! And Mother simply giggled, like Katie.' Her adult face reflected the anguish the teenager had felt.

'That must have been bad,' Maggie agreed, looking as if she'd hardly heard, 'but your mother's such a warm person; she had room for everyone. And she didn't disapprove of teenagers. She actually liked them – think how rare that is!' She gazed down the lane as if looking into the past. 'If anyone was my role model as a mother, your mother was.'

'She always had time for other people,' Louise agreed, her mind continuing bitterly, But not the time for me.

Louise had been the outsider, the unwanted one. She was the fourth child, and after three daughters her parents had been desperate for a son, even her father, who generally didn't mind much about anything. But Louise arrived, a girl again. The entire family mourned; even the little girls, then eight, six and three, were upset. It had been decided that this fourth child must be the last, and four was more than they had intended. Her father, a middle-ranking civil servant, had enough of a struggle to provide. But four years later her mother was pregnant once more. An accident? Apparently not. They admitted, after many years, that the lure of a son had still possessed them. Sheer folly, Louise thought, remembering secondhand toys, passed down clothes, shared baths. But the baby was a son and much had been the rejoicing. Except by Louise. She didn't dislike Austin, but she did dislike the little attention that had been hers as the youngest being withdrawn. It was at about this time that she learned to read. There were plenty of books in the house, even if they were old and battered: Louise took them under the dining table, the safest and quietest place in the house, and retreated into a separate world. She was there, eight years old, reading Mrs Gaskell's *Cranford*, when the final child was born. 'You've got the knack of having a boy now,' the older girls had urged their mother. 'Have another.' When they peered under the table to tell Louise it was a girl, she laughed. But oddly, so did the others. After all, they did have a brother – and the new baby was sweet, dear little soul. Katie received all the attention due to the youngest from big sisters who had reached the cooing maternal stage, while Louise perceived the shocking unfairness of life and moved on to read the child's version of *David Copperfield*.

'Perhaps you're afraid of a baby coming between you and Simon,' Maggie mused.

'Perhaps,' Louise said. But on considering it, she thought not. She was afraid children would come between her and what she wanted to do, to achieve, as all her sisters and her brother had once done. That was the real, the insoluble problem.

At the cottage they went in through the back door to the kitchen.

'Sit down, Louise. Push things out of the way.'

The mixed clutter on the table was oddly similar to the mixed clutter of Maggie's clothes, each object colourful, interesting, yet unrelated. Her garments this morning were in layers, some strangely patterned and ethnic, others home-spun, home-dyed and hand-knitted. She put the vegetables on to cook and then poured them both a stiff gin and tonic. Louise sat, pushing aside vases of dried flowers, a saucerful of pebbles, a large ammonite, two half-eaten jars of heather honey, several finger paintings and assorted small socks.

'Mother's ruin!' Maggie said wryly, tipping her glass back. 'Wonderful for the bad days, though. Listen, Lou, you loathe the thought of being pregnant, but honestly it's not that bad. To me it's something amazing. All right, you probably feel nauseated in the early stages and lumbering at the end, but have you thought of the pure creativity of the process? Within the confines of your own flesh, you are making a new being. That's an awe-inspiring feat. More wonderful than Michelangelo sculpting his "David". That can't walk and talk and think.' Her face took on an expression of almost religious intensity. 'When I'm pregnant and I walk in a crowd, I look at all the flat bellies around me and I pity their owners. They're empty. They're nothing. I have the future within me. It's the most wonderful feeling of power. And it permeates me all through those months.'

'Hubris,' Louise said, but smiling and moved in spite of herself.

'Pride, yes,' Maggie returned. 'I suppose – well, it's the equivalent of the arrogant pride that a stud of a man feels in his sexual powers. We're not supposed to possess it. Penis envy is what women are supposed to feel. But pregnant, I feel exalted.'

They were silent, Louise stunned by a vision entirely new to her, by the unexpected thought that she might not, after all, have wholly fulfilled herself if she omitted an experience of such life-shaking importance.

Maggie moved among her vegetable pans, slicing and salting and tasting. Then she slopped more gin into her glass and sat at the kitchen table beside Louise. 'And breast-feeding. Some women don't like it; they complain of smelling of milk, of being endlessly damp with it. But I always knew I should like it – and I do. It gives you a most satisfying feeling – I can't think of the right word . . . not sexy . . .'

'Sensuous?'

'That's it. Sensuous. And there's the symbolism, too. Giving the very best of nourishment to a child from a secret well that is part of you, a fountain of life . . .' A pause, her eyes remote. 'I remember your mother with your little sister. She was the first woman I ever saw breast-feeding; people used to shut themselves away as if it were something shameful, but she made it beautiful – she was all still and serene and smiling . . .' She stopped, choked and turned her face away. 'Oh Christ, how embarrassing, Louise, I'm getting all poetic and sloppy. And with you, of all people!' She picked up the glass and drank in an effort to control her emotions but the effort was in vain. She choked again, crashed her glass down on the table in a flood of gin and burst into sobs.

Louise stood awkwardly and put an arm round the heaving shoulders. 'It's all right, Maggie. Say what you want to, cry if you want to. You have to get it out of your system.' She tried to hug her, but the shoulders were resistant.

'No, don't,' Maggie gasped finally. 'I told you, be bracing. I'm sorry. Truly, I didn't mean to do this to you.' She sat up, throwing off Louise's comforting arm. 'Gin speaking.' She fished in pockets and sleeves for a handkerchief, failing to find one.

In silence Louise fetched her several sheets of kitchen paper. Maggie mopped and blew and mopped again.

'I'll tell you,' she said, rising to fling the sodden paper into the bin and return to her saucepans. 'You may as well know what this is all about. It isn't about Felicity – well, it is, but not entirely. It's . . . you see, I thought I was pregnant. I was more than a week late. And then this morning I knew I wasn't, and it was hell, sheer hell.'

'But if you really want another baby, you can try again,' Louise said, puzzled.

'No, I can't! Jack doesn't want another. You see, I was cheating on the pill and he's cottoned on to it.'

'How?'

'He knew I was late, didn't he? Every fourth Friday I've been starting . . . so when I didn't he was first surprised, then suspicious, then furious.'

'Oh Lord!'

'Yes. We had some nasty arguments over it. But that was nothing to the explosion this morning. Louise, he was pleased when my period came. He actually smiled! I came out of the bathroom and told him and he said: "Thank God!" I yelled at him. I was a real bitch. I threw everything I could lay my hands on at him – toothmug, clothes brush, water glass. I yelled what a filthy uncaring bastard he was. He hit me!'

'He hit you?' Louise was appalled.

'He smacked me on both sides of my face. I suppose I was a bit hysterical. And the boys were upset. They wanted to know what the racket was about . . . they were shivering . . . Toby started crying.' She wiped tears away angrily with the back of her hand. 'He had to do something.'

It was all beyond Louise's comprehension: the overpowering emotions, the anger, the violence – and that this should erupt at such a time, so soon after the death of their two-year-old daughter from meningitis. She had believed their relationship to be rock solid. Now she saw cracks, chasms even, opening between them.

'But why all the argument? Would having another child be

so awful?' A thought struck Louise. 'Would Jack worry that you might make another child just a substitute for Felicity? Sorry, but it has to be said.'

Maggie nodded vigorously, fresh tears splashing down to spit noisily off the hotplate. 'That's his excuse. That all I want's a replacement for her, and that would be psychologically damaging for both the child and me. But it isn't that. I want another child for its own sake, and preferably a daughter because I want one of my own sex. Felicity was lovely . . . she was so different from the boys . . . even at two she was my friend and she wanted to help me. I miss her so much. I always shall. Jack wants me to look forward, not back. He keeps saying so. But forward to what? To the boys all going away to prep school, to being alone? Felicity wouldn't have left me, she'd have stayed. Without her there's a great black hole – and I keep falling into it. And there's nothing and no one to save me from it.'

She stabbed vegetables vengefully with a knife as if it were Jack she was attacking. Then she stooped to take the casserole from the oven. While she stirred and tasted it Louise puzzled her words. There were aspects of this quarrel she didn't understand.

'But you did have four children. Surely . . . after six months, a year maybe, if you still wanted it, well, he'd give you another child?'

No reply, while Maggie crashed about with dishes and lids. Then, explosively: 'No! No, he wouldn't. You see, Jack never wanted Felicity. I had to cheat on the pill to get *her*. He was *furious*. He even suggested an abortion. He came round in the end, but no, he won't have another.'

Louise was stunned. She searched desperately for words, thinking, I'm not the right person to deal with this, not from the opposite end of the spectrum of female desires, as I am; the only thing we have in common is cheating on the pill. She said: 'But he did love Felicity.'

'Oh, yes. Who couldn't? He's not that bad.' She carried her casserole through to the dining room, returning to say: 'It's the expense. Four children don't fit into the back of a car. Three do, just. Worse is the thought of school bills. But he paled when I said children didn't have to have expensive

47

schooling to lead a happy life. He said he wouldn't bring them into the world to give them second best.'

'Understandable,' Louise said gently.

'Not from where I stand,' Maggie retorted. Then she grinned at Louise in unexpected and endearing ruefulness. 'I'll have to take a lover. If any man but Jack would have me, fat and depressed as I am. That's something to say in his favour, isn't it? At least he does still fancy me.'

Louise studied her. She was fat, as she had remarked, but she had the fleshy voluptuousness of a Ruben's model, and, looking at her lovely capable arms and her generous breasts as she stooped over Toby, who had come running in to demand orange juice, it occurred to Louise that she would have few difficulties in finding a lover.

Maggie looked up at her, catching her eye and straightening. 'Lou, on a different matter – I'm just a selfish bitch who wants her friend to come and live near her. But my selfishness apart, mightn't it lead to a break-up with Simon if you insisted on staying in London?'

'I don't know. I haven't tried it yet.'

'Well, I'm anxious about it. Truly. Good men don't grow on trees, as they say. They have to be searched for, dug for, like truffles. Rare and toothsome when you find them. Some women never develop the right nose, they dig up rubbish every time. Don't chuck Simon – you'd regret it.'

'That,' Louise said, 'had occurred to me also.'

Jack and Simon appeared in the doorway.

'Are we actually going to eat some time this afternoon?' Jack asked.

Louise had an instant urge to throw something at him, followed by a leap of fear that Maggie would, but she merely straightened, moved to the oven, said sweetly: 'Right now, darling, if you'll carry these plates in for me,' and slid a pile from her oven-gloved hands into his.

'Ow!' Jack howled and took them at a run to the dining room, returning shaking his fingers. 'They were hot!' he complained.

'But you were in such a hurry,' she smiled.

Simon took the gloves from Maggie, picked up a large vegetable dish and silently carried it out, returning for more.

Louise watched him with a gaze heavy with all that preoccupied her, while voices echoed through her mind: *'Better a husband in Basingstoke than in Peru'*, *'Commuting's a rest period'*, *'Hubert the horrible husband'*, *'Good men . . . have to be searched for . . . like truffles'*. In a sudden rush of affection for his basic decency, Louise went to Simon and put her arms around him from the back, pressing a cheek between his shoulder blades.

'We'll put the house on the market on Monday, shall we?' she said, and avoided seeing the radiant transformation of his face.

But no babies, she vowed mentally, or not yet, not for a long time.

Chapter 5

Brozie poured sherry into a kitchen tumbler and took several gulps. Once she had believed in God's help; not any more. Sherry, not God, would give her strength. Its sweetness, its warmth, the defiance implicit in the hidden bottle, they combined to sustain her. She swallowed, choking down tears and alcohol. Hubert was being horrible again. She shuddered and recovered. Self-pity was a waste of time; work was the answer, getting on with the job. First job was the washing.

It was a cold but sunny morning in late-March, with a brisk wind chasing stray lambs' tails of cloud across the valley. She would hang the linen in the garden; it needed the antiseptic value of the sun's rays and a freshening blow. She lugged a basketful out and struggled to peg the billowing sheets to the line. Hubert had wet the bed again. It was the third time. He refused to admit his incontinence when she spoke of the sodden sheets, shouting that she was disgusting, claiming that she must have had a leaking hot-water bottle, or, alternatively, had spilt water from the glass on her bedside table: 'Careless fool that you are!' He refused to consult the doctor. 'If anyone should, Brozie, you should.' He detested the local doctor; as well as being female, she was the wife of the rector, facts which offended his most cherished shibboleths.

Was Hubert's problem something to do with the cancer? Brozie didn't believe so. He was drugged with sleeping pills, incapable of arousing himself when the need came. He was secretive about it, but she'd checked the bottle. A treble dose or more he took now, in terror, she knew, of the wakeful frightened nights. In the early days she had left the warm bed to make him cups of tea, but he refused her comfort, would not admit the fear. This morning, when the seeping wetness woke her, she had hastily got up, looking back at his humped form in repugnance and dislike, wishing that if the cancer were going to kill him, it would get on with it. But how did he get the pills? Not from nice Dr Jane Field. The chemists' labels showed addresses in Wiltshire or Sussex. Several times recently he had taken himself off in the car, refusing to explain long absences from the house. Had he made his way to surgeries there, signing himself in as a temporary patient on holiday to obtain the drugs that gave him relief from terror? She didn't know. She didn't care. But he must drive her into Basingstoke to buy a rubber sheet. And she must make up a bed in the spare room for herself; she would not lie in Hubert's reeking piss another night.

She picked up the laundry basket, heard familiar sounds and swung round. There was an outburst of squabbling in the heronry on the river bank. That birds with the herons' capacity for standing in motionless and silent dignity for so much of the year should rear their young in communities of noisy antagonists each spring, never failed to fascinate and amuse her; forgetful of the chill wind, soothed by their nonsense, she stayed to watch the combatants.

The shrill sounds of the telephone broke her trance, sending her running to the house. It might be Charley; she must get to the telephone before Hubert. As he reached out she snatched it up.

'Jus' me!' the deep voice growled. It was Charley.

'Good morning!' she replied. 'It's for me,' she told Hubert.

He grunted and shuffled away.

'Where are you?' she asked. Charley rushed around southern England, to Basingstoke, Southampton, London and on, attending meetings here, clinching deals there; he had business friends and colleagues everywhere who were involved in what he called his little sidelines. Inevitably he ran into hold-ups. That was when he would ring her on his car telephone. To keep us cheerful in adversity, he said. In his mad working life it was a great way to keep in touch.

'I'm on the M3,' he told her now. 'Road-works. Two mile tail-back, I reckon. Stop, crawl, stop, crawl. Just past the Bracknell turn-off. I'm behind a lorry that's furiously farting diesel fumes at me – jealous of my chic motor, I reckon – if I suddenly stop speaking you'll know I've been asphyxiated so dial 999 for the rescue services, okay?'

'Okay,' she said, and found herself giggling.

'Hey, Brozie, I did a terrific deal yesterday, just an off-shoot to another negotiation I'm involved in – made myself fifteen hundred pounds. Not bad, is it?' He explained the deal, something to do with computer software some company director acquaintance had been searching for; Charley had played middleman, fixed the whole thing up, made everyone happy and taken his cut. 'It's all a matter of inside knowledge, keeping in touch with folk, knowing where they're at, what they've got. I've a brain like a computer for storing these facts and I can pop them up on my mental screen just when they're needed.'

'Marvellous,' she said.

'It is, isn't it?' He was like a small child in his glee. 'It means I can finish ordering the bedroom carpets at The Old Barn. I've worked most of the weekend in London, now I'm going to take the morning off and trundle round the shops.'

'What fun!' Brozie had never bought a carpet; the first Mrs Hamilton's speckled fawn broadloom still covered the floors it had been bought for thirty-five years ago; it was due for its annual spring-cleaning scrub shortly; it wouldn't improve it much, nothing could.

Charley had an idea. 'Hey, you come to Southampton too. You could visit my office development with me, help me choose my carpets and maybe do some shopping on your own account. How about that?'

It sounded wonderful. The car . . . those brilliant new offices she'd heard about . . . the alluring department stores. She could buy Hubert's rubber sheet without having to plead with him to drive her to the shops. He wouldn't let her drive, didn't trust her. But he would be furious.

'I'd love to, I'd really love it, Charley. But there's Hubert –'

'So what? Would it make you happy? Right. You should

52

be happy. Everyone should be happy – like me. I'm always happy! Sod Hubert!'

Sod Hubert – Charley's rude words invariably made her giggle and feel frivolous. Just for once, she would. 'Right. I'll come.'

'See you shortly then. Oh, and make me some coffee, please. I've had no breakfast. Bye!'

No breakfast! She imagined him devoting the incisive brilliance of his mind to the engineering of business coups, quite forgetful of the need for regular meals to keep his big frame going. She'd make him a toasted bacon sandwich as well as coffee. Since he'd moved into The Old Barn six weeks ago he'd often come sidling round her kitchen door, untidy, unbothered, mocking Hubert, cadging coffee and a chunk of one of her pies – Britain's best, Charley said. His girlfriend, a tall, languid blonde called Melody, was only around at weekends, and neither of them, from what Brozie had heard, had culinary aspirations higher than shoving a supermarket quiche in the oven. Ridiculous! Brozie relished feeding him. He was like a particularly kindly nephew, she told herself; one who bought her chocolates, mended her front door bell and oiled her gate, and was so confident and full of fun that he transformed even driving her round the village to deliver the parish magazine into a festive occasion. He liked her herons too. She finished the sherry in the tumbler, turned on the grill and darted happily about her kitchen.

In the kitchen of Walnut Tree Cottage Louise was drinking champagne and feeling at once cross and decadent. It was three days since the move and her third bottle. It was the one thing that kept her from screaming and throwing the myriad objects for which she had yet to find a place. Simon had prescribed it on day one, pressing a cool glass into her hand as the removals men came past her in a never-ending stream, carrying boxes and furniture and pot plants and yelling: 'Which room, luv?' as they passed. 'First bedroom!' she said. 'Dining-room, sitting-room, second bedroom – no, third!' There seemed to be a dozen men, though there were only three. But they were indefatigable. They dumped furniture anywhere in the rooms, returning for more. Louise poured champagne down herself like medicine, leapt up and down the stairs, ran from room to room. 'Up here, over there – no . . . yes . . . there! Careful, Christ, be careful – that's precious.' Champagne gave you energy, kept the blues at bay, so Simon told her kindly. He had been leaping like a goat himself, taking the stairs three together, drinking from the bottle when he had a moment spare.

From time to time he told Louise how well it was going and she said: 'Mmm!' non-committally. He'd said that all along. They'd done well in finding a buyer for the house in Notting Hill within a week, done wonderfully well over the price, unbelievably well in the time scale of exchange of contracts and completion dates. So Simon said. Not well in Louise's terms; she was dizzy and reeling from the speed of it all as well as the champagne. She couldn't believe they were already here in Hampshire, in Abbotsbridge. Like an emergency operation, it had been over almost before she'd had time to fear it. She steadied herself with a hand on the uneven wall and wondered about her powers of recuperation.

Early mornings were the worst time. She opened her eyes, not to the high white Victorian room that she had loved, but to the low ceiling and heavy beams of an earlier age looming oppressively over her as she lay, speechless with misery, thinking how much she hated this place. The chintz curtains at the mullioned windows particularly repelled her, so pretty, so floriferous, so jolly.

She had insisted Simon should return straight to work, despite his offer to take the week off with her. 'Not when you've just started an important new job!' she said, pushing him out. If she must live here she would sort the cottage out alone, placing her treasured possessions with care, considering where each of her pictures would be best displayed. Simon would bang hooks in at random and be hurt by her anguish; worse, he would be happy, stopping at the windows to appreciate the views, breathing deeply in the soft air and raving about the robins' spring song.

After a second glass of champagne she felt strong enough to complete the organisation of the kitchen, concentrating on making the routines of cooking simple, finding the right places for packet goods and tins, for her decorative jars and Simon's copper-bottomed pans. She liked the kitchen; it had a flagged floor and white walls and while it looked cool it was in fact cosily warm and it smelt of herbs and spices. She found the job surprisingly soothing and when it was done felt the stirrings of a sense of achievement. She put a bowl of fruit on the table, ran into the chilly garden to pick a bunch of daffodils and put them in a blue jug on the dresser. She poured herself another glass of champagne and leaned against the warm Aga to admire the effect. It was good.

She moved to the sitting-room. The Maddens might like to wallow in chintz – and Simon too, since he'd been keen to buy their curtains – but this room should reflect her style, be cerebral not gushing. She stood on a stool to remove the rumbustious roses twined with ribbons that flourished themselves at the low windows and the change in light and space was dramatic. A pleasant long low room, but its beams dimmed the light. Plain white curtains? No, too stark. It needed shades of pale, then; natural colours in a subtle mix – oatmeal, barley and the slate blue of the carpet – a background for the vibrant colours of her paintings. And she remembered the guest room curtains from Notting Hill, retained for a possible future house because she loved them so: a light honeysuckle shade. They would be too long . . . she hesitated, regretful of their graceful length, then braced herself to shorten them. She thought that this room could never be elegant, but it did occur to her that it could be a sanctum, its thick walls enclosing a peace and seemliness which she had not known in her over-crowded childhood.

Comforted by the image, she began to heave and push at the furniture, arranging her deep sofa and her Davenport and Simon's pedestal desk where she wanted them, putting her twin rush-seated corner chairs on either side of the great hearth, lifting armfuls of books from packing cases and organising them on the bookshelves that filled its alcoves. Full marks to the Maddens there, at least. Books were as important as pictures; Louise handled them with love.

At lunchtime, unexpectedly hungry, she found an elderly yogurt languishing alone in the fridge. She must visit the shop.

Abbotsbridge Post Office and Village Stores startled her. After the crowded anonymity of the London supermarkets, to be assessed with open curiosity by its customers – two gnarled old men, three gossiping housewives and a damp toddler – was disconcerting, while to be pressed with offers to deliver her goods or get her special orders was positively unnerving. The shop was larger than she had expected, the elderly charm of its Ye Olde Forge frontage abruptly changing to a long breeze block extension invisible from the street. Mrs Chubb – 'Call me Nancy, everyone does!' – ran the groceries while her husband, Les, presided over the twin cages of post office and off-licence with lugubrious distaste. He detested the forms involved in the first and resented the miserable pittance he was paid for dealing with them, while as for the alcohol, too much of it was drunk by the young and loutish, he said. Nancy, a heavily jolly and garrulous woman whose face had the shinily wrinkled look of an over-baked apple, played up to him while playing him down to the customers.

'Disgraceful, the way things are managed nowadays,' she told Louise as she helped her locate items she didn't need, 'but there, we believe in giving a service to our little community. We take the rough with the smooth.'

'And our money! Get us pensioners in for you to fleece, don't they?' one of the old men commented, leering happily at Louise over *The Farmers Weekly*.

Nancy's wrinkled apple face turned sour. 'Want something do you, George? Or just having a free read of my magazines?' She took his money dismissively. 'Some folk!' she said, as he clumped, muttering, from the shop. 'Still, nice to have new people like you in the village. I saw you move in Tuesday. Want any dogfood, do you? Just by your elbow. Coco Pops for the family then? No family? Well, you've time yet, haven't you? Nice place to bring up a family, your cottage. The Maddens, they made it lovely, just like in the glossies.'

'Bread,' Louise managed curtly. 'Cheese.'

'Camembert? St Agur maybe? I got those in for Mrs Manningford at the manor last week, special . . . on that fridge shelf, look.' She stopped abruptly to give an enthusiastic greeting to a man entering the shop, a tall man in a fawn covert coat. 'Well, good morning, sir! We don't often

56

see you in here, the busy life you have. What can I do for you today?'

'Nothing, thank you,' a deep voice responded repressively, 'nothing until you've finished serving this lady.'

Mr Manningford from the manor, Louise deduced till he turned and she saw the dog-collar.

Nancy Chubb hastened to introduce them, her knowing looks implying close acquaintance. 'Our rector,' she said. 'And this is Mrs Fennell, the new lady from Walnut Tree Cottage.'

Louise stiffened. She was Louise Bennett, a person in her own right, nobody's adjunct. Explanations were tedious, but now she felt wrong-footed. And the twin facts of her own drift into agnosticism and the Church's drift into acknowledging any state considered generally socially acceptable did nothing to relieve her annoyance. And where had Nancy learned the name Fennell, anyway? From Maggie? The Maddens?

'Thomas Field,' the rector said, shaking hands. 'Welcome to Abbotsbridge.' He was in his early-forties, with a long, strong-featured face under a thick thatch of prematurely white hair. In contrast his eyes, deep-set and intensely blue, were those of a young man. His skin had the ruddy tan and tiny wrinkles of one who spent most of his time outdoors. 'A delightful cottage, that,' he added. 'With a beautiful garden. Are you a gardener?' He had an air both assured and enquiring.

'No. 'Fraid not. Neither of us is.'

'Perhaps you'll become inspired. The Maddens,' he said in a judiciously neutral tone as he selected half-a-dozen packets of vegetable seed from a rack, 'used to open their garden to the public in early July every year. With teas. For charity.'

'For the church restoration fund,' Nancy beamed, her fingers flashing over the till keys as she dealt with his purchases. 'Very important that. The manor, the rectory gardens and Walnut Tree Cottage.'

Panic rushed over Louise, a cold sweat of nervousness brought on by her own feelings of inadequacy, feelings that had gripped her irrationally, but horribly, ever since she had

57

agreed to move to Hampshire. In London no one cared who you were or what you did, but they expected things of you here – the Church, the WI, the horticultural society – you had to be involved, a part of a true old-fashioned community, Simon said, that was the point of country living. She knew nothing of flowers, barely the names of the most obvious. If she dug over the beds she would be certain to jettison valuable plants, preserve the weeds. How could she open her garden to knowledgable countryfolk without appearing a total fool and a fraud?

'Not this year,' she said hastily. 'Maybe another time.' Put it off, and perhaps with luck it would come to be forgotten.

With his hand on the door he said hopefully: 'If you'd like any help or advice, I should be delighted to assist. Indeed it would be a pleasure. I'm always passing on my pastoral calls.' He added wistfully: 'The daphnes and the anemone blanda will be exquisite at this time of year . . .'

Louise was non-plussed. Which would they be? She recollected various patches of colour in the garden, but she'd never looked closely. 'That's kind of you. I'm sure I'll need advice. Goodbye.'

She finished her shopping and took her wire-basket to the check-out.

'The rector's wife's about your age,' Nancy informed her chattily. 'They got married five years ago. We thought he was all set to be a bachelor, but no, all of a sudden he goes and marries this young doctor.'

'A doctor?'

'Our GP. Surgery's in Brambourne. She and a chap, they cover all the local villages. Come to that, the rector's got three parishes – us, St Thomas at Brambourne and St Michael at Litton-in-the-Marsh.' She dropped her voice to tell Louise about his wife and the strains Nancy reckoned her busy life put upon the equally over-burdened rector. 'Hardworked like he is, she ought to be helping him in the parish, but it's him as helps her. Two small children they've got now, and there's one of those foreign girls living in, but I don't suppose he's any too happy to leave his precious kids with a scatty Swedish blonde all day . . .'

Louise knew she shouldn't encourage gossip, but the

information was interesting. She said nothing and continued to load her basket.

'It's Mrs Hamilton who has to deliver the parish magazines and run the flower rota in the church, and her with a sick husband and all. I'm surprised the Church allows its rector's wife to ignore her duty like that – but then the Church has no rules about anything these days, does it? Raves in the naves, everybody kissing for peace, homosexual priests – all that sort of thing, not nice at all. My Les says they'll be making buggery compulsory next and the bishops'll barely bleat. What I say is, a sin's a sin, and the Church should get up and say so, don't you agree? Mind you, our rector's all right, a smashing man, a lot of the older ladies really fancy him, quite put out when he married, they were!' She laughed her jolly laugh. 'That'll be fourteen-pound seventy, dear.'

Louise paid for her goods and made for the door.

Nancy's voice followed her: 'Don't forget we do deliveries. Just drop a list in and it's every Friday. I do the runs myself, so you can be sure . . .'

Louise had a vivid picture of the sharp eyes peering through the cottage windows and swore to keep her curtains closed on Fridays.

Arabella Manningford arrived on the fourth day. Louise was up a step-ladder removing the detestable frilly pelmet from the bedroom window and saw through the panes a Mercedes draw smoothly up outside the garden gate. Its owner's legs emerged first, perfect legs ending in expensive and beautiful shoes. She stood, and following the line of her body upwards Louise saw a dark suit of the most immaculate cut, a Hermes silk scarf, hair of a glossy chestnut and a face which could only be described as patrician. Louise drank her in, a thirsty soul at an oasis. She was in her late-thirties and was the epitome of London elegance, of all that Louise admired in the smart and cultured women who formed so important a portion of the public who visited the Holbrooke Collection; the sort who in their beautifully modulated tones murmured: 'Darling, the Sèvres, exquisite, isn't it? Such wonderful, such unbelievable colours . . . Do look at that picture,

Fragonard, so high-spirited . . . just think how delightful, what fun, in one's dining room . . . You saw poor Geoffrey's work at the Summer Exhibition? . . . Dinner next Wednesday . . . Goodness how I covet that Boulle table . . . Yes, we must remember to give a donation . . .'

She was startled from another world by the doorbell and stumbled awkwardly downstairs, aware of her dishevelled hair and grubby jeans.

'Hallo,' the voice said, a husky voice, warmer than she had expected. 'I'm Arabella Manningford. I live in Abbotsbridge House and I've called to introduce myself and welcome you to the village. Is this a frightfully inconvenient moment?'

'No,' said Louise, showing her into the sitting-room. 'Well, I was up a ladder, but I'm grateful to be down because I'm frantic for a drink. Have one with me – coffee?'

'I'd love to but this must be a flying visit. I'm driving up to Kensington to lunch with a friend. My weekly day off. Goodness, what a transformation, one wouldn't believe it could be the same room!'

'It's not complete,' Louise said, nervous lest her under-stated style should not meet with the Manningford approval.

'It's terrific – the coolness, the simplicity. Those ebonised corner chairs with the rush seats – the old Morris factory, of course? – those curtains. A feel of the past without slavish imitation. Heavens, what a marvellous change from frills and flowers and Birmingham horse brasses nailed to the beams!'

Louise laughed. 'That I won't do!'

She went to make coffee and returned to find her pictures being scrutinised.

'Fascinating,' Arabella Manningford said. 'I love those semi-abstracts, the essence of a subject without the photographic detail, the tremendous swirl of colour. Did you inherit them or choose them?'

Inherit? Louise almost laughed as she recollected the two reproductions of thirties Cornish artists' work that were the sole salute to art her parents had ever afforded. 'I prowled galleries in my lunch hours and went to the Royal Academy Summer Exhibitions, and on the rare occasions when I could afford what I liked, I bought.'

'You bought well. Though that's only my opinion, I'm not madly knowledgeable. Lucky you to have the opportunities to prowl – now wait, I remember, you're a friend of Maggie Easton's. She told me you had a job in London and that you'd be commuting back to it. What do you do?'

Louise told her.

'The Holbrooke Collection? How perfect! The very thing. You don't have to answer now – I promise I won't bully you! – but would you seriously consider giving a little lecture to the WI? I'm the chairman, for my sins, and we're always on the look-out for people like you. There's a fixed vision of us that's all cakes and home-grown vegetables, but it isn't so at all. Slides of the beautiful things in the Collection would hold us riveted – we have a need for beauty, a need to get away from the commonplace. We meet in the evening, so no worries about your work.'

'Well, I suppose . . .'

'You will? How very kind. We'll talk dates in a week or two. Perfect coffee. Mmm, blissful. I envy your life, you know, I'm a Londoner manquée myself. Brought up there largely. God, how I missed it at first, still do. Hence my weekly day off – time for friends, fashion, all that's happening . . . theatres, concerts, exhibitions. The stimulation of lively minds. I shall come to one of your lunchtime lectures, I truly shall. Give me your next dates.' She fished in her handsome leather bag for a matching leather diary; a tiny gold pencil flashed in the slim, expensively ringed hands.

How could someone like Arabella possibly envy her? Louise wondered, watching the pencil jot. 'But you wouldn't want to return to London, not with all you have here, the house, the estate, everything. Would you?'

To her surprise there was a sigh, a rueful smile, a shrug. 'We used to have a place in Chelsea, but we gave it up. James never had the time for it. He said. His life is wholly here and no alternative. I knew that when I married him, of course, but I don't think I took in the full implications. Now I've developed a life of my own – my children, the house, the WI, the local Bench, the church, the playgroup – I've no lack of occupation! London or rural Hampshire? I can fit in to either. But then women are adaptable. We're chameleons, we alter our protective colouring – our clothes, our habits, even our accents – in a way men can't or won't.'

'And women twine like ivies into relationships, women like me, anyway,' Louise said slowly. 'They dislike being alone.'

Blue-grey eyes examined her. 'You wear a ring, but not a wedding ring. Are you about to get married?'

'I don't know,' Louise said, glancing down at her left hand. She added sardonically: 'A commitment to the idea of commitment perhaps – but I'm far from certain about the current scene.'

'A commitment to commitment!' Arabella Manningford said with a wry twist of the lips. 'Sounds like the *difficult situation situation* our local social worker lectures us about! But when you've taken a good look at the village I hope you'll stay, married or not. A purely selfish wish, of course.' She put down her coffee cup, glanced at her watch and leapt from her chair. 'Goodness, I must fly! Maggie told me you'd reservations about your move, but for heaven's sake, villages like ours are hardly wholly agricultural these days. There are four farms here where in James' grandfather's day there were fourteen – and only a handful of people employed on them. And if Abbotsbridge isn't to dwindle away it has to accept commuters and weekend cottagers – though, please God, not the dreamers of a rural idyll that never existed, nor the young Sophies in aubergine jodhpurs and cashmere cardigans whose partners come home from the City to dress in hairy tweeds and Barbours that never see a thorn bush! We need realists with alert minds and outside interests, your sort of people. And if I can adapt, you can too!'

Louise sensed, more from her tone than the actual words, that she did not, as most of Louise's acquaintance did, view marriage as a shackle to tie women to the home and a lesser role, but rather as a sensible method of ensuring inheritance, of preserving the seemly charm of a certain way of life. She suspected that the mental outlook from Abbotsbridge House would differ as much from that of the terraces of Notting Hill as the physical. Hadn't Maggie said that she was the granddaughter of an earl? Commitment was as much a part of her heritage as noblesse oblige.

Elated nevertheless by the unexpected pleasure of her conversation, Louise waved Arabella Manningford off to the M3. It was a full half-an-hour later that it occurred to her with what skill, what charm, she had been induced to address the Women's Institute – and, she presumed, not even for an honorarium.

Chapter 6

As the first week went on the pain of the move subsided and Louise found herself becoming curiously fond of the cottage. It was always warm, always peaceful. It accepted the furniture, blending with it, gleams of light from the flickering log fires in its great hearth glowing on polished surfaces. Louise abandoned champagne and kept coffee warm on the Aga instead: working about the cottage, altering and hanging new curtains, arranging each room to her own satisfaction, was stimulus enough. Then there were the unexpected delights of the garden and its March flowers. In Notting Hill she had resented the cost of florists' mean bunches, limiting her purchases to special occasions; now she found herself filling the rooms with great bowls of flowers. This garden bore no resemblance to the London garden of her childhood with its scuffed grass, its stunted sickly shrubs and its sour-smelling soil. Sometimes she wandered out into the thin early sunshine simply to look, sipping her coffee, seeing a difference every day as more daffodils and narcissus – and strange exquisitely scented shrubs that were entirely new to her – rushed into bloom. She would stoop and finger them and inhale deeply. There were always wood pigeons cooing in the trees, and there was a robin who hopped near her, looking up at her with dark and shining eyes; later she saw a second robin, brisk and flirtatious, and watching them she discovered the half-built nest in the ivy on the old flint and brick west wall.

During the week neighbours called. Maggie came regularly with young Toby on their way back from the village playgroup. She sank on to a kitchen chair, drank Louise's gin and complained that Jack was supervising her taking the pill every night – 'Like a small child with nasty-tasting linctus! But I'm not going to be made better. It's my body and I want a baby in it!' She tried to make a joke of it, but her eyes were full of pain.

Louise remembered her friend Josie, an expert in baroque works of art now fast becoming a baby-burping expert. She told Maggie: 'Some women develop migraine-type headaches on the pill – then the doctors make them abandon it. Other methods of contraception aren't fool-proof, are they?'

'Christ,' Maggie said fervently. 'You're brilliant, Lou. Thanks!'

The haunting nervousness Louise felt with local people about her lack of horticultural knowledge did not extend to Maggie and she took the opportunity to ask about her unknown flowers. When she had left Louise would walk round the garden once more, savouring the names on her tongue – grape hyacinth, hellebore, pulmonaria, pulsatilla . . . When the rector came on a pastoral call and looked wistfully through the window, and that odd woman Brozie Hamilton came in her tweed hat to deliver the parish magazine and hint about flowers for the church, she ushered them out and absorbed still more names as they exclaimed over the beauty and the scent of the Viburnum farreri, the daphnes, the Spiraea arguta. Louise ventured to Brozie that the latin names were off-putting. 'Not at all,' she said. 'They all describe the plant or tell a story. See that weeping willow by the river? Salix babylonica!' 'Oh,' responded Louise, enchanted, ' "by the waters of Babylon we sat down and wept." I do like that!' And she picked Brozie a big bunch of narcissus. It gave her an extraordinary sense of pride and ownership to do so.

As she became more accepting of the cottage, she began to feel that perhaps the move from Notting Hill might be bearable after all. But on returning to work she found the transition from one world to the other both exhausting and exasperating. The journey was far from the restful interlude Charley St George had so airily described and really, she told herself, to waste some fifteen hours a week in travelling was ridiculous. She gritted her teeth, she said little to Simon, she learned where to wait on the station platform to maximise her chance of a seat, she learned to avoid the train bores with their endless DIY details, and the train groper who pressed himself against her in the crush; she was determined not to be defeated into babies and domesticity.

Easter came, the weather was fine, and on Easter Monday half the village, it seemed, went to the point-to-point at Hackwood Park, a few miles away. While traffic on the six-lane M3 flashed uncomprehendingly through its cutting below, up on the great green meadow of the Park there was a slower, more traditional scene. From mid-morning onward there came a steady influx of cars, Range-Rovers and horse-boxes lurching their way along the lane and over the grass, to park in rows beside the racecourse.

The air was warm and sweet, the first real breath of spring. Louise and Simon had followed Maggie and Jack in their Volvo Estate, and as Louise wriggled from the car and stood up she found the scent of the crushed grass and the earth as heady as wine. The sun was shining, sparkling on the glossy rows of cars and lancing its beams into the woods behind them to pick out the shrill green leaves on the bushes and gild the smooth trunks of the beech trees. Simon turned off the car engine and above the sounds of voices talking she could hear the song of a lark as it spiralled upward. It irked her that the bright scene should be so full of light and life and she feel so remote from it.

She sent a swift assessing glance among the women, anxious lest she had committed any sartorial faux pas, relieved to see that her casual trousers, shirt and pullover outfit was standard, as Maggie had said.

At first Maggie's suggestion of the point-to-point had been one to reject, something alien to plague her with her ignorance of the rural pursuits of the shire counties. Louise still blushed to remember her one and only visit to a farm. It had belonged to her grandmother's cousin, a traditional small Kentish farm. There had been apple blossom and fluffy chicks and lambs. Louise had cooed happily along with her

66

sisters – until the depths of her ignorance had been revealed. Seeing some soft brown cows in a paddock, she had asked how much milk they gave. It seemed the sort of question she should ask. But the elderly cousin stared at her. 'None, love. Not yet. They're only heifers.' 'Oh. When do they start, then?' A great bellow of laughter: 'Ho, not till they've had their calves. You won't give milk till you've had a baby, will you?' Her sycophantic sisters and brother had giggled too, though Louise could have sworn them equally ignorant. The notion that cows had to calve regularly to produce milk was a novel one: she'd thought them a form of milk-producing machine. Worse was to come. Reviewing her idea of hens, she attempted a joke about the cock's happy role in egg production. The cousin slapped his sides with mirth: 'They don't need a cock – they simply lay, poor deluded creatures! Dear oh me, where have you been all your life, girl?' The illogicalities of nature had Louise totally confused. And her confusion became a family joke that never palled with the telling. She feared being a joke at the point-to point. Horses? She'd never even sat astride one. She had anticipated the event with dread.

It was Charley St George, encountered on an evening commuter train, who had made her feel better about it. He told her how point-to-points were races for horses from the local hunts, over big fences and water-jumps. It was good relaxing fun taking a picnic and gnawing chicken bones and drinking wine in the sunshine with your friends first. Her ignorance would be no bar to enjoyment, he said, he'd explain it all, he'd enjoy that. She must arrange with her friends to park by the finishing post and save him a place if she didn't see him first.

Louise looked along the line of vehicles parked by the course; boots were open, rear doors flung back, wicker hampers and cold bags were being dragged out, canvas chairs and picnic tables erected. More cars were sweeping up and disgorging laughing people who jumped out and dashed across the grass to meet their friends, exclaiming, catching hands, kissing. Children milled around them; labradors and English spaniels were ordered to sit and be tethered. She saw no gleam of scarlet paint, no Charley, not yet.

A weather-beaten woman appeared before her, pushing some sort of thick pamphlet at her with a confident beam. What were these?

'Race-cards!' Young Hugh left the friends he'd been chasing about with and came to Louise's rescue. 'Daddy! How many do we want?'

Jack was talking to Simon, two tall assured men in tweed jackets immersed in business; they were hopeless once they got together nowadays. Neither reacted to Hugh's yell.

An extraordinarily elderly Landrover rattled over the tussocky grass, heading for the space she'd saved. Louise raised her hands to stop it, saw that the large male at the wheel was Charley himself and skipped aside.

'Hello!' he bellowed. He jerked on the brake, flung open the door and jumped out to give Louise a smacking kiss. 'You're here! Great! Race-cards? How many do we want? How many are we?' He whipped out a wad of notes from a hip pocket and paid for a handful, combining handing them out with a 'Hey, good to see you again!' for Maggie, and with introductions all round.

Jack and Simon shook hands with Charley with a formality which seemed out of place among the picnics and children and horses and reminded Louise of sniffing stiff-legged dogs. They wanted to repay him for the race-cards and looked put out when he waved them aside. Two women emerged from the Landrover, the first a willowy girl who appeared all beige, from her long straight hair down through the thigh-length knitted beige top with its leather and gilt belt on her hips, to the matching leggings and the beige suede bootees on her long narrow feet. Her complexion, too, was beige, verging in places on green. Charley put an arm round her shoulder with bearish affection and introduced her as Melody Monday. She shook hands limply. Behind her was Brozie Hamilton, looking quite at home in her tweed hat and her green wellies.

'Your husband not with you?' Maggie asked her. 'How is he?'

A flicker of complicity seemed to pass between Brozie and Charley, a complicity tinged with humour.

'He's all right,' said Brozie. 'He refused to come, didn't

feel up to it, but I've left him with a casserole and a baking potato in the oven.'

'I persuaded Brozie to take a day off,' Charley said complacently. 'She never has one and she deserves it.'

'I haven't been to a point-to-point for twenty years,' she told them. 'Not since I married Hubert. Such a change.'

Melody clutched at her belly, grunted, 'Ooof!' and scrambled into the front seat of the Landrover, muttering something at Charley as she went.

'Gin!' he said, adding: 'She's got cramps. Usual monthly problem – she goes through hell for about twelve hours. Hitting the gin bottle's the only solution. Doctors,' he added largely, 'are useless.'

'For Chrissakes, Charley, shut up and get me the gin!' Melody snarled, her eyes closed and her face screwed up.

'She's waspish with it, too,' he said. From the back of the Landrover he poured her half a tumblerful of gin with a dash of tonic.

She drank the greater part of it as if it were water, held it out to be topped up, then huddled down in her seat, clutching the glass like a talisman. 'Now go away and leave me to die!'

'Okay,' he responded equably, and turned back to the others. 'How about food?' he asked.

The men passed glasses of wine around, the women busied themselves with the hampers. Maggie had made an excellent raised veal and ham pie, Brozie contributed an unusual chicken liver pâté – 'It's the generous hand with the brandy bottle that does it!' Charley commented – and Louise's spiced chicken joints were fought for by Maggie and Jack's three small boys. The adults helped themselves indiscriminately to something of everything and stood around munching and talking.

'Is that Landrover yours?' Maggie demanded of Charley, gazing with amazement at its mud and rust. 'Not the sleek outfit we expected!'

'Something different, isn't she?' he responded. 'I went to a car auction the other day – sometimes you can pick up a bargain and sell it on at an amazing profit – and there she was. I've always wanted one for the country.'

'It's held together with barbed wire and electric flex,' said Jack spitefully. He loathed being in the vicinity of anything so shabby as that grubby and disreputable vehicle; clients of his might be present and associate it with him.

'I shall restore it,' Charley said grandiosely. 'It'll be a good project for my weekends. And when it's done, it'll have antique value.'

'Christ,' Jack muttered. 'You must be out of your head.' He picked up a bottle of burgundy and went round replenishing the glasses.

'What's Melody's view?' asked Maggie.

'She doesn't mind. She never minds what I do. She spends half the weekend asleep, anyway.'

'But you – don't you ever stop working?' Brozie wanted to know.

'Not if I can help it. There are too many fascinating things to do in life, you have to cram them in. It's boring otherwise, anyway, and boredom leads to depression.'

'You've never been depressed,' Brozie scoffed, holding out her glass to Jack for more wine. 'Have you?'

'I know what it's about,' Charley admitted. 'But I've conquered the brute. Absolutely.'

'I wish you'd teach me how,' Maggie said. Despite the words she looked for once relaxed and cheerful. The fresh air and the wine had brought unusual colour to her face and her hair was attractively tousled.

'I will,' said Charley, eyeing her with admiration. 'With pleasure.'

Jack turned from refilling Brozie's glass, his face tight. He began to say that the traumas of bereavement hardly equated with mental illness but Charley interrupted him, his big hand raised. 'Hold it!' Loudspeakers were booming a voice across the meadow. 'Runners and riders for the first race. Hell, someone, anyone, where'd I put my race-card?'

Everyone dived for pencils and pens and started marking off their cards. Charley showed Louise how and then with urgings and laughter and an enthusiasm that was infectious, he collected Brozie, Maggie and the three boys and took them to inspect the horses as they stalked round the paddock. Louise stood squeezed beside him in the crowd, vividly conscious of the great size and power of the gleaming horse-flesh that passed and repassed before her awed gaze, deeply respectful of the sangfroid with which their attendants led these head-tossing giants. There were six horses for the first race. At first they all looked much the same sort of size and configuration, but then as Charley talked to her and gestured, his fingers stabbing and his words tumbling over each other in a torrent of mingled instruction and admiration, she began to perceive that they differed, that as he said, the chestnut was not only a handsome colour but also heavily muscled, that number 6, a neat bay called Pocket Rocket, was particularly alert and excited, and that the grey which had first aroused her admiration was what Charley called stringy. So how did you pick a winner?

'With a pin,' Brozie suggested.

'With difficulty,' Maggie offered.

They laughed.

Charley pulled his great body up to its full height and raised his thick eyebrows in mock reproach. 'With my help, how can you doubt Louise's success?'

'Will you give her a guarantee?' Maggie asked.

There was more laughter.

On Louise's other side a husky voice with a Hampshire burr claimed her attention. 'This the first time you've bin to a point-to-point?'

Louise looked round. A short and rounded woman was tilting an untidy greying head up at her, her eyes alert with interest.

'Yes,' Louise admitted. 'It's the first time.'

A warm mottled hand lay on Louise's arm; the little woman murmured confidentially: 'Then I'll give you a tip, my dear, and you can show your friends you know what's what too. You put a tenner on Bronze Beau and you'll do all right.'

'Bronze Beau?'

'Number eleven, look.'

Number eleven was neither bronze nor particularly beau, he was a brown horse ambling round, looking bored.

'Deceptive,' Louise's new friend said happily, reading her mind. 'My son runs the stables, like. So I know. An' Mr

71

Getliffe's riding him. He's a great rider. Back 'im in the third and fourth as well and you might find you're on to a good thing. Rob Getliffe. Bye! Have a nice day, dear.'

'Well, thank you,' Louise said, startled and touched and hardly knowing what to think. 'Thank you very much.'

'Right!' said Charley in her ear. 'A glance at the bookies' boards and then on to the Tote. Picked a winner yet?'

'I'm backing Bronze Beau.'

'You must be mad,' said Charley.

Simon stood beside Louise as they waited for the race to start, eyeing her uneasily. Since the move he had been happy, uplifted in the mornings by the sight of cows standing hock deep in mist as he drove along the river valley, and at dusk by the cawing rooks circling the untidy nests in the great avenue at Abbotsbridge House, and he longed for Louise to feel as he did. His encouragement had opened the world of fine art to her, now he had this special world to give her. Originally he had been certain that time only was needed to convince her of the desirability of the change; he had put up with her grumbles – she had always been given to female mutterings of unfairness – but on occasions he had glimpsed a real distress on her face that could not be dismissed as the fatigues of moving or commuting. It worried and depressed him. He wanted to spend the rest of his life with her, to marry her, for God's sake, to have children with her. But there was the blight of her inexplicable aversion to living in the country. When he had returned each evening of that first week to discover all she had achieved in the cottage in the hours of his absence – order regained from chaos, the tranquil simplicity and beauty she had created in each room – he had believed that she was settling in, that like some displaced animal her new habitat was claiming her. But still there were frowns, and silences, and he remained uneasy. If only today she could put her prejudices aside and enjoy the fun of the point-to-point, perhaps she might discover that rural life was not so alien and inexplicable as she seemed determined to believe it.

A raised voice made him look round. Jack was demanding the immediate descent of his sons from the roof of a nearby

Range Rover, on which, along with a pair of similarly blond small boys, they were cavorting to the imminent danger of life and limb and the vehicle's paintwork. 'Oh!' they wailed. 'No! Please!' The Range Rover's owner shrugged amiably; provided they all sat peacefully they could watch the race from their vantage point.

'Sit, boys!' Jack commanded, as to exuberant puppies, and watched them subside. 'I apologise for my sons' thoughtless behaviour,' he added.

My sons. How Jack relished and repeated those words. His sons, living emblems of his virility, proof of his potency. Simon wished that Louise were about to give him similar proof. In the hidden corners of his mind anxieties were lurking. For months he and Louise had been trying for a baby and nothing had happened. Her periods were regular, her family clearly fecund. In an area where he had always been supremely confident, he was now concerned. Could it be his, Simon's, fault? Was his fertility low? Was his technique wrong? His mind ranged through hitherto unconsidered problems. After reading a magazine article at the dentist's he had changed from Y-fronts to boxer shorts and lowered the temperature of his bathwater. He read the *Kama Sutra* and experimented with previously unthought of positions. Louise had seemed surprised but acquiescent, even enthusiastic, despite the contortions. She had always been an eager contributor in bed – though now he came to think of it, there had been less of that in recent weeks. In the mornings she got up early to catch the train, and in the evenings there were mutterings that the journey had tired her. He hoped that his superb sex-life would not dwindle either in quality or in quantity at this important juncture. He was resolving to look discreetly in the bookshops for something that might aid their procreative efforts when there was a yell of: 'They're off!'

He must watch the race. He and Jack had backed the favourite, the grey. A sensible choice, Jack had said, since they had become so engrossed in their conversation that they had neither visited the paddock nor checked the horses' form. They had been talking of his, Simon's, work. It was going well, absorbing him throughout each day. It seemed

73

the clients he would be dealing with – was already dealing with – were impatient, successful men and women who would keep him on his mettle, while the work was at a level he'd rarely tackled before. And Jack, with his solidly established background of clubs (golf, cricket, Round Table, Lions) and useful business acquaintances, was already introducing him to a host of worthwhile contacts whilst weaving him into his own network.

The horses and riders swept past on their first round of the course, bunched closely together, a pounding mass of colour and majesty and straining muscles. Where was his horse? He peered as they rose to the next fence – lying second and jumping well. Good.

'Mine's only in fourth place,' Louise said in a disgusted tone.

'Well, you never know,' he encouraged her absently. 'Tactics. Don't want it to get to the front too soon!'

It had been a good tactic of his to change firms, it would get him to the front in the rat race of life. Louise had queried caustically: 'Big frog, small pond?' but Shergold & Stent were not small, they were as big almost as his last firm, and growing. He would grow with them: it had been made clear that he had been recruited as a potential equity partner and that he intended to achieve in the minimal possible time. He had specialised by choice and by training in taxation; he loved the unsullied clarity of figures, but more, he enjoyed advising people on their financial and business affairs, interesting people who needed his expertise; he was fascinated to compare their figures from year to year, watching them winning or losing, striving, if he could, to help them make it the first. He was, he told himself with a wry smile, a people person. He had been given an unexpectedly good office – modern rosewood furniture, big leather chairs, indecently healthy plants rearing up from expensive urns – suffusing him daily in a cloud of well-being. But the contrast with his home life made him restive; it even made him feel guilty.

Louise was jigging up and down beside him and muttering beneath her breath. The muttering grew louder: 'Come on, Bronze Beau, come on!'

Simon stared, then swung round to see three horses rise

almost simultaneously to jump the last fence, land, and surge up the course towards them.

'Come on, Pocket Rocket!' Charley's bass roared deafeningly from beyond Louise, to be echoed by Maggie and Brozie.

One of the jockeys was using his whip, the others were busy with their hands. God, it would be a close-run thing; Simon added his voice to the rest. The grey he'd backed and the bay, Pocket Rocket, appeared to be neck and neck in front . . . no, looking quickly across he thought the brown might be gaining on them . . . He leaned forward, but the angle of vision made it impossible to see clearly . . . the horses flashed past the winning post, feet pounding, divots flying, and Louise grabbed his arm.

'It won!' she said in a voice of pure astonishment. 'My horse won!'

Louise won a hundred and fifty pounds on the first race. 'Beginners' luck!' everyone chorused condescendingly, teasing her. When she won forty pounds on the second race (she had heard a large and knowledgeable-looking woman in a headscarf like the Queen's comment that Young Sprig was 'a damn' good goer'), and somewhat larger sums on the winners of the third and fourth, by backing their rider, Rob Getliffe, as she had been instructed, they murmured: 'Unbelievable luck!' and looked stunned.

Hugh, who was allowed to bet in a tiny way with his father, comforted himself that all the other grown-ups' losses were larger than his. 'Bet your wallet's skinny now, Charley! How much have you lost?'

'Ten, twenty, forty and eighty – what's that make?'

His tongue in the corner of his mouth, Hugh concentrated. 'A hundred and fifty. Wow!' he added, awed. 'How'd you do that?'

'I double my bet each time I lose. That way, when I do win I get it all back with a vengeance!'

'Unbelievable. The swiftest possible way to disaster!'

Louise smothered a giggle at Jack's appalled look. No, he would never exceed the parameters of his meticulously planned life with Charley's gambling or any other of his nonsensical flamboyances.

'I'll win eventually,' Charley said confidently. 'I always do.'

He walked over to the Landrover to peer in at Melody. She was lying huddled in the front seat, her face half-obscured by a damp tangle of long hair that clung in strands to her pale skin. She was clearly asleep, her chin sagging towards her chest.

'Passed out, poor cow,' he said. 'Thank God. Now she'll sleep the worst of it off. She'll be okay.'

Eddie was pestering Maggie. 'I'm starving,' he moaned theatrically.

'Hot dogs!' Charley suggested. 'All round. How about that?'

Three sets of round eyes focussed on him, avid as hungry puppies. 'Yes!' they clamoured.

Within seconds Louise found herself rounded up, together with Maggie and Brozie and the boys, and heading for hot dogs – 'No, thank you!' – followed by a home-made sweet stall for fudge – 'Mmm, delicious!' – for the Tote to collect her latest winnings and then to the tents crammed with country clothing for Charley to buy himself a padded shower-proof waistcoat: 'For fishing on chilly days. They actually carry my size here!'

This garment paid for from a wad of notes hardly diminished by his losses, he turned his attention to his companions. There were hats piled on a table by the entrance to this tent, smart hats to combine with country wear. They had shallow felt crowns and stiff neat brims and Louise had particularly noticed several of the stylish younger women emerging from their Mercedes and Volvo estates sporting similar designs.

'You need another hat,' Charley told Brozie, and pouncing on some burgundy-coloured ones, found her size, removed the Harris tweed from her head and settled the new hat at the right angle with triumphant panache.

'Like that!' he said. His gaze shot to Maggie. 'What do you think?'

Maggie nodded, laughing. 'You couldn't beat it,' she said.

Like the green tweed, the hat transformed the lanky, ordinary-looking woman whom no one would notice into someone of character, someone of a style which, if eccentric, was nevertheless noteworthy. 'You are clever,' Brozie said with affection, and pulled out her purse.

The clothes in the tent were attractive; not the sort Louise would ever have thought would lure her, but with her own purse bulging with her winnings she felt unexpectedly drawn to them; they were what was worn here, what looked right. A waistcoat like Charley's would be just the thing to pull on when she went to pick flowers in the garden – and so would a pair of the green wellies she could see piled in a corner. With mingled advice and approval being called from the others she bought them, and added a bright silk scarf that Charley found, poppies and corn rioting on a rich blue ground. It was a thousand light years from anything she would wear in London – but London was not here.

Outside the tent a wind had sprung up, light but cool, blowing long thin streaks of cloud over the sun. Louise shrugged on her waistcoat and tied her new silk scarf round her neck. Hugh was anxious to run to the paddock to view the horses before the next race and time was running short. He tilted his face from his mother to Charley: 'Quick, we've got to go!' he urged them.

Louise told them to go; she wouldn't be trying her luck again today – that would be tempting fate! Brozie said ruefully that she'd better not either, for the opposite reason – her eye and her luck were totally out. Still, and she sighed and smiled, she was having a wonderful time.

They found Simon and Jack reviving the unfortunate Melody with coffee from Thermos flasks. Someone had to look after her, Jack said righteously. Simon looked round and widened his eyes at Louise's new clothes. Melody wanted to know whether Charley had won lots of money yet. 'He usually does,' she said in her vague drawl, a thin, elegant hand pushing back the hair from her face. 'We have a terrific meal out afterwards.'

Arabella Manningford came past, accompanied by three of her handsome children and two labradors. She called to Louise: 'This your first point-to-point? Back any winners?'

'Four in a row,' Louise called back.

'Heavens!' she said. 'You've found your feet quickly!'

Louise felt as though she had been given an accolade, then acknowledged with inward mirth her own snobbishness.

'You wouldn't like a kitten, would you?' Arabella asked. 'The tortoiseshell who mouses round our outhouses is bulging ominously.'

'No, thank you,' said Louise. She had never possessed an animal and had no wish to do so.

Charley, Maggie and the boys did not return until after the last race. Then they arrived triumphant. Hugh held a pound between thumb and forefinger and flourished it above his head: 'I backed the winner!' he shouted, swaggering towards them over the turf. Charley, unbelievably, had won nearly two thousand pounds. 'I told you my system worked,' he boasted to Jack, and Melody echoed him: 'It's amazing!' He had bought the boys a candyfloss each which they were demolishing with glee, their eyes shining above sticky blobs of the stuff. 'Great kids,' he said. 'They deserve it.'

'You'll rot their teeth,' their father muttered, unimpressed.

Maggie, laughing and shaking her head at everyone's questions, said that she'd only won enough to cover her earlier losses, but Louise saw that her step had a buoyancy she had not seen for many months and she looked as though all her senses had been given a stimulating alcohol rub.

Hubert had worked himself into a fit of fury by the time Brozie returned. As she opened the front door he was there to grab her wrists and drag her in, digging in his fingernails. He often hurt her now. He hated her to go out without him, specially with Charley, but he refused to leave the house himself. He wanted her to be buried alive, like him. But Charley was right, that mustn't happen. She rubbed her smarting wrists. Hubert's nails left marks on them, like nails of another kind. Stigmata. But why should she be a martyr, crucified for his affliction? He was shouting at her, but she shut her ears to the abuse.

As she shook herself free he snatched her new hat and flung it across the hall. She darted to its rescue and went into the kitchen, shutting the door, leaning her back against it. Heat poured over her, scalding her face scarlet, but the unpleasant symptoms of her time of life were nothing beside her husband's problems. Poor Hubert, veering for years between anger and terror. Now both had swelled up to monstrous proportions, filling his brain, the anger predominating – anger that she was escaping the torment he was suffering, anger at the realisation that her sympathy was almost gone, that only the stoic patience of years was left – and now wearing dangerously thin.

Euthanasia, that was the answer. Mercy killing. Charley had seen it. 'Bop him on the head,' he'd said. To end Hubert's life would be a kindness. It was what she should have done for her parents, for her mother, dying by slow inches of kidney disease, for her father, like Hubert, tormented by cancer.

She had watched them die, helpless and wretched. She had never intervened to ease their pain. Why not? To let an animal suffer as they had suffered would bring convictions for cruelty; it should be so for humans too. Had she stayed her hand because she had loved them too much? Or not enough? She had thought about it many times over the years, but the answer had never come.

Euthanasia was forbidden by law. She must find a way to evade the workings of the law.

The Church forbade euthanasia too. Yet surely God would understand the need for Hubert's death? She was fanning herself with her hat, frantically, but the heat was retreating now. She put it down gently on the pile of his glossy books that Charley had given her to read and gave it a little pat. Perhaps it was God who had seen her daily fight against depression and sent Charley to cheer and advise her?

Suffering was wrong; cruelty was wrong. To be merciful was right. She would be merciful to Hubert. She had only to think how.

Chapter 7

When in mid-May Jack and Maggie were dressing for their dinner party that evening, he complained that he'd no idea what to wear.

'What did you stipulate on the invitation cards?' he demanded, standing in his socks and underpants and staring at the amazing sight his wife presented.

'I didn't send cards,' said Maggie with aggravating nonchalence, flinging a couple of ropes of amber beads over her head. 'I telephoned.'

She was wearing a flowing loose silk pyjama outfit in swirls of golds and greens. At least, Jack prayed it was silk, not the polyester he deplored. It was deplorable enough as it was – frivolous and gaudy. No dinner jacket could ever look right beside that. He scowled.

'So what did you telephone?'

'Casual. Friends and neighbours, what else? Wear the cashmere pullover your mother sent you.'

He supposed he could. But he was put out. Casual, that was the epitome of Maggie. Once he had found her easy going good-nature and her untidiness attractive, relaxing. He was younger then. Now as he rose in his profession and acquired gravitas, he wished she would learn a similar dignity, go to the hairdresser's, wear Jaeger suits and sit on committees. But she seemed to be heading in the opposite direction: a sad and messy earth mother whose eyes constantly reproached him for not wanting more children – until tonight, when suddenly, shockingly, she appeared as voluptuous and seductive as an houri.

His temper was not improved when the door knocker sounded the arrival of their first guests and she told him that the Colebys, wealthy landowning clients of his from the next village, had cried off two days ago on the excuse of his raging hayfever. So whom had she invited in their stead?

'Charley St George and Melody,' she said over her shoulder, and opened the door to them before his expletives could blast through the cottage.

Their other guests, the rector, Thomas Field, his doctor wife Jane, and Simon and Louise, arriving hard on their heels, Jack pulled himself together to be a good host – he prided himself upon the warmth of his welcome, the quality of his claret and the sympathetic interest he brought to bear upon his guests' interests and concerns – but it took some time for his annoyance to evaporate. To invite the Colebys had been his idea. Reprehensible of Maggie not to have told him when they cried off; far worse to have invited those extraordinary people. The noisy Charley was no man for Jack's network, and Melody, unlike Charlotte Coleby, Cambridge graduate and descendant of an ancient local family, would never co-opt his wife on to charitable committees, or influence her in a sensible way.

His guests settled with drinks and striking up conversations, Jack sat down to reflect that someone had to influence Maggie; she couldn't moon over babies all her life. It hurt him too, to remember little Felicity; he was shocked how sharp the pain was even now; but life had to move on. Jack had no desire to push his wife into a full-time career; being a wife and a mother took up too many hours to make the combination with work anything other than a horrific strain; he'd seen that in his clients enough times. Women in that dual role could be single-minded about nothing, inadequacy was forced upon them, and then guilt over their short-comings turned them militant and aggressive towards their husbands. But charity work would be just the thing to give Maggie proper interests and some status; when the boys were all away at school she could even come to sit on the local Bench.

He looked at her. She was sitting on the sofa next to

81

Charley, whose notion of casual was nearer to a builder's mate showing his bottom cleft than the Armani wear that Simon sported. His jeans were inadequate to his great size and Jack could have sworn he saw burrs, yes, real burrs, sticking to them, while the frayed shirt was crumpled. Bad to be prejudiced by appearances, but there were limits. Maggie, far from being repelled by the sartorial short-comings, was leaning towards Charley, listening to him with her lips slightly parted and a look of fascination on her face. Reluctantly Jack listened too.

Charley was responding to Jane Field's interest in a new-comer to the village by telling her he was a publisher – staggering information. Asked if he had inherited the business, Charley laughed and shook his head. No, he'd set it up himself. The name was odd, and nobody seemed to know it. Simon leaned forward to murmur something about capital investment but Charley's hands brushed the idea away in a wide gesture of dismissal and he explained that he was in subsidy publishing; no need to tie up large sums. The punters, he said, all put their money up front; the contribution he and his partner made was the investment of their expertise, their eye for a book that would sell, their ear as to how the market was moving. There was not only the publishing company, there was their latest baby, Reflections, booksellers and distributors. Both were successful, growing, and would continue to grow. Now telly was so terrible people were turning back to books; they were mining a rich seam.

He leaned back, the shirt straining its buttons over a large stomach and parting shortly above the waistline to reveal a triangle of hairy skin. He was expansive, confident, explanatory. There were creative writing classes springing up all over the place, on top of these there were workshops, summer schools, weekends, days – you name them, folk flocked to them. And they all dreamed of publication: Icarus Publishing made their dreams come true. Charley was the marketing director; that took him out of the office, moving around the country, able to take advantage of other money-making opportunities that came his way.

In a pause while he gulped at his drink, Maggie spoke. 'You're a property developer, too, aren't you?' she asked.

82

'Brozie Hamilton told me she'd seen a site down in Southampton.'

She sounded like some doting wife encouraging the object of her marital affections to show off his brilliance, Jack thought. She never did that with him. Not that he'd want her to – too damned embarrassing. He sifted through remarks calculated to silence Charley; every one was a bludgeon. He discarded them rather than shock his guests and then, as Charley's voice soared once more, grimly regretted doing so.

Yes, Charley was a property developer – that and publishing were the twin concerns that were poised to expand till they became the corner-stones of his great business empire. He spoke of his future and waxed eloquent. He told his listeners of the great tycoons of the past and how they had built their vast companies and their limitless fortunes. He spoke of Richard Branson, of his business acumen, of his flair for perceiving gaps in the market that could be profitably filled and how he elbowed his way into them, of the range of his exciting ventures. With the recession receding Charley was ready to take advantage of the markets that were reappearing: he foresaw for himself a similar future. At times he was solemn with the immensity of his vision, his voice sonorous and rich, then suddenly he would be witty, flippant, laughing at himself, playing with an idea, flinging it into the air where it sparkled with the joyous light of his imagination, letting it ascend into the dream castles that were the true realms of his fancy, to capture it again with a deep chuckle. He would be successful, rich, powerful; he would use any means to gain his end, but when it was achieved he would retire to his country estate and its trout stream and his philanthropy would rival a Nuffield's. It was impossible to distinguish the light-hearted notions from the true substance of his beliefs, but from the look of his audience no one cared. He was brilliant, he was wild, capricious, irresponsible – what did it matter? Laughing, protesting, entranced, they hung on his words. Even Jack was torn between exasperation and admiration: such fluency the man had.

At dinner the fluency was unabated. Charley was seated between Louise and Jane. He was fascinated that Jane was a doctor; she didn't look like one, he said, eyeing her with a grin that expressed his delectation of her tawny pageboy hair, full sensuous mouth and sturdily attractive figure, yet village gossip told him she was a good one. He wanted to know about her practice and her children, and how on earth she managed to combine medicine with motherhood and marriage to a parson.

'Caring for the community body and soul, between you,' he said, leaning back for Jack to pour white burgundy into his glass. 'Body and soul. Quite an undertaking!'

'It takes a sensible au pair and tight organisation,' Jane admitted. 'I'm a fiend for lists, and reminders to Thomas lie all over the house. Too often we're playing box and cox, one out when the other's in.'

'We do meet at times,' her husband observed as he spooned up his cucumber soup. 'Births and deaths connect us.'

'Deaths, certainly. Thomas needs my certificate before he can bury the body.' She sipped her wine appreciatively. 'And what village gossip are you referring to? Most that comes to me is either crude or rude.'

'Nancy Chubb,' Maggie said with a mock shudder.

Melody spoke unexpectedly in her high drawl: 'I reckon Nancy's secretly hooked on sex. I caught her deep in a lurid blockbuster when the shop was empty one evening. She nearly jumped out of her skin.'

Sex? Charley put down his soup spoon. Sex, he proclaimed, had become the great passion and fashion of today. 'And not just in blockbusters. Sex is no longer the quick bedroom bonk the Victorians knew, but a leisure pursuit with all the accompanying literature and gimmicks. What's the betting that sex aids, like other games equipment, won't be available in the sports shops soon? Vertical jogging is out; horizontal jogging is the new health craze. Training manuals are available by the thousand – call them soft porn if you like – and training videos – otherwise known as blue movies! I have a vision. I see the day coming when sexual performance will receive recognition as man's oldest and greatest sport . . .' His imagination was again whirling with wild ideas; he seized upon preposterous notions and embroidered them till his listeners were helpless with laughter.

'There'll be competitions, league tables, races . . . sex will be included in the Olympic Games. Imagine the categories – sprint, high jump, under-water . . . not to mention the marathon!' Here Maggie abandoned her attempt to clear the soup plates and leaned weakly on the table. 'Superman will be replaced by supervirility man with muscles in a different place. Imagine a future Mr World, judged by the development of his alternative equipment!'

A whoop from Melody made Jack jump and stare as she leaned back in her chair, her long neck pulsing with her mirth. She was wearing a knitted silk suit in pearl grey, her hair was pulled into a bunch high on her head and woven with silver ribbons and her arms jangled with silver bracelets. Jack had privately viewed her as sleek and scornful and sophisticated. Now he saw a little girl in the clutch of the giggles. 'Oh, Charley,' she gasped, 'how do you think up such wild things?'

Jack looked with apprehension at the rector, but he was laughing too, no hint of remonstrance on his face. Jane, Louise, Simon . . . they were all caught in the glittering webs that Charley wove; they greeted every word as brilliant wit. Jack let himself utter a low chuckle, then pushed Maggie away from carving the Beef Wellington. 'That's my job, go away and get the vegetables,' he ordered her. It was embarrassing to look at her, flushed and gasping and mopping her eyes with a napkin.

The rest of the meal was sheer penance, but his wife and his guests were encouraging the nonsense, and there was nothing he could do to stop it. Jack was out of control of his own dinner party and the unusual nature of this situation left him confused and irritable. Not that you could call it a dinner party, not this amorphous mixture of social levels and dress. He circled the table replenishing the claret glasses. Like the useless bubbles in the champagne he detested, insubstantial stuff that got up one's nose, Charley was a bubbly unprofitable sort of person; Jack preferred something of more solid worth. He despised Charley for the atmosphere of levity, for the lack of serious informed talk on a level that left one feeling uplifted at the end of the evening, benevolent even, colleagues turned into friends, friends introduced to people who would interest them, might be of use to them. Flippant rubbish about sex achieved nothing.

Yet when he saw Maggie relaxed and laughing on the sofa with her coffee after the meal, his heart smote him and he had to acknowledge that at least the fellow had cheered her up. Despite her short-comings he was fond of his wife. He could not contemplate her present unhappiness with equanimity; he wanted to help her, if not in the foolish way she demanded. His earnings would not allow that. Since the recession fewer clients went to litigation, and when they did, they mostly settled out of court; they took longer to pay, too. He had not discussed this with her, not wanting to worry her, but he was quietly making retrenchments. There could be no second holiday abroad next winter, and he had cancelled his order for a new tweed suit. Did she realise the burden of the school fees he would start to bear in September? For three children they would be heavy, for more impossible.

Maggie rose to refill the coffee cups and he watched her. Perhaps her outfit wasn't so bad after all; it was colourful, different. She had let her figure go, but after all those babies some deterioration was inevitable, and she still looked quite handsome when she made the effort. Desirable, in fact. He smiled as he held out his own cup to her. He would make love to her after these people had gone, they could leave the clearing up till the morning – the boys woke them early anyway. At the thought of her soft flesh his own stirred and his mood, like hers, improved considerably. He had enjoyed very little by way of fleshly comforts recently; tonight could definitely be propitious.

Maggie was sitting next to Jane Field now. Good, she was circulating as she should, and she might find the opportunity to consult Jane about her headaches. Maggie had suffered headaches ever since Felicity died, but recently she had been complaining of stunningly nasty one-siders. Louise had suggested they could be migraines. Tension was the cause, no doubt, outside interests the solution. He would get hold of the Colebys soon, perhaps arrange a joint visit to the theatre in Winchester. He could include Simon and Louise, introduce Simon as he'd intended. He finished his coffee and got up to offer his guests a brandy, ending with generous measures for the rector and Simon. Jack remembered Simon as a skinny little new boy at school when he himself was in the sixth form: they had each come a long way since those days. He was glad he had put Simon in touch with Shergold & Stent; it had done them both a bit of good and it was great to have his friend living near. He had looked after Simon at school and would continue to do so now. He was fond of Louise, too, a smart and sensible girl who believed in women contributing. He had heard her agreeing with the rector that she and Simon would open their garden to the public in July. Her influence on Maggie would be excellent.

'An unusual evening,' Thomas Field commented, as, back in the rectory, he and Jane checked on little Flora and smaller Lucian asleep in their nursery, and then undressed for bed. He felt relaxed, slightly drunk and agreeably amorous. 'But a highly amusing and pleasant one.'

'More lively than the usual village entertainment,' Jane agreed, kicking off her shoes and stretching lazily. 'What an extraordinary man that Charley is.'

'Mmm. Not,' Thomas observed in a dry and neutral tone, 'a man of reticence and responsibility.'

'No.' Jane chuckled and began to peel off her clothing. Her voice muffled, she added: 'Fun, though. For the occasional evening. I shouldn't care to live with him, far too exhausting.' Her head emerged from a tight-fitting black and gold top and she shook her hair vigorously. 'I'm not surprised that girl Melody spends half her time in bed, as he said.'

'How much sleep is it he needs? Only four or five hours a night?'

'Around that. Like Maggie Thatcher. People with excess energy and all those extra hours can cope with levels of work that would defeat us ordinary mortals.'

'So you think he could achieve his ambitions?'

'Oh, that I don't know. He might. Everything he said was exploding with ideas, prophecies, determination, innovation . . . and confidence, all intimations of success. But chronic over-confidence, like pride, can lead to a fall. He could be a touch manic. I shall watch with interest.'

Having divested himself of his trousers, Thomas sat on the edge of the bed to remove his socks. 'His girlfriend is very different. I tried to talk to her, but . . . a parson? Not her scene. She eyed me sideways and said little. Either she thought me a bore or that I'd find her boring – perhaps both. Charley spoke of her as an interior designer, as if she ran her own firm, but she's more like a Girl Friday to some chap who specialises in the Chelsea and Kensington set. I forget the name but it was one she expected me to recognise.' He removed his shirt, flung it at a chair and sat back naked to watch his wife reach the same state.

'An inert girl, Melody,' Jane commented, taking off a gold necklace. 'One of those to whom things happen, not one who engineers happenings. But she's excited by Charley and all his plans, and the thrills and possible spills of living with him. She likes the presents, too. She told me how generous he is. The silver bracelets, the chains round her neck . . . all from Charley.'

'I wonder what she gives him?' mused the rector.

Jane reached behind herself to unhook her bra. 'Well,' with a grin, 'the obvious. But also, I would think, rest. No hassle. Someone who goes along with him admiringly, uncritically.'

'How very dull,' Thomas said. 'Even dangerous. We all need critics.' His wife was not merely a sounding-board for his difficulties with argumentative church wardens or help-less single-parent families, she was a very real help in times of trouble. She listened to him while rolling out pastry or bathing the children, put her trained and needle-sharp mind to the problem, asked questions that focussed his mind on the points at issue, tossed out a tart comment or two, and then let him reach his own conclusions. He rose from the bed to stand behind her, cupping her breasts in his hands. 'You're never dull. And I appreciate your criticisms – well, some of them! Your earthy views are a good reminder to me not to idealise my work. Stay still – no, let me do that.' He slid her briefs down her legs and held her while she stepped out of them and kicked them away, then he pulled her soft bottom hard against his body. 'And I can't imagine,' he added as she leaned lasciviously in return against him, twisting her head back and round to kiss him, 'I can't imagine Melody's half as exciting as *you* are in bed, Dr Field.'

'Ooh, ah, oh!' Simon climaxed with grunts of pleasure, kissed Louise on the tip of her nose, then rolled off her to lie blissfully back. 'Lovely! That was terrific! I took rather longer than usual,' he added in extenuation of what had been a distinctly protracted performance, 'because I wanted to build up to maximum jets. There should be millions of sperm inside you now and it's the absolutely right time of the month.'

'Yes,' Louise said flatly, passing him the paper tissues.

'Days thirteen and fourteen are the most important.'

'I suppose so.'

'A pity you came before I did; a simultaneous orgasm is best.'

'Mmm. It would be.'

'Now, stay on your back and pull your knees up – yes, right up like that. Hold them there. Half an hour should be enough.'

'What?' she almost screamed. 'Half an hour? At one o'clock in the morning? But I'm sleepy, Simon, I've eaten well, drunk even better, and with the tiring life I'm living, I damned well need my sleep.'

'But to give our baby-making the optimum chance of success this is what we have to do.' He leaned over her affectionately, stroking her shoulder. 'You don't begrudge it, do you?'

Maggie was in a relaxed mood as she and Jack went upstairs to bed, grateful that he had not bawled her out for substituting Charley and Melody for the Colebys, pleased he had suggested leaving the mess from the party till the morning and dealing with it together then. She could go to bed on a high note. She was tired, but her tiredness was of that mild and not unpleasant type that accompanies contemplation of a job well done. She thought she might even sleep well for once.

'I shouldn't care to live with someone who simply lay around all day, like that girl Melody,' Jack remarked. 'What a dead weight. And she hasn't two ideas in her head to rub together.'

'She's quite pretty, though,' Maggie said vaguely, forbearingly, sliding out of her silk top and trousers. 'Decorative.'

'What good's being decorative in life's great scheme of things?' Jack protested. 'Nothing positive in that, no more than an ornament or a cushion. And she's no cushion, she's bony as a flat fish. Imagine making love to that!' He tugged off his clothes vigorously.

Maggie smiled, pleased by the implied compliment and by his evident amorous intent as he walked round the bed to take hold of her.

'Well, look at you!' she said, adding slyly, 'I reckon bedsprings'll be bouncing in Abbotsbridge tonight after all Charley's romancing.' She leaned into his embrace, enjoying the hard feel of his body, the muscles and the big bones against her own soft bulk. She had felt distinct physical reactions herself from the talk from which Jack was now benefitting, though naturally she was not intending to tell him that. She wondered what love-making would be like with Charley, such a very large man – would he perform the act with the vitality and lusty enjoyment he brought to all else in life? Then she realised with shock that she was fantasising about herself locked in passion with Charley and glanced up in guilt at her husband, thankful that the images were hidden in her head.

Jack had stiffened, slightly but noticeably, at her mention of Charley. 'You're my wife,' he said. 'I love you. I don't need Charley's smutty nonsense as a sex aid. You turn me on. Come on, gorgeous, get between those sheets.' He released her, gave her an affectionate push towards the bed, then remembered a matter of urgent importance. 'Here,' he said, 'have you taken your pill? Better take it first in case you forget – you know what you're like.'

Abruptly tense with antagonism, she went to get it from the bathroom cabinet, half-choking as she forced it down with a gulp of water. How could he spoil the joyous natural urges of their bodies with something so unnatural, with such a total disregard for her feelings, her needs? She would have another 'headache' tomorrow, let Jack do tonight's clearing up – serve him right – and on Monday she would go to see Doctor Jane. Migraines on the pill indicated a possibility of strokes – Jane would stop her prescription at once. With an old-fashioned method of contraception like a diaphragm it might be possible to contrive an 'accident'. But when? She wanted a baby tomorrow. She walked on leaden feet back into the bedroom. Desire was gone. Simple, lovely desire had been shorn of its simplicity by his brutal reminder. Her heart pounded the words of her frustration and anger: *sterile sex, sterile sex, sterile sex.* For an hour or two she had been happy listening to Charley, enjoying his wonderful plans and his comic patter; she had felt normal, lustful, sensing a return of the zest for life that was something she would once have had in common with him. Now it was all erased.

She stared at Jack, watching her expectantly from the bed. How easy life was for him: a set pattern, the rules exact and trusted to give the desired results, rules that sent him and his sons and his sons' sons no doubt, in years to come, to the right schools, into the right professional careers, married to the right women, breeding, background and education all carefully matched. All uncomplicated, decent, honest people – and wholly uncomprehending of what drove women like her. The rules did not encompass large families whose members teemed in happy conjunction with one another and with their friends, eating, talking, sharing, loving, in an untidy and generous warmth of companionship. That would be excessive. 'Italian!' Jack called it, with all the Englishman's scorn of mediterranean foreigners and their catholic immoderacy, their sunny lack of forethought.

She lay down beside him on the bed and arranged her body for their encounter. No point in denying him; that would only lead to a row and there had been too many of those lately. She let him perform as he would, her body wooden, her arms automatically holding him while mentally her rejection was total. She felt assaulted, violated by the body floundering upon hers, and worse, he seemed completely unaware of her lack of response.

When it was over she turned out the light. Soon she heard the deep steady breathing that told her he was asleep, replete and contented. They had lived together for almost ten years, made four children together. How could he dismiss her needs and her pain so totally from his mind? Fail so wholly in understanding despite her screams for help? He might have been a stranger she had brought in from the street.

Maggie turned away from him, plummetting into the black hole of her despair, tears of loneliness and grief for her dead daughter soaking silently into her pillow.

Chapter 8

When the weekend was over and Monday arrived Louise was relieved. Work would be a gentle diversion, virtually a relaxation, after the stress and labours of the last two days. When Simon had not been planning what to do if she failed to conceive this month – 'We'll have to get a good consultant and we'll both need tests!' – he had been organising the readying of their garden for its public opening in seven weeks time. At least that distracted him with an alternative form of productivity. They must have a system, he said, and a timetable. He would take charge of the lawn, which must be watered with weed-killer, scarified, aerated, fed, as well as mown and trimmed twice a week. Lurking horrors like daisies or dandelions he would remove by hand. It must, he said, be of a perfect velvet texture to set off the beds and borders, Louise's responsibility. These contained gorgeous shrubs and herbaceous plants which should be at their stunning best then, but there were gaps that must be filled. When Louise murmured of marigolds or petunias he blenched, speaking instead of nicotianas and violas, stocks and heliotrope. Gardens were subject to fashion every bit as much as clothes, and what attired them must be right. He had been studying books and magazines and he had spoken to the rector and Arabella Manningford. One must not over-weed or dig in the summer months; that would destroy seedlings one wanted, such as primulas or foxgloves, and to have immaculate, worse, regimented borders would be suburban. The aim was subtlety, texture, scent, the effect a casual natural beauty.

If the theory was hard, the practice was painful. Louise

93

was aching as she sat in the early train. Her back ached from hoeing and weeding, her shoulders and neck from spraying the climbing roses that clothed the garden walls and the house. Her head hurt, too. That was from the sleepless nights worrying over Simon.

She felt unhappy, at times very unhappy, at the lie she was living with him. Yet she had no intention of telling him the truth. Or not the whole truth. At times she had almost blurted out her aversion to having a child at this juncture, almost decided to plead for time, then caught her breath in horror at the arguments it would cause. There would be endless philosophical discussions of the meaning of life and its continuance through the ever-renewed generations, there would be his distress and hurt. Simon was a monogamous man who wanted to live within the bond of marriage with her, in total faithfulness and trust and honesty; he would come to suspect the reasons for her barren state, and then, and then . . . She shuddered. Their relationship would be changed, vitiated. It was too late, in any case, to win the fight she had avoided many months ago: his desire for a child had become an obsession, a desperate imperative that he would find impossible to relinquish, even for a year or so. Yet how much longer could she go on with the farce that was enacted every time they made love? In those circumstances desire vanished; instead she felt nasty, traitorous. She was betraying Simon every time she took one of those damned pills. Deceiving and hurting him. Why, oh why, had she ever put herself in such a position? If Simon had not been so insistent in the first place the deception would not have been forced upon her. She told herself he was as much to blame as she was, then castigated herself as a liar. She held to one thing: she must have time to consolidate her position at work, to be certain that she would be welcomed back and encouraged still to rise after the baby's birth. Another year, that was what she needed. It was impossible to see how she could have it.

The train slowed, stopped. Louise hardly noticed. The wheels of her mind whirred hopelessly round, going over and over the same track.

Work, she discovered when at last she arrived, was to be no gentle diversion. The Holbrooke Collection had a new director, appointed three months previously. Not an easy man. The previous director, a woman of both scholarship and wit, had been tough but kindly. During her nine-year reign a major programme of repairs and additions to the fabric of the building which housed old Matthew Benedict Holbrooke's collection had been completed and the atmosphere of the dead and gone that had settled dustily over its brilliant artefacts banished. Redecorated, the rooms were brighter, the lighting discreet but excellent; the pictures, the porcelain, the antique jewellery, the furniture, all glowed with deeper, richer, more subtle colours. Regular exhibitions were now held in the added galleries, both of works that had previously lurked in the cellars and attics and those on loan from elsewhere; these exhibitions added both to the museum's income and its fame. They also generated an unbelievable amount of toil and dispute. Aylmer Littlejohn, the new director, exacerbated both. Under pressure to make decisions he would either become aggressive or vanish, leaving Louise struggling to calm her exasperated colleagues.

Today he burst into her office from his as soon as she arrived.

'You're late!' he shot at her.

'Sorry, but it wasn't my fault,' she said, dumping her bag on her desk. 'The train was delayed.'

'You should come by the earlier train.'

'I did,' she snapped back. She had been up since half-past six, the journey had taken half as long again as it should do and her mind was aching from an excess of unproductive self-examination. 'The line was being repaired – unwarned.'

The director gave her a frustrated look from hot and blinking brown eyes. He was a rather short man, with faded mouse-coloured hair and heavy brown eyebrows. He had a high and shining forehead and a long and shiny nose; his mouth was long, curving and weak. He was a man of immense erudition and culture and almost no administrative ability. Louise could not understand how the trustees could have appointed him. She could only assume that the fame of his scholarship and his publications together with his length of service had made it impossible for them to ignore his merits and appoint elsewhere. When he spoke of particular

95

pieces in the Collection to her he did so with a gruff love and a total understanding that was endearing. In day to day work he muddled matters, issued contradictory orders, lost his temper and was generally impossible. He never apologised; he considered it a weakness.

He flung letters and files in an untidy sprawl across her desk. 'You'll have to deal with these,' he said. 'Petty niggles about petty matters I've no time for. Oh, and the insurance demands for the Renaissance exhibition we're planning for March next year are becoming outrageous – just when I thought we were reaching joint agreement on our security strategy. More meetings, more discussions! Dear God! Lay them on, will you? I'm off out.' He turned on his heel to remove himself at a trot. A misogynist, he never spent more than a minimal time with Louise.

She scurried through the door after him, heels clacking. 'Where will you be if anyone needs to get hold of you?' she called at his rapidly retreating back.

Aylmer Littlejohn wagged a hand without turning round, nipped sideways into gallery two, Baroque Works of Art. His voice floated back, disembodied: 'Here and there, here and there. I'll telephone later, he back by three.'

Louise had neither sight nor sound of him for the rest of the day. She warded off the man from the V and A with whom Aylmer was having a protracted scholarly row over the provenance of a Boulle console table; she dealt with an irate workman who was being 'Hassled and harassed something shocking' while he completed plinths and show cabinets in gallery six; she calmed the printers who telephoned to ask how they were to produce a catalogue as for tomorrow when it was still missing two illustrations, discovering and dispatching the missing items, and composed and dictated three agendas and fourteen letters.

Throughout the hot and busy day she was conscious of anxieties over Simon throbbing in her head. She felt his vulnerability to the unhappiness she could inflict – was inflicting – as a piercing pain in herself. It wrenched at her, intrusive and insistent, spoiling her concentration on her work. At times it infuriated her so that she cursed and determined to ignore the whole thing, to suppress it. She was not used to being so involved in another person. Until the move she had successfully compartmentalised her life into work and home, savouring each. There were the pleasures of the Holbrooke Collection, her wide and detailed knowledge adding to her delight in a painting by Rembrandt, a Meissen bowl, a chair by Robert Adam; the more cerebral gratifications of neatly completed administrative work. Then there were the pleasures of her life with Simon, the small ceremonies of their delicious dinners, their mutual enjoyment of Mozart or Bach, sleeping together. Now everything was under threat.

This baby he wanted, this child, it would make her present life impossible. She would have to take the later train to Abbotsbridge tonight, she had left at dawn this morning. How could she do that if she were responsible for some helpless yowling creature? She would become second-rate at work, as harassed and hassled as this morning's unfortunate workman. Why, oh why, had Simon had to move to Hampshire? And yet . . . She would have second thoughts about moving back to London these days. Living in the country was quite different from her early imaginings and fears.

Spring had been a revelation. After the mud and dun colours of winter she had been relieved by the vivid greens emerging in the April hedgerows and entranced as the trees in turn burgeoned into full leaf, from the first pale slim leaves of the willows to the final splendour of the lime avenue at Abbotsbridge House. She had found celandines and primroses and wood anemones on the banks of the lanes, and later she had laughed as the swifts screamed in races round the church tower and exclaimed at the brief blue flash of a kingfisher across the river. Simon had identified them because they were new to her. Everything was new, like the point-to-point which had been such unexpected fun. There had been no wild animals, only the rabbits she saw on her early drives to the station and two hares boxing on the downs. The resentment and resignation of the early months were gone: the cottage and its garden had taken a hold on her heart; they were a new dimension of her life with Simon, aching back or not, and he was full of praise at how swiftly she had adapted.

But she would be hassled and harassed in the cottage, with

dirty nappies and endless feeds. Her research done and her notes made, she prepared her lectures there. Babies left no time for peaceful thought and original contributions. Worse, there would be an au pair girl, like the Fields' Swedish blonde, or an expensive nanny, living in. What would become of their secret and splendid love life then? No more rollings on the hearthrug to thunderous sounds of a Beethoven symphony or couplings on the sofa to Vaughan William's 'Lark Ascending'. Louise caught herself up. That was not their lovelife today. Sex now was baby-making, a chore as charmless as a factory process, neutralising the electric thrills between them. Babies interfered with everything. She folded her arms on her desk and sank her dark head on to them. Oh hell, hell, hell, hell.

The telephone shrilled through her thoughts, ringing for the seventeenth time that day. Dear God, she'd lost concentration yet again. She lifted her head, pushed back her tumbling hair and answered it.

As she emerged from Basingstoke station that evening. dull with exhaustion from working late and then standing the entire way in the train, she heard herself hailed.

'Hey, Louise!' Charley came charging up to her, a battered briefcase in his hand. He was wearing a suit crumpled from the heat and his tie-knot was at half-mast to allow an open neck to his shirt. He ran a hand through already rumpled hair so that it stood on end. 'Thank God I saw you. The Porsche's in dock being serviced and the Landrover refused to start this morning. Jesus, what a day! Be a love and give me a lift home.'

'Yes, of course. Come on.' As the car nosed out of the car park she asked: 'How's life in the publishing business?'

'Ergh!' he grunted. 'Disaster area. Forget it. Tell me about your life instead.'

'Disastrous too.'

'How's that?'

'Oh, a difficult day at work. But that's a minor part of the problem. It's decision time in my life and I can't come to grips with it. I just go round and round in resentful circles.'

Charley grunted, setting his bulk more comfortably in his seat. 'Go on. Decision on what?'

They were heading west. The evening sun shone brilliantly in a sky only faintly streaked with radiating white clouds, making Louise blink.

'Having a baby, damn it.' Why was she telling him this? The need to confide in someone, to air her case in front of a neutral judge, pushed her on. 'Well, what do you think?' she demanded irritably when she had finished, without, naturally, confessing her deception of Simon. 'The whole situation's impossible, isn't it?'

'I don't see why,' he said. 'You've got it all jangled up inside your head. Start from first principles. It's your life, you've got to live it. Hell, we only have one go on this earth, it isn't a rehearsal for the next, no one believes that any more. So . . . do what's right for you. Trouble with you girls is, you're all muddled up with notions of virtue and caring. You're pre-programmed to support your man's self-affirmation, you won't stand out for your own.'

'But Simon will be so hurt,' she muttered. 'Bitterly disappointed.'

'Won't you be if you muck up your career? Put yourself first, you'll be a better person for it in the end. Enlightened self-interest.'

'Where's the enlightenment?'

Charley chuckled. 'Christ, Louise, you don't strike me as lacking in fire under that quiet exterior. You're bright – look what you're achieved already – you can aim for the high places. But reaching the menopause as a career woman denied success and struggling not to detest your teenage brats – well, I reckon you'd turn into a bitter old bat.'

'Thanks!' she said, but she laughed. Charley had a gift for making everything sound simple and easy. Before his lavish confidence mountains crumbled, and the seas rolled back. Simon would never want a bitter old bat. She must, like the citizens of Hobbes' *Leviathan*, pursue her own felicity, for her salvation – and Simon's – would lie, not in the denial of her character, but in its fulfilment. Once Louise had thought that becoming a lecturer would fulfil all her ambitions. Now she saw ambition expanding with her expertise as if in obedience to some strange form of Parkinson's Law. As fast as she gained each summit so new glistening pinnacles came into view. She could write learned monographs, become a trustee, a director, achieve an entry in Debrett's *People of Today*. She had a right to a degree of fulfilment; her years of study and effort had not yet been repaid. She must persuade Simon to understand. Tonight.

Still smiling at Charley's firm disposal of her problems, she turned the car into the ivy-banked lane that led down to Abbotsbridge village and took her foot from the accelerator, letting the car's own momentum and weight carry it almost silently on. The familiar magpies flew up from the inevitable squashed small corpse, narrowly missing the car; on the right James and Arabella Manningford were cantering their horses up the turf beside the lime avenue, their shadows long across the grass. The valley was cool and very quiet, infinitely remote from London. Louise's headache was almost gone, the tension knotted in her shoulder muscles unravelling.

She was signalling to swing down the little lane that led to Charley's Old Barn when he leaned forward to stop her. 'Ah, no, stop, would you? I nearly forgot, I picked up a prescription for Brozie and I must let her have it. I'll have to walk back.'

'It's all right,' Louise said. 'I'll drive you.'

He demurred, but she insisted. He'd been helpful to her and he did look tired.

Answering her door, Brozie peered round Charley and gave a brief wave before taking the little white chemist's bag he pushed at her. In the evening light her sallow face looked yellow and drawn and she seemed almost embarrassed to see them. Perhaps it was because of the old man who appeared round the side of the house and stopped still under a holly tree to stare with baleful eyes. Louise had not seen Mr Hamilton before; she thought he looked deadly ill, grey and hunched.

When she opened the door of Walnut Tree Cottage the cool beauty of a flute concerto and the warm scent of food hit her simultaneously. Simon emerged from the kitchen to take her briefcase and kiss her.

'You had to work late? My poor love. Was it you I saw drive past a few minutes ago? Who was that with you?'

'Charley St George. I gave him a lift from Basingstoke.'

'Ah. Funny chap. What you might call ebullient! I'd be a bit nervous if I were in partnership with him, all that excess of confidence.'

'Would you? He sounds as if he has it all under control.'

'Hm.' Simon had on what Louise dubbed his accountant's face. 'I've one or two clients in property development; they caught a nasty cold in the recession. Property development is stressful, highly complicated and risky. It's far more complicated than the average person looking from the outside perceives. For example, the legal documentation, which is usually called a finance agreement, generally runs to three hundred odd pages – it takes a day to read the thing.'

'Brozie said at the point-to-point that she'd seen what Charley was involved in, she said it was smaller than she'd expected.'

'Did she? Yes, that would figure. Anyway, the developer has to be a Mr Fixit and ensure he has his tenants all lined up, not easy these days. He needs great powers of persuasion.'

'Charley has those all right,' she said tiredly.

'Yes!' Simon gave a snort of amusement. 'And the necessary gambler's mentality. Well, if it's successful, it's a highly profitable business. Maybe he'll do it. Maybe he will become a millionaire. Here, honey, why are we standing around? You sit down and have a drink and I'll dish up. Dinner's almost ready.'

She sank on to the Knole sofa and he poured her a glass of light white wine, knowing without asking just what she would like. The contrast with Brozie's miserable home life and Charley's return to the empty Old Barn (no Melody during the week), was overwhelming. Simon was so thoughtful, so kind; her heart moved miserably within her. He said he'd had a particularly good day. He had bought two new CDs and several bottles of wine recommended by a local wine merchant because he felt so cheerful. He hoped she liked the Mozart. She murmured that it was lovely.

It was hard to speak, her mind was so obsessed with what she had to say. With him in this mood she must seize her chance, but she wished more desperately than ever that she had never deceived him; their arguments, however protracted and

101

hurtful, would have been over long since, she could have been enjoying his affectionate solicitude with a free and open mind, looking forward to the oriental lamb, his special dish, which she knew from its spicy smell he had cooked for her tonight. Now she felt it would choke her.

As he dished up he told her he had eaten lunch with one of the senior partners at work. They had had an absorbing conversation, wide-ranging. It had encompassed matters of EC regulations affecting their industrial and farming clients; later they had discussed the Conservatives' present taxation policy and analysed the Chancellor of the Exchequer's recent speeches at the London Guildhall and elsewhere in detail. 'Really stimulating,' said Simon. Quentin Stent had seemed impressed by his views and the breadth of his knowledge. 'And,' Simon concluded triumphantly, 'he said how happy the partners were with what they had seen of my work so far.'

Louise congratulated him; she was truly pleased how well the move had worked for him. At the same time she felt an awful jealousy on her own account for the male simplicity of his career's steady development. No looming gaps for him, no clinging impediments. She forked oriental lamb into her mouth and chewed resentfully. Hers had no such sturdy independence. Still, it was not his fault she had been born a woman. But then he didn't have to increase her difficulties, either. Her mind swung from one consideration to another, hazy now with drink and the tiredness that seemed to be increasing with food, rather than the other way round.

His cheerful face, smiling at her across the table, made it difficult for her to find the words to make her communication. She would say: *'Simon, I'm sorry, but I must have another year at work before I take the break for a baby . . .'* No, that was too harsh. *'Simon, I've been thinking, wouldn't it be better for the two of us if we waited a little longer, just a few months . . .'* She ate, thought, swallowed with difficulty. She opened her mouth. 'Simon . . .'

'Hey, Louise, my lovely one,' he interrupted, 'how about us having one of our weekend breaks in June? We'll holiday in Greece in September as we planned, but I reckon you're under par now. You're looking strained and miserable, sounding it too. How about Bath? We've never been there.'

'Yes,' she said weakly, 'yes. That would be great.'

Tears clogged her throat, made speech impossible. Her strain and misery came from what she had been struggling to tell him. She felt hunted by the need to be honest, but he had made it impossible; to do it tonight would be a peculiarly refined form of nastiness. If only he were not being so especially affectionate; if only he had groused about her lateness or left her the cooking so that she could have felt aggrieved, then she could have braced herself to the ordeal; now it was beyond her.

Perhaps, she thought, perhaps when we're in Bath the opportunity will come. She would wait a week or two longer, do it when she felt less overwrought.

Over the following days it was a relief to have pushed the problem into her mental pending tray, for to have had an atmosphere at home as well as the rapidly developing difficulties at the Holbrooke Collection would have driven her to breaking point. Indeed she did reach breaking point on Wednesday, the breaking of a coffee cup. Aylmer Littlejohn was incapable of leaving well alone. The summer exhibition had been all planned and set for its opening next month but in a storm of blood to the head he had come up with the most brilliant notions, so he assured Louise, that he had ever had. His ideas for restaging certain exhibits were, while purely cosmetic, designed to cause maximum disruption for everyone concerned and make nonsense of parts of the catalogue now being printed, a point he had not considered. Louise set herself patiently to argue him out of his changes before he could wind up her colleagues, already tired from the hard work and late meetings of recent weeks, to screaming point. It took her two days, with brief intervals of peace while he brooded in the galleries concerned before returning with fresh wind to the argument. 'You have no vision!' he lectured her. 'Where's your artistic eye?' he yelled, and, worst of all, on the deepest note of reproach to which his reedy tenor could drop: 'You lack the scholarly approach!' So by Wednesday afternoon curators and security staff alike were beginning to show the whites of their eyes when they saw either Aylmer or Louise approach; they knew something was wrong, something disastrous was brooding about the rooms. At length Louise thought she had him pacified with a couple of minor changes of position and lighting – until he interrupted her break for coffee mid-afternoon in a last ditch attempt to reinstate one of his wilder notions. 'Call a meeting!' he barked at her. Louise was standing by her desk, she had no time to sit down. 'No!' she almost shouted at him. 'It can't be done! Oh, surely you can see the impossibility now!' And she made a violent impatient gesture with her hands, quite forgetting the coffee cup which flew from her fingers to shatter against the wall beside him, spattering the wallpaper, the carpet and his trouser legs with coffee.

They stared at one another in silence, identical expressions of amazement on their faces. Then Aylmer turned on his heel and marched out. He did not appear again that day, nor had Louise seen him by the time she met her friend Josie for lunch the following day.

Josie was an older colleague who had constituted herself Louise's mentor. She had a brilliant mind and a breadth of knowledge Louise could only marvel at. She was highly esteemed at work, indeed, predicted by some to be the next director, when she unexpectedly found herself pregnant. A fortnight before the birth she married her partner of many years, an architect. 'Might as well do the thing properly,' she said briskly. The baby was born on her fortieth birthday. 'Life begins . . .' she observed and laughed. She was planning to return to work in ten weeks' time, when the baby was six months old. Louise decided she must talk to her. Urgently.

Josie had managed to seize a table in a secluded corner of the wine bar that was their rendezvous. Four-month-old Lucy was in a baby-seat beside her.

'I had to bring her,' Josie said, laughing at Louise's face. 'She'll need a feed soon. No, I couldn't ask a friend to give her a bottle, she's breastfed.'

'You're not going to feed her here?' Louise was appalled.

'Why not? It's quiet enough and my back's to the room. Say hello!'

Louise bent over, feeling foolish. Large blue eyes stared at her, then light illuminated them, the lips broke into a toothless smile, the whole body swirmed with delighted greeting.

'Hello!' Louise said. 'Goodness, she's quite a person, isn't she?'

'Of course,' Josie said. 'She's so gorgeous I could eat her. Now what's this I hear about you throwing cups of coffee at the Director?'

'Oh God,' Louise groaned, 'who told you?'

One of the curators, finishing his lunch just five minutes earlier, had given a lively account before he darted back to work. 'From what I hear,' Josie said, 'he's being a pain, a fussy old woman. General verdict is, hurray for Louise. You did what no one else dared.'

They had a pleasingly ribald conservation about the reasons for the director's tantrums and about various eccentric Holbrooke Collection personalities over their food and then Louise drank coffee while Josie fed her Lucy.

'So tell me,' Josie said, lifting her dark eyes from contemplation of the child fastened to her breast like a glugging limpet, 'why the frantic demand to see me? Was it purely exasperation with the awfulness of Aylmer, or was there something else?'

'You're too clever by half,' Louise grumbled.

'Go on.' Josie lifted the baby on to her shoulder and patted its back. It responded with a belch of quite extraordinary volume for so small a mortal.

'Good God!' said a beautiful young man about to seat himself near to them, and moved away looking revolted.

Louise shook with silent mirth to the point of near hysteria. 'That,' she gasped, recovering, 'that's my problem! How the hell can I fit a baby sensibly into my career, without wrecking it? When should I do it? You know me and you're learning the difficulties. Advise me, please!'

Josie attached Lucy to the other nipple and then surveyed Louise. 'Your lectures are going well, I hear, but you should get a few more under your belt before you take time off. A year of them in total should establish you there.'

'You think that's enough?'

'Yes. Frankly, get on with it. I was far too old. At your age you can work till you're eight months pregnant. You'll want the full six months off afterwards, but that's not too long an absence. Aylmer's bound to curse and rant, but once you're back everybody will swiftly forget you were ever away.'

Louise remembered Maggie's words. 'Did you feel exalted when you were carrying Lucy?'

'Feel exalted? God, no! I wondered what the hell I'd done. I felt as if my body had been taken over by an alien life force, an incubus sucking away all my energy. It lurched around inside me, kicking me night and day . . . . But once my Lucy was born . . . well, they call it bonding, don't they? *Now* I'm exalted if you like, *now* I adore her! The difficulty is going to be dragging myself back to work. Lucy will have the best nanny money can buy. That's essential. Ours is due to start next month.'

Louise nodded and fell silent. She was calculating time. A year of lectures under her belt . . . she could work until she was seven or eight months pregnant . . . Say three months under that plan till she gave up the pill. A nervous thrill ripped through her body. To commit herself that soon? Dear God! Josie had spoken with enthusiasm and love of her child, despite, so she had earlier told her, once having vowed she would never submit herself to the ties and stresses of motherhood. Louise must brace herself. Should she openly ask Simon to give her that extra time, to stop his pathetic doomed efforts so that they could return to the robust enjoyment of sex for its own sake? No, ridiculous to cause arguments and possible suspicions just for that short time. Charley had said she should do what was right for her, and she would. Why should she consult Simon? It was her body, her career, not his. On that timetable she could continue to deceive him; somehow she could hold him off from fertility tests and the messing about with temperature charts that were his latest suggestions. Just a few more weeks. She felt breathless and slightly sick.

Chapter 9

'I'm late,' Jane Field observed to Thomas as she joined him in the rectory kitchen at nine o'clock in the evening. She did not apologise.

'Very,' Thomas agreed, stirring a spaghetti sauce (Selma the Swedish au pair did not cook). 'The children went to bed long since. They were plaintive because you hadn't kissed them goodnight, but I read them a Thomas the Tank Engine story and they went off all right.'

There was no reproach in his voice; neither of them picked at the other. Each accepted the odd hours their jobs demanded and worked within their constraints, faintly amazed at the other's acceptance of what many might have dubbed intolerable. When Jane remarked during a dinner party at which the archdeacon was present, 'Sundays are hell in our house!' there were scandalised titters and eyes turned from archdeacon to rector, but instead of frowning Thomas laughed, conceding that with three congregations competing for his services, two lively children and his wife frequently on call, it was no day of rest. Still, he said, they muddled through it somehow. He smiled at Jane, who, slightly flushed, grinned back. The archdeacon's wife, a tart and exceedingly competent woman covertly known as Mrs Proudie, remarked later to her husband that it quite put her off her food to see two people leer their affection so publicly.

Neither was ambitious. That, the Fields agreed, was their saving grace. If Thomas had aimed for a deanery or Jane had needed to move from one hospital to another in pursuit of a consultant's appointment, their life would have been impossible. Instead, if Jane dreamed of a roomy and modern surgery, or Thomas wondered if he might become a rural dean, neither was affected by more than a moment's wistful envy of those who achieved such heights. They lived and worked in a community that was not a constantly shifting segment of a larger one, a dark city place whose harsh houses and grey streets soaked up what light pierced its grimy trees, but one remote from such situations, settled in a gentle valley under a wide sky, where everywhere there was shape and colour, in hedgerows and fields and hidden grassy dips, in the warm brick and thatch cottages of the villages. They drove along lanes familiar to the Romans and the Saxons to visit parishioners and patients who were known neighbours and friends. They were contented.

Jane helped Thomas to dish up the food and they sat down at the big mahogany table in the dining room in the usual awkward trio with Selma. Jane's face expressed a sombre weariness.

'What is it?' her husband asked. 'A bad day? Something gone wrong?'

'Sharon Nutt lost her baby. A simple miscarriage, no problems, but she's very upset.'

'Oh poor girl. I'm sorry. I'll visit her, shall I?'

'I wish you would. That inarticulate lad she lives with won't be much use to her and she's the sort to want to talk out the whys.'

'I'll go tomorrrow. What else?'

'Oh, nothing really. Just this afternoon's surgery seemed weighed down with those sad sorts of problems that aren't purely physical.'

'Tell me,' he said softly.

She glanced at Selma, but she had turned her blonde head away. As a staunch atheist and a healthily squeamish young woman, she found her employers' conversation, what she could understand of it, both dull and repellent. Nor was living in a foreign country remotely as exciting as she had hoped: the Fields threw no wild parties, they had no yacht or swimming pool, there were no sophisticated young men around to seduce her, she had abandoned hope even of the interesting wickedness of an affair with a priest. She liked the children and the bronzed village boys who made up in energy for what they lacked in savoir faire; the rest, she made clear, she endured for the sake of the glamorous job on the pop scene she was convinced she would land when she had fluent English. No, she was not interested in her employers' chat.

Jane thought, eating slowly. In her consultations with her patients, there was rarely the time to explore their lives or their states of mind as she would have wished, so that the worries she wanted to communicate were as much intuitive as factual. Besides, there were lines of discretion both she and Thomas had to draw in their work.

Eventually she said: 'Brozie Hamilton . . .'

'Poor woman. She's kept going for so long one almost forgets how terrible it must be for her to live with a man under sentence of death. The strain's not making her ill, is it?'

'I don't know. She had a nasty sore place on one wrist which needed antibiotic treatment. Scratched by a bramble, she told me, infected somehow, and the creams she'd tried weren't working. She looked odd, awkward, and she was sweating. I wondered if she was running a temperature, but it wasn't that, and then I thought, stupid me, probably her age . . .' She pushed her plate away and glanced at the au pair.

Selma sighed, collected the plates and ambled off to the kitchen to find the fruit, biscuits and cheese which almost invariably ended their meals because no one had either the time or inclination to make puddings.

'Did you ask her?'

'Oh, yes. She admitted to some menopausal problems – headaches, insomnia, hot flushes – but only after I pressed her. Amazing that there are still women who think it neurotic to admit to their troubles, isn't it? It was perfectly bearable, she said with dignity. When she came over hot she simply breathed deeply and waited for it to go. I said I trusted the new drug I'd prescribed was helping with Hubert's broken nights and she agreed that it was. I asked if she would consider taking anything herself but she said, No, that Hubert's restlessness had been what spoiled her nights and gave her headaches. She had no need for the crutches of drugs.'

She broke off as Selma came in with the platter of cheeses and trailed out again for biscuits. It was impossible to persuade the girl to use a tray and carry several items at once; she had her ways and nothing would shift them. But she was good with the children, and since that was why she was there, Jane and Thomas bore with her.

'Go on.'

'I don't know,' Jane said fretfully. 'I don't even know why I'm telling you this . . .'

'You want me to visit her too,' Thomas suggested, smiling.

'Yes . . .' doubtfully. Then with more assurance: 'Yes, I suppose I must. There was something about her that wasn't right, but I can't analyse what. It sounds horribly unprofessional, doesn't it?'

'I should visit her more often, and Hubert, too,' Thomas said. 'My conscience smites me. I'm a coward where Hubert is concerned. He will attack me about the spinelessness of the Church of England and demand to know when I'm going to make a stance on modern morality, meaning modern immorality and a hell-fire sermon. Last time I was there I was told he was sick of the Church burbling about compassion but never mentioning blame or shame. Liberal thinkers are a lot of bleating woolly-minded sheep, he said, they muddle the sinners with the sin. I opened my mouth to say, "True," but before I could utter it he was off on to women priests, "The idiocy of the millennium", and could I imagine his fool wife running a parish? In front of Brozie, too! I said mildly that I had often thought she would make an excellent deaconess and fled before he could break a blood-vessel. Ah, thank you, Selma. A ripe Camembert, what a treat.'

'He hates having a woman doctor,' Jane said. 'Resentment oozes from him like sweat. I reckon he sticks to it just so he can die on me.'

'Darling, don't be gruesome.'

'Sorry. At least Brozie has Charley St George to cheer her up now. He's given her half a dozen of those books he publishes, a couple even signed by their authors. She brought one to read while she waited at the surgery, a thriller set in post-war Czechoslovakia with a glossy cover all guns and blood. She said she'd never read anything like it in her life!'

'I shouldn't think she has. How kind of Charley.'

'He gave one to Maggie Easton, too, by way of a thank you for the supper party. That, I'm told, is about a woman in America who had such an insatiable urge to have children that she ended up with thirteen, some her own, some adopted – and made a million dollars writing a funny book about them all! She says it's amazing, wonderful. She can't imagine why other publishers rejected it.'

Jack wished Charley had rejected it. He wished Maggie had never met Charley and never seen that infernal book. He wanted to tear it up, burn it, throw the ashes in the river. Maggie had laughed till she cried over it, but her tears were not always of mirth. She was very erratic and strange these days and it was upsetting the children. Toby had thrown a tantrum, actually lain on the floor and kicked and screamed, over breakfast this morning. Jack had come down for his own quick coffee and croissant before going off to his Saturday morning foursome of golf and had had to jerk the boy off the floor and smack his bottom. And then Maggie had virtually thrown a tantrum over the smack, screaming at him of physical abuse. Ridiculous. The last thing a man in Jack's position needed was riots at home; it was enough to give a chap an ulcer or a heart-attack. And all the noise and nonsense had been over the hard-boiling of an egg that Toby had wanted soft to stick toast soldiers into. Soldiers? Not the thing at all. Babyish. Vulgar.

Jack threw his golf-clubs into the back of the Volvo Estate and drove off up the lane more quickly than usual, conscious that he was late and tense. The usual lightness of heart that his Saturday morning's game brought him was absent and, he thought, not surprisingly. He had important decisions to make. They'd kept him awake last night, sweating and anguished, till finally he had crept from bed to drink a double whisky and returned swearing not to think of them again. Often if he shelved knotty problems overnight he found the road he must take was clear as the morning light when he woke. Not today.

He swung the car on to the main road and struggled with his new and perplexing puzzle. Doctor Jane Field had taken Maggie off the contraceptive pill, telling her, so Maggie reported, that there were contra-indications to its use. He supposed Jane knew what she was doing, but how the hell were they to prevent the advent of yet more children? From the start Maggie had objected to any and all forms of contraception – they spoiled the act of love, they made her sore, they gave her cystitis. But they had to be meticulously careful: Jack groaned to remember how he had once boasted to Simon with complacency: 'I only have to flick my trouser leg and she's off!' Nothing to be complacent about now.

He could have a vasectomy, he supposed; it might be that was the only answer. But the very thought of the operation made him sweat. He would be mutilated, no longer a full man. Like those peculiar souls who craved a sex change, calling themselves women when they were really mutilated men. No, he wouldn't fancy a vasectomy, he'd just have to trust Maggie. But could he trust her? Twice he had found her out in her folly and deception. He needed absolute certainty . . . but the knife? Oh God! His mind was a treadmill he'd lurched on before, round and round again.

At last he was parking near the clubhouse, looking at the car clock, annoyed that he was late who was never late. He jerked himself out of the car, conscious that he was in quite the wrong mood to benefit from the pleasant combination of mental stimulus and bodily relaxation that the game generally gave him. He lost two balls in the rough and one in the water and his partner was unforgivably rude to him. The worst thing, Jack thought, as he hurled his clubs back into the rear of the car, was that there was no one he could confide in, no one to advise him, not even their doctor. It was dreadful to think how much Jane Field knew of his married life in any case. How could Maggie have put him in such a position? Well, her at least he must talk to, right now.

On Sunday afternoon Maggie visited Felicity's little grave, as she always did. She went alone, walking round the side of the church, the flowers she had picked from her garden cradled in her arms as once she had held her daughter. Roses and delphiniums and white achillea. Felicity had loved flowers. "Lowah' was the first word she had learned after dad-dad and mum-mum, her tiny forefinger pointing, her eyes bright. Maggie filled the heavy vase with water, arranged the blooms with careful hands, inhaling their scent, the sun hot on her back. When she had finished she put a hand on the turf that blanketed her daughter and rested it there for a moment. Felicity, dead a year this week.

And Jack had chosen this time to speak of vasectomy.

She sat on the grass, her back against the side of Felicity's little stone. Kindly stone, thick and sturdy, returning warmth absorbed from the sun. She often sat for an hour, taking strength from its strength, breathing quietly, a little sad. And at times Felicity was with her, not down in the close darkness where her flesh crumbled, but suffused among the golden insects dancing in the sun and the living rustling leaves on the trees, her spirit waiting to be born again. And then Maggie spoke to her softly, or sang her the nursery songs she had loved and often demanded in those last untroubled and happy weeks.

How could Jack have a vasectomy, deny her the spirit of love? Again she pressed her hand against the ground. Mother Earth – Earth Mother. The very point of existence was to procreate; she was drawn to medieval paintings of fecundity and rich harvests, she loved with passion all young and growing things. She must have her baby. But she had lost the battle of words; Jack would not give in, secure in his armour of commonsense. Tears flooded down her cheeks. She looked about herself wildly, seeing a thicket of gravestones. Beneath them lay generations of husbands and fathers, dust now, useless and gone. Once Jack had that operation he would be of no more benefit to her than the dead men, his sperm useless and gone.

She trembled with the urgency of her need; she would go to any lengths, use any subterfuge. There was no virtue in endurance of the inevitable, for the inevitable did not exist, only the power of the human spirit. The woman in Charley's book had the right spirit; she and her man had only been rich

113

in love, but they had outfaced the critics who lashed them with their tongues as foolish and greedy and irrational, and thirteen children had returned their love and thanked them. Maggie did not want thirteen – just one little girl.

'I will do it,' she said aloud, her voice breaking with the intensity of her passion, 'I will do whatever I must,' and the sun dried the tears on her face.

Behind her, near the great dark yews, an old man and his wife scrubbing a lichened headstone raised their heads to look at the woman by the child's grave who wept and spoke to herself; they caught each other's eyes and looked serious.

The village store had a late night on Friday, and passing it on her way home from the station Louise remembered she had run out of salt and flour and stopped. Those could not be left until tomorrow's big shopping expedition to Basingstoke. The shop was quiet, only old George Nutt propped against the shelves having his usual surreptitious read of Nancy Chubb's magazines before reluctantly paying for a *Farmers' Weekly*.

Nancy was perched on a stool by her check-out in a new fuchsia-coloured blouse over lime green polyester slacks. On her face was an expression of pained forbearance, which Louise rightly attributed to a battle between the desire to snap at George and dislike of a shop wholly empty of customers.

'Been working late again, Mrs Fennell?'

Louise stiffened, nodded, hesitated, then said briskly: 'In fact it's Miss Bennett.'

'Oh? Oh!' Her face registered the rebuff and her lips folded in on themselves. 'Well, I'm sorry, I'm sure. I just take it for granted . . . marriage. Out here in the country . . . I suppose you young people do what's best for you . . .' She found it impossible to express her views, the need never to antagonise a good customer inhibiting her. Finally she said in a voice full of meaning: 'Such a very *nice* man, your . . . your Mr Fennell.'

'Yes, he is,' Louise said tightly. 'Thank you.' Simon's niceness, his own desire for marriage, daily reproached her; she didn't need Nancy as well.

Nancy turned her attention to George, now ready to buy his *Farmers' Weekly*. 'How's your granddaughter, then? Still feeling badly? I said to Les, poor Sharon, I said, it's really hard to lose a baby. Give her my sympathy, won't you? Tell her I know how she feels.'

George grunted, delving in his pocket for change. 'She's down, right down, that's what she is. What with her mum and Wayne being out at work it's my Marlene's looking after 'er. That's fair enough, I said, but what about my tea?'

'Have to get your own, won't you?' Nancy said cheerfully. 'Tell you what, get Marlene's too, give her a surprise.'

George looked revolted. 'Got to be joking,' he said. 'Wouldn't know how.' He picked up his magazine and left, banging the door.

'Mean old bastard!' Nancy yelled after him with unexpected venom. She ran Louise's items up on the till, then said, her voice flat: 'Their Sharon had a miscarriage. I lost three meself that way. Wasn't going to tell George, none of his business. But I do know how young Sharon feels. It hurts . . . in your head . . . it just hurts and hurts. Sometimes you think the pain will never stop.'

Louise was shattered. She had never thought of Nancy as anything other than an adjunct to the checkout point, never suspected a vulnerable and aching human under the fat and insistently cosy exterior. This unsuspected human aspect left her feeling inadequate and unthinking.

'I'm sorry,' she muttered, and fumbled to pull a note from her wallet.

Nancy took it, smoothed it and laid it in the drawer. Looking away, she said: 'Your friend Mrs Easton, she still hurts. It's a year ago yesterday her little girl died.'

'I know. I'm seeing her tomorrow.' She wanted to give Maggie sympathy and support, though she was hopelessly unsure how. 'You remembered the date very exactly.'

'Yes,' Nancy said, counting change into her hand. 'It was the day my sister became a granny. Proud? Made her life over again, never hear the last of little Darren. Funny, isn't it – strange, I mean? God gives one, God takes one, it doesn't make sense, not any way you look at it. Mrs Easton, never been the same since. Sits in the churchyard and talks to her dead child. Not healthy that. You didn't know? Oh, yes. Better she remembers she's got three living still, count her blessings. If I could be in her shoes I'd thank God singing every day of my life . . . but there, I can't be and it's no good crying over what can't be changed. Maybe she should get counselling. We managed without it in the old days but I've heard it helps some.'

'Counselling?' Maggie said scornfully. 'I don't want counselling, you know what I want.'

They were sitting in her untidy kitchen, and she was making camomile tea for them both in long glasses, with lemon.

'You've made no progress in the baby direction?'

Louise watched her. From Nancy Chubb's words she had been expecting to see some pale half-mad Ophelia murmuring sad songs, but Maggie was flushed from a game in the sun with her boys and appeared her normal self.

'No, no progress. Well, I'm off the pill, that's something, but now Jack's talking of having a vasectomy.'

'No!'

'That's what I yelled! He said he didn't know if he could trust me.'

'And he can't.' It was a statement.

'Certainly not!' Maggie began to laugh, a nervous giggle. 'It's war between us, Louise. Oh, it's fought with English phlegm and a stiff upper lip and the usual half-strangled embarrassed utterances because otherwise it gets emotional and we can't have that, can we? But it does have its funny moments. I must tell you this, Louise, I've got to tell someone.' She giggled again, but her eyes had gone pink. She looked defiant.

'What?' Louise asked, her dark eyes sympathetic.

'The nurse at the surgery fitted me up with a diaphragm. Jack insisted. I can't say I use it with all due care, and oh dear, I seem to forget the spermicidal gunge that goes with it more often than not. But I'm still not winning over that suspicious sod of a husband of mine. Last night he's his usual randy self, asks me if I've got *it* in! Oh yes, I say. But then he says that by his reckoning it's my fertile period, so we'd better use double protection. And he digs a packet of condoms out of his trouser pocket and puts one out ready for use. Condoms! I was ready to murder him. Then Toby calls out in his sleep and Jack goes to settle him. No time to find pins or sharp scissors, I have a go with my nails. No luck, needless to say. Back comes Jack – what was I doing? Oh, just looking, I say innocently, funny sort of colour, isn't it? 'Cos it was! Hmm, he says, turning out the light ready for the usual routine, and then, would you credit it? – he tests it. Blows it up, all puffing and straining, and Louise, it's glowing! It was luminous!'

She choked over her camomile tea.

'I screamed. I said I wasn't going to make love to a man with a luminous dong – no way! He got so agitated he let go of the ballooned-up thing and it darted round the room like some mad Tinkerbell, farting air as it went!'

'Oh, oh!' Louise gasped, laughter shaking her. 'Oh don't, it hurts! It's unbelievable! Why luminous?'

'He thought of condoms at the last minute and nipped to the Gents in The Bull. That's all they sell and he reckoned it was a desperate case!' She was giggling with a kind of guilty rancour, but the sounds that emerged were nearer to tears.

Louise pulled herself together, alarmed by the threat of hysteria. 'It's not funny,' she said. 'Not really. Not for you, love. I'm sorry.'

'It's stalemate. Huh, there's a word – stalemate! Useless, ineffective. Christ!' She banged her fist on the table.

They sat in silence, sipping their tea. Louise saw now the anguish she was in, the desperation for which the chatter and the jokes were a poor smoke screen.

Maggie turned her ravaged face to say almost accusingly: '*You* see your identity as lying in your status as an intelligent achieving woman. In your career. For you, relationships and children are secondary matters; for me, my children *are* my career.' A short laugh. 'Strange how profoundly women's expectations have changed in the last century. Once the family was every woman's career, a large family too. Now that's frowned upon as selfish, excessive, inconsiderate. The family must be limited to curb population growth, even destroyed as part of an outdated paternalist system. What's to happen to women like me, women who have a yearning to

117

care, not for Jack's adored charitable causes, however noble, but for their own flesh and blood? Tell me, just tell me, what about us? What about me?'

'I don't know, I honestly don't,' Louise said with loving anxiety. 'You've totally lost me there.'

Chapter 10

The thought of Maggie's desperation troubled Louise all through that weekend. Spurred by a very real concern she decided to speak to Jack – then jettisoned the idea for fear of making matters worse. It was certainly none of her business and she suspected that he would be infuriated by Maggie's revelations to her. Yet even as she travelled to Waterloo her failure to intervene caused her a profound sense of unease.

In the whirl of the week's activities at the Holbrooke Collection the Eastons were relegated to the back of her mind, there was no time for them. Aylmer Littlejohn's determination to be awful was attaining histrionic heights. Louise had apologised for the coffee cup incident, explaining that it was an accident; Aylmer had never accepted her apology, though shrugging as she tried to sound genuinely contrite, dismissing it as a bagatelle. This it clearly was not: nobody, but nobody, treated him like that and got away with it, his subsequent actions insisted. He interfered with her work, countermanding instructions she passed on from him to workmen or security staff, denying that they were his orders; he failed to meet appointments she noted in his diary, saying that they'd not been there when he'd checked that morning; it came back to her by various channels that he was complaining of her inefficiency and difficult behaviour to curators and trustees. At first she had been taken aback, even at times apologetic, wondering if she had misheard his directions or he had misunderstood her. She had taken endless care to soothe the staff's injured feelings at the extra work the constantly changing arrangements produced, but as the days wore on the resigned nods were changing to an exasperated: 'For Heaven's sake, stop apologising and get it right next time!' And even, 'If you're having a nervous breakdown, Louise, go and have it somewhere else!' Slowly she recognised the sheer double-edged brilliance of Aylmer's nastiness: the critic stood up at a well-known lunch venue had savaged an article of his; he'd been due to give detailed reports to two committees which he'd now given himself time – just – to complete in time for the reconvened meetings (something of which only Louise was aware); those lumbered with excess work were colleagues she knew he disliked – and he loaded insult upon injury by telling third parties that much of the muddle was of those colleagues' making.

'Killing two, even three, birds with one stone!' Louise complained to Simon. 'You know, I believed people were normally only vile under pressure or through mental illness, but Aylmer is pro-active in nasty manipulation, he goes for it with both hands.'

'Darling, aren't you becoming a bit paranoid?' he protested.'Their inefficiency may be the reason he dislikes those particular people.'

'No,' said Louise, brooding over the matter, 'they're actually among the most efficient. Besides – hey, think of this, Simon – he re-directs the criticism of his own failures. They, and above all, I, become the source of his administrative cock-ups while he basks in sympathy over the poor quality of his staff!'

The following evening she telephoned Josie to bring her up-to-date. She was not without manipulative skills herself: since Josie was a possible, no, a probable successor to Aylmer, and no great admirer, she would be grateful to be warned of the sour atmosphere that was developing in the great galleries. But as she spoke she became aware of a strange quietness on the other end of the line. A prickle of apprehension ran down her spine. 'You've heard from Aylmer recently, ' she stated.

There was a pause. 'He has spoken to me, yes,' said Josie.

Louise reflected swiftly, then spoke in her briskest voice. 'Well, as I was saying, things have not gone as smoothly as

120

one would have liked over the past weeks and inevitably people are shifting the blame around like a game of pass the parcel, but I shan't bore you with the details, you've better things to think about. Sufficient to say that Aylmer and I are sorting it out. How is your dear little Lucy? And when do we see you back?'

With luck, after that anything the director had said to Josie would seem like petty fretfulness. She had, after all, herself described him as a fussy old woman.

Remembering that she had once heard Jack say that he made his clients sign a proof of their instructions to avoid arguments or even litigation later, she followed the same line with Aylmer. After a morning of detailed and frequently contradictory decisions and 'Well, what do you think then?' being regularly and irascibly fired at her, she presented her final note for his signature. His non-plussed expression was pure farce. He ran his hands through his scanty hair: 'Don't be ridiculous!' he blustered. Louise gave him her most charming smile, spoke in her most charming voice. 'We have had misunderstandings once or twice recently,' she said gently. 'It doesn't help the reputation of either of us. I want to be sure I'm conveying your exact requirements.' Forcing himself, Aylmer made two alterations, then signed. Louise thanked him. 'You see?' she said. His coldness towards her increased, but the mistakes diminished.

It was a relief to Louise. She was having a particularly difficult week. Repairs were being carried out on the line between Woking and Basingstoke, delaying trains. She had to leave the cottage at an hour that in her opinion simply shouldn't exist, returning late and exhausted. In addition this was the week of her lecture to the WI and she had to organise slides and check the equipment available for the village hall with Arabella Manningford as well as give up an entire evening. Worse, her next lunchtime lecture was scheduled for the following week and Aylmer had insisted that she broaden its scope, necessitating meticulous research during her lunch break and work till the small hours at home.

Thank God for the weekend in Bath. As Simon drove her westwards through the bright summer morning she replayed the events of the last week through her mind. Aylmer

121

stopped in his nefarious tracks – but would it be temporarily or permanently? He had need of a scapegoat for his inadequacies and thinking about it, she saw that she was the obvious person, involved as she was in almost every aspect of his work. Had he the grace and the character to do a volte-face and lean on her? Might she persuade him to that? She doubted it; he was not a man used to working in a team, certainly not in tandem, never with a woman. Spiteful little homosexual, she dubbed him, then grimaced with reluctant amusement and played with euphemisms . . . sentiently challenged, vertically challenged, sexually different! Aylmer found refuge in political correctness. His sexual orientation was in fact a matter of indifference to her; there were many men she admired working in the world of the museums and galleries who had similar inclinations; she simply wished he had normal male confidence.

How pleasant it had been by contrast to deal with Arabella, to arrive at the village hall to find everything perfectly organised, to be introduced as a personage and gracefully praised. The village women, as Arabella had said and she had doubted, had loved her talk. They sucked in ecstatic breaths at Meissen and Sèvres porcelain, they murmured in wonder at the splendour of mahogany or intricate inlays, they giggled at details of the private lives of their previous owners. 'Tremendous!' Arabella said afterwards. 'You pitched it at exactly the right level – erudite without being earnest or over their heads, and never condescending.' She had heard some of them planning a joint trip to visit the Holbrooke Collection: 'Though God knows how the poor loves will manage it, tied as they are to the humdrum by children and chores and jobs.' She said she would repeat the visit she had made in April – when was Louise's next lecture? 'Oh, and Simon and you must come to drinks on a Sunday morning, to meet James and become properly acquainted.' Simon had been delighted, not only at the chance to see the glories behind the magnificent façade of Abbotsbridge House, but at the enhancement to their social stature, the potential valuable clients he might meet. His gratification did something to relieve Louise's mind, ever-troubled by her deceptions. Her lecture was a form of amendment, like her efforts in the cottage garden, and it was somehow reassuring that both had brought their own pleasures.

Driving towards a weekend free from chores or responsibilities was soothing. Simon had switched on the radio to a Vivaldi horn concerto and was humming to it in bursts of good baritone. As the tribulations and pressures of the week started to retreat, pleasurable thoughts of great architecture and someone else's cooking took their place. Dear Simon had arranged this and she turned to look at him with affection. He sensed her attention and smiled ahead of himself.

'You know what I think?' he said. 'I think we're going to have a wonderful time.'

Bath was magnificent. Sun poured down on them from a cloudless blue sky, illuminating the honey-coloured beauty of the Cotswold limestone buildings, the smell of hot stone vying with freshly-mown grass and sweet whiffs of suntan oil. They had arrived early and prowled the city at a leisurely pace, leaning on a balustrade to admire the Pulteney Bridge over the Avon and the swans whose wakes shivered its elegant reflection, then moving on to the Circus, the incomparable Royal Crescent, the Assembly Rooms and Queen Square. They were silent in the face of the fine Palladian buildings – what was there to say? They knew each other's thoughts, they sighed in delight, they smiled, it was enough. The streets became crowded with Saturday morning shoppers and tourists, the temperature rose; neither mattered. They stopped for coffee as delicious and hot as the day, they browsed in bookshops, picking up tourist literature and swopping information. 'Sam Weller declared that the taste of the waters here was "like warm flat irons",' Louise informed Simon, while he retaliated that the early Christian Church, far from approving the Romans' desire for cleanliness, regarded baths as a worldly luxury which should seldom be permitted. 'Saintly possibly, smelly distinctly, those monks must have been!' In the cool Abbey Church after lunch they held hands, they read the flowery eulogies on the memorials, they burst into peals of laughter. As finally they wandered in a daze of amazement round the Baths and stared into the murky waters Simon was glad neither of them had been there before. We show each other things, he thought, together we find new dimensions to our awareness of the great and the precious in life. Several times he told himself that he would remember this day as one of the happiest of his life. He felt blessed.

They drove to the country house where they had booked to stay for the night with the car windows down and the hot air thick with odours of summer, dry and sweet. The house was not an hotel but one of a group of similar houses across England and Wales whose owners discreetly provided bed and breakfast with dinners, 'As good as the Gavroche!' said Simon, after a meal in the Peak District of quite exceptional quality. To stay in one of these places gave the feel of a country house weekend, passed perhaps with the friends of friends. No sharp red-nailed receptionist, no bored or boorish waiter; instead an atmosphere that was quietly tranquil.

'It's a wonderful room,' Simon announced for the third time as, pleasantly dizzy with good food, Chablis and lust, they undressed for the night. 'If it were my own house I wouldn't change a thing – it's perfect.'

He looked around himself with a smile. The house was a weathered Queen Anne manor and the bedroom was filled with beautiful things: a gleaming walnut chest of drawers and tallboy, a big old bed with a cane bedhead intricately woven, needlework pictures on the walls, old bell pulls still intact beside the pale grey marble fireplace. On a table by the window was a jumble of interesting objects: several antique boxes of varying shapes and sizes, a snuff box with a river view on its lid set within an oval edged with blue enamel, a silver partridge, a small blue and white porcelain vase filled with white rosebuds, and two family photographs in elaborate silver frames.

Simon fingered them, standing half-naked in the warm room.

'Beautiful and valuable.' Louise stretched and shed her blouse.

'One day I'll buy you things like these.' He caught hold of her. 'Hey, I want to do that.' He stood behind her to unhook her bra and slip it off, then he slid her briefs down her legs and held her as she stepped out of them. 'You're beautiful and valuable!' He fingered her breasts, caressing the hardening nipples, and she leaned against him in voluptuous enjoyment. He would take this slowly, drawing out the pleasure to the exquisite extreme. His fingers explored down the deeply expanding and falling ribcage to the soft curve of her belly and the long length of her flanks, stroking them reflectively. His hand quested into the warm darkness between her legs, the finger tips touching, probing, becoming urgent.

'Mmm,' she said, deep in her throat. 'Yes . . . yes!'

He turned her towards him for a kiss, his hands holding the curve of her buttocks to press her against himself – and then she pulled away.

'Ugh, Simon, Stilton!'

A small shock, cold air on the warm skin that had been against hers. Louise hated the smell of Stilton. Damn, he should have remembered. But why did she have to be so fussy? He loved that cheese.

She was laughing. 'It's no aphrodisiac!' she pointed out.

'I'll clean my teeth,' he offered grumpily, and went into the bathroom.

There was no toothpaste in his sponge-bag; he must have forgotten it. Double damn! He'd use Louise's, though he didn't like the flavour. He opened her sponge-bag and put in his hand. What was this? Something vaguely familiar . . . a plastic card of pills, each marked with the day of the week. Pills taken from it – Wednesday, Thursday, Friday . . . The blood seemed to be draining downwards from his body, leaving him shaking and sick. He stared at the . . . the *thing* as if his eyes would vapourise it. This couldn't be true. The evidence stared back at him. Anger flowed through his veins like hot lava across a plain.

He stood in the doorway holding it out. 'What the hell is this!'

Her lips moved. A flash of horror, of guilt, and she stepped backwards. 'Oh God, Simon, it . . . I wanted to tell you!'

So it was true! His stomach flopped over heavily, robbing him of breath. Louise, his Louise! His heart was pounding so loudly that he could hear it, pounding into his shocked and incoherent mind the thought that she had lied to him, time and again . . . not only lied to him, lived a lie. She had lain on her back, clasping her knees to conserve his sperm, and all the time she had been deceiving him; there was no hope of life for them within her, only death. He could not have been more shattered if he had discovered her fornicating with another man. The hot lava of his anger burned into him, replacing shock with searing pain. Hardly knowing what he was doing, he advanced towards her, brandishing the packet of pills. She edged backwards; he kept going, pushing her across the room until she was backed up against the marble fireplace. Then he hit her.

'You bitch!' he breathed. Transferring the packet to his left hand, he slapped her across the cheek with his open right hand, once, twice. With the second blow the marble shelf caught her below the shoulder blades and her head swung back to hit the frame of a picture with a crack that penetrated the reddened mists of his anger. 'Christ!' he said.

She cringed sideways to avoid him. 'God, Simon, I'm sorry, I'm sorry!'

The fear that he had cracked something vital in her receded, but he could not hit her again. The need for violence volcanic inside him still, he smashed his fist into the wall behind her instead, yelping with the brutal shock of pain that shot through his knuckles and up his arm. Louise caught his wrist and held on to it with the strength of urgency.

'Don't,' she said. 'Please, Simon, don't! Stop it!'

He backed away from her, sat down on the bed, corrosive thoughts of her deception made more destructive by the thought of how foolish he must look sitting there in his boxer shorts and socks. The last faint withdrawing throb of his desire goaded him. Boxer shorts! He'd bought them to aid his fertility – how Louise must have been laughing at him all these months. But he should not have hit her; he had never hit a woman in his life, it was a terrible thing to have done. He nursed his knuckles, his arm, pain of every sort hammering its way through his veins, but worst of all, choking his head and his throat, was the pain of his humiliation.

'I'm sorry, Simon,' she said again. 'I'm so sorry. I never meant to deceive you, I never meant you to know . . .'

126

'No, I'm sure you didn't. What a laugh, letting me wallow on top of you, month after month, knowing my efforts would be useless. Did your friends all laugh too?'

'It wasn't like that,' she cried frantically. 'You mustn't think –'

'How do I know what it was like? Shall I tell you what it was like for me? Shall I?'

'If only you'd let me explain!'

Simon dug his nails into his palms, searching for the words that would blast her with his pain. 'Sod your explanation, you thoughtless, blood-sucking bitch! You made me feel incapable, less than a man. I'd begun to believe I was sterile – do you understand that? I wanted to know . . . but I was frightened to find out. So night after night I tried and hoped – and then I sweated and feared. That's what it has been like.'

'That's awful,' she blurted at speed. 'But listen. I was only doing it for a few months –'

He overrode her words mercilessly: 'Now I know it was your fault. Relief? I wouldn't know. Because what I know now is that the woman I loved and trusted couldn't be trusted with one of the most important matters of my life.'

The thought of having a child with her had been wonderful, warming. It had combined with his delight in moving to the country and with his growing pride at his career development to make him feel euphoric, triumphant, a giant. In his simple philosophy, felt rather than articulated, it held the true meaning of his existence. To copulate, to breed, to know that the bloodlines would continue, one's genes be found in future generations, that was what drove the rutting stag to fight for his harem, the randy tomcat to range his neighbourhood. For men and women though, there were other facets to life: he and Louise would strive to instil in their children their own desires for achievement, for steadily seeing through the years the quality and value of life improve; they would inspire them too, he hoped, with a love of literature and history, of great music, of fine art and architecture. He had been irradiated by these thoughts; he had believed – assumed, he now saw, that Louise had felt similarly. His sense of loss was immeasurable.

'I was going to stop taking the pill in a couple of months. Our child would have been born in late-spring or early-summer.'

'Really?' A red-hot needle of scorn. 'Easy to say that.'

'It's the truth! I wanted my career to be more established before I gave up work. That's all.'

'So month after month you played along, lying to me, making an idiot of me. There's no reason on earth why any-one should do that, even to an enemy. Am I an enemy?'

'No! Oh God no, Simon! Never!'

'Then I understand even less why you treated me like this.' He got up heavily from the bed, retrieved his trousers from a chair, tugged them on, shrugged on his shirt and zipped it in. He slipped on his shoes.

'I wanted to talk to you about it,' she said feverishly, 'But it always seemed to be the wrong moment.'

'Rubbish.'

'Darling, I promise you – '

Simon turned to leave the room, opened the door. Louise ran after him, putting her hand on his arm. He shook it off. She remembered she was naked and shrank back behind the door.

'Where are you going?' she cried in a low voice, terrified someone might hear.

'Out.'

'But any minute the house will be locked up. You'll be locked out.'

His voice was sharp as a singer slipping off key. 'Isn't that what you want? What you've done? You've locked me out.' He slammed the door. She heard him go down the stairs and out into the summer night.

She pulled on a nightdress, wondered whether she should dress. She stood listening hard; Simon wouldn't . . . surely he wouldn't . . . drive off and leave her? In the far distance a dog barked; an owl whoo-hoo-hoo'd, the sounds ebbing and returning eerily as it drifted near the house: no sounds of an engine. She flung herself on to the bed, turned off the light and lay staring into the half-light of the June night. The min-utes passed, turned into hours. Remorse and horror at what she had done to him ground into her, pulverising her with

128

regret. So lightly had she been destructive, not pausing to think her actions through, affected by Charley's easy optimism, his casual approach: 'It's your life, you've got to live it . . .' 'Put yourself first . . .' No, she thought, not his fault, hers. What did he know of their relationship? She had clung to the words because they were what her selfish soul craved. Worse, so blind had she been in her enlightened self-interest, her belief in the moral superiority of self-affirmation, that she had aired her dilemma with outsiders while shunning all discussion with Simon. Please God he would never know that – it would be the final pain, the final betrayal. She could hardly conceive the pain she had inflicted already. Bitch, bitch, bitch! She flayed herself with his words, turning her head into her pillow, sobbing with shame, self-scorn and anguish. The terrifying possibility flamed like a red-hot coal lodged in her breast that their relationship might be over, his love dead.

The owl, busy in the last pale light of the moon, made weird and mournful sounds. Louise sat up. Where was Simon? It must be past two. She switched on the light – twenty to four! Ouch, her head hurt. She must have drifted off into a half-sleep. She pulled on slippers and ran out to find him. There was just enough light on the stairs; she manoeuvred the bolts of the big front door by feel. The night smelt of cows and roses.

He was asleep in the car, the front seat tilted back. His profile looked stern and withdrawn. She opened the door to touch him timidly.

'Simon? Simon, wake up.'

He opened his eyes, frowned, focussed. 'What do you want?'

'Darling, you can't sleep out here. Come up to bed.'

'I prefer not to sleep with you, thank you.'

'Simon, please don't be so cold to me. Please, please come back inside and have some proper sleep. Then we can talk in the morning.'

'I have nothing more to say to you.'

'But I have. So much. So very much. I want to apologise to you. I want to tell you how much I love you. I want to explain . . . everything.'

He was silent, still looking ahead of himself, his face rigid.

Terror hit Louise once more. 'You've always been fair – be fair now. Give me a chance to tell you.'

'I see no sense in explanations. The facts speak for themselves, and the facts you have admitted.'

'There's the fact of our love. I love you and I always shall.' She wanted to sob out to him: We were so happy all day – can all that laughter and warmth and understanding between us be destroyed by a packet of pills? But she knew that it could. She shook, her knees weak. 'Please listen, Simon. Please.'

He misinterpreted her shiver. There was dew on the car windscreen and the air was chill. 'You'd better go in, you're getting cold. Oh, very well. We'll both go in and talk – though what difference it will make I can't imagine.'

In the room there was a mini-bar discreetly tucked in a corner. She found whisky and poured a measure each. The neat spirit made her gasp but she prayed it would brace her. Simon had sat down on the edge of the bed and was staring at her, the tumbler clasped in both his hands as if it might warm them, stop the shaking that she saw was afflicting him too. She found it difficult to select the right words; her throat was constricted and she was afraid of bursting into tears.

He said in a tight voice: 'No wonder you pushed aside my talk of marriage. Just a passing fancy, was I? Someone to fill in time with while you kept your options open?'

'No!' she said vehemently. Pause, deep breath: he had given her the opening she needed. 'No, but there was a time when I felt you were taking certain options away from me. You accepted the offer from Shergold & Stent in Basingstoke, you made an offer on the cottage, both without consulting me. On top of that you wanted me to have a baby before I was ready . . .'

'Oh?' he interrupted. 'So you punished me with deception in return. We couldn't have talked it over rationally? Oh no! Nothing so normal.'

'No! Not true. If you remember, we did talk it over, but you were insistent. You must have children before you were thirty. You refused to give me the extra year or two I needed to establish my career.'

'So then, not having the guts to put your foot down, you had fun making a fool of me.'

'Didn't you make a fool of me? But I haven't held that against you as you'd know if you'd just listen!'

Words were poisoned darts now, tossed from one to the other. Their eyes met across a room that was filled with harsh breathing.

'Go on.'

'Simon, I think I must have been out of my mind, but arguments are hateful and I decided to avoid this one by quietly continuing on the pill. Then came the move. I certainly didn't want to be pregnant during that upheaval, and then, well, Aylmer Littlejohn became the director, and, and . . . he hates me because I'm a woman and a better administrator and I show him up and I was terrified he'd find some way to get rid of me if I had to be away for six or eight months, and Josie said I should do at least a year of the lectures to establish myself there – though I could do them when I was pregnant so . . .' she was gabbling faster and faster to try to get it all out before she burst into tears '. . . I was going to chuck the pills in the month after next – ' a huge tearing sob ' – and I never wanted to hurt you but once I'd started it became harder and harder to tell you, and I could see you were getting worried and I loathed myself but then I thought it was only a few more weeks . . .' a flurry of sobs '. . . and I do love you and I want to stay with you.' She had to stop to steady her voice. She detested the loss of control. She found a tissue and snuffled into it with as much dignity as the bubbling wetness would allow. She lifted her head: 'And have a child with you. Now.'

She had a deep sense of surrendering to forces stronger than herself. Commitment. She had done it at last, burned her boats, tied herself down, ruined her career, probably ruined her figure too. She thought he had no idea of the enormous step she was taking, one she had dreaded and shrunk from for months, years even. She was doing it from love.

There was silence. He seemed to be weighing her like some object he was considering purchasing. Did he see her differently now? Did he consider her damaged goods, despite her explanation? Just a few hours ago he had called

131

her beautiful and valuable. In the dim room she shivered again with fear, troubled by an aloofness he'd never shown her before. His violence, his blows on her face, had been easier to cope with: she understood the force of his fury, even acquiesced in it as a fair response to her duplicity.

'Simon?'

He said nothing. She caught the glow of his eyes in the first light of dawn. She sank to her knees beside him. He drank the last of his whisky and put the tumbler on the bedside table without ceasing to watch her.

'Simon, say something. Please. Say you understand. Say you forgive me.'

He said slowly: 'I don't know. I'm still in a state of shock. I need to think about it.'

'I want to comfort you,' Louise said, meaning that she craved mutual comfort. She put her arms round him, feeling the rigid coldness of his body. 'You're icy, you should get into bed, let me warm you. Come on.'

He simply sat, staring ahead. Afraid, she shifted as close to his body as she could, conscious of pain in her knees at contact with the hard oak floorboards beneath the worn and ancient Axminster carpet. She locked her hands behind his back, pressing her cheek against his. Slowly he lifted his arms to hold her. Relief flooded her. The feel of his face with the early stubble of beard, the texture of his shirt, the scent of him that was soap and skin and a dying echo of aftershave, was all infinitely familiar, deeply moving. She lifted her head and the first light of the rising sun lit the room with a thin but brilliant ray. Everything about him was suddenly more intensely real, more personal to her. It was as though she had passed through an invisible door into a more instinctual and glorious world, interjacent to that of hard knowledge and experience and success, and yet quite separate, an Elysium of pure vision and feeling. She sensed the smallness and meanness of herself die away. She repeated, calmly now, knowing it was true: 'I want to have your child.'

She moved her lips across his cold face, wanting to warm it, seeking his lips, her tongue caressing. Abruptly his arms tightened on the flesh of her back, his head was pressed against hers, lips contacting fiercely, too fiercely; she could taste blood as he ground her teeth against them. He slid from the bed to the carpet; with one hand still holding her he unzipped his trousers, jerked his clothes out of the way, her nightdress up, and then he was entering her. She was unprepared, it was too sudden; he hurt her. 'Please!' she gasped, but he continued, the thin texture of the carpet beneath her buttocks no protection from the hard floor boards into which he was ramming her, his penis pounding in and out, rutting like some untamed animal, some stag asserting his rights, claiming his dominance. It was frightening, painful, exciting. She climaxed unexpectedly, violently, the electric shock of it shooting through the soles of her feet, her fingers, the top of her head. 'Ahhhh!' she cried out, and then he flooded her with a great groan and came to rest inert on top of her.

Chapter 11

The morning of Hubert's death was wholly disconcerting for
Brozie. Everything concerned with it was unexpected. She
had anticipated that sleep would evade her that night, as it
had for many nights, but she awoke late from a dreamless
sleep to an enchanting morning of sparkling sunshine and
birdsong, the scent of roses drifting in through the wide
flung windows of the spare bedroom where she now slept.
For a second or two she lay smiling to herself, then the
serenity induced by the solitary untroubled night was shattered by the remembrance of her husband: Hubert! She flung
on her dressing-gown, paused with her hand on his door-
handle, pushed it open, stood to see. 'Hubert?'

She had expected wide-staring and accusing eyes and
tumbled bedclothes, but he lay on his back, eyes closed, bedclothes smooth to his chin. No crepey neck, no lunging
Adam's apple, no angry eyes; the lines on his face strangely
smoothed out. As self-conscious in her actions as an actress,
afraid of invisible eyes watching, judging, she touched his
hand – icy – then passed her fingers round his wrist. No
pulse. Dead. She laid the hand down, her eyes fixed on his
face. He looked quite unlike her horrible Hubert: an image
came into her head of the marble Henry Manningford lying
on his fifteenth-century monument in the village church –
pale, dignified, calm. Why had Hubert never been like this in
life?

What happened next? Anxiety stabbed at her. She must
ring Dr Field, start the long rigmarole and panoply of death.
A familiar clutch of nausea was followed by the terrible heat

and sweat of a hot flush; she waited, breathing slowly, for the beast to retreat. No, no intruders yet upon her peace. Nobody must come until she had immersed her sticky unpleasing body in a cool bath. Then she must dress, have a cup of coffee. Dignity and calm, she warned herself, dignity and calm.

Coffee inside her – black to keep her mind sharply clear – she forced herself to the kitchen telephone. Even as she dialled the surgery she could see reminders of Hubert all round the room: his elderly, much-mended shoes waiting to be cleaned by the back door, a grubby handkerchief on a chair, the tin of bitter chocolate biscuits that his false teeth scrunched – had scrunched – so noisily every teatime . . . Horrible, repellent now . . . She almost retched. She would carry his most intimate things to the bin with tongs.

'Yes? Yes?' the self-righteous receptionist was saying insistently.

Brozie forced her thoughts to cohere. 'Could I speak to Dr Field, please?'

'Well, I don't know if that's possible just now.'

'It is important.'

'Dr Field is very busy this morning,' the woman said reprovingly. She was bossy, armour-plated in self-satisfaction; if she could, she would have stood patients in line in the waiting-room, called them to the doctors by number. 'If your call's not urgent, then please ring at four o'clock like our regulations say, or better still, make an appointment.'

To her horror, twenty years of repressed anger and bitterness welled up in the normally mild Brozie and sharpened her voice to armour-piercing steel, so that she stabbed back with sarcasm and words she'd never even contemplated using before: 'Oh no, not urgent, you cold uncaring cow! Only that my husband's dead in his bed, so he can't go anywhere or need any treatment, but I want the doctor and I want her now. So get off your fat arse for once and get her – fast, damn you!' Then the nauseating tension that had gripped her stomach broke and the sweat of another hot flush burst through the crimsoning skin of her face to mingle with the unexpected tears that poured down her cheeks.

The rector was well acquainted with his wife's occasional

withdrawals into the recesses of her mind while she sought the answer to some medical conundrum, and when she appeared for lunch long after it was finished, abruptly told him that Hubert Hamilton had died in the night, and answered his queries – as to how Brozie was taking it and when he should best call on her – at random or not at all, he deduced without difficulty that her mind was mulling over the event, probably with an excess of self-criticism. Jane took all her patients' deaths, even when expected, even if they were approaching their century, as a personal blow. She believed with Donne: 'Every man's death diminisheth mee'. He knew she had expected Hubert to be around in all his many-faceted awfulness for months yet. He sat admiring the way the sunlight was streaming through the open long windows to gild her tawny hair, watching her eat a ham salad, aware that if he asked her in fifteen minutes time what she had eaten she would not be able to say. The children were playing a game of lions among the legs of the dining table, crawling exuberantly round, growling. Thomas waited, eating black grapes one by one. Jane would tell him her problem when she was ready.

At a nod from him Selma slouched off to make coffee, something she did do well. On her return Jane pushed away her plate and accepted a cup, clasping it in both hands, brooding over it. At last she spoke.

'You know I said there was something not quite right about Brozie the last time I saw her?'

'Yes, I do remember.' He turned. 'Selma, take Flora and Lucian into the garden to play quietly, please.' Not all the subjects of Jane's musings were fit for other ears.

She put down her coffee cup. Her eyes, dark and intense, swivelled to his. 'I couldn't think what it was, then afterwards a thought came to me. There was a . . . a feeling of death about her. That sounds dramatic, but it wasn't. There was a distance, an avoidance of eye-contact. She spoke with detachment about Hubert which she never normally did. The terminally ill sometimes become detached in that way, they enter a world of acceptance, of resignation, even serenity. Not Hubert, never Hubert. He railed in fury against the slowness of medical research to the end. But do you remember Dorothy Lees?'

His brows descended to a frown. 'She killed herself.'

'Yes, and I saw her just two days before, quite by accident in the lane. That something not quite right about Brozie . . . suddenly I realised she reminded me of Dorothy. As if she had passed through a great mental turmoil and emerged at the other side. I was in bed, on the point of sleep, when it came to me and I jolted awake: Brozie was depressed; Brozie was contemplating suicide. But what could I do at midnight? I comforted myself you were to visit her. I convinced myself I was imagining things. But now I'm terrified I wasn't. Thomas. . .' Her voice dropped almost to a whisper. 'Oh, darling, this is the awful thing – I believe Brozie killed Hubert. It wasn't her own death she was calmly facing, but his.'

He stared at her for several seconds. 'How?'

'A mixture of barbiturates and alcohol. Not difficult – you wouldn't need much.'

'Barbiturates?' he repeated.

'Mmm. Soneryl. Hubert wasn't sleeping. Hasn't been for ages . . .'

'I remember your telling me – and that his tossing and turning was upsetting Brozie.'

'He'd constantly complained that the sleeping pills I prescribed were useless so I reluctantly put him on to that instead. Pressed, Brozie told me he was drinking whisky all evening, that she warned him he shouldn't and was yelled at for her pains. He asked her did she want to deprive him of all his last pleasures in life? My own gut feeling is that she got him fuddled on purpose, then gave him a further dose or doses.'

'But what put you on to this? Why on earth should you suspect her?'

'Intuition? I don't know . . . A prickle between the shoulder blades. An absence of any other explanation. Nothing wrong with Hubert's heart that I'd ever discovered . . . not in the physical sense, that is.' Her voice was wry.

Thomas looked at her, serious and tender and concerned for her in her trouble. 'Little right in any other sense.'

'That doesn't mean . . .'

'No. Never.'

'Something else. A book – one of those that Charley St George gave her. It was on top of a pile in the kitchen by the telephone. I had to make various calls and while I was waiting for the connections I glanced at the top novel. Thomas, it was about a man whose wife had terminal cancer, painful cancer, and how he secretly assisted her to euthanasia – and then had to defend himself through the courts because her doctor insisted on post mortem tests. It was done through the deepest love, the blurb said, and went on about how the novel was a brilliant and searching re-appraisal of the arguments for and against euthanasia.'

'In other words, the arguments for? A reversal of the old saying: "Man proposes and God disposes"?'

She gestured helplessly. 'I imagine . . . but I don't know, I haven't read it. And I can't read Brozie's mind, either.'

There was a long pause while he directed his own mind to what could have been in a parishioner's for whom he had always had a deep regard. 'I cannot believe she would,' he said, his voice level and low and definite. 'She is a good and kind woman.'

'She could have considered it a kindness.'

'So it would be. Kinder than God. Kinder than you could be.'

'You want to comfort me . . .'

'Of course. But very well, look at it logically. What would a post-mortem show? An overdose? You said it wouldn't take much. Then did he take it or she administer it? Who is to say?'

'Hubert clung to life like a gnarled old limpet.'

The rector spoke slowly, choosing his words with care. 'The Church believes that the process of death should not be one of distress, but of preparation for another world; as you said, a time of acceptance . . . even of gladness. It is a time when relationships are of importance – it can be a time of healing. But Hubert made no use of the time he was given, he had no conception of resignation, or of a healing and peaceful transition. Only anger held him up, held him to life. But anger is stressful and wearing. Possibly he'd had enough. Or possibly something did go wrong with his heart. A post-mortem could only cause trouble and offence in the village.'

138

'Oh hell, I know, that's what's so awful!' She put her elbows on the table, clasped her head in her hands. 'But I can't have my patients doing away with each other.'

'The demise of one terminally ill and critically grumpy old codger is hardly going to lead to a riot of mass slaughter in Abbotsbridge, sweetheart.'

She giggled weakly, then clenched her hands in her hair, wild locks erupting between her fingers. 'I can sign the death certificate – he died within fourteen days of having visited the surgery,' she said in a muffled voice. 'But, oh darling, it's so horrid to think such a thing and not to *know*!'

Brozie's day became ever more odd and disconcerting. The weather was hot and wave after wave of sweat drenched her. Drinking herbal tea to calm herself only made her burn the more. She leaned at the kitchen sink to splash her face with cold water till embarrassing dark splodges showed on her navy blouse to echo the dark rings in her armpits. To change was impossible: she could not, would not again enter that room which her dead husband's presence dominated.

It seemed an eternity before the men from the funeral parlour came to take the body. The doctor came and went and came again. The death certificate, she said, she had to have the right form. A woman normally warm with sympathy, she was distant and coolly professional, her questions exact, probing, once upon another in swift succession. She sat in Hubert's chair, a Queen Anne wing chair, like so much of the furniture in the house a relic of the antiques and furniture restoration business, and Brozie sat opposite her, unnerved that she should choose that particular chair, trying not to look at her in it. Instead she fixed her eyes on her hands, swollen a little with the heat, the veins standing out slaty blue above the flesh, pressing the fingers together to still their trembling and struggled to answer as accurately as she could. Finally she lifted her eyes to meet Jane Field's, and told her of Hubert's nightly terrors and his frantic need during the last months for more and more aids to help him sleep. She was dreadfully tired and her voice now had all the quiet calmness she needed. The doctor heard her out, her young attractive face very still, wholly concentrated. She spoke only once, to ask if Brozie could show her any of the bottles containing pills she claimed Mr Hamilton had acquired elsewhere.

Brozie shook her head. 'I don't know,' she said, blotting her hot face with a tissue. 'His drugs were his business. If there are any left they'll be on the top shelf of the old commode on his side of the bed.'

The doctor looked at her, then walked straight up the stairs to return with her hands cupped round five or six little bottles. Her face seemed at once grim but relieved. She nodded to Brozie.

'He was very foolish,' she commented, 'and you were foolish to let him.' She signed the death certificate and then instructed Brozie to visit her at the surgery: 'To discuss hormone replacement therapy. You say you can manage without it, but I believe you need help badly.'

The man from the funeral directors was younger than Brozie expected and he was caring. 'We believe in a *caring* service,' he explained. 'In a time of bereavement and sadness we're here to make sure that everything is done exactly as you would want it, but above all, as the departed would have wanted. Care and dignity are our passwords.'

Despite her attempts to refuse, Mr Fudge swept Brozie up to the bedroom and Hubert in a torrent of persuasive words. He knew she would want to be present to see how his colleagues handled Mr Hamilton with caring and gentle dignity. First, of course, he'd explain what would be done, so she wouldn't be forced to ask. The deceased was tenderly wrapped in a sheet, then placed in a cover and taken by stretcher – with all due decorum as you'd have a right to expect – to their private ambulance. Then to their Chapel of Rest, open for visits at *any* hour. His words flowed over her in a warm and syrupy flood. Hubert would have detested Mr Fudge: *Sycophantic little toad*, she imagined his spirit snapping. But Brozie liked him, liked the firm hand holding her elbow, the gentle brown eyes in the grave face; a chord was struck, she knew he was sincere. Now he was withdrawing his men: she'd like a minute alone to say goodbye, he knew, time for a last kiss. Horrorstruck, she opened her mouth in denial, then closed it as he tipped out, nodding. She must not disappoint Mr Fudge.

She stood beside the bed. 'Goodbye, Hubert,' she said and bent to kiss his cheek. It resisted her, cold and hard as marble. She straightened. It was silent in the room, cool and grey. The discreetly drawn curtains were outlined in blazing light. Sparrows broke into a noisy squabble outside. Hubert would never squabble again. She looked at him once more and felt no sense of his spirit. The sparrows flew off and the silence intensified. He was utterly departed. Down by the river she heard the distant voices of children playing. She had a new life before her; she was free as the children. Free.

She opened the door. 'Thank you, Mr Fudge,' she said.

She had anticipated peace after the men had left with their burden: she had seen herself drinking tea in the empty kitchen or wandering her quiet garden, nipping off a faded flower here and there, watching her herons in their heronry. But people . . . she had never expected all the people. When her parents had died a few friends had called, a very few. Most wrote, like her few distant relations, then forgot her. She had been horribly alone. But now the doorbell and the telephone rang endlessly. The rector, Mrs Manningford, Nancy Chubb, Maggie Easton, the other ladies who were on the church flower rota – they all called and brought flowers. Each time she was at the sink, deep in leaves and stems, and dried her hands only to find herself smothered in affection and still more flowers.

The rector brought a mixed posy from his garden, Nancy Chubb arrived in her van with tins of food: 'Well, you won't want to go shopping until the funeral's over, will you?' and blindingly bright orange roses. Arabella Manningford appeared with lilies and spoke of guilt: 'Now you mustn't feel guilty!' she began and Brozie fixed her eyes on her in painful concentration. Could she possibly . . .? But then she found herself being hugged and told how terrible that lady had felt at the death of her father – 'I hadn't telephoned for a fortnight and he went suddenly and all I could think of was how much I wanted to tell him I loved him and I couldn't. And now it can't be long before my mother . . . well, I send her letters every day I can't see her. All of us who are left

141

feel guilty – sins of omission, you know – but you mustn't reproach yourself, Brozie dear, because we all know how good and patient you've been!'

Maggie arrived with an armful of delphiniums and her son, Toby. Brozie was unused to small boys and expected to find him equally tonguetied, but he looked up at her with round eyes and confided: 'What God does when he flies you up in the sky, is he holds on tight and pulls you up in a parachute. That's how he took Felicity, isn't it, Mummy?'

Maggie smiled. 'Why do you think God uses a parachute, my treasure?'

'Well,' Toby said seriously, 'if he flew you up in a plane or a helicockter it would break His house, but a parachute is smaller an' it's soft.'

'You're right,' Brozie said, half-gasping. 'You must be. Clever boy!' The thought of Hubert in his crumpled pyjamas floating ever-upward and away in the hot July sky appealed to her so much that she found herself torn between hysterical giggles and tears and only calmed herself by scrabbling through several cupboards for yet another vase.

But when, three minutes later, Charley St George rapped and came in through the kitchen door to say: 'Hallo, Brozie, what's this I heard at the village stores? Finally got rid of Hubert, have you?' the tears of stress and tension won and she dropped her sheaf of delphiniums and burst into sobs she could not smother.

'God, Charley, how can you be so tactless?' Maggie hissed.

He was unperturbed. He stepped forward to hold Brozie in his bearlike grasp and patted her bony back comfortingly. 'It's the shock,' he observed. 'A hell of a day for you. It's all right, you know.'

All the tense core of her that had built into a hard icy lump melted in the curious warmth and unconcern that radiated from Charley. She leaned her head against his shoulder, letting herself be held by him as nobody had held and cuddled her, not since her father when she was small and hurt her knees. She stopped sobbing but the tears flowed on, seemingly endless, drawing out with them the hate and the fear and the misery.

'Oh dear,' she said, at last trying to loosen herself from his grasp. 'Oh dear, how embarassing . . . I'm so sorry.'

'You need a hanky.' Charley's arm was still round her shoulder. With his free hand he hauled a green-spotted piece of cotton liberally streaked with black out of a trouser pocket and surveyed it with dismay. 'Ah, I was repairing the old Landrover again . . .'

Maggie found a clean tissue. 'Here – this do? Charley, isn't your Porsche back on the road yet? It's about time.'

He grinned. 'I love the way you bawl me out. Yes, as a matter of fact it is. Just. Like my Porsche, do you? Brozie likes my Porsche.'

'I do,' she agreed, giving her eyes a final wipe, 'it's exciting.' And her sallow red-splotched face relaxed into a little smile as she thought of the amazing changes the car and Charley had brought to her life.

Maggie smiled too, turning to Toby who was looking apprehensive from seeing a grown-up lady crying. 'Here, Toby, you climb on this stool and help Brozie and me arrange the flowers. You're a Porsche man, aren't you?'

'Mmm!' Toby said fervently, handing his mother a stem covered in white blooms. 'That one next, Mummy. Charley's car's nicer'n our cars.'

'I'd happily drive an estate car if I had kids,' he said unexpectedly. 'Haven't found anyone to have them with yet, though. Hey, Tobias, like me to run and your mummy home when you leave?

'Yes, *please!*'

'We'll have a cup of tea first, though,' Charley decided, 'and some of Brozie's amazing cake.' He handed the kettle to Maggie to be filled. 'I came to ask you if you want me to take you anywhere tomorrow, Brozie?'

She turned, the ninth bowl crammed with great blooms held in her hands so that she peered between leaves and flowers, muzzy almost from post-trauma and the scents that were filling her nostrils.

'I don't know,' she said vaguely. 'What does one do? There must be a hundred things to deal with but it's more than twenty years since I had to organise a funeral.' A stupifying heat rolled over her without warning, seeming to

143

remove any last vestiges of competence from her brain. She plonked the flowers down on the table, grabbed a damp towel from a hook and pressed it to her cheeks and forehead, for once not caring who noticed, drawing indescribable relief from its clammy coolness. There would be so much to be done, she could not think even where she should start on the multitude of decisions and arrangements: she cringed at having to decide times and places, at the remembrance of forms and certificates, hymns and headstones, at incomprehensible interviews with solicitors and bank managers. Terror struck her at the realisation that she would have to drive the car to cope – but Hubert had always driven, she had not touched it in years.

'Arrange the funeral, prove the will,' Charley was saying in his deep voice. 'Make lists tomorrow. Telephone all the right useful people. I'll come round early and give you a start. I can drive you anywhere you need . . . till mid-morning, that is.'

Brozie took the towel from her face. 'But your work?'

'I'm taking the day off, I'd planned for a break today and tomorrow. I told my partner he can get on with it, sort things out himself for once.'

Relief ran through her like a cooling soothing stream. Dear Charley. So big, so solid, so kind. Someone with his masculine savoir faire could sift through all the financial and organisational difficulties in no time.

When Maggie and Charley left her half an hour later Brozie let her front door stand open to catch the breeze and found herself listening to their voices as they sauntered towards the Porsche that was half-hidden behind the hedge.

'This is the weather,' Charley was saying, stretching luxuriously in the heat. 'I hope it'll last through tomorrow.'

'Of vast importance, is it?' Maggie asked half-mockingly. 'What do you plan to do beneath the sun then?'

'Go to Goodwood,' Charley said with complacency.

'Not the races again! Over on the downs in the sun? I envy you – it'll be gorgeous.'

'I'm going to a party tomorrow!' Toby boasted, twisting his head up to Charley. 'And I'm having lunch with my friend Matthew too!'

'So you are,' Maggie said, 'I almost forgot. What fun – and a free day for me as well.'

'Come with me to Goodwood, then!' Charley commanded.

'Oh, I couldn't, Charley,' she protested with a vigorous shake of her head and a hiccup of nervous laughter. 'No . . . Heavens no! Whatever would Jack say?'

Chapter 12

She was still determined to say no again the following morning, though Charley had ignored her refusals, laughing at her and saying: 'Nonsense, you're longing to come. Relax. Someone like you was never intended to be all buttoned up and miserable – you know you love the horses, we'll have tremendous fun!'

She stood by the casement window of her bedroom mid-morning gazing out. She could feel summer's beauty intensifying in the deep blue sky, in the hay-scented faint breeze that touched her cheek, in the piercing and repetitive sweetness of a thrush's song. Bees were working in the roses on the cottage wall, a persistent busy hum; a pair of peacock butterflies danced an entangled path across her vision, and the sights and the sounds reminded her that summer was short, but it was here now, in all its deepening warmth and perfumes and luxuriant growth, not to be ignored or taken for granted, but enjoyed, savoured, relished, for it would be over all too soon. She looked up the lane to the distant hills and felt a wayward softness and longing deepen in her. Chores had no meaning on a morning like this: to abandon everything and drive into the sunshine was wickedly tempting. When a flash of red and a throaty roar caught at her consciousness she snatched up a pair of sunglasses, her bag and a shady hat, and was out of the front door and running down the path to the car before she had time to think what she was intending.

As they drove away from the village along the empty top road she stretched and breathed deeply and relaxed. She was certain no one had seen her. She laughed low in her throat at her own daring and folly.

'I must be mad,' she said. 'Quite mad!'

'Good,' Charley said. 'I like my friends to be mad – mad and happy, like me.' He accelerated to overtake a Jaguar and continued down the country road at eighty.

'So fast!' she said, at once apprehensive and excited.

'We're a bit late,' he told her. 'I had to sort out various problems for poor old Brozie. Still, while she was finishing with the solicitor I bought us a picnic – it'll save time. Hopeless arriving seconds before the first race and then having to fight for food. This way we eat in peace.'

A picnic? Tucked in a quiet glade? Out on the hills? A qualm of guilt now. Easy to chat and laugh and keep him at arms length in a crowd. Safety in numbers. Not totally safe where Charley was concerned. Such a big, determined man – and determination was dangerously attractive. Her thoughts rose and swooped wildly, like the birds from before the speeding car; they glanced at various implications, flying to Jack and babies and hastily away. But Charley said they wouldn't have much time. Besides, such vanity to imagine he would want to seduce her, fat and sad as she was these days. He drove Brozie all over Hampshire, nobody could imagine anything more than simple friendliness there. He was a kind man, concerned for her, Maggie, wanting to lighten her day, glad of her companionship when Melody presumably was working. How delightful. How wasteful . . . Stop, push away the disturbing thoughts. Enjoy the sun and the speed and the moments of excitement when the Porsche dashes past slower, more mundane cars, watch too the passing chalk downland that comes just after Winchester and see beyond like a spreading map the expanse of wheatfields and lush meadows flanking the river Itchen, anticipate the sounds and sights and excitement of Goodwood.

Charley was talking about making a mint at the races, and how he'd been studying form in the papers; he would guide Maggie, he insisted, no nonsense about choosing a horse because she fancied its name or its colour. They would be scientific, and science combined with his system and the luck he betted she'd bring would do the trick, make him enough to pay the bills, and more.

She looked in surprise at his profile. 'Pay the bills? I thought you made more than enough to do that!'

Shadows flickered across his face as they dashed beneath trees, great sycamores and beeches. He shrugged. She thought he looked faintly sheepish. He lifted a hand from the wheel to wave minor setbacks aside.

'Cash flow difficulties. In a business like mine they come and go.'

'Is it real trouble?'

A snort of scorn: 'No! No way! Just my partner, Tony, working too slowly. I've had the accountants in to sort it out, don't think I'm fool enough not to do that! Tony's got to pull his finger out, get the books published more quickly. And we have to expand. Can't expect to make a profit if we carry on piddling about like we are.'

'Do the accountants think expansion is the right course? How can you do that if you've cash flow difficulties?' Maggie was no business woman, but it sounded strange in her ears.

Charley glanced at her and smiled suddenly. He began to talk, fluently, easily, as he always did, explaining how his business worked. She did not understand quite all that he said to her, but as they drove a picture began to emerge that made some sense, even to her untutored mind. He had set up the business with a friend. This friend had been at school with him, brilliant, absolutely brilliant he was, though the masters detested him because he mocked them, because he was never seen to work hard, because despite this he came top in the examinations. 'Made them look fools,' Charley commented with scorn. Tony had gone on to university, taken a degree in business management; clued himself up on economics and accounts and such matters. Then he worked for various firms, including a big publishing conglomerate where he had been moved from department to department: 'His bosses were always jealous of him!' Charley chuckled. Tony reckoned he knew a good book when he saw one, he understood the publishing scene inside out, and he had been furious when sure fire winners he'd recommended were turned down as 'An old theme badly reworked!', or 'Not suitable for this imprint'. He and Charley had met a publisher fellow at a party who was in vanity publishing and making a bomb and their eyes had met above glasses raised in glee. They had planned at school to go into business together, this would be it.

The start had been easy, great; the postman had lugged typescripts of every sort up to their offices and they had chosen only the best, publishing them to the highest standards. 'Really beautiful, as you've seen,' said Charley. He had insisted on it, that was the way to make their name. But recently authors had started complaining: there had been trouble over clearing picture copyrights; a printing firm Tony had used and trusted had done substandard work, claiming it was what they were asked to quote for, three books had had to be entirely reprinted and at Icarus Publishing's expense – 'That wiped out some profit, I can tell you!' One way and another a log-jam of unprinted work had developed and Tony maintained he was unable to clear it because he spent too much time dealing with idiots who moaned about crises that were none of his making.

The accountants had combed through all the figures – took several expensive and unproductive days over it – then came up with their answer: Icarus Publishing was not trying to publish too many books, quite the opposite; the present level of production meant that the overheads were not spread widely enough, so, production must be raised. They should trawl for someone with an extensive knowledge of publishing to work with Tony, and perhaps also a freelance editor who could work from home, not to overload their offices. All stages of production must be properly monitored, with regular checks and counter checks to avoid further expensive delays and mistakes. The inflow of money from new authors would kick-start the fresh systems Tony had designed following the accountants' advice, and in no time the log-jams would be cleared, cash and production flowing.

'So,' Charley observed, 'it'll all be great, once Tony's got things sorted. He'll have to get off his arse for once and pull his finger out – I'll kick him from here to eternity if he doesn't – and I've told him so. No problems on my side of the house; the accountant was amazed at how I'd managed to persuade even the big boys among the bookshops to stock my stuff. Marketing man of the year, that's me!' And he slammed into lower gear to cut up a large and stately Mercedes, making Maggie laugh aloud.

It was enlivening to hear Charley sound cheerful and expansive even in the face of difficulties. Not like Jack with his recent messages of doom and gloom. Lines creased between her eyes as she thought of her husband's fears for his practice in the current economic situation, the way he had analysed it after the row that had erupted over the condoms, the way he fretted over the household accounts. They all lived comfortably enough, she had never wanted expensive holidays or high fashion clothes. She was suddenly assailed by a rushing wave of anger against Jack for mulling over miseries that might never happen, a wave of furious repugnance at everything about him: his well-cut tweed suits, his old school tie, his over-trimmed hair, the spreadsheets that spewed from his personal computer, the rules that governed their sex life.

Charley slowed behind a horse-box and was momentarily silent, waiting for the opportunity to overtake it on the narrow country road. His full lips were slightly apart, his eyes lively, glancing before and behind. She gazed at his tanned skin, his ruffled bear's pelt of hair, the low-slung knot of his tie at the open neck of his shirt, the crumpled linen jacket with its sleeves pushed up, wishing Jack could be equally casual.

Then as Charley spoke again with enthusiasm, this time to say what a pity her sons couldn't have come to the races too, all three were such fun kids, so a different wave came over her, warmly, slowly, dissipating the faint tension of guilt that she was here in the car with him, making her laugh and say: 'Where would they have sat? On the roof? In our laps? No thanks. We're better off without them, just being us!' not caring what implications he might read into her words.

He dropped his hand to lay it, warm and heavy, on her thigh, then snatched it away to swerve the Porsche round the horse-box and zoom on over a long straight stretch and up once more into downland.

He was telling her of a new granny writer who had spilled

150

the beans about her wild life as a flapper in the nineteen-twenties and who wanted her autobiography published her way and no other, whose salacious revelations would cause a tremendous furore in the media – 'Wow, you wait and see! I'll make sure we send you an advance copy!', when unexpectedly he braked hard and turned on to a rutted chalk track that led upwards between tangled saplings and brambles and wild clematis and out on to a wide green stretch of downland. He stopped almost immediately.

'Can't take this car any further – bottom it disastrously. We'll carry our picnic up.'

He hauled out a Marks & Spencer bag that bulged promisingly, an aged plaid rug and then a big bottle swathed in tissue paper. They walked slowly, he still telling her of his granny author, wild and comical stories that made her laugh so much she had to stop for breath. The sun was high and dazzling in a sky of endless blue depths and somewhere up in them larks were trilling. She was hot, but it was a pleasant warmth, except for the heat of her legs. She was wearing tights; she wondered why . . . perhaps she had always intended to go to Goodwood . . . and she smiled to herself.

'Here,' Charley said, leaving the white line of the path and striking upwards, then sideways and over into a curious small shell-shaped declivity that cut into the flank of the down. Three thorn bushes screened it from the path below and its base was smooth and level, its grass close-cropped.

'Sheer genius,' Maggie said, and relaxed down on to the rug that he spread.

'Of course,' he said, seating himself beside her and opening the bottle deftly with a pop and a fizz. 'This, I'm afraid, will not be chilled, and I don't have any glasses, but I can't believe you're the sort to cavil at minor details.'

'Not when I'm hot and thirsty, and not when it's champagne,' she agreed, and tilted it to her mouth. It was cool and delicious and a part of her mind noted that you couldn't tell how much you had drunk like this, and the thought seemed not alarming but gloriously humorous and she drank again before handing the bottle to Charley.

While he toasted her she swiftly reached beneath her skirt

and wriggled out of her tights. 'Too hot!' she said, and flung them aside.

'Much,' he agreed. 'Ridiculous!'

He put the bottle down with care on the grass. He ran his hand down one sun-warmed leg, fingers caressing.

'Careful,' she warned him. 'Don't start something you can't control.'

'I know what I want to start!' There was laughter in his voice; there always was, disarming, beguiling, reckless.

Grasshoppers were chirping, above them the invisible sky-larks warbled endlessly; all the lovely heat and beauty of the day was in their sounds. She lay back in sensuous luxury, her eyes closed against the sun. His big hand was surprisingly gentle as it ran back up her leg, her thigh, and she felt a vibration of response – hot, urgent, throbbing – rush through her body. He leaned and they kissed, gently at first, then catching fire, recklessly, hungrily, a turbulent devouring. She pulled away, short of air, racing blood and racing mind a battlefield of conflicting needs.

A pause. Great sighs sucked in breath.

'Where's Melody today?'

His hand was hot and still on her thigh. 'Melody? She's in Paris, wildly busy. Has been for weeks. The big break-through, she calls it. Some chap with millions – got a house in Gloucestershire and another in Kensington and now this flat in Paris she's the chance to do over. She's gone. I rarely get to see her now.' His rumbling bass sounded amused: 'She slept so much of the time it hasn't made much odds.' His hand tracked upwards. 'But I could do to see much more of you . . .'

His fingers undid blouse buttons, moved to a breast. Once more the rush of feeling seized her and she turned her body to press hard against him as the kissing took over. Her last coherent thought, killing all others, was of the wonder of his great nakedness. No rubber, no pills, no gunge, no nothing. Just naked skin against naked skin within.

They missed the first race at Goodwood after all, but Charley was unperturbed. Normally, he said, he would treat it as if he'd backed a loser, and double his stake on the next, but he could hardly do that now, could he? Maggie was the winner of a lifetime!

As they stood by the paddock rails his hand was on her shoulder; as they stood in the pushing shoving crowd to place their bets his arm was round her waist; and as they cheered their horses on his hand massaged her bottom. When from time to time in the hot afternoon she broke away to lean on the rails and fan herself with her race-card, his eyes stroked the ample curves of her body and lingered on her long firm legs, shapelier than a first glance at her might indicate, for her gardening and games with the boys had kept them taut and slim. She was beautiful, he told her, and she knew she was. She was metamorphosed from the unhappy housewife counting pennies at the village shop into her old self, sparkling and carefree, and she charmed herself, too.

He said she was bound to bring him luck. He said it of four races but each time his horse lost by a nostril to the favourite. Charley never backed at short odds, not worth it, he said, the pathetic winnings you got. Nor would he bother with each way bets. On their last race he emptied his wallet on to a lively grey called Swivel Eyes at sixteen to one and held Maggie's hand from start to finish. She could feel his agony of tension in her cracking bones. Swivel Eyes' antagonists boxed him in on the rails and his jockey only managed to free him to nip to the front in the final yards. He won by a head. Charley let out a great shout and waved triumphant fists in the air. 'Done it!' he roared. 'Sixteen hundred lovely ones! Now I can live!' And the crowd laughed and roared with him.

Louise was determined to arrive early at work on that particular day. It was essential if she were to give time and thought to her lunchtime lecture and yet keep one jump ahead of Aylmer Littlejohn, anticipating and preventing any hitches in the smooth opening and running of an important exhibition of ceramics next Monday. But again British Rail was repairing the line and the trains were running twenty minutes late. In the crowded state of her present life she never had the luxury of having time on her side, could never relax and feel that her desk and her life were clear of encumbrances; circumstances, it seemed, invariably plotted against her.

One encumbrance, at least, she comforted herself as she peered down the line from the platform, had been removed from her life – the backaching labour on the garden. The day of the charitable opening of the Abbotsbridge gardens had come and gone more than two weeks since and it had been successful. As the last visitor left Louise had drawn a rapt breath of pleasure that far from disgracing herself as she had imagined, she had been praised for her breadth of knowledge by earnest enquirers after names of the specimens – 'Exquisite, quite exquisite, and so unusual!' – in the borders of Walnut Tree Cottage. Simon had been gratified, too, so pleased at their success in drawing visitors and donations that for a short time he had dropped the coolly detached manner he had used with her since their weekend in Bath and its revelations, and given her a hug.

The train appeared. Louise positioned herself strategically, and nipped beneath a large businessman's arm to jump up the steps before him, ignoring his indignant: 'Hey!' and sprinting for the one vacant seat.

Simon had barely spoken to her on that dreadful Sunday. After an exhausted late sleep – they had almost missed breakfast – she had yearned for healing talk. But his remoteness had been so unnerving, and so unnatural in a relationship always characterised by its ease and warmth, that she had barely managed to keep even the most shallow pretence of normality going, uttering remarks that made her blush for their banality simply to break the thickening ice of their silence.

In the afternoon they had visited the Holburne of Menstrie Museum in the Sydney Gardens to see the collections of porcelain and silver, Italian maiolica and bronzes, and the interesting furniture and old master paintings that she had been wanting to see for years. She had anticipated real enjoyment together with Simon, but instead of the normal exchange of comments and the questions he would have put to her here where her expertise would add spice and illumination to their discussion, there was no more than the occasional frigid nod or 'Really?' as she made her appreciative observations. She wanted to share, but he would not share. Despite the warmth of the day her hands had been cold, her face pale from the tortured beating of her heart; she was more miserable than she could ever remember being in all her life. Briefly alone with him before an array of miniatures she had pleaded: 'Please talk to me, Simon!' 'What have we to talk about?' he replied in a voice that pierced her, and the florid face of Beau Nash blurred. 'Ourselves,' she had managed, reaching blindly for his hand, but Simon was already walking from her sight to study Famille Vert vases.

During the following week normality had appeared to return, but it had been surface only. They ate together, spoke of indifferent matters, shared a bed, even had sex. Perhaps, Louise thought, this was how many marriages were – polite, distant, not antagonistic, but never loving or involved either. She found it terrible, loathsome. She was involved with Simon, now, painfully, whole-heartedly, as she had not been before, so that when she wanted to scream her frustration with the present impasse at him she restrained, choking back the words, because she did not dare. Instead she made for him the little gestures he had once made for her, the savoury dinners, the new CD, the bottle of wine, a book called *Old Villages of Hampshire*. Simon said, 'Thank you,' smiled briefly and returned to self-contained detachment. Sometimes the sense of loss was too much and she cried, but not in front of him, in case he should despise her. She went into the immaculate garden instead and cried over the Félicité et Perpétué roses whose name seemed so beautiful and sad and remote.

A hand was creeping under her buttocks; it pinched; she leapt up, nearly lurching across the gangway with the motion of the train. The train groper was leering at her. She might have known. She glared at him, waited for the hand to withdraw. 'So sorry,' he was saying, 'couldn't find my pen, thought it might have rolled under . . .' He met the full fury of her eyes, stopped and cringed against the dusty window. She sat down, turned her back and struggled to concentrate on her lecture notes.

Aylmer Littlejohn did not appear all morning. She checked his diary, checked the galleries, checked with the staff. He was nowhere and no one knew when he would arrive. Louise cursed and chewed her lip. She must see him to rearrange certain dates, one of them a trustees' meeting, because Aylmer had double booked himself for both and refused to alter the other arrangements. Her lunchtime lecture would mean a late lunch, she wouldn't be back until two-thirty at best and Aylmer had to be in Hampstead for three-thirty . . . She must pin him down and send the letters today, or she knew who would be blamed for any ensuing chaos.

At the end of the morning still no Aylmer. Louise left a red-inked 'Urgent' note on his desk and went to gallery six to start her lecture, shrugging with exasperation and wishing she didn't feel so tired. She had felt oddly limp the last two days and not quite herself. With the stress Aylmer put her under and her agitation over Simon it was not perhaps surprising.

There was the usual group of people waiting: one or two older couples clutching guidebooks and looking earnest and faintly overwhelmed, a few jeans-clad students with intelligent faces and unkempt hair, and two tall and immaculate middle-aged ladies exclaiming in carrying tones about the awfulness of the traffic in Kensington Church Street. Beside them and causing her heart to sink stood a trustee Louise did not care for, a tall desiccated man with pinched features, and another man whose face was only vaguely familiar but who looked equally dour. Their appearance made her tense but it also put her on her mettle. Were they here to judge her?

She smiled, greeted her audience and had finished her opening remarks and gathered her listeners around the first display case, containing Sèvres porcelain, when she was aware of two further people coming into the room and standing behind her. She moved to one side to allow them a clear line of vision and began her lecture on the Collection's porcelain, speaking of hard and soft paste and the production problems encountered in making such rare and beautiful objects, mentioning also the histories of the most notable pieces – 'A gift for Madame de Pompadour' and 'Specially made for the Empress Catherine of Russia', and drawing attention to the fresh and bright and seemingly very modern

colours used. Her audience nodded and murmured interestedly: not a bad audience, she noted in relief, the tall ladies
were particularly appreciative with their exclamations of
'Amazing!' and 'That turquoise – one would think it had
been produced yesterday!' She led them into gallery seven
and now there was Meissen for their delectation.

She explained how the rediscovery of the secret of hard-
paste porcelain at Meissen had been the result of a Saxon
nobleman, Count von Tschirnhausen, a man of great energy,
forming a partnership with a clever young man called
Böttger whom he had been supervising. She was adding that
Böttger had been intended to work as an alchemist for
Augustus the Strong in a struggle to make gold, when she
found herself being interrupted.

'What was particularly clever about Böttger?' It was the
dour-faced man standing with the trustee, John Cobbold-
Black.

'He was knowledgeable about metals and meticulous in
research. Not only did he solve the mystery of the composi-
tion of hard-paste porcelain, but he also created a wholly
new colour, a reddish-violet lustre derived from gold which
we see here –' She pointed with her hand only to be stopped
again.

'Was hard-paste porcelain all that was produced at the
Meissen factory?'

'No, both stoneware and porcelain were produced at the
same time –'

'And were the same decorative techniques used on each?'

He had a hard face, long and pointed, toothy and inquisi-
tive as a cartoon rat. 'Motifs modelled in moulds as reliefs
were used on both, and if you'd all care to look at this elegant urn-shaped vase here –'

'What sort of ornamentation?'

Twice she had tried to deflect him, twice he had refused to
listen. Had Rat-face been a tourist she would have been firmly repressive at this stage but he appeared to be a friend of
Mr Cobbold-Black. Dare she snub him? She spoke in her
most dampening voice: 'I shall be coming to that in just half
a minute. Now, do please look at the brilliant colours of
these dishes here. After Böttger died in 1719 the King was

157

pressing for new colours and styles of decoration which were realised by Johann Höroldt, Böttger's successor. You can see here and here how the beautiful single ground used, blue, turquoise or yellow . . .'

She was gesturing towards the Meissen pieces in the cabinets and speaking rapidly to deter further interruptions, when she saw in its glass a reflected movement from the door behind her and twisted her head. Yes, it was Aylmer, peering in. But even as she recognised his face he was gone, whisking away into the darkness of the landing. Had he acted on her note? She turned back, listened for the echoes from her mind – where precisely was she? Rat-face was twitching his long nose . . . Ah, the Höroldt period and that beautiful yellow. She opened her mouth but within seconds her voice collided with another snapping series of questions.

'What about muffle colours in the seventeen-twenties?'

'How were the enamels fixed?'

'How was that delicate gilded lacework achieved?'

Like some terrible oral exam, she thought, and was struggling to reply and expound for the interest of the group as a whole when a wave of nausea hit her. The room was overwarm, there was no air to breathe . . . the yellow ground that had rivalled the Chinese 'Imperial' yellow turned sickly, vile; this was the third degree; the room swirled around her . . .

A cool and perfectly modulated female voice sliced through the questions to say: 'Please could this gentleman leave his catechisings to the end of the lecture, and not interrupt Miss Bennett?'

It was a voice she knew. Her hand on the cabinet for steadiness, Louise turned. Arabella Manningford, eyes heavy-lidded, eyebrows elevated, was looking from her tormentor to Louise.

The authoritative-looking man next to her, in his early fifties and upright in an expensive light-weight suit, concurred: 'An excellent suggestion. Then the rest of us can hear what we came to hear – Miss Bennett.'

Louise could have fallen on their necks and hugged them, and was shocked by the emotional reaction, so out of her normal character. Her tormentor's nostrils flared and con-

158

tracted, but he stiffly inclined his narrow head to this request and shut his trap of a mouth. She took a long slow breath; the dizziness and the nausea were retreating. Her heart was pounding, her legs were melting jelly still, but the colours of the Meissen had returned to their normal beauty. She forced a smile, said to Rat-face: 'Please do ask me any questions you wish after the lecture. I should be delighted to assist you!' – thought with pleasure how condescending it sounded and continued with her talk, this time to more than normally fervent murmurs of appreciation. There was a clear feeling that something untoward had occurred and her audience had been put out.

Afterwards Rat-face left without speaking, following the desiccated John Cobbold-Black from the room. The Kensington ladies redoubled their assurances of their delight and interest in her lecture, the elderly couples said, 'Yes, absolutely, you know. Quite fascinating!' in flustered friendliness and the students muttered: 'Yeah, wild, great. Thanks!' and all backed out with half-salutes.

'You look terrible!' Arabella Manningford said bluntly, surveying her. 'Are you all right? Seriously? Then you must come and have a stiff drink and a sustaining lunch with us – you clearly need both. No, no argument, you're coming. And right now. Oh, and this is an old friend of James' and mine, Alexander Cockroft – Louise Bennett.'

'Hello. How do you do? I've got to . . . I'd love to . . . how very kind you are. I must just leave a message for the director, Mr Littlejohn . . . collect my bag from my desk.' She pulled herself together. 'If you would give me a couple of minutes, please, then I'll be with you.'

No sign that Aylmer had read her note. At once despairing and furious, she left messages with two curators and a secretary, hurriedly brushed her hair – Arabella had the crisp sort that always looked immaculate – and rejoined her and her friend.

They took her to an expensive restaurant a couple of hundred yards away, one Louise had heard of but never lunched at. Its cool and shadowy exclusiveness, its white roses and billowing white tablecloths, the Puligny-Montrachet '86 that they pressed her to sip steadily, 'You look most unwell still and this is guaranteed to revive!', all were balm to her sore soul. She revived like a drought-smitten plant in rain, straightening her shoulders, smiling, then laughing at their imitations of the man who had cross-questioned her.

Over smoked salmon Alexander Cockroft spoke of him as 'A weasel, an unpleasant little weasel!'

'Funny you should say that,' she said. 'I saw him as a rat. With a scaly tail. I saw it clearly, twitching with malice. And when I visualised it, I wanted to giggle. It kept me sane.'

'You did well,' he told her. 'And your lecture was excellent. I mean that sincerely. Do you know him? Is he some dealer?'

'I have no idea who he was, but the chap he was with I recognised as a trustee. Not an outstanding one; he tends to cry off from meetings.'

'A trustee? Who allowed a friend to behave like that? Incredible. Indeed disgraceful. How very extraordinary.' He frowned, then smiled and said dismissively: 'I expect the fellow squabbled with his wife this morning.'

The droll dry way he spoke made Louise chuckle. He signalled to the waiter to refill her glass. 'You look better, but a touch more of this won't hurt. Was it the heat that upset you? A rare month of it we've been having, but the forecasters say it will last no longer. Storms tonight herald its end.'

He was kind and urbane; clearly someone from the Manningford's own world of wealth and culture. As she ate Emince de Volaille Andrée he asked about her position at the Holbrooke Collection, appeared genuinely interested in her work in the organising and running of exhibitions, and from his comments upon her lecture and the porcelain and pictures in the Collection, she saw that he was both knowledgeable and perceptive. He was a collector in a small way, he told her. Arabella said he had lots of lovely things: 'Including a little Turner that makes my mouth water!'

After coffee he said he must rush: 'A meeting at the Ministry.'

'I must go too,' said Louise. 'Work calls. A delightful lunch, and thank you.'

'I shall write to your director,' he said, 'congratulating

160

him on his excellent lecturer. And I shall mention the nuisance of the trustee's unpleasant friend.'

Louise said she was grateful and meant it whole-heartedly. The thought had occurred to her that the man might have been led to test her by Aylmer and Mr Cobbold-Black. It was an unpleasant thought and one she tried to suppress as unworthy, but nevertheless it lurked at the back of her mind. Such a letter would really rock Aylmer back on his heels.

Outside the restaurant Alexander Cockroft hailed a taxi and was gone. Louise wanted to know what he did.

'Alex? He's a general.'

'A *general*?' Unbelievable. Whatever would Aylmer make of that?

Arabella looked in surprise at the incredulous tone of her voice, then observed briskly: 'You mustn't be affected by the way the media present the armed services, you know. Like old black and white films, they're half a century out of date. Modern army officers mostly have degrees; they're widely travelled people who love books, music, art, the same as anyone else.' She kissed Louise on the cheek. ''Bye, my dear, take the rest of the day easily. Catch the early train home for once.'

The stone steps to the George I building and the stairs to Louise's office seemed endless. She pondered why she had been feeling so peculiarly limp recently. She had not been sleeping at all well, and she had been over-pushed . . . and then Simon . . . Wait a minute, time of the month . . . Surely she was due? Overdue? She couldn't be. She ran to check on her calendar. Three or four days. The pill no longer keeping her regular? She had taken it only for five days in this cycle, then stopped. Could she be . .?

Pregnant!

There was a note on her desk. Aylmer had given her the information she needed. Why had she been so fussed about that? What did it matter?

A baby. It could well be. The child Simon wanted.

She could not wait – she must know now. Go to the chemist's, buy one of those kits. Test!

She turned and flew from the room.

Chapter 13

There was a storm coming, Brozie decided, standing by the French windows in the late afternoon and looking out across her garden, a summer storm, it would clear the air and water her poor wilting plants. The valley was silent. Cumulus clouds were building up above the hills, their tops brilliantly tipped with light, their undersides dark and ominously heavy. She thought how dramatic they looked and how much she would like to paint them; perhaps she would take art classes, learn to paint in water colours. She could do things purely for her own pleasure now, as Charley had said. Was that lightning she could see? She leaned against the doorpost, fanning herself with a magazine, a lovely glossy magazine that told you how to make your house beautiful. She would read it tonight and make plans for the future.

Despite the heavy heat she felt far better than she had yesterday. With Hubert out of the house and the people now calling to see her intent only on giving solace and assistance, her mind was easier. Charley had been specially kind and helpful this morning. He had gone with her to register the death, then accompanied her to the solicitor's and the bank, asking in his unbothered way the questions she hadn't dared frame, and finally, briefly, to the shops. He had been anxious for her, but his questions had drawn from the solicitor the assurance that Hubert had left his affairs in good order: she had never had much doubt of that, but it was a relief to have it confirmed. Yes, everything was hers now and she would be comfortably off. Hubert had even built up an investment portfolio all unknown to her, though he had always insisted that money was short. She knew no details yet, but she could relax, not worry.

'Terrific,' Charley enthused as they left. 'So give yourself treats. You've never lived. Live now!'

She would too, she would have fun. She never had run her own life, never learned to spend money, never had any. And always she had been with older people, dealt with sickness, done without holidays. She could visit the Lake District, go to the Scottish Highlands. She might have enough money to go abroad, to Florida or Bali or China where the wealthier folk in the village spoke of going. To see the Great Wall of China and the Terracotta Army would make up for a lifetime of deprivation.

Brozie had already taken her first steps into freedom: she had eaten a fillet steak for lunch, her first since childhood, eaten it with new potatoes all minted and smothered in butter, and watercress, lots of watercress, and she ate it relaxing in a canvas chair under an apple tree in the garden, finishing with a deliciously wicked chocolate and coffee torte smothered in cream. She had bought all sorts of food that Hubert had banned, rushing from supermarket to off-licence before Charley went off to the Goodwood races. She had savoured the succulent steak, saliva flooding into the mouth that had been dry for days. She could hear Hubert now: 'A fillet steak? And all that butter? Can't afford such extravagance!' And again as she munched the watercress fresh from the Hampshire beds: 'Only a fool would eat nasty bitter weeds from the river!' Butterflies had fluttered past, colourful in the sunlight, and she had seen insects dancing above her borders. Hubert would never eat out-of-doors in case something bit him. Tonight she would wash down her meal with a glass or two from one of Hubert's prized bottles of wine that he had never allowed her to touch. 'You have no palate, that vintage would be wasted on you.'

But she must not take major decisions until she knew where she was. Everyone was warning her of that: the rector, Mr Fudge, the kindly church flower ladies, and in remarkably similar words. She would not take decisions yet; she would dream instead, dream and write lists.

In the supermarket she had snatched up a pad of paper specially for the purpose together with a brightly coloured

163

5-pack of files for correspondence about the funeral and probate, and for the running of the house that Hubert had always done. She would start afresh, organise everything her way, show that she too could be efficient. Hubert's nasty dusty box files would go in the attic.

The storm was coming nearer, the birds had fallen silent. Heat and dust were thick in her nostrils and there was a sulphurous glow of half-light transforming the familiar view into something of almost menacing beauty. She stared in fascination. Yes, she must learn how to capture those colours, using pen and ink to mark the intensely clear-cut outlines of trees, fields, hills, and the church tower, unnaturally near in the stillness.

Single large heavy drops of rain began to fall, pockmarking the dust. Brozie closed the French windows and the heat inside intensified. Hurry up, storm, she urged silently, blow your winds through the valley, clear the air, set the water racing in the trout streams. She mopped her sweating face with a handkerchief and turned her attention to her lists.

Put pen, paper and ruler on a little table beside her chair, make a cup of tea – no, ridiculous, far too hot . . . she would have a glass of the white wine she had been chilling for this evening. Little treats, she told herself, admiring the imposing label on the bottle, little treats. She sipped, rolled the wine around her tongue; delicious. She sat down, took up her pen, wrote 'Things to be Done' and underlined it. Then she wrote, 'Buy paints' and 'Find out about art classes'. A pause while her eyes wandered the worn and shabby room to rest upon Hubert's special chair, hating it. Thunder rumbled outside, scattered raindrops hit the windows. That chair had been covered in a hard-wearing brown rep twenty years ago; the material represented everything she detested most about him. Throw the chair out, her feelings urged . . . But her sensible mind protested that would be wicked. 'Re-cover wingchair', she wrote. Inspired by this thought of change her mind jumped on and she added, 'Paint outside of house in pale parchment – get estimates', leaned back and laughed aloud. The ugly brickwork that for twenty years had offended her would be hidden, the house made over as hers. Now ideas were crowding forward . . . 'new carpets, new curtains', she wrote. She could spend a day looking in the shops, Charley could take her. She would buy more of the magazines her heart craved, study the clever rooms she saw in them, send off for free leaflets and samples of materials. She foresaw weeks, even months of enjoyment. And Charley would share her fun as she had shared his in choosing the carpets for The Old Barn; fun was twice as good when you shared it, especially with someone young and full of ideas like him. A lightning flash made her jump. The room was darkening, she switched on a table lamp. Charley had so much spark and energy you could light a whole town from him.

She picked up her glass and the wine inside trembled at her excitement. Thunder spoke in the distance and she went to the window. The sight outside was magnificent in its barbaric splendour. Sheet lightning lit up the low line of the downs, the black limbs of the willows by the river were waving wildly and the rain was lashing down. The room was stifling; the heat rushed into her face, burning it. She opened the French windows, not caring about the rain that blew in on the old carpet. She grabbed the wine bottle, pressing its damp and dusty coldness against her cheeks. Then she poured again and emptied her glass in great gulps and the elemental excitement outside seemed to run down her throat and through all her limbs.

She wanted to dance in the rain. She would dance in the rain. The wind and the rain would cool her in a second. But first, off with her overheated clothes! Laughing aloud she struggled out of her blouse and skirt, her damp and clinging slip; then flung away her sandals, her bra and her knickers. Out on to the flagstones, and the icy lash of the rain made her gasp, then shout aloud with relief.

She ran awkwardly across to the lawn. No one could see her, here near the house, for the great conifer hedges that stretched on each side for thirty feet and took the light from the sitting-room had been planted by Hubert to block out the neighbours. Death to the Leyland cypresses – put that next on the list! But in the meantime . . . Brozie tipped her face up to the sky, flung out her arms and began to dance, first slowly stepping, then wildly, passionately, a middle-aged

165

bacchante, the grass squelching mud between her toes, the water pouring endlessly over her shoulders and down between her breasts. Round and round she twirled, careless of the thunder and lightning that crashed and flashed over the valley, free to do exactly as she wanted for the very first time in her life.

Twenty minutes later, towelling herself down in the bathroom, she laughed until she hiccupped, wondering what on earth her neighbours would have made of the sight had they caught a glimpse of her. Goodness, she did feel wonderful. The storm was moving away now, rumbling in the distance. She padded to the bedroom to dress in fresh clothes and made another mental note: change bedrooms: she had not slept in here for months; she never would again. She would throw out the sombre Victorian marital bed: not only Hubert but his first wife had died in it. She had discovered about his wife several weeks after she had married him. Hubert never had understood what all the fuss was about; it was a good bed, he said, and would be valuable one day. The room smelt sour. She flung open the window and the rich clean scents of wet grass and jasmine and roses rushed in.

Brozie leaned on the windowsill. The sun was coming out from behind the receding clouds and drawing a myriad points of light from twigs and leaves and the wet curves of the lane. A blackbird taking an energetic bath in a puddle caught a miniature rainbow in his splashes. She watched in idle pleasure.

In a minute she would start to carry her clothes to the guest bedroom and the ornaments and pictures that would turn it into her room. That room faced the river and the morning sun, so bracing and welcome at the start of the day, especially in the winter. The more she thought of the idea, the more pleased she was. She would rise on frosty mornings to see the river steaming mistily behind reeds stiff and bright with rime. She would paint that too. She sighed happily. She would put a little oak bookcase in there and fill it with her favourite books, to read in bed: Trollope's Barchester novels, Flora Thompson's *Lark Rise to Candleford*, Gilbert White's *Natural History of Selbourne*, Vita Sackville-West's gardening books, and all of Jane Austen. Old-fashioned and so restful.

A red car was coming down the lane, she thought she recognised the sound – yes, it was Charley, speeding along as usual. She wondered how he had enjoyed Goodwood, and whether he had won anything. There was someone in the car with him . . . she peered . . . yes, a woman. Naughty Maggie! Dear, oh dear! Had she been to the races after all? And would she tell that good but dull husband of hers? Her eyes twinkled appreciatively. Oh, Charley, you wicked man!

More cars were coming, quite a rush hour. Mrs Manningford in her big Mercedes. Brozie liked the Manningfords; they took a proper interest in village affairs and invariably gave flowers generously for the church. Far better to have folk at the manor who knew what was what than show business people or pop stars with their parties – all very exciting, but not useful, not properly useful like the wealthy ought to be, as her father used to say. Nancy Chubb in her van, doing deliveries and collecting gossip; Brozie withheld judgment there, the scales varied from day to day; sometimes Nancy was surprisingly kind but you always had to watch how you trod. Who was that in the little Peugeot? That girl Louise who worked at the Holbrooke Collection in London. That was somewhere Brozie could visit now, another treat. Louise was one of these modern girls, living with a man but not married to him. Sensible. If Brozie had given Hubert a trial run her life would have been different, oh, so very different. Louise was in a hurry, dashing through the puddles like that.

Louise parked her car outside the cottage and leapt from it. Then she stopped with a jerk and stood by the billowing yew hedge and stared unseeingly in front of herself. She had rushed home determined to fling herself into Simon's arms, to have an emotional show-down, to end this cruelty through assumed indifference he was practising on her. But then the vile thought struck her: perhaps the indifference was genuine. He had not been indifferent on that terrible night; violent emotions had raged in him. Was his distance now a form of armour against further hurt, while he waited for her to

167

prove her whole-hearted involvement, or was it from dislike? Had some condemnation been passed by Simon, some resolution been made of which she was ignorant? Was he waiting for her to recognise the inevitable? The retreating storm rumbled ominously, increasing her unease. She chastised herself mentally for not having broken through to him before. Had the passing of time, far from lessening his anger and hurt, raised new barriers?

She would know nothing without speaking to him. He was in the kitchen. That disconcerted her. And listening to some soprano shrieking Wagner on Radio 3 – worse. She loathed Wagner. In the train she had visualised him sitting on the Knole sofa, reading. He would look up; she would sit close, take his hand, confide her secret; she'd seen his face brighten, a mutual flinging of arms, bliss . . . Mills & Boon, she saw now, ridiculous. Simon was vigorously chopping onions, his back towards her.

He looked up briefly, said: 'Oh, hello, had a good day?' and returned to the onions.

She stood in the doorway, willing him to turn. She said, her voice vibrant with meaning: 'Simon, I've got news. Exciting news.'

He picked up a garlic clove and put it in the presser. 'Oh?' he said, his hand squeezing so ferociously that the bones stood out. 'Promotion at work?' His face was still averted, his voice expressionless.

Of course his mind would swoop on that: he thought she was more involved with the Holbrooke Collection than with him.

'No. Oh no. Something far more important.'

She could hear the sarcasm in his voice even above the shrieking soprano. 'You've been invited to write a learned monograph on Meissen in the 1720s or some such fascinating period?'

He believed she valued porcelain higher than babies. She had, but now she'd changed priorities. His back was wooden. She ran across the kitchen, switched off Wagner, forced him round to her, held his face between her fingers.

'Simon. Darling Simon! It's . . . I'm pregnant! We're going to have a baby!'

168

'A baby?' Startled disbelief.

'Yes! Isn't it amazing? Isn't it wonderful!' She wanted to warm his coldness, gather him up into her excitement, repair, renew, transform. Her voice urged triumph and emotion and new beginnings. The sun came through the window behind him, flashing brilliantly on its raindrops, haloing his head but leaving his face a dark blank.

'How can you possibly know?'

'Three days late . . . I took a test. I could hardly credit it, so I rushed off and bought a second test. *Yes* both times! Darling, it's incredible but it's true. I'd hardly started to take the pill this month, so it happened straight away. You must be a terrific stud!'

'What? Oh!' His arms came round her. 'A baby! Us, a baby! I can't quite believe it, but I suppose I might learn. Oh, it's fabulous!' His voice cracked.

He held her, he hugged her, he rocked her. He turned his face and the sun illuminated his joy. Her legs felt weak; she was limp with relief. Mills & Boon was marvellous. He let her go and she saw he'd been hugging her with the garlic presser.

'The garlic, . . . oh, Simon, my jacket will stink.'

'It doesn't matter, I'll love you just the same!'

A teasing sentence he had often used: the emotional reaction that had surprised her earlier in the day flooded over her again and tears poured down her cheeks. 'Oh, lovely, lovely Simon, I adore the slushy things you say. Oh Lord, I'm crying. How idiotic, I hope I'm not doomed to weep my way through this pregnancy.'

'Say you don't mind it!'

'Mind what? The garlic, the weeping or the pregnancy? Oh, darling, I'll put up with anything now.'

'You can't send Hugh away to prep school this year,' Maggie said feverishly, scrubbing her big jam-making pan under the tap with great splashings and flourishings. 'It's wrong. Boys that young shouldn't be taken away from their mothers.' She swung round from the sink to face him. 'And I can't take losing him now. I just can't. Write to the headmaster and change the date to next year – better still, change to a day school.'

169

'No. He's booked and that's that. Besides, you've bought his uniform.'

'I haven't bought a thing.'

'Then you should have.' Jack looked at her with disfavour. 'And don't talk so over-dramatically. You won't lose him. It's not like the old days, we can see him regularly and he'll have weekends at home.'

'Hugh will hate it. He'll miss me and be lonely. He'll cry into his pillow at nights like I used to do after my father walked out. It was horrible.'

'But I haven't walked out and he'll have lots of new friends of his own age. I never cried when I went off to school, I enjoyed it.'

'Why are you shouting about me, Mummy?' Hugh asked. He sidled into the kitchen and eyed Maggie apprehensively. 'I want a biscuit. I don't like you being cross. I haven't done anything.'

His father sighed and said in a carefully neutral voice: 'We were talking about your new school. You don't have to go there, you know. We can still stop the plan if you don't like it. What do you think?'

Maggie turned from the kitchen sink to stoop over him, adding quickly: 'You must say what you really think, Hugh. Not what you think we'd like to hear. It would be no trouble to stop it, no trouble at all.'

'But I want to go,' he said with prompt indignation. He sighed and looked exactly like Jack. 'I keep telling you, Mummy, it'll be fun. Now, can I have a ginger biscuit, please? Thanks.' He disappeared.

'You see?' Jack said.

Hugh and Toby were built in his image, even the gentler Eddie would never rebel. She must have another child, a girl, to be hers. She looked at Jack in hatred and when he had gone out she telephoned Charley.

Chapter 14

Towards the end of August Charley threw a party: 'Just a casual supper party,' he said, telephoning all his acquaintances at the last minute. He suited his reasons to his guests. 'A belated house-warming,' he told Louise, 'time you gave one too!' 'To celebrate your new life,' he said to Brozie. 'An early harvest festival,' he informed the Manningfords. And for Maggie, 'To rejoice in the glory of you, you gorgeous thing!'

As Simon and Louise walked through the gathering dusk to The Old Barn the evening air smelled damp and there was a fine mist gathering along the valley; later there would be dew on the stubble left by the still circling combine harvesters. Simon remarked that summer was slipping into autumn, he could smell that special yeasty fruity scent of straw and michaelmas daisies and apples. Louise nodded and smiled and looked about. Swifts were wheeling above the church tower and rising high into the air, but there seemed fewer of them, rosehips and elderberries were appearing in the hedgerows, and the pale seed-heads of Queen Anne's lace were stiff along the banks; subtly, slowly, the face of the country was changing. Autumn, a new season in the country, a fresh experience. A year ago she had lived in London, had never known elder trees or country flowers. She looked forward to the flaming leaf colours Simon described in the beech woods, to watching pheasants gleaning in the stubble fields, to clearing the garden and making bonfires. Already they were sitting together on the sofa at night looking at colourful bulb catalogues and planning for the spring, for drifts of anemone blanda, for fritillaries under the walnut tree, and aconites, too. And with the bright new flowers would come their baby, in April.

'Feeling all right?' Simon asked. He was always solicitous for her now.

'Not bad at all,' she said.

Not entirely truthful. She felt tired and faintly queasy; that she invariably felt queasy when her stomach was empty was something she had been forced to come to terms with in recent weeks, as she had with the dragging tiredness, the sleepiness that overcame her at inconvenient moments and the swelling sensitive breasts. She did not feel herself, that was the truth. She had telephoned her mother to tell her of the approach of a fifth grandchild and was overwhelmed by the delighted congratulations: 'Well, I'm thrilled – I never thought you would!' and the advice. This was strong on vitamins and the importance of serenity, but useless on the dreary symptoms: 'I always felt amazingly well when I was pregnant – it's all in the mind, you know.' Louise's sister Katie went further: 'Morning sickness and nausea demonstrate rejection of the child.' 'But I want the baby!' Louise protested. 'Not subconsciously!' Katie insisted. She was planning her first child for next year; Louise decided it would serve her right to be sick too and consulted Maggie, who gave real sympathy and help: 'Poor love – I'm always like that in the early stages of mine. Sip sodawater and get your nice Simon to pamper you.' Simon was tremendous. When, her face green, Louise wailed to him: 'This takes all the gilt off the gingerbread!' he not only consoled her with words, but, a practical man, provided thermosfuls of soup for her to take to work, homemade vegetable soup which soothed her ominously lurching stomach.

Already The Old Barn was full of people and noise; Charley must know half Hampshire, Louise decided. Simon rang the bell and they walked in through the open door. Guests were milling all over the ground floor, drinking, trumpeting greetings to one another, examining Charley's house and its furnishings, gesticulating and laughing. Charley was nowhere, but on a heavily carved oriental table, of the sort generally known as Aldershot-style, lay a gaudily painted tin tray holding assorted glasses and goblets of red and white wine. Louise hesitated; Simon helped himself to a goblet of red, sipped, blinked and muttered from the side of his mouth: 'I shouldn't bother, darling.'

Louise swallowed. 'I think I'll look for mineral water,' she murmured, and took a circuitous route through a huge living room towards what she had to assume was the kitchen door.

The room was extraordinary, she thought, as she squirmed between suited or silk-clad backs, dodging dangerously waving glasses. It was galleried at one end, but at the other rose to the full height of the one-time barn, revealing great beams and rafters and dwarfing furniture which resembled the miscellaneous remnants of a giant junk-shop sell-off. She saw shabby Victorian buttoned day-beds on bulbous turned legs jostled by rattan coffee tables; glossy red Ryman's filing cabinets flanking an Edwardian wash-stand with a marble top, lanky rubber plants in battered brass coal scuttles, 'fifties wrought-iron standard lamps leaning drunkenly, a pair of negro-boy statuettes and a sedan-chair in the last stages of decrepitude. On the walls African masks and embroidered shawls fought each other and Chinese rice-paper paintings for attention. It was amazing; it was crazy; it was fun.

In the kitchen, which was modern pine and surprisingly ordinary, she found Maggie shredding lettuce for a tossed salad and Brozie grating Parmesan cheese over huge amounts of lasagne, while Charley teased a half-grown black labrador and intermittently opened bottles.

'Ah, Louise!' Charley said, kissing her with enthusiasm. 'What, no drink? Have some of this white.' He held up a bottle.

'Don't!' Maggie said. 'Don't be fobbed off. It's terrible.'

Charley looked as hurt as his cheerful ruddy face would allow. 'I got acquainted with it in France last year; I think it's superb. Old Les Chubb got this lot in for me at a special price.'

Maggie and Brozie groaned. 'That would explain it!' said Maggie.

Louise said quickly that mineral water was what she sought.

Maggie lifted her eyes from the bowls to which she was now adding watercress and cucumber. 'You look grim,' she observed. 'Something fizzy needed fast, Charley love.'

He ambled across the room, patting Maggie's plump and silken pyjama-suited bottom as he passed. He picked up a glass and rummaged in a large, rumbling and aged fridge. 'Like my dog? Cerberus, he's called. Came from the Manningfords – very well-bred.' The labrador puppy bounded over to Louise and sniffed up her skirt.

'No! Down!' Louise commanded, backing away and wondering if she actually was going to be sick this time. Why had she never noticed before how disgusting dogs smelt? And why did they always sniff in that indecorous fashion?

Maggie intervened swiftly, one hand pushing a tumbler of Perrier water at Louise, the other slapping the dog's muzzle away. 'Stop it, Cerberus!' she commanded. 'That's not well-bred at all. Louise, the loo's on your right down the hall, but go somewhere quiet and sip this, then you may not need it.'

Louise decided that the loo was probably the *only* quiet place to go. She slipped down the hall past knots of grinning people, shouting to make themselves heard.

'. . . Nancy waves red rags,' someone yelped, chortling, 'but if they attract any bulls she drops them – a coward at heart!'

'. . . Very hard to keep one's mind raised to the glory of God when the depredations of death-watch beetle make one wonder why He should have cursed His world with such a menace,' the rector was saying to James Manningford, 'but Charley's been wonderful. He's squeezed four-figure cheques from the most unlikely people . . .'

'Not a bad harvest at all,' a man with a peeling red nose conceded. 'Mind you, it's not all in yet . . .'

The loo. Peace and safety. Louise slid in, locked the door, leaned against it and sipped her Perrier, swallowing hard. The icy liquid slid fizzing down; slowly the monster released its clutches and her stomach subsided. She breathed again. Every day this last week she had expected to disgrace herself in public; somehow she never quite had. She drank a little more. Heavenly cool water, soothing and calming. God, that was better. A near-run thing. She straightened and stared.

Before her on a low table stood an elaborate gilded Victorian bird-cage, complete with stuffed parakeet. She blinked. On the wall to her right were old sepia photographs of Edwardian belles, all hourglass figures, bare shoulders and rounded bosoms – presumably there for the delectation of the gentlemen using the china. For the ladies, facing the other way, there were similarly faded studies of small children, solemn and big-eyed, all lace and huge hats, posed against velvet drapery. She began to smile: they were both comical and enchanting. Propped in a corner was a cane fishing rod. And on the wall opposite were bookshelves piled with reading material, a catholic mixture of magazines and books. Louise saw that Charley's interests ran to antiques and cars, to architecture and wars and fishing, Biggles and Rupert Bear. She was feeling much better, almost normal. She had no use for the elaborately decorated blue and white china, the varnished mahogany throne of a previous era. (Where on earth had Charley found that?) Louise straightened herself, pulled the clanking chain for form's sake, and went back into the hall, where Charley turned from pouring wine for the rector and Jack to ask her if she was all right.

'Yes, thanks,' she said, adding, 'I like your loo!' to divert him. She did not want the world to know about her pregnancy yet.

'Great, isn't it?' Charley enthused. 'See my cane rod? It's antique, a beaut. Lend it to you if you like, you too, Thomas. There's no better cure for the mad rush of modern life than a quiet evening on the river. Solitude, birdsong, room to ruminate, and if you're skilful – or lucky – trout for dinner. Whenever I can I get out on the Test or the Itchen. I found that rod in a junk shop – hold on!' He ducked into the lavatory and emerged flourishing it, his guests flinching. He displayed it to the rector. 'I like rummaging in junk shops, you can often pick up a bargain and sell it on. This rod's worth a lot, I reckon, but I bought it for nearly nothing because the proprietor hadn't a clue of its value.'

'It's a handsome old thing,' the rector agreed, handling it.

When Louise enquired if fishing weren't an expensive pastime, Charley grinned. 'Not if you know the right people. Only nouveaux-riches need to splurge money on everything.

I do favours for my friends and they pay me back in the manner I always intended! The Manningfords let me fish that superb stretch behind Abbotsbridge House from time to time, and the Colebys their stretch, too. I was brought up round here. My father's an estate agent and auctioneer, he and my grandfather before him; they know the value of knowing people, of good friends.'

For a moment he sounded like Jack. Were all men the same? Should she start consciously networking too? No, she hadn't the time. Louise excused herself and went to find something to nibble in the great main room, to ensure her stomach remained quiescent. She found sesame-seeded bread sticks stuck in a jug and bit into one with relief. Maggie and Brozie were edging round the sides of the room carrying trays of cutlery and plates. Charley came pushing his way between the guests, his bottle of wine held high, to murmur something in Maggie's ear which made her laugh softly and drop her eyes; he touched her hand and moved on.

Doors were open to the garden; the room was hot. Louise slipped out into the cool evening air, finding a long table covered with a white cloth out on the paving stones. It was surrounded by a mixture of old rattan chairs (had someone in the family lived in the Far East?) and two or three folding directors' chair (so suitable somehow for Charley), giving the impression of a film set. Illumination came from a lamp on the house wall whose light was surrounded by small creamy moths. The sole object on the table cloth was an arrangement of coppery dahlias and silvery leaves in a bowl bearing the mark of Maggie's hand. Louise sank on to a chair.

Maggie and Brozie emerged from the house in haste, carrying their trays. They dumped knives and forks and plates, and great bowls of salad on to the table.

'We can't conceive,' Maggie said, pushing back flopping blonde hair from her forehead, 'how Charley would possibly have managed without us.'

'No,' Brozie agreed. 'He hadn't even ordered extra glasses and plates till we took him in hand. Half this stuff is ours.'

They sounded like adoring acolytes, complacent in their ministrations. 'Who cooked the meal?' Louise enquired.

'Why us, of course!' Maggie said.

'Charley can't cook,' Brozie added. 'I often have to feed him.'

'But he sings for his supper,' said Maggie. 'Brozie drove so rarely in her life with Hubert that she'd almost forgotten how – Charley's teaching her.'

'He's patient,' Brozie said smiling, 'even when I scrape things.'

They picked up their trays.

'Food shortly,' Maggie promised Louise. 'And save us seats out here, will you? I love to be out in the night air.'

As they hastened back into the house Simon came out.

'I lost you,' he said reproachfully to Louise. He sat himself down in a rattan chair beside her, picked up her hand and planted a kiss in its palm. 'All right?'

'All right,' she agreed and thought that everything between them was so now. The show was back on the road, their eyes met, they touched, they smiled. In the past his open affection had been an embarrassment, fretting her, now every gesture was a benison. Once, to her own amazement, on her return from work she had found herself walking into the church and wanting to give thanks, but when she entered the dusky building and walked up the echoing nave she found she had no idea of prayer; finally she sat for some time in a pew quite simply savouring her happiness, enjoying the odour of faded flowers and the darts of late sunlight that caught on brass rails and stone and stained glass, letting her thoughts float upwards. And wandering back along a side aisle afterwards she had noticed a memorial to an ancestral Manningford couple, born more than two centuries ago, an earlier James with his Susannah, who had died within days of one another at a good old age. *Their Love was Disinterested, their Affection mutual, their Benevolence sincere and enlarged by Hospitality,* the marble proclaimed. At once amused and touched she thought that was how to live and how at last to die. She was full of sentimentality, she who had once scorned such feelings.

Thomas and Jane Field strolled out, followed by Arabella and James Manningford.

'I hope food appears soon,' Arabella remarked. 'My

stomach is horridly deflated and flapping against my spine. Louise, how lovely to see you. Do tell me, have you heard anything further about that lecture we heard that was so rudely interrupted? I told James about it, and he was quite as horrified as Alex Cockroft and I were. Did you complain?'

'No, I didn't – I didn't need to. The general must have been exceptionally swift in writing because a letter arrived the following morning. Aylmer Littlejohn was impressed that I knew General Cockroft, and very taken aback. He came through to me with the letter in his hand. He told me how well the general was known for his expertise and scholarship, how very much admired. He was anxious to assure me that no one had been testing me, so anxious it was quite funny.'

'I'm glad to know of it.'

'Oh, yes. None of the trustees or their friends, he said, would ever wish to disrupt an expert's talk; it must have been wholly unintentional.'

No one could have been more careful than him in the following days. His manner had been ingratiating and there had been no 'mistakes' in their dealings, no 'forgotten' appointments. The nastiness of the occasion had almost been worth the relief from Aylmer's harassment, though she suspected the truce would not last; she did not believe his dislike and jealousy had in any way amended; he could not meet her eyes now. Had the little episode been instigated by him? She had no way of telling.

'If you have any further problems you must let Alex know,' James Manningford said. 'He is sufficiently influential in your world to make any intervention felt.'

Louise thanked him and pondered the subject of networks once more.

People came out juggling with plates of food; Simon departed to discover its source; with the éclat of one performing a particularly brilliant conjuring trick, Jack introduced Louise to Charlotte and Harry Coleby, who turned out to be friends both of the Manningfords and the rector. Suddenly everyone was shaking hands or exchanging smacking kisses. Harry was a landowner and a judge, Jack volunteered. Charlotte, her expensively natural coppery hair

178

backlit by the lamp, was fascinated in turn to learn from him that Louise lectured at the Holbrooke Collection; such a marvellous place, she must have a scholarly mind. She sounded genuinely admiring. She, Jack told Louise confidentially, was big in children's charities work in Hampshire; she had recently been awarded the OBE. She was, he added with admiration, a serious woman. If she were, it was not immediately apparent: no grey flannel skirt, no home-knitted cardigan, no drab skin-coloured tights here. Her silken trousers and flowing shirt were the ultimate in sophisticated high-fashion and the latest muted shades, aubergine, putty and taupe.

'Arabella says your lectures are well worth hearing,' Charlotte said. 'You'll see me in your audience very soon.'

Simon appeared, accompanied by Maggie and Brozie, all laden with food. Behind them came Charley, clutching bottles of wine, which he dumped on the table. Louise sighed with relief for her plaintively growling stomach. Lots of lasagne, good, plenty of tossed salad, too: she piled her plate and began to eat, careless of appearing greedy. Simon plonked himself beside her in a director's chair; a hand absently fondled her knee.

Charley lowered his bulk to sit on her other side and began to shovel up food like mechanical digger at a pile of in-fill material. Beyond him was Maggie, her body relaxed into her chair, her head thrown back, her legs thrust out in front of her in exaggerated exhaustion. 'Whew!' she said and thrust her hands through her untidy blonde hair before picking up her own plate. 'No, Cerberus,' she said to the hopeful dog. 'You've had yours and this is mine. I deserve it.'

'Maggie the Trojan,' Charley said. 'Tremendous performance, terrific food! Thanks!' A big and hairy hand went out to give her thigh a pat. Their eyes met, they smiled.

Eye contact, touching, smiling, that's how we signal the show's back on the road, Louise thought, an icy tingle running down her spine. Have those two got a show on the road? She moved her eyes cautiously to look at Jack across the table to her left, and observed the bleak look of dislike he cast at Charley.

Then something in the still and alert posture of Brozie

beyond Jack caught her attention. From being flushed when she and Maggie had arrived with the food, Brozie was now pale. Doctor Jane Field was speaking, saying something apparently to Judge Coleby, collecting the attention of those around her. Death? Was she speaking of death? In front of one so recently widowed as Brozie? Euthanasia. A strange subject for a party.

'The House of Lords' committee on euthanasia rejected it,' Jane was saying, 'but that hasn't stopped it from being the latest enthusiasm of the trend-setting lobby. Rub out your nearest and dearest when they become too long in the tooth to be useful – put them down like a pet dog that's a bore to nurse.'

Charley looked up from gulping his food. 'Euthanasia's not such a bad idea. One thing to be sentimental about the old and sick, but I had an aunt who was riddled with cancer – screaming for death, poor old bird – and no one had the guts to help her go. If an animal were tormented like she was you'd be in trouble with the law for causing unnecessary suffering. But your hypocritic – sorry, Hippocratic – oath,' he grinned with mischief, 'prevents you doing the right thing, so you pretend it must be wrong. Isn't that it in a nutshell?'

Jane's tawny head reared up and round; she riposted quietly, but with a voice as precise and cutting as well-tempered steel, posing her own questions: 'Do you expect the carers to turn into killers as and when it suits society? Doctors believe in the value of all life, they're trained to preserve it. Would you want the doctor you pray will help you to wield the lethal syringe?'

'Oh God, yes, if I were in the state old Auntie was. That was the ultimate help she wanted. She'd have finished herself off if she could, but the poor love was in hospital where the idea was to keep the patients going as long as humanly possible – not humanely possible. Looks better on the statistics for cancer cures, doesn't it?'

Brozie's strange speckled eyes were flicking from one to the other.

'Some doctors are unwilling to let nature take its own course,' Jane said shortly, 'but then they're afraid of being sued if they don't strive to the very end. And miracle cures have been known – how about those?'

180

'Darling, not over dinner, please,' her husband pleaded softly.

'You should read the book I've just published,' Charley told her, ignoring Thomas, 'it's a wonderful novel on exactly that subject – a powerful plea for mercy for those con-demned to endure intolerable pain. *Some Loving Act* it's called – from Shakespeare, you know . . . "death which commits some loving act". *Anthony and Cleopatra*. A hus-band whose wife asks him to shorten her sufferings, and unlike most of us moral cowards, he has the guts to do so . . .'

'Ah, yes,' Jane interrupted. 'I saw it at Brozie's very recently.' She turned to Brozie. 'You've read it, haven't you? And what do you think? Did your husband Hubert want help to die?'

Brozie sipped and turned the wine over on her tongue before she answered. Then she gave a faint, almost scornful smile and spoke dismissively: 'Hubert had cancer for many years. He never complained of pain, but there was no recog-nisable quality to his life either. And he was deeply fearful of the pain which might come at the end.' She replaced her glass on the table and met Doctor Jane's eyes. 'We never dis-cussed death itself; he was not a man to dwell on such a sub-ject. All I can say is that he was lucky that his heart failed before his worst fears were realised.'

'And the book? What was your opinion on that?' Jane's voice pushed at her.

The questions were sharp-edged. Louise was startled at Jane's lack of tact, disturbed herself by the whole subject. Suppose her baby were to be born damaged in some way, suffering even – would she have the courage to end its suf-fering? She looked at the rector's still and observant face, at the taut tendons of Brozie's neck. There was an atmosphere here she did not understand.

'The book made an emotional and moving plea for mercy in a particular situation. As Charley said, it takes courage to do what that man did.'

'It does, Brozie, and I lacked it,' Arabella Manningford said softly. 'My mother had a stroke about a year ago. Her mind was alive, her body useless, and her speech had gone.

181

She'd always asked me not to let her end her days as an incontinent old nuisance, but to help her go in dignity. I never had the courage and I despise myself for it.'

'Nonsense,' Harry Coleby said. 'You were right. The law was made for very good reasons. To change it could open the floodgates to crime.'

'Precisely,' Jane nodded. 'Dangerous precedents.'

'I'm afraid so,' her husband agreed. 'Now hospices . . .'

'Nonsense!' Charley roared, and by pure force of personality and volume of sound silenced the others. 'Not with proper safeguards. It's ridiculous to keep alive those who want death, especially on this overcrowded planet. Nowadays we pour out millions of pounds prolonging the lives of the terminally ill and the inhabitants of the geriatric wards. If just a third of these were taken out by euthanasia – their choice, mind – we'd save something like fifteen per cent of our National Health bill. Think of that! Think how our taxes would go down, hey Jack, hey Simon?'

'How revolting,' Jane said, 'to value life in money terms.' She added crossly: 'Careful, Charley, you're leaning towards the values of Hitler's Germany. Perhaps you'd advocate sterilisation of the unfit also?'

'An excellent idea,' he said with glee. 'Since your husband's Church doesn't object to abortion, why should it object to that? A sound and sensible move. Start with HIV-infected people – stop them giving birth to doomed and suffering children, go on to the proven useless mothers whose every child has to be taken into care, and the mad. Why not? And if the politicians had that put into law, the Church would promptly go along with it – wouldn't it, Thomas?' He grinned happily. 'As with divorce, abortion and homosexuality, all anathema until recently.'

Maggie began to laugh. 'Stop winding everyone up, Charley, do!'

He smiled back at her. 'And how about castrating criminals, too?'

Louise noted that the awfulness of his opinions, which in a less relaxed and cheerful man would be obnoxious, were somehow counteracted by his smile, that clever arrangement of facial muscles which combined with his mischief to give the strange illusion called charm. But however amusing he contrived to be this was the wrong discussion for a party, and from their shakes of the head and embarrassed looks others thought so too.

Brozie collected plates, her angular body stiff and awkward. 'Puddings!' she prodded Maggie. 'Cheeses.'

'Goodness, yes!' Maggie said and leapt up. 'Come on, Charley, your guests are being neglected.'

By the time everybody had acquired their strawberries and cream a sort of general post had occurred. Jack, who had been determined to sit with Charlotte Colby or Arabella Manningford, found himself instead flanked by Brozie and an unknown female of indeterminate age. Brozie was a good woman, no doubt about that, but she could never by any stretch of the imagination be thought to be high-powered, and Jack preferred women who were powering themselves somewhere. He turned therefore, though without much hope, to his other neighbour. She had covered her well-upholstered person in tight fuchsia-coloured satin, adding a great many dangling bright gold chains. The whole hurt his eyes; he averted them. A polite man, however, he opened the conversation.

'Do you come from one of the local villages?'

'Oh no!' she said, as if the very idea were comic. 'Andover. My husband has a factory there – kitchen cabinets.'

'Oh. Really?' A labrador sniffed at him; he pushed it away.

'And you?' The question plopped into the short silence like a solitary fish angling to be caught.

'I live here. In Abbotsbridge. Solicitor.'

'Ah, yes!' She gave him the vigorous nod of one who now could appreciate all facets of his life. She smiled. Jack did not smile back. 'Have you known Charley long?' she asked, slapping the labrador heartily.

'A few months.' With reluctance.

'Oh, I've known him for years. Absolutely years. No. Down, boy, that's enough. A lovely man, isn't he?'

Jack's eyes wandered to where his wife was again sitting

close to Charley. She was laughing at one of his jokes, her head flung back, her throat quivering. She never laughed at his own jokes like that. She'd spent most of the day here, organising Charley's party, leaving him, Jack, to look after the boys, even to bath them ready for bed. It really was too bad. People would begin to think . . . things. He knew there would never be anything in it. Of course not. But these days . . . well, people could assume heaven knows what. Charley was rising now to pour another round of drinks; he served himself first, Jack noticed. He hoped the filthy stuff would choke the man. He looked at his neighbour and said nothing.

She, it seemed, took his silence for agreement as to Charley's loveliness. 'A rogue, that's what I tell him he is,' she confided, 'a charming rogue. He used to go out with one of my daughters, once. Very close they were – like that!' She showed him crossed fingers, then sighed. 'But there were problems. She's always confided in me – she told me.'

Far more interesting now, this woman. Jack nodded, his tone inviting: 'Yes, one can see. Charley's liveliness . . .?'

'Like being on a roller-coaster, being with him was, Debbie said. One month all red roses and expensive meals out, then whoops! Hardly enough to eat, bills piling up and peculiar men at the door. Fun he was, and generous – you'd hardly believe. But in a proper long-term relationship you want stability, don't you?'

'Of course,' Jack agreed, his mind buzzing.

'I think he's settling down now. Well, I hope he is for his poor parents' sakes. They say he'll grow out of his wild ways, given time, but personally I wonder.' She rambled on, telling him how Charley would ring her up from all over England – and abroad, too, sometimes. He knew how lonely it was for someone like her now all her little brood was out in the world. It was lovely to hear his voice saying: 'Jus' me!' on a dull morning. She was one of his staging posts when he was driving around for his business; she fed him regularly, and in return he'd mend things her husband hadn't time for. 'Such a kind man,' she sighed. 'You have to forgive people like him, don't you?'

Charley arrived to pour more wine into Jack's glass; a different bottle this time – a guest's contribution perhaps. Jack drank; that was more like it. He drank again, stopped Charley from moving away by thrusting out his glass for more.

'Where's Melody?' he demanded loudly. 'Left you, has she?'

Charley shrugged, unabashed. 'Couldn't meet the challenge of my dynamic personality! Perhaps fate intended it – now she's in Paris with a new man and she's becoming a stunning success, got herself in all the magazines.' He walked off into the house.

Brozie had disappeared; where her head had been he saw Simon's. Louise was pregnant, Jack remembered, he must congratulate Simon: poor fool had been yearning for a family. Still, Louise was no Maggie, she'd probably stop at one. He told Simon he was glad for him, emptying his glass with a flourish to emphasise the point.

'But keep Louise away from Maggie, for heaven's sake. Mustn't encourage my wife.' Charley had left the bottle on the table. Good. He poured, drank, and took a deep death. 'Women like the thought that they belong to an opp . . . oppressed minority and have to fight for their freedom to breed or not as they want – the right to their own bodies, they call it. But lemme tell you, 's an outmoded concept. It's men now who have to fight for their rights.' Simon was giving him an odd look. He went on, getting more angry as he spoke: 'Women hold the whiphand. They give or withhold as they please. They keep the children nine out of ten times after divorce. They're making men suffer now. Not fair. Hypocrites.'

He brooded. When he looked up, Simon had vanished and in his place was Louise. It didn't seem to matter. In their present burgeoning self-complacency they were interchangeable. He told her sourly: 'You know why Maggie really likes being pregnant and giving birth? Because it gives her status. It's a time when women get everyone's attention – the whole world fusses round them, coos over their babies. It gives meaning to their existence like nothing else. Maggie's no fool, she could get status elsewhere, in voluntary work, for example, but she's intellecshually idle, she'd rather breed.' He stared into his three-quarter empty glass, stuck in his little finger and fished out a small insect. 'Breed like the bloody greenfly!'

'She only wants one more child,' Louise pleaded. 'She says there's an empty black hole where Felicity was.'

Jack shook his head vehemently, then wished he had not as giddiness attacked him. 'Know something?' he asked darkly. 'Tell you something. Wouldn't be satisfied with jus' one. Never be satisfied. Even when Felicity was alive she had this wistful line about another lil' girl just waiting up in heaven for us to call. Thought you were her friend, Louise. Tell her she's got to stop somewhere, sometime. Tell her its got to be here and now. Right bloody now! No, in fact I'll tell her. Take her home and tell her. Time we went anyhow.'

'It's early yet,' Louise said, startled. 'You don't want to break up the party.'

Breaking up the party was exactly what Jack wanted to do. He would have liked to break other things also. He rose ponderously to his feet.

'Baby-sitter,' he said in explanation to the floating faces of Arabella Manningford and Charlotte Coleby opposite. 'Baby-sitters always got to be cherished.'

He went to find Maggie.

'Go? Now? You have to be joking,' she said. 'I'm a hostess here, Charley's hostess for the night. I'll be the last to leave.'

Chapter 15

Two and three-quarter hours later Jack finally managed to winkle Maggie away from the house and into the car. The bubbling irritation that he had expressed to Louise had settled into a seething discontent, not at all improved by a returning sobriety induced by the awfulness of the drinks on offer. He had promised the baby-sitter to return her home at midnight; now he would not only have to pay for more than two hours' overtime but face the delayed journey with her, and as could be expected of a niece of Les Chubb's, Janice had an outsize capacity to make the car reek with disapproval. But she had been the only minder available.

He opened the cottage door on to a chaotic scene: discarded shoes, bats and balls littered the hall, blazers had fallen off their pegs, even the prints on the walls hung crooked and the cat had been sick in a corner. The living-room was little better: jigsaws upset on the rumpled rug before the fireplace, crumpled drawing paper, crayons and toys flung anywhere, stained abandoned mugs cluttering the mantelshelf. He had complained as they left for the party; somehow it was far worse coming home to it.

Silently Janice rose from a sofa, but the sight of her rigid back as she picked her way through the jumbled house to the front door made him cringe. In the car he tried to apologise; she did not speak.

When he got back Maggie was drifting around in an aimless daze. He suggested in a tight voice that some tidying up might be in order.

She looked about herself, seeming to observe the mess for the first time. 'Does it matter? At this hour?'

'It's a disgrace. I can't live like this. I feel ashamed.'

She said in aimiable unconcern: 'I spent half the day at Charley's. I can't do everything.'

'Then you should do less for Charley. And,' he added in meaningful tones, 'persuade the man to do less to you.'

She stood very still, staring at him. 'What do you mean?'

He shot a glance at her astonishingly blue eyes and looked away. He was embarrassed for her and for himself. 'I can't believe you haven't noticed. He puts his hands on you. He touches you. All over.'

She picked up the empty log-basket from the hearth and began to sling toys into it. 'Not all over,' she said, bending to rescue a battered pick-up truck and straightening again, her face pink.

'He touches your arms, your knees, your bottom. I've seen him. You even let him hug you.'

She had reached the jigsaw now; she picked up the pieces with care. 'He's a physical sort of man. He likes to hug his female friends. He hugs Brozie.'

That was true. 'Well, I'd rather he didn't hug you.'

'Or touch me on the parts you regard as particularly yours?' She was smiling now, flashing him a look of mischief.

'Yes,' he said truculently. 'He can leave you alone.'

'You're surely not jealous? No, you couldn't be that!'

'Of that clown? Certainly not.'

But her look of reproachful concern reduced him to the small-boy status of one rebuked by Mummy for refusing to let a friend play with a favourite toy. He struggled to maintain his sense of grievance. At home she slopped around the place, depressed and slovenly; when Charley was around he cheered her in a way that Jack despised. He himself could not be light-hearted and irresponsible as the bachelor Charley could; God knew, he had responsibilities. And people's imaginations would whirr from seeing her cook for Charley. He remembered reading that in some West African tribes, for a wife to do work for another man was considered a more heinous crime than infidelity. He understood vividly those men's reactions.

188

Jack needed to feel better than all his acquaintance to feel at ease with himself; the more convinced of his superiority he felt, the better he became. With an admiring wife's support, his household well run, his children demonstrably more bright than his neighbours' and his career progressing ever upward, no one could be more decent, more concerned for others, more generous in spirit and in cheques, but with all that he valued now coming under attack, he felt his life's foundations rocking, saw moral chasms opening to threaten him. Assault occasioning actual bodily harm. He gloated at the thought of blood flowing, he, a mild-mannered solicitor. He had fantasies of punching that great bear of a man, Charley, on the nose for daring to fondle Maggie; he would have liked to take a stick to her for permitting it without the retort of a slap, or at the very least, a public rebuke. But Maggie remained unbothered – and, he thought with vexation, while he himself paid for his fishing, men he admired gave Charley free rein on magnificent stretches to which he had no access! Jealousy, rancour and violence warred with the love inside him.

He looked at his wife in amazement and fear at his own emotions. She was straightening the rumpled Kashan rug with her foot and collecting a mug on each finger of one hand as she made her way to the door, at the same time adjusting her clever flower arrangements with the free hand: the economy and swiftness of her movements had achieved a transformation from chaos to charm within minutes. All was made fresh once more. He sighed. He could not argue with her any further; she was not responsible for the awfulness of that leering dubious fellow. Really, the man was rather pathetic. Not a single item of value in that ridiculous done-over barn, no silver, no oriental rugs, his furniture a laughable collection of junk. Not a man of property in the Galsworthy sense, but a boastful man of straw. Ridiculous to think of Maggie in connection with anyone like him. Surely.

By way of a hairshirt for his suspicions he went to find kitchen paper to deal with the cat-sick in the hall, taking several pieces.

'Thanks,' she called to him as he finished his task with

distaste, 'but don't put that muck in the kitchen bin, put it down the loo.'

He obeyed, flushed the loo and turned to wash his hands.

Maggie appeared in the doorway, her arms still full of toys. She really must get a grip on the boys. Good habits, formed early, were of the essence.

'You are good to deal with that muck,' she said softly.

'I know,' he said, rubbing his hands dry on the towel.

She grinned. 'I can see your halo, newly burnished, top quality.'

'Mmh.' She was trying to get round him; in her own way she was apologising for neglecting him all day; she did care for him. Irrationally he was mollified.

He turned to leave but she was obstructing his way, her body jammed next to his in the confined space. She was warm, soft, faintly scented with that delectable smell that was at once the essence of summer and the essence of Maggie. The toys clattered to the floor and she lifted her arms, chuckling. He clutched her, clamping his mouth on her enticing lips; her plump hips swivelled to meet his, her hands pressed him hard against her, sounds like purring coming from deep inside her. The anger and misery that had lanced through him all evening dissolved; warmth and desire rose and spread in him, permeating his mind and his body. She was his, his and no one else's and he would have her as Charley never could.

'Let's go to bed!' he said thickly.

'Yes, let's !' she whispered, and seized his hand to tug him upstairs.

He took her in haste and she responded with the same urgency, meeting his desires with hers, climaxing in unison with him. Afterwards, his tension dissipated, he was conscious of a familiar sense of comfortable affection and trust. Maggie was not perfect, but then who was? When he thought of the divorce cases that were dealt with by his partners he shuddered with horror and reminded himself he must be tolerant.

It was not until he was on the edge of sleep that he realised he had not used a condom as he had recently decided was essential on every occasion. A shock of horror jerked him awake. What stage of the month was Maggie at? He calculated, paused, figured again. No, it should be all right, she was well past her fertile stage. But then, his mind told him, surely she must be due? Overdue? Another bolt of horror, more unnerving, more violent. He tried to remember exactly and failed. Tried to reassure himself that women's biological rhythms could be upset by coming off the pill. It could only be by a day or two . . . it must be all right with the precautions he had been taking. Mustn't it?

The grandfather clock downstairs struck four. Somewhere across the field an owl was hooting, lonely and melancholy. Finally he fell asleep, only to dream over and over again of a house lost in a swirling mist from which there came the despairing wailing of abandoned and unloved babies left to starve. The sounds echoed and re-echoed in his head.

Brozie was euphoric. Such a splendid morning, all sun and roses. Such a lovely party last night, so lively, so much friendliness. There had been a few unnerving moments with Doctor Jane, but she could remember being very calm and collected – full of dignity, as she had instructed herself. She wondered . . . then shook her head. No menacing thoughts, no nasty recollections should spoil her happiness. Breakfast in the garden, in a sheltered spot in the sun; a Sunday breakfast to savour at leisure, her boiled egg done to perfection, the white set, the yellow runny. Fresh coffee, too, the toast of that granary bread she relished, and her own homemade marmalade, made from a mixture of oranges, lemons and grapefruit, sharp and delicious on the tongue. Little pleasures, little treats. And oh, the bliss of not having Hubert's grumbling monologue over the *Sunday Telegraph* as he indulged in his daily hate session against all politicians.

She rose to scatter her toast crumbs. 'Robin, robin, robin!' she called. He arrived suddenly, in a flurry of self-importance. Good boy. This was a new robin, a youngster from one of last year's broods. Perhaps he was the son of the robin she had found dead on the day she met Charley. If so, he had taken over his father's territory; nature abhors a vacuum.

Dear Charley had brought her home in his Porsche at

191

nearly half-past three in the morning. The stars had been out, and an amazingly dramatic full moon. A strange silent hour, with a distinct scent all its own, sharp, cold and clean, of crab apples and wheat-straw and river water. She had never been up so late in all of her life – or only to nurse the dying. Parties had never interested her parents, they were quiet retiring people, and as for Hubert, well, he'd been middle-aged and staid when they'd met and he'd despised what he called frivolity. Brozie yawned contentedly. Such fun to be frivolous, such fun to drink till you felt deliciously dizzy, and to listen to all the clever light-hearted talk and watch Charley and Maggie flirting – so outrageous he was, but it was only nonsense, and it was good to see Maggie's eyes brighten and her face crinkle into mischief again after all she had gone through with the death of that dear little girl.

She picked a half-blown rose to tuck in a buttonhole, packed her breakfast dishes on to a tray and whisked them indoors to wash up. Oh, how well she felt, how much better on the HRT. Doctor Jane had been right: no insomnia now; she woke fresh as a small child, full of anticipation for each day, planning exciting and new things to do, planning her treats. Steadily the improvement had increased, her hot flushes vanishing, her taut nerves relaxing. She had first noticed the improvement on the day of Hubert's funeral, just the thought of which had made her rattle with nerves and shiver with dread before. Yet she had been calm and in control and it had passed without unpleasantness. Indeed, the rector and Mr Fudge had shown her such concern and kindness that they brought tears to her eyes, tears that might otherwise have been missing. And so many people from the village had turned up, and she knew it had been on her behalf, to support her, not for poor Hubert. She had felt blessed with friends. She was blessed also in knowing that she had no money worries. How extraordinary that was: Hubert had been so secretive; she had never for a moment suspected that he had regularly made investments out of the retirement income he denounced as inadequate. Why, he had railed at her over her hats as if they were going to bankrupt him, insisting on the necessity for ever-greater retrenchments. When she had run her eyes down the list of Hubert's stocks and shares she had felt quite strange, felt almost as if someone were playing a practical joke on her. Not six figures but substantial. And they were all true, all to be hers. 'A touch staid,' was how the bank manager described them, 'but sensible and safe.' They had, he told Brozie, performed steadily even during market downturns and their capital value overall had appreciated. If she wished to make adjustments to her portfolio, the bank would, of course, be happy to assist her.

Charley had made her laugh. 'Go to the bank for advice?' he had exclaimed in horror. 'Dreary one! No, you enjoy your money, invest in something a bit different, something way out and wild for a change.'

'Me?' she said. 'I've never been way out and wild, I wouldn't know where to start! A shrinking violet, that's me. Anyhow, what sort of thing do you mean?'

'Oh, I don't know,' he said, 'but there must be dozens of possibilities. Hold on – let me think!' A pause while he devoured a slice of the date and walnut cake she had made for him, slurping it down with coffee as if he'd neither eaten nor drunk for twenty-four hours, then bit into a second slice. 'Try these for size,' he said exuberantly, showering crumbs: 'Number one. Invest in a young race-horse! Imagine the enjoyment of visiting the stables and watching its progress, or going with parties of friends to the races, collecting your wins and then rushing off for a celebration dinner!'

Snobbishly Brozie visualised herself standing in the sunlit paddock of a well-known race-course, talking knowledgeably to her famous trainer and jockey while patting the arched neck of a handsome tail-swishing chestnut, the hot favourite, the cynosure of all eyes. But this alluring picture was rapidly replaced by one of a tailed-off nag, its coat dull with sweat and foam, stumbling over the last fence to skid to a fall, breaking a leg and stunning its unfortunate rider. This picture was horribly vivid.

'No,' she protested, mocking her temporary folly. 'Oof, Charley, the risks! Horrors! Hubert would rise from his grave to haunt me if I did that! Number two suggestion?'

'Buy into property bonds, then you could have almost free holidays two or three times a year – places like Florida,

Spain, Italy, Greece – a different place each time, your own place, all laid on and looked after for you, and from them you can go out and explore all those countries' great architectural beauties, their hills and their histories, sit in cafés where great painters and poets have sat and talked, see the scenes that inspired them. I'd do it myself,' he added grandiosely, 'if my money weren't already wholly tied up. Another idea – invest in a shop or some other business, put in a manager, always have an interest. A flower shop, that would use your expertise . . . or an antique shop. You'd love it! Or – wait for it – best of all a hat shop!'

As she stood now at the kitchen sink, peeling potatoes to roast round the leg of new Welsh lamb for Charley and herself for lunch, Brozie chuckled at the memory. So much nonsense, so much wit. Charley's exuberant life-style, abounding with activity, impatient of caution, was bracing as a fresh wind. Being with him made her feel reckless and vital and young again. And he had changed her world: like the Arabian Nights of her childhood, he brought her excitement and the freedom of a new charmed world, unknown, brightly coloured, exotic. She saw vast desert sands, ancient civilisations, the splendours of the orient – Bali, the Great Wall of China, the Taj Mahal; could she just see those she would die blissful – all the mountains of the earth travelled with him on his tongue and she scaled the peaks of human possibilities. Endless opportunities were available to her now. She would contemplate all the alternatives – and she sighed happily in anticipation of the hours of enjoyment that would bring – and suddenly, in a burst, it would come to her what to do.

Nearly time for church. She switched on the oven, then darted out to her herb patch to pick mint for a mint sauce, nipping on past scented buddleias bright with butterflies to where runner beans rioted over their supports and vegetables of every sort swelled in immaculate rows. She selected beans and a small beauty of a cauliflower with perfect creamy curds. In his racing and flurried working week she knew Charley often succumbed to the lure of fast food, horrible greasy beefburgers and similar stuff oozing lurid sauces. Today he would have country food, packed with goodness.

With the lamb safe in the oven Brozie straightened. Now,

194

where was the dashing new hat she had bought for the autumn, to catch the eye of the congregation?

Fifty yards from the church Nancy Chubb appeared alongside her and they panted up the rise together.

'Good morning, Mrs Hamilton. Only just in time this morning, aren't we? Not like you to be late. Sleeping on after that party, were you?'

'No,' Brozie replied shortly. 'I've been busy.'

'Oh? Got folks for lunch, have you? Many people coming?'

'Just Mr St George.'

'Ah. Yes, well, I see that car of his outside your home a lot. Can't miss it, wherever it is. Feed him, do you? He has a way of getting people to do things for him.'

'He's a kind man, he does a lot for me.' How was it Nancy always put her on the defensive?

'Yes, he is kind,' Nancy agreed. Her tough baked apple face collapsed into unwonted softness; she smiled reminiscently. 'When Les was laid up with that ankle of his last month, he helped me shift the heavy stuff in the store room. Dunno how I'd have managed otherwise. An' funny? Had me giggling till I nearly 'ad an accident. Helped you get driving again, didn't he? I saw. See Mrs Easton in the car with him too. Not teaching *her* to drive, is he? She knows already. I wonder what he's doing with *her*?'

The voice was all too innocently enquiring, the eyes averted.

Brozie felt herself stiffen and straighten. She wanted to flay the woman for impertinence, to lash her with words like Hubert at his most abrasive, but they had reached the church gate now and there were too many people around. Instead she said in the breathless voice of one who has not been attending:

'Oh, look, isn't that Miss Hunter in the church porch? Talking to Mrs Manningford? I've been wanting to see her . . . Yes, yes, it is. What luck! Harvest Festival, you know, Nancy. So important to get the details settled early on. And I must speak to Mrs Easton too. So good she is. Excuse me!'

The drawing-room at Abbotsbridge House was stupendous,

Louise thought, staring with admiration as the Manningfords' Sunday morning drinks party drew near its end. The walls were lined with what must be the original silk hangings, the heavily faded colour now more dusty pink than rose-red, but still delicately pretty. As in the church two hours earlier, she had a feeling of continuity, as if the past were still imposing its energy on the present . . . in the kindliest way. The furniture, the pictures, the ornaments, had charm and variety, but they were the accrued choice of generations rather than a whole designed and executed by one person. The nicely figured walnut of Queen Anne days had never been rejected because a Georgian squire was acquiring shining mahogany, while a Regency beauty painted by Sir Thomas Lawrence in her high-waisted silk stared out from her picture frame at a bobbed young person in nineteen-thirties taffeta on the opposite wall. The petit-point chair seats, footstools and samplers too, were clearly the work of several centuries of female Manningford hands. She sipped her mineral water while listening with only half an ear to Arabella Manningford's apologies to Simon and herself for not having had them over to the house sooner.

'. . . because of my mother's death,' she was saying. 'I've been up to my eyebrows – and it is rather gruesome, don't you think, to go through one's parent's underwear, or her yellowing old love letters?'

'Hmm? Oh, yes,' Louise said with sympathy. 'Gruesome – and embarrassing. How horrid for you. Have you very much more to sort out?'

'Oh, a ton, an absolute ton. I wilt just to think of it. And so little time. With half the world off on holiday I've had to do many more days on the Bench than normal, and then my darling children have been underfoot for weeks and I do like to give the poor loves some attention, plus we spent three weeks in Italy – which was gorgeous, but one can't achieve order out of chaos from Tuscany, can one?'

'Oh!' Simon interrupted, looking downward. 'A cat! I wondered who or what was nudging my leg!' He bent to stroke a half-grown grey kitten.

'Keziah!' Arabella exclaimed. 'Kizzy, you shouldn't be here! Sorry, Simon, she's supposed to be a yard cat, but one of the children must have let her in again. She's most insistent on human company. Beatrice, take Kizzy out, please. Oh, and Thomas, wine for Louise.'

The Manningford boys were, Louise judged, in their mid-teens, the two girls about twelve and ten. They were helping their parents' housekeeping couple to circulate the drinks and the food, well-trained children. Now the twelve-year-old Beatrice looked unexpectedly mulish.

'Kizzy hates it outside. She cries. Why can't she come in?'

The half-grown kitten was in Simon's arms now, responding to his advances with a purr as throbbing as the diesel engine of a London taxi. 'She's enchanting,' he said. 'Do let her stay.'

Arabella's eyes measured her daughter and glanced at the amused Simon, who was rubbing behind ears. 'Oh, very well, Bea. Just for now. But no more attempts at inserting wedges or I'll have her put down!'

The boy Thomas nudged his agitated sister aside, offered Louise more wine, then corrected himself, 'Oh, no, you were drinking Perrier, weren't you? Just two seconds, please.'

'Perrier?' Arabella queried. 'You were drinking mineral water last night. I noticed. We all heard the bans being read in church this morning – congratulations, Simon. But is there cause for further congratulations? Could it be . . . you're not pregnant, are you, Louise?'

Louise nodded, holding out her glass to Thomas.

'How exciting for you both! But how are you feeling? Queasy? Poor you. Wonderful creatures, babies, but they do pull one down.'

'Babies?' Charlotte Coleby swung round from an animated conversation with Jack Easton and James Manningford about the nuisance the fishing antis had become locally, throwing over her shoulder: 'Fish liberation they'll be calling it next! But they don't come near when Charley's around – he chucked three of them in the river last month and he's so large he petrifies them!' She looked at Louise. 'A baby? You are? How lovely, but combined with your career how daunting. You do intend to keep working?'

'Certainly I do.'

'Straddling two worlds at once. But all that travelling? Phew!'

'I envy Louise,' Arabella said. 'I should love to have a career. I'm tired of being a kept woman.'

'What nonsense!' James Manningford joined them. 'What do you mean, a kept woman? You work for me and God knows you do enough for the community. Besides, you have your own income.'

'Unearned,' Arabella retorted, 'and hardly vast, darling. Besides, times have changed – unearned incomes aren't considered Politically Correct. To be chic one must be personally successful – in cash terms. Mind you, I can't imagine how Louise will cope over the next two years. She'll need the perfect partner and the perfect boss. How's Simon rate, Louise?'

'Pretty highly,' she said, looking round for him, but Simon had retreated with Beatrice and the gambolling grey cat to the end of the room. 'I can generally rely on him.'

'More than two-thirds of us can say,' Charlotte remarked. 'I can rely on Harry with certainty only in one capacity –'

'To be elsewhere when urgently needed!' Arabella returned, laughing.

'How did you guess!'

'He's cloned with James! And your director, Louise, what's his name? Aylmer Littlejohn? Will he understand if you have problems?'

'I doubt it,' she admitted, and a ripple of unease ran down her spine, a cold feeling she had every time she contemplated the ordeal of telling Aylmer she was expecting a child and would be claiming statutory leave of several months. 'He's unmarried for a start, and not one of life's sympathetic characters. His view of my living in Hampshire is that it demonstrates a most unhelpful attitude of mind.'

'Oh, lord, what a silly man!' Arabella said.

A longcase clock with a silvered dial struck the quarter before two.

'Goodness, I must run,' Charlotte said. 'Come on, Harry, lunch!'

Waving them goodbye, Arabella put a hand on Louise's arm and said softly: 'Before you go I must have a word with

198

you. Would you mind if I asked your advice on various pieces of furniture I've inherited from poor old Mama? I'll happily pay for your time. I don't want exact valuations, I'm having that done for probate, but what I do need is to know what is intrinsically worth saving and putting somewhere in this house, and also what I could well jettison from among our present furniture. Would you?'

'It sounds interesting,' Louise said. 'And I wouldn't want payment.'

'No, no. We'll keep it on a business footing,' Arabella insisted. 'Come and have a first look in the attics. I shan't keep you long.'

Louise was ushered into a room as big, she thought as she stared, as the entire ground floor of any of the village cottages. Beneath its raftered and cobwebbed roof it was packed with old furniture, trunks, toys, pictures and a host of other objects. A gilded harp trailed broken strings on the dusty floor; handsome old mahogany chests of drawers were flanked by abandoned marble washstands; two faded silk-covered couches were piled with marble busts, leather-bound books and long-silenced clocks. On the right-hand side of the room an area of sizable rectangular shapes was covered in old blankets: Arabella tossed these aside to reveal still more furniture.

'These were my mother's,' she said. 'There's more in the next room.'

Louise drew in her breath. 'She had some superb pieces.'

'Yes, I know. But some may be showy yet relatively valueless. Others should be put on show. I need to know before I arrange a sale of all the junk.'

'I'd love to advise you,' Louise said.

Voices from downstairs were calling Arabella and she left hurriedly. Louise followed her at a more leisurely pace, pausing first to run her hands lovingly down the legs of a Chippendale vase-stand and examine the drawer and the rule-joints of a Sheraton Pembroke table. 'Unmarred,' she murmured, 'virtually unmarred.' And she pondered how delightful it must be to live amid such an abundance of rare objects that one could actually choose whether or not to keep them. It did not occur to her to envy the Manningfords; her

199

own expectations in life fell far short of any such aspirations to wealth or property; it was enough simply to be consulted.

When she arrived in the big hall she discovered that Simon had gone out ahead of her. Arabella kissed her good-bye with a faintly guilty air and a million and one thanks for everything, an effusion of gratitude that James echoed and which struck Louise as excessive until she reached the car and found Simon and little Beatrice placing a wickerwork basket on the rear seat, a basket which jerked and mewed.

'And just what is that?' Louise enquired ominously.

'It's Kizzy,' Beatrice told her, her eyes shining. 'Simon said he'd love to have her, and he was sure you wouldn't mind. You see, Mummy won't have her in the house. She says we've too many dogs and cats as it is and they're awfully damaging to the furniture and things. And I'm terribly pleased you're going to have Kizzy because she's quite the nicest and funniest kitten we've ever had and now I can be sure she'll be loved.'

Louise knew when she caught. She sat in silence back to the cottage while Simon, slightly drunk, recited poems in praise of cats and rehearsed the merits of children growing up with animals.

Finally she spoke: 'I never had an animal and I'm far from convinced that every child needs a flea-ridden furry friend to grow up balanced. You feed her, Simon, you groom her and de-louse her and all the rest of it. She's your cat. And don't ever play a trick like that again.'

Charley was late for lunch, later even than he usually was. Brozie began to worry whether he had forgotten to come, or even whether he might be pinned under the Porsche in a ditch somewhere.

When he did arrive he apologised, but did it in so abstracted a manner and with his hair springing up from his scalp in such disorder that she knew something major had occurred in his life.

'What kept you?' she asked, rapidly carving the now over-roasted lamb. 'Nothing too disastrous, I hope?'

'My partner,' he said, leaning over the table to pluck crisped bits of meat from the dish and pop them in his mouth. 'My bloody partner, Tony. He's a disaster area all on his own.'

Brozie lifted succulent lamb on to sizzling plates, pushing dishes of roast potatoes and beans towards him. She hated him to be stricken with worries. He should always be her insouciant Charley, his aura of happiness wrapped round him like an invisible cloak. She longed to put all his bothers to rest; at least she could feed him.

'Cauliflower cheese,' she said. 'Gravy and mint sauce on your right. So what's Tony done – or not done?'

'Five books should have been printed this last month,' he said, furiously piling spoonfuls of cauliflower cheese on his plate. 'Their authors had done their proof-reading, the amendments had been made and double-checked. Did they go off to the press? Yes! I took them there myself. Spent three days in Basingstoke supervising it all. Were they print-ed? No!' He thrust food into his mouth like one starving, carried on talking as he ate. 'Tony'd forgotten to pay the invoice for the last lot of printing so the stuff all sat there waiting. And the bloody-minded sods never sent him a reminder.' He swallowed hard. 'Never said they wouldn't print, either. In the meantime, far as I can make out, Tony put it out of mind and concentrated on creating systems for his new computer – devised, would you believe it, to stop this sort of thing from happening!'

'But are they going to be printed now? Straight away?'

He stopped his piled fork halfway to his mouth and put it down. 'No. That's just the hell of it. What happened is . . . Tony forgot that bill, spent the money on special software for the computer when his own systems wouldn't work and God knows what else. Now all the authors are screaming for their books and we can't get them printed because he's spent us not just up to our overdraft limit but over it and the mean sods at the bank won't play ball.'

'Heavens,' Brozie said. 'That sounds terrible. What will you do?'

'Well, Tony reckons we've been undercharging some of our authors. It's true, too, they're getting their books pre-pared and printed at bargain prices. Hell, we had to undercut the opposition at the start to get the punters. But they'll have

201

to put more money up now.' He filled his mouth with food once more, chewing gloomily. 'Maybe I could persuade the printers to go ahead with a part payment on account – after all, they let us down with sub-standard printing on four books. That cost us. They claim it was Tony's fault, but I reckon with a bit of my clever negotiating I could make them feel guilty and screw a compromise out of them. Once the stuff's published and selling we take twenty-five per cent of what comes in to cover the cost of sales and distribution – that goes to Reflections, our distribution baby, but it'll make the bank feel better; it could come in useful. And I've got an amazing relationship with the bank manager, far better than Tony: I should be able to persuade him to raise our overdraft limit. Trouble is, Tony's probably already gone to him and mucked the whole scene up. In fact I'd take a bet on it they'll be demanding a hefty cheque too. That we're a thoroughly sound venture means nothing to these bank managers. Double hell. They'll just have to sweat for their money if that's the way of it.'

Brozie ate her lamb without tasting it. Poor Charley, so concerned and upset through none of his own fault. He always worked hard and from the start she'd felt uneasy about that partner of his. She struggled to think how she could help him. She was conscious of inadequacy, of a lack of comprehension; though he had been frank in explaining his problems, business finance was to her an incomprehensible maze. Faint threads of thought drifted across her mind, unclear, yet disturbing.

Finally, dishing out apple crumble and custard, she just had to ask: 'Your office development – isn't that nearly completed? You haven't mentioned it and I can't help wondering . . .?'

'Ah, I sold it, Brozie. A bit of luck. It was completed as far as I could go. I'd intended to lease it but in the end it seemed sensible to realise the investment. A chap made me an offer and I closed with it – after I'd negotiated him up a few thousand. With Icarus Publishing on my back I wanted my mind clear. Yes, it was all finalised last week.'

'Oh,' she said blankly. 'Couldn't you put the money from that into the publishing?'

'No,' he said, with a regretful shake of his head, 'no way. I've other demands for what I got on that.'

'You did make a good profit? You should have done, all that work.'

He spread his hands and moved them up and down meaningfully. 'Not so bad,' he said, 'Not so bad. But too many other developers have got in on the act and there's something of a glut. I can't complain though.'

'Oh, good,' she said vaguely. A tremendous idea was forming in her head. 'Charley, why can't I . . . I'd really like it if you'd let me . . . *why shouldn't I invest in your publishing business? Could I?*'

For a long moment he stared at her. Then the familiar enthusiasm lit his face. 'That would be terrific, Brozie,' he said, 'really terrific.'

Chapter 16

Louise groaned as she padded to the bedroom door at five o'clock in the morning of a chilly September day. She was shaky from fright and she felt terrible. At least the howls and shrieks of women in childbirth which had tormented her sleep were unreal – the banshee wails had come from the cat as she demanded entry. Keziah had no time for gentle mews, when she wanted anything she let the world know; Simon reckoned she had Siamese ancestry. As Louise opened the door Kizzy took in the situation, nipped sideways to avoid retribution, broke into fervid purrs and scuttled past Louise to head for the bed.

'You're a horrible cat,' Louise hissed as she flopped back into bed and dragged the duvet up to her throat. 'A pain in the neck, a demanding little beast. I can't think why we put up with you.' Keziah snuggled behind the bend of Louise's knees and her purrs increased in volume till the bed shook. 'Daughter of Job, indeed,' Louise muttered. 'Ruddy cement mixer.' She sipped water from her bedside glass to remove the sour taste from her mouth and composed herself for sleep.

It seemed only seconds later that a crash woke her. She started up to see Kizzy sniffing interestedly at the alarm clock now on the floor.

She shook Simon. 'Kizzy. Your cat. Wants attention. Feed her, for God's sake.'

'Whassa time? Not six yet? She can wait. Go t'sleep!'

Louise rolled over, shut her eyes, prayed for sleep.

It was some sixth sense that alerted her to imminent danger, but she turned just too late to catch the glass teetering at the edge of the beside table: it fell and its contents were flung across her face and all over the pillow.

The worst of it was that Simon laughed; laughed himself silly, gasping what an intelligent, special, amazing cat they had. Louise threw the wet pillow at his head and told him to shut up or they'd be divorced before they were married.

'Sorry, darling, but surely you can see the funny side?' he protested.

'Maybe one day I shall. Not now. I feel too sick. Just feed that awful moggy, will you, and get me a cup of tea and a dry biscuit? This time I know I'm going to die.'

By the time Louise had bathed and dressed she felt, if anything, worse. The tea lay leaden in her stomach and her head ached.

'Don't go to work,' Simon said, hovering by the front door.

'I must,' Louise said. 'Aylmer has an important meeting this afternoon and I'm taking the minutes.'

'Up to you, then. Perhaps you'll feel better soon.' He went.

Louise cursed men, cats, babies and her fretful stomach, and decided to try sitting quietly for ten minutes. She dragged herself to the sofa in the sitting room, sat back and awaited events. Kizzy jumped up beside her.

When she made for the lavatory it was in haste, retching as she ran. Nothing came up. She waited, shivering; the emergency passed. Something nudged her leg; she looked down to see the little grey cat peering up at her. Louise felt unexpectedly warmed and comforted.

'Thanks for your concern, cat,' she said.

Her stomach was marginally better. She remembered she had a lunch date with Josie, now back at work. Louise needed hot career advice and who better to understand her dilemmas? Morning sickness was all in the mind, her mother said: very well, she would command her mind, catch her train and cope with cool competence with all that the day and Aylmer Littlejohn could throw at her.

By exceeding the speed limit all the way she made the train, but had to stand. She glared at the impervious men immersed in their *Telegraphs* and *Expresses* and longed for the day when she would be vast enough to impel the offer of a seat. She thought with loathing of all feminists who had ever refused such offers.

The train clattered, lurched and heaved as it headed for Waterloo; Louise's stomach ignored the commands of her mind and began to lurch and heave with it. She headed with speed for the lavatory. It was engaged, it would be. She rapped on the door. 'Please hurry!'

At last the door opened and a male figure appeared, still ostentatiously zipping itself. 'In a rush, dear?' it leered at her.

Louise's stomach growled. She tried to push the man aside, failed, and vomited down the trousers of the train groper.

Josie, like Simon, laughed at her discomfiture. This time Louise grinned back. 'Served him right, horrible creep.' The occurrence had been unpleasant but her stomach was the better for it, her sense of humour restored.

'So when's your baby due?'

Josie looked different – power dressing, that was it. The black linen suit with its shoulder pads, the crisp white blouse, the swinging leather bag large enough for a notebook, all spoke of the boardroom, all told you to forget her motherhood, here was a woman striding to the top.

'My baby? Next spring. All Fools' Day, I'll bet, in view of today's exhibition. It'll certainly fool around with my life from now on.'

'Not if you organise it on a sound basis. I'm finding the return to work easier than I thought – and, oh, the bliss of mental stimulation after a desert of nappies and wind! I'm even relishing argumentative trustees and stormy meetings. Not that I don't adore my Lucy – you know I do – but I long for her to talk. Well, here's to an easy pregnancy!' She raised her glass and drank.

They were in the same wine bar as on the last occasion they had lunched together, but this time without little Lucy. Louise wondered if she would one day feed a baby in so public a place and failed to visualise the event: she still found it impossible to imagine herself as a mother. Was that normal? To plan for the unimaginable was hard, but plans were essential if her life were not to be wholly disrupted. Childcare was the key. She asked Josie about hers.

'Nanny's wonderful,' Josie said briefly, 'if one can bear the self-righteousness. No question but that I know nothing. Also damned expensive. Worse for you where you live.'

'How do you mean?'

'She'll not just want a car, she'll have to have it, and at your expense. Nannies expect a social life for themselves and their charges, you know. And they're competitive. Our Eunice's last family had a boat on the Hamble and a house in the Dordogne. They holiday'd three times a year, plus skiing. She's slumming it with us.'

'Help!' Louise thought of the superb flat in The Boltons that Josie and her husband inhabited, and winced. A nanny or any baby-minder in Walnut Tree Cottage would be a squash and she'd never budgeted for a car. Did Simon with his accountant's knowledge understand the true expense? Many people managed with an au pair, but Simon had ruled that out. 'Some teenaged girl who can barely speak English? She might be marvellous – but she could equally be murderously inadequate. Not for my child. No way, darling.' To afford the paragon Simon wanted Louise would need promotion and a large rise and her pregnancy would prevent that. And that brought her to something she needed to discuss with Josie.

'You don't think . . . having a child at this stage will mess up my career too much?' She took a deep breath, ventured: 'Do you think I could do well? Aim high?' She longed for this senior colleague to say something bracing and encouraging.

Josie's eyes, clear blue eyes like her Lucy's, examined her thoughtfully. 'Difficult question. How am I to say? You've come to your present position on an odd track, and you've done well. You want me to be honest? You're bright, I don't know about brilliant. I believe you to be sound. Persevering. As yet you lack something. A certain confidence, a certain standing. An aspect missing from your childhood upbringing, perhaps? Maturity may bring it. It's what's lacking in Aylmer to some degree. He appears to have no real conception of himself as one in command, a person of worth. He is ill at ease except with objects, ill at ease in the present. He lives with objects, in the past. There, of course, he is brilliant, untouchable in fact. It's why he is where he is. You have time, my dear Louise. I shall watch your development with interest.'

Louise was taken aback; this damning with faint praise was not what she expected. A barman appeared with their food and fiddled about with cutlery. He gave her time to think. When he left she spoke slowly.

'I appreciate what you say about Aylmer. You've been frank; I'll be frank in return. Josie, it's damned near impossible to display confidence or develop a persona while working with a man who is so insecure in his own ideas and plans that he frequently countermands them. And so . . . absentminded, shall we say? that he forgets to inform me of such changes. It undermines my standing with colleagues. I . . . I've wanted to raise this for some time, but I hesitated, mainly because I hoped things might improve.'

Josie was eating her seafood, her eyes on her plate. Now she lifted her head to give Louise an indecipherable look. 'I think you had better give me chapter and verse.'

For a split second Louise wavered, weighing consequences. 'Don't make waves,' Simon had advised, 'never rock the boat. Sort out disagreements over time.' This she had struggled to do. Aylmer was now more or less under control, never easy, but bearable, just. But recently there had come a change of attitude among those she worked with most closely, nothing specific yet she sensed distrust, saw raised eyebrows, doubtful looks, a tendency to check and double-check her memos, her decisions. She was convinced Aylmer was behind this. With a pregnancy to hamper her, days like today of ill-health and soon the regular hospital appointments at awkward times, minor hiccups and exasperations could become major. Without a friend to back her, she could be swiftly down-graded in everyone's estimation. Trying not to sound paranoid, she told Josie of her problems.

She gave examples of the countermanded instructions, the appointments she made that Aylmer failed to meet, then blamed her for, the interference with her own spheres of

208

work. She ended on a rueful note: 'You know what I've been forced to do for my own protection? I take a formal note of everything decided between us and make him sign it.'

A pause. Josie put down her fork. She remarked in a neutral tone: 'I had heard it was the other way about.'

Louise had begun to eat her own food, now cold: she almost choked. 'I don't believe what I'm hearing . . . just repeat that, will you?'

'He spoke to me of your carelessness and refusal at times to check back on matters that had been queried. He was worried that your move to Hampshire had forced you to over-stretch yourself. He said he was forced to protect himself.'

'But Josie, that's not true!' She was first incredulous, then appalled. She bit back the screams of anger, the desire to throw the cutlery; she waited for her flush of distress to fade. How dare Aylmer tell such a lie? But she must word her rebuttal carefully. 'I think . . . I believe you must have misunderstood him. Aylmer said something like: "I sign a note of what's been decided" and it was natural you should assume it was he who wrote the note.'

'Perhaps.'

Her voice was too neutral, Louise thought sourly; it's Aylmer she believes, not me. 'I can assure you, Josie, it was an idea that came from a solicitor friend when he was speaking of his clients.' She bit the words off one by one. 'The mistakes are not mine.'

Josie said: 'You put me in a difficult position.'

'I see that and I'm sorry for it.' Louise gave her a brief smile and a shrug. She ate a few more mouthfuls of the quiche her empty stomach had been craving not many minutes ago, then pushed it aside in revulsion.

By moving first Aylmer had pre-empted any defence of hers. Was he planning to be rid of her? He disliked her as any man would dislike a person who was intimately acquainted with the mistakes he had managed to shuffle off. Looking back, she saw that she should have been protective of him, foreseeing difficulties and preventing him from making blunders, reminding him at frequent intervals of appointments or deadlines to be met. But she had been accustomed to his predecessor's razor-sharp mind and brisk efficiency.

209

She had expected that the new director would guide and encourage her – though she prided herself upon her competence. That it might be the opposite way round had not occurred to her. But for the first time she was deeply concerned. She had nothing to go on beyond intuition and the faint stiffness and withdrawal she had sensed in her telephone conversation with Josie of a few weeks ago, which today had become so horribly reinforced, but she was certain there was method behind Aylmer's nastiness.

If she made a formal complaint she could only appear paranoid, for to accuse the director of manufacturing false stories to destroy her credibility within the Holbrooke Collection would stretch the belief even of Josie, as she had made clear. There was something Louise had learned in childhood battles: never to show hurt, never to appear weak. If people cannot hurt you, they have no power over you. She would practice stoicism; she would shrug off Aylmer's treachery. She would demonstrate to everyone her full capabilities.

In reply to Josie's query she said: 'No, I won't have a coffee, thank you. Just a glass of mineral water.' Why had she never realised before what nauseating stuff coffee was?

'I didn't care for coffee when I was pregnant,' Josie remarked. 'Specially not in the early months.' Her voice was sympathetic.

In a brilliant flash it came to Louise. Aylmer was being underhand and manipulative, creeping around, sneaking behind her back with lies – the sort of behaviour men alleged against women – well then, she would use sexist ploys herself, she would use her condition and her wedding plans to command sympathy and understanding. If this was war, and a dirty war, she had to counterattack somehow, and these were her only weapons. But she would not be treacherous, she would not be telling lies; her hands would be clean. She had intended to swear Josie to secrecy on her pregnancy, to acknowledge it herself only when it became obvious; moreover she had vowed to tell no one of the wedding to avoid fuss, to continue to call herself Bennett at work. But now everything had changed.

'My early weeks haven't been too bad,' she told Josie.

'This morning was unusual. Anyway, only a week to go and Simon and I are off on holiday to Greece – or rather, on honeymoon. By the time we get back I'll be fine.'

Josie reacted just as she should. Her carelessness in putting down her cup slopped coffee into its saucer. 'Honeymoon?' Her face broadened to a smile, her shoulders under the smart linen jacket relaxed at this new and acceptable line of conversation. 'You're getting married? Just like we did when the infant came. How lovely! Next Saturday? You should have let us all know.'

'It's only recently been arranged. Besides, I didn't want to cause a stir. It'll only be a tiny affair, immediate family and a few friends. But I'd like you and your husband to come. Could you?'

'We'd love to. But any wedding causes work, as I remember all too well. You must be under pressure; you should have let us know. Well now, we must all buy you a present. What would you like? No, I won't embarrass you – I know you well enough to guess your tastes. And, wait a minute . . . it's too late to arrange a party, but how about the staff taking you out for a little celebratory lunch on Friday? No, no argument, I'll definitely lay that on. Heavens, and I thought you the modern sort, as I once was, who'd swear she'd never marry! But we're right, you know, absolutely right. Commitment for the child's sake. Tremendous!'

Louise was hard put to it not to laugh.

Chapter 17

She had no desire to laugh at the Eastons. Louise could never relax happily in the toy strewn muddle of their cottage and this evening was the worst yet. The three boys were out in the evening sun playing some awful yodelling form of obstacle-race over canes and ropes and overturned seats on the lawn, but almost every toy they possessed must have been on the sitting-room carpet. Jack made clear his hatred of this sort of physical muddle by lashing out with his foot at anything that came within reach, finally stooping to hurl several trucks and engines in the direction of a large box and cursing when they missed. Maggie glanced at him. She was clearly on edge herself, but her reaction to his snarls was of a smirking and head-tossing dismissal. Contemptuously she threw a few toys herself, her aim accurate. Then she sat down with an ostentatious air of fatigue.

Jack's good manners prodded him into producing drinks, after which he removed sufficient submachine guns and plastic dinosaurs from a sofa to enable him to drop down beside Louise and ask after her work.

'So so,' she said dismissively.

He pursed his mouth. 'Under pressure, are you? That director of yours? Simon was telling me the other day he's being difficult.'

Before Louise could shrug this off Simon intervened with: 'He's a shocker. Tell Jack what you were told today, darling.'

Louise gulped wine. 'It was nothing, just a bore.' Leave it, Simon.

'No, it wasn't. It's horrific. You could do with advice on how to handle it. Jack, this man Littlejohn has been so erratic she's been forced to get a confirmatory signature from the brute on every decision taken. Today she heard from a senior woman friend that he's putting it about that Louise's inefficiency forced to him devise the notes and signatures for his own protection. Put her in an intolerable position.'

Jack grunted out a few questions, told Louise: 'Trying to be rid of you. Standard sort of ploy.'

'But why the hell should he want to do that?' Simon protested. 'Louise is ruddy efficient. I should know.'

'Afraid she'll show him up? Or maybe he has a friend he wants to slip into the post.'

'Both, I bet,' said Louise with fury. 'He inherited me from his predecessor and he hates my being more effective on the administrative side than him. We haven't got on from day one. He has a wide acquaintance in our world – he'd know dozens of men he'd prefer to work with than me.'

'Precisely. So you're being manoeuvred out.'

'But what you're suggesting,' Simon said, 'well, it's constructive dismissal. Louise could resign and take him to court.'

'You try proving it,' Jack said tersely. 'I don't know that much about employment law, not my scene, but on what you've told me Louise wouldn't have a leg to stand on.'

'So what does she do?'

'Up to her – but protect her back better than she's done till now.'

A glum silence fell in which the boys' voices from the garden sounded raucous and loud. Jack rose, flung wide a window and bellowed. Silence fell within and without. Louise wished they hadn't called; the atmosphere in the house was as electric as an approaching storm; the very air smelt of burning. Pre-dinner drinks, Maggie had suggested, so that they could discuss the wedding, for which she was to organise the food, an idea which filled Louise with gratitude. But it was not the moment for sentimental talk of nuptials. What, she wondered, was Jack so furious about and Maggie trying to brazen out?

Maggie suddenly opened her mouth to say: 'Help, I can smell my dinner ruining itself!' and fled from the room.

The smell of burning had intensified. Louise hastily followed her out.

* * *

213

'Pregnant? You're pregnant? Well!' Louise blew out a long awed breath. 'I suppose you're over the moon? Yes! But what about poor Jack?'

'Rabid with fury!' Maggie splashed water into her burned dry casserole dish, which spat and sizzled violently. She surveyed it with a critical eye, poked the meat about with a spoon. 'That'll be edible, just. I shoved the thing in the Aga when you arrived and left the blasted lid off!'

'Sounds as efficient as your use of contraceptives!' Louise commented tartly, adding: 'And don't change the subject. When's it due? A month or so after mine? Then you must have known for two or three weeks, and Jack's not slow. So what's this evening's row about?'

Maggie eyed her sideways. 'Jack went to the stores for tonics and mineral water and that interfering bitch Nancy Chubb remarked what fun I seemed to have riding around in Mr St George's Porsche. Jack came home and hit the roof.'

'Oh, my God. Of course, you told him it was all Charley's kindness to your boys . . .'

'Of course.'

'And was it?'

'Was it what?' Maggie fenced.

'All kindness.'

'He's a very kind man.' She grinned.

'So it wasn't. I was pretty sure at Charley's party that something was going on – he's nothing if not obvious. But Maggie! Hell, I can't believe . . . The baby – it isn't Charley's, is it?'

'Keep your voice down!' Maggie hissed.

'Is it?'

Maggie looked at her and shrugged. 'How should I know?'

Louise sat down with a bump on a stool and put her head in her hands. 'Oh my God!' she said again. 'Poor old Jack.'

'I told you I'd take a lover.'

'He doesn't deserve this. He really doesn't.'

'I gave him three sons. They're what he wanted – though he'd have preferred them pre-formed at the rugger and cricket stage. Now it's my turn.'

'Suppose it's a boy?' Louise enquired crossly.

'At least it'd be another baby. But it won't be, it'll be a girl. I know it will.' She tossed her head, picked up a notebook and pencil and said bossily: 'Now look, shut up before we're overheard and let's talk about your wedding food. We haven't got much time.'

Louise enjoyed her wedding in the village church of St Swithun and pondered how contrary life could be. Once she had thought it unlikely she would marry, but should she ever be so foolish as to put her life wholly in one man's hands then she would do it at a smart London Registrar's Office, accompanied only by a select band of friends. Now here she was in a mediaeval church, not in white silk or satin, true, but but in an off-white shantung suit, swearing to all sorts of out-dated notions, and somehow, in thrall to the rector's quiet voice, to the centuries-old words, to the still air seething with the scent from Brozie's great vases of flowers and the warmth of many friends – even the sound of her mother snuffling into a handkerchief as the last of her six children stood before the altar failed to annoy her. She stood very still beside Simon, feeling the muscles beneath his sleeve warm against her shoulder, letting the ancient verities of the wedding service impress themselves into her mind, and she felt as she had on the first occasion she had entered this church, that these words and hymns were being absorbed into the beams, into the walls, into every part of the ancient fabric, as similar hymns and services and anthems over hundreds of years had been impressed upon them, to remain there to eternity. And now he and she were a part of that whole. Then as they walked back down the aisle, past the smiling faces and out into the September sun, Louise thought, It's *we* now, *us*; a couple, an entity, how extraordinary . . . but how right.

Watching their guests milling about the cottage and its garden, laughing and talking, Simon found his elated feelings settling in layers.

How pretty Louise looks, how enchanting. My wife.

I wish it were tonight and us in Greece.

. . . *Licence my roaving hands, and let them go,*
Before, behind, between, above, below.

215

Come on brother-in-law, father-in-law, circulate the champagne.

How subtle of Louise to introduce that Josie woman to Arabella Manningford, her fervent admirer.

Food time soon? Better check on the kitchen front . . .

Hell, Charley's in there with Maggie. Divert Jack at all costs!

'Such a handsome house we saw on the way in to Abbotsbridge,' Josie told Arabella. 'Palladian, quite perfect, down an avenue of ancient lime trees. My husband's an architect, but he didn't know of this handsome example. Can you tell me who owns it?'

'Certainly. It belongs to the Manningford family.'

'Oh, but surely you . . .? Then it must be yours? It is! Then I must tell you how much I envy you. I was going to ask whether it was possible to see over it, but I suppose . . .'

'If you have the time to spare, why not come and have tea with us after the reception?' Arabella invited her. 'We enjoy admirers!'

'How very kind. I can think of no more pleasant way to end the day.' Josie was impressed,

'You clearly can't be a local person, you must be one of Louise and Simon's London friends – or are you family?'

'I'm a colleague of Louise's at the Holbrooke Collection,' Josie owned.

'Then *I* envy *you*. We're most impressed with Louise. She and Simon only moved here last winter, yet already Louise has made her mark in the village. Their garden was exhibited to raise church funds in July – did you know that? Yes, coming from what Louise calls purest ignorance she's gained an enormous amount of plant knowledge. We were worried that cack-handed amateurs might ruin what has always been one of Abbotsbridge's treasures, but quite to the contrary, she is building on to what was. And her slide lecture on the Holbrooke Collection to the Women's Institute was a tour de force. They voted hers the best in three years.'

Josie blinked. 'She's a good lecturer.'

'Superb. As for us personally, she's updating the inventory of our furniture in the most efficient way and telling us all sorts of fascinating things about the pieces that we should have known and didn't. She must be a treasure for you, a perfect treasure.'

'I envy you your children,' Charley told Maggie. 'My dream has always been to have a vast family and a loving laid-back wife like you to come home to. Jack doesn't know when he's well-off, doesn't even start. He grumbles at the boys. He tries to clip your wings. I've seen him, I've heard him.'

'Lay off Jack,' Maggie said. She slapped the dog's muzzle away from the table and the food. 'And you can lay off too, Cerberus.'

'Come here, Cerberus,' Charley ordered. He leaned over to pull the dog's ears and massage his shoulders. Cerberus looked blissful. 'He's a super dog. I shall start training him as a gundog soon: the Manningfords and the Colebys are bound to invite me to shoot with them. When I've made my pile I shall have a country estate with shooting and fishing. Then I'll relax, enjoy my family while I'm still young, go to the races, maybe own a race-horse or two for the excitement, perhaps even breed horses. I shall have plenty for the children to ride, that's for certain. Hard work's great when you're young, living in the fast lane, wheeling and dealing. But not when you're over forty, then's the time to relax and enjoy it, with your family, of course. Not to get all sober-sided like poor old Jack, always in a stuffy business suit, counting every penny and fussing over the the cost of education.'

Maggie began removing clingfilm from dishes and bowls of food, comparing his outlook with Jack's as she did so, to Jack's detriment. She glanced at Charley, leaning comfortably against the fridge, untidy even in a suit and tie. To be with him was so easy: all that unruffled calm, the unbothered happiness. Even when Jack was celebrating a success he could never truly unwind, he was always plotting the next move, establishing new contracts, discovering useful facts. Nothing came naturally to him. Charley made more friends just through being Charley.

She sliced garlic bread at speed and said: 'You wouldn't be like Jack, then, horrified at the thought of a further child?'

'No way!' He looked up in shock. 'Are you pregnant then? You are! Christ, it must be mine!'

217

'I don't think so,' she said, shaking her head. 'No, no it isn't!' She retreated back from the table as he came towards her. 'Charley, don't touch me. No! No! Someone'll see. Brozie'll be here in a second.'

'They'll all have to know sooner or later. You're mine now!' He reached for her.

'No!' she said in a low but penetrating voice, shoving him so hard away that Cerberus barked. 'Can't have a scandal on a wedding day!'

That deflected him. He retreated two paces to stand staring at her, grinning his satisfaction. 'I've never got anyone pregnant before. Not that I've been told about. Nice to know the machinery works.'

'You don't know it's yours,' she said in a fierce whisper. 'Now go away, Charley, do. Jack's suspicious. Sharp eyes have seen us together too often. Whose? Who do you think? Nancy Chubb at the store!'

'That marvellous mart for the exchange and evaluation of gossip? No one would seriously credit old Nancy – would they, Cerberus?'

'Trouble is, her information's normally good. They would, they'd love to. Go away, Charley and stay away – and lock Cerberus in your car.'

'The garden looks wonderful,' Louise's mother told her, admiring the vivid blue of ceratostigma against silvery artemesias and red fuchsias. 'I do think you're clever, remembering all the plant names. Don't you, Katie?'

'Mmm,' her sister said, unimpressed. 'I'd loathe all that back-breaking digging myself. How are you going to manage after the baby comes? What with your work and commuting and everything else on top, you'll never see the poor brat, let alone play with it.'

'It does seem hard,' her mother said. 'You mustn't do too much, Louise, Simon wouldn't want you ill from doing too much.'

'I'll manage somehow. It's boredom kills me, not work.'

Kizzy came hopping from one paw to another across the lawn towards them, patting at a late butterfly. It fluttered out of reach; she jumped a lavender bush and tried unsuccessfully to look casual.

'What a pretty cat,' Louise's mother exclaimed. 'Whose is it?'

'Simon's. At least, she came as Simon's but she reckons she's mine.'

'But you've never liked animals,' Katie protested. 'Or babies.'

Kizzy strolled over and wound her way in and out of Louise's legs.

'Not other people's smelly rodents in my bedroom,' Louise told Katie, picking Kizzy up, 'but an intelligent friend like a cat is a quite different proposition. She knows when I'm feeling sick or tired and she sits beside me purring her sympathy.' Kizzy put a paw on Louise's shoulder and looked smug. 'I'm sure one's own baby becomes a friend too.'

'Oh, it does,' her mother said, 'it really does. You always were perceptive, Louise. I'm glad you've seen that.'

Jack was drinking steadily to ease his torment. He was talking, or rather half-listening, to a chap called Austin, Louise's brother, who was in management consultancy, in a senior position for one so young. Seemed he'd done work for some damned big companies, some of national significance. A knowledgeable fellow, worth cultivating. He'd been going round with the champagne, ensuring it flowed as it should. Jack held out his glass for more. 'Thanks!' he said, nodding. Normally he despised champagne, but this was first rate, relaxing him. It eased his temper too that Charley was chatting up one of Louise's sisters instead of chortling in a corner with Maggie. He supposed it was kind of her to have offered herself and Brozie to do the wedding food, but it was a bit off that she'd started appearing at local gatherings in the light of a servant, some waitress or something, rushing about with dishes of food. It denigrated her. And him. And she wasn't even paid for it. Jack wasn't sure whether that was good or bad, but it was a niggling irritation.

The vast, the overwhelming source of his torment was the thought of the coming child. Why hadn't he ignored Maggie's hysterics, had that vasectomy? His finances would never stretch to all the additional expense. Worse was the jeering voice in his head hinting it might not be his. 'Such friends they are,' Nancy Chubb had said in that insinuating voice of hers.

Had they been more than friends? He'd been so careful over contraception she couldn't have become pregnant. Or could she? He'd forgotten to use a condom once: could he have forgotten on another occasion? Maggie said so. She'd teased him about puncturing the beastly things, too. And 'forgetting' her own precautions. What tricks to play on a man! But preferable to giving him another man's child. No, no, he couldn't, he wouldn't believe that. She was his Maggie, his wife, he loved her. Did she still love him? Oh God!

'Give me some more champagne,' he ordered Austin. 'Now, tell me about Pierce & Morgan. Been able to turn them round, have you? I've clients who obtain component parts from them . . .' One worthwhile thing about champagne, it loosened people's tongues.

'Amazing food, terrific champagne,' Charley said happily to James Manningford. 'Just the sort of send off I'd like one of these days.'

'Planning to marry, are you?'

'Could be. I rather fancy myself as a family man. I'm getting to the age when I ought to settle down.'

'Well, The Old Barn's big enough for a family. But talking of The Barn, Charley, that cheque you said you sent us never arrived. I know the post's not brilliant . . .'

'It's ruddy awful. I'm sure I did send it – I remember writing it . . . But anyway, there's absolutely no problem now – I've got a backer. Yes, Icarus Publishing is being re-vitalised, underwritten, money no object. God's in His Heaven, all's right with the world. I'll write you a cheque right now. Oh, no, I can't, left the old cheque book at home.'

'Never mind,' James said hastily. 'Quite the wrong time. Just let us have it when you're passing. Oh, hello, Kizzy, you're looking very well.'

'One of the most delightful weddings I've been to,' Josie said to Louise as she kissed her goodbye. 'Such a charming village setting, such a pretty garden, such lovely people. Now, have a good relaxing honeymoon. I'm sure the fortnight off will restore you to your old competent self and we can look forward to seeing you back.'

220

Chapter 18

As a fine September gave way to a damp October Jack fought with contrary feelings. He found it impossible to make up his mind about his wife's behaviour. Outwardly he went about his daily life as if all were normal, his face without expression, but inwardly he continued to be torn with pain and suspicion and jealous love. In the great game of life he had prided himself on being ahead; now he found himself a loser, and a loser in the most vital and fundamental sense. Most of the time he could convince himself that Maggie would never have succumbed to Charley's blandishments, but that she could have cheated him, Jack, for a second time over the conception of a child, devastated him. Maggie had scorned his beliefs, his caution; she had made fools of them both. He cursed the personal fulfilment movement that had always attracted her, the fanaticism for self-affirmation at every level, no matter what the costs to others. But the baby must be his own, it must. The infidelity had been mental, not physical. He was not the sort for seething jealousies simply because some gossiping village woman made remarks that hurt, madness lay that way. Nevertheless, others of a malicious persuasion might find enjoyment in mouthing similar inuendoes.

He must stop Maggie seeing Charley, scotch the rumours. The man's whole way of life was hazardous, ridiculous. What had that woman from Andover said of it? A roller-coaster ride. Jack pondered. Publishers he'd known were quiet fellows, not loud-mouths who boasted of endless dramas, high flights of success or terrible let-downs; they were not seen flashing vast untidy rolls of notes, they paid with discreet credit cards. It might be worthwhile to enquire into Charley's financial standing and his antecedents through certain of Jack's contacts. At his office the next morning he made telephone calls, arranging to meet two chaps for lunch, a third for a round of golf at the weekend.

Afterwards he set out his work on his desk, but he had seldom been less inclined for concentration. The day was grey and felt as though it had been so forever; rain blew intermittently against the window. The year was moving towards winter. He was cold. When he attempted to write his fingers felt stiff, his stomach hurt and his mouth was dry. He managed to do what he must, but from time to time he found himself staring out at the rain and wondering why fate had sent him such afflictions. He did not go out for lunch as was his normal habit, but sent for sandwiches, and the taste and the texture of them in his mouth was repellent so that he had to force himself to eat.

He could not bear to live with suspicions, could not bear the sound of his own voice, raging, harsh, using words that were meant to stab and leave a lasting sting. It was terrible to have made Eddie cry out to him to stop, sobbing, sobbing.

Maggie had not stabbed back. She had teased, mocking him. 'So I went to the races with him? A half a day of fun, in a public place. You have female clients, you're closeted all afternoon with them in your office, do you roll around on the carpet?'

'And seen in his car, time after time?'

'I like his car. So does Toby, he thinks it's great.'

'Leave the boy out of this!'

'But I can't, he was in it, every time! We all had fun. Don't make such a meal of things, Jack. Throw off that old school tie, unbutton that stuffy shirt, loosen up!'

He had been exasperated to find her so unconcerned, shaking with a fury that led him to shout at her for a self-absorbed fool who cared nothing for his position or his feelings, who undermined all he was striving to achieve for her and the boys, who'd drive him into bankruptcy with her greed for babies. Yet even while he was shouting and Eddie crying a part of him was reassured – mockery was hardly the reaction of a guilty woman.

Perhaps if the family were to show a cheerful solidarity no one would believe the Chubb woman's insinuations. He must give nothing away, not make himself a laughing stock. He remembered from his schooldays a line by Thomas Hardy: 'We probably wouldn't worry about what people think of us if we knew how seldom they do.' And now there was the unborn child to consider. He flexed his aching shoulders as though to ease a great burden they carried. He swallowed the last corners of bread, washing them down with bitter black coffee. Then, wearily, he concentrated on the disputed clauses of the contract before him.

By three o'clock the rain had lessened and the clouds were lighter. Jack saw how in places the wind was tearing them apart to reveal a smeared blue lining. A watery sun blinked over Basingstoke's wet roofs. At four o'clock he stopped work; the sunlight was clear and steady and he had had enough. Eddie possessed a big new kite, a recent birthday present; they could go to the common to fly it. It would be something to do together – though it was a pity Hugh couldn't be there. Still, his masters were pleased that he had settled so easily at prep school. Maggie had made more fuss about his going than Hugh had.

As Brozie poured her first glass of wine each evening she was prone to ruminate on how different her life had become from anything she could possibly have visualised in the last twenty years. The narrow bounds against which she had struggled with barely visible results (permission, grudgingly given, to run the church flower rota or the local flower show), had been replaced overnight by wide horizons against which she saw herself poised in the style of some film star of her youth, irradiated by sunlight after her tribulations, taking her first steps on the road to some glorious future. Brozie's future was a partnership in a publishing business. She sipped wine and rolled the words over her tongue. A business partner. A sleeping partner, that man Tony called it, but Brozie had no intention of sleeping. She was waking up to new possibilities. She would become a reader on the fiction side, subjecting the typescripts to a rigorous examination, dissecting their authors' plots, their structure and their style of writing. She would visit the offices regularly, ask to see their accounts and discuss them with the accountant. It was all coming to her now in her fifties: Icarus Publishing and Reflections. She felt she knew this new life, had known it for ever; it was her birthright that had been stolen from her and now was returned. Her father had always said she was intelligent and would make a good businesswoman; she'd wanted to help Hubert, but he had never so much as contemplated the thought. She had gone over the Icarus accounts with Charley's accountant, an earnest young woman, and she had spoken to the bank manager at length. He had congratulated her on her sense in examining this new project in detail. More importantly, he had said: 'I am satisfied the businesses are viable or I would never have allowed the overdrafts to run on so long.' Brozie toasted her future.

It was pure chance that Louise entered Josie's room at the time she did. It was her third day back at work and she needed to discuss the Renaissance Exhibition planned for next March, the pictures, the statues, various artefacts. She was determined to keep Josie briefed on its progress, both as a subtle compliment to a probable future director and to ensure an ally against Aylmer's sly warfare. She found the room empty, the desk clear but for Josie's open desk diary. Was she away for a meeting, a day, or longer? Louise peered. 2.30. Monthly Meeting? But that had been scheduled last January for each first Thursday, not Wednesday – help! as it had been here, Thursday scribbled out. Louise flashed a glance at her wrist: 2.40. She rushed to her room, seized a file from its cabinet, reached the door, stopped, turned for something else which she ran to grab, then headed for the Conference Room, anger mounting. She was secretary to this particular committee, due to take the minutes. How could the meeting have been re-scheduled without anyone informing her?
Faces were raised, necks swivelled round as she stalked in. The faces were reproachful, stern, mouths were pursed.
Louise pitched her voice loud and clear: 'I am most sorry

224

to be late,' she said, 'but I have to say that my discovery of the change of date was purely fortuitous, a bare three minutes ago.'

Eyes examined her and passed on to Aylmer.

'I did inform you,' he said on a gently forebearing sigh.

The eyes returned. 'No,' she told them, 'I was not informed.'

'I pencilled it into your diary,' Aylmer said quietly.

'No such entry is in my diary,' Louise returned equally quietly.

Aylmer shrugged. 'Well, there's no way we can check your desk diary now. We were late starting, waiting for you . . .'

Louise pulled the desk dairy from the file, opened it and showed the page to the two people sitting nearest, Josie and a senior curator called Matthew Rider.

'No entry for today's date,' Rider said, and Josie nodded.

'Thank you,' said Louise. 'I felt I should make that point.' She sat down, the open diary pushed out in front of her so that others could see. 'Well, shall we get on with the meeting?'

It was with distaste that Louise left the Holbrooke Collection three hours later to make her way back to Hampshire. A fretful wind was twirling dead leaves and shreds of rubbish beneath a dark and lowering sky, and by the time she was halfway to the underground station lancing rain was cutting her face with icy blades and making rats' tails of her hair. She struggled through the pushing ill-tempered crowd, buffeted and shivering. A memory of the monthly meeting blew across her mind.

'A bit pointed in there, weren't you?'

'I had to pin Aylmer down, Josie.'

'Did it matter that much? You were only ten minutes late.'

'I refuse to suffer for his mistakes.'

'Airing minor disagreements in public will hardly convince him of your merits.'

It was not the point. Aylmer knew her merits; he wanted to deprecate them, to denigrate her. His cunning was endless, his spite could never be countered. It gave her no help to protest now, if protesting itself was an offence. The brief flare of her triumph was dead. Feeling cold and wretched she let herself be carried downward on the packed escalator into the dusty grey bowels of the underground. This was not how she had seen her career developing last January. Then she had been confident, picturing her future as a figure of rising importance in her world, known for her professional acumen as well as for her capacity to share with an audience the range and profundity of her knowledge, in lectures that sparkled with wit and perspicacity and taste. She had visualised writing articles for glossy journals, even lecturing on television. With her developing success she could have afforded the expensive and elegantly understated clothes that subtly underlined it. To fit a baby and a nanny into such a life – in London, as she had thought – could have been smoothly achieved.

The platform was crowded and grew more so as she waited, back aching, head beginning to throb. She stared hopelessly along the dark tunnel beyond her. She was not living in London, but in Hampshire, facing as always at the day's end the stresses and traumas of commuting. If she continued to work she would have no time or energy for Simon or the baby, nor would she gain financially by her endeavours. She had done her sums now: the costs of the train and a nanny and the car she'd need would take almost every penny of her salary. Nor could she claim anything back against tax. Louise loved the country life now, she loved the cottage and her garden, full this month of asters and chrysanthemums, brightly coloured berries and leaves. But what benefit could she expect from it?

The train came at last, a blast of dry air preceding it, blowing her damp hair against her cheek. A surge of humanity carried her on and wedged her in its midst, pinning her between cursing men who jammed their briefcases and their umbrellas into her spine, and worse, her precious belly. Commuting in bad weather was hell and winter was coming. From now on she would travel to and fro in darkness and rain, seeing Abbotbridge only at weekends. The thought was depressing; the energy she needed to drive her on was nearly gone. Why had that maniac Charley told her commuting was a rest-cure and betrayed her into this misery?

She hung on to a strap, swaying with the train. If Aylmer could work with her in harmony, if he came to depend on her, it would all be worthwhile. Hell, was she asking for the moon? If he simply accepted her presence and let her get on with it, that would be sufficient – but he never did. Jack was right: Aylmer planned to be rid of her; he probably already had some man friend lined up for her place. He knew nothing of her baby yet: she anticipated his reaction and flinched in advance.

She could leave work, of course, and please Simon by remaining at home for the next few years; she could deal with nappies and iron little clothes and clean shelves and talk endless baby-talk . . . All those things she'd vowed she'd never do. Whatever she did, she saw, she'd be savaged by the usual female guilt: guilt at wasting her degree, her expensive training, her career opportunities, or guilt at neglecting her husband and baby, the cottage and the garden. Neither course was fit to be contemplated. The train headed into darkness, taking her spirits with it.

At Waterloo she hurried along the platform, her eyes searching the crowded train for an empty seat. Suddenly there was a banging sound and she heard her name bellowed:

'Louise! Louise! Over here!' Charley St George was behind a window, mouthing and waving. 'Had to come up for the day and I thought I might see you,' he said complacently. 'So I saved you a seat.'

'Thank God,' she said, collapsing beside him. 'I'm finished, I never could have stood all the way.' She divested herself of wet scarf and gloves, disposed of her briefcase on the floor. 'Why did you tell me commuting was restful? Is life worth this fearful waste of time?'

'Disenchanted?'

'Entirely. Every damned aspect.'

'But I thought you revelled in your work?'

'I did. I still could do. But I loathe commuting and I loathe my boss still more.'

'Giving you hell? What's he done?'

She told him briefly and he responded with suitable indignation.

'Stupid bastard. What a creep. You shouldn't stand for it.'

'I don't if I can help it. But too often I can't. He's the Director, he's God in our small world.'

'Then you should get out. Resign. Tell your Director where he can stuff his job! That's what I'd do. You shouldn't go on commuting now you're pregnant, anyway. Bad for you, Louise, bad for the baby.'

'Resign myself to domesticity? Horrors! I've never been that sort. Work locally? Not a chance. My line of work is highly specialised – London specialised.'

He looked non-plussed, unusual for Charley. 'You're doing that inventory for Arabella Manningford. Couldn't you find more of the same?'

'Most unlikely. Arabella's is a one-off.'

'She thinks you're ace,' he observed. He dug in his battered briefcase for a greaseproof paper packet, extracting from it a vast pastry concoction smothered in raisins and sticky sugar.

'She's pretty knowledgeable herself.' Louise watched in fascination.

'My treat after a hard day!' Charley said, pulling off a glutinous chunk and pushing it at Louise.

The train started with a jerk. To her surprise Louise found herself accepting the offering, even enjoying its dripping sweetness. She licked her lips and sucked her fingers with a childlike satisfaction.

'Good, hm? Feeds the brain when the blood-sugar level is sinking. Now the ideas'll start to flow towards a job you could do.'

He settled his big body more comfortably in his seat and folded his hands across his substantial middle. A blur of suburban houses flashed beyond his head, blue slate roofs giving way to ruddy tiles, terraces to semi-dets; gardens became larger, autumn colours flickered.

Louise shifted uneasily in her seat. In Aylmer's latest plot, in his silences and evasive eyes today, she had seen depths of antipathy that had no connection with his need for an administrative scapegoat. There was a corrosive chemistry between them that could not be slaked by any show of efficiency or helpful efforts on her part, something that brought out all his innate misogyny. He and Josie could tolerate each other because their spheres of work rarely overlapped; a toadying minion of a typist would be beneath his disdain, but she, feminine Louise, working at close quarters, inextricably interwoven in his days, was his hair-shirt in these days of political correctness; someone he could not shift, an unbearable irritation. Her hopes that her pregnancy would bring support now seemed ill-founded; this afternoon her colleagues had looked sideways in embarrassment. Simon had always assumed that she would abandon her work for their children's years of infancy; she had thought in terms only of her statutory leave of absence. With everything combining against her his option began to look the more beguiling. Yet it was not what she wanted.

'I have it!' Charley exclaimed, making her jump. 'You open an antique shop, no, an antiques gallery, and combine it with a picture gallery. Sell both in the same space and double the profits. How's that?'

'Alluring,' Louise admitted, 'but I've no money.'

'You could find a backer, borrow from the bank. Or you could sell your clients' stuff on a commission basis. I had a girlfriend who did that. No need for any investment, she simply raked in the dosh when the stuff sold. Just think about it, Louise – and listen to this . . .'

She had the specialised knowledge, she had the skill and the taste. Charley created a picture in her mind of beautiful rooms in an old building in Winchester, the lettering on the shopfront a dignified gold on deepest blue, faded carpets of a bygone era on the floors – 'You'd sell those too, of course!'; each room furnished with antiques from whose patinas elegant lamps would draw deep and subtle gleams; pictures on the walls in regularly changing exhibitions, pieces of porcelain placed here and there as in a real house – 'No jostling junk shop look' – the total effect one of timeless charm and style.

She saw it; she saw it all. The parties every two to three months that would inaugurate the latest exhibitions of pictures, with well-dressed clients and dealers sipping from tall glasses – 'Pimm's and champagne in the summer,' said Charley, 'and mulled wine for Christmas and the New Year!' – and circling the room in that state of delicious inebriation that would assuredly draw forth a rash of red spots upon the pictures and sales for the alluring objets d'art and the furniture. She saw how the fame of her shows would grow, drawing more and more buyers reassured by her excellent taste and her expertise. There would be something to suit everyone: special exhibitions of modern oil colours and acrylics by famous local names, at other times country views within the county, or Victorian cottage and farm pictures, or recent water-colours, or ... or valuable prints from Georgian and Regency times. There would be furniture that would be of use as well as beauty. And couples who were drawn in by one item would stay to look at others ... and buy ... and buy.

Louise was excited by all the ideas, caught up in Charley's flights of fancy into a wonderful dream; they had arrived at their station almost before she knew it. But behind the fantasy was always the knowledge of its unrealisable nature. As they walked to the car park she told him so.

'But I have no money, Charley, and neither has Simon. We've put our everything into the cottage, and more. We have to play catch-up now.'

'I think I could find you a backer,' he said, looking both mysterious and complacent. 'Perhaps even two. I always know useful people, and I can use my powers of persuasion. Don't give up the idea yet – you never know. Oh, and Louise, be a love and give me a lift back. The Landrover's electrics are lethal – I've to sort them at the weekend – and the Porsche's in dock for a big service.'

'Sure,' she said, unlocking the car. 'Hop in.'

'Stop at Brozie's, would you? She's had Cerberus for the day. I'll pick him up and take him home on foot. We'll enjoy the walk together now the rain's stopped.' He swung his bulk into the car and the entire vehicle seemed to shudder.

'Does Brozie have the dog every day?' She nosed the car out.

'Heavens no! Poor love. No, just when I've no car. I can't lug him around on tubes and buses, you see.

'No. Of course not. What were you doing today? How's the publishing world flourishing?'

'Today I had a meeting with some fool woman who's

230

making a fuss about a book of poetry we published for her. One of those idiots who change their minds twenty times about what they want and then blame you when it goes wrong. And expect you to pay for it. This one's talking about lawsuits, but we know she hasn't a leg to stand on. The solicitor and I sorted her out, I reckon.' For a moment he sounded tired and dispirited, then he revived: 'Still, overall we're doing well. Orders coming in, books rolling out . . . We've been stunningly busy this month. My partner, Tony, he's had to slave on into the evenings. He's moaning about it, but I've told him to shut up if he wants to make big money. We've the chance now and there's no lack of authors out there. We've a new writer, Sammy Squire, who Tony's tremendously excited about. I haven't read him yet, but he does thrillers. His first won a prestige prize but his stupid publishers turned down his next two so now he's turned to us – Tony couldn't put his latest typescript down, read on till four in the morning. That shows you.'

Louise rolled her window down and inhaled the soft newly-washed Hampshire air that rushed in. It was chilly but sweet, scented faintly with apples and grass and damp leaves, specially welcome after the stuffy train and the dank smell of London.

'Do you read everything you publish too?'

'No. Impossible. I read some, dip into others. Poetry never. I'm a doer, not a reader. I haven't the time. I leave it to Tony; he's the one who knows.'

'But not the one to sort out your legal problem today? I thought you were the marketing man. Wouldn't that be his side of the house?'

'Suppose so,' Charley admitted. 'Still, I always do it because he hasn't the time. Besides which he's a hell of a temper when someone tries to play him up or take him for a ride. He's a bright lad and he can't understand why others don't see things as sharply as he does. Me, I've the tact and the charm. So I sort the trouble-makers out. Give them a bit of soft soap, you know! Then we can reach a compromise – without giving anything away.'

'Oh,' said Louise. 'Ah. Yes, I see.'

At Brozie's house she dropped him off.

He got out, straightened himself, then stuck his head back in the car, stooping his great body awkwardly. 'Thanks for the lift, Louise. Don't you dare give up on our brilliant ideas,' he told her. 'I'll be speaking to a potential backer tonight and I'm ready to bet that within ten days or a fortnight we'll have something satisfyingly concrete thrashed out.' The door of the house opened and Cerberus hurtled out to greet his master with barkings and leapings around and yelps of delight. Charley fended him off as he concluded: 'You hang on – I reckon this is one of my most brilliant schemes yet. I wish I had the money for it. Still, I'll be your marketing adviser, okay?'

'Right!' she said, laughing as he struggled to extricate himself and calm Cerberus's ecstasies. 'That's agreed. 'Bye, Charley!'

The telephone rang just as Louise was leaving the house for the train next morning.

'It can't be for me,' she told Simon. 'You take it!' But nevertheless she hung on in the cottage doorway, poised to dash off.

'It is for you,' he called from the sitting-room. 'Arabella Manningford.'

'Oh? Odd, at this hour.' She picked up the telephone. 'Hello?'

'Good morning, Louise. I'll try not to keep you long but I thought I must say a few quick words about this antiques and picture gallery idea. Do you know, I'm distinctly taken with it! Charley St George was rather persuasive last night and I am looking for something I can take a proper interest in – the hands-on approach he calls it – rather than dull old stocks and shares to invest my poor old mother's money in. How hooked are you on the proposition?'

'I . . . I was taken by it,' Louise replied, struggling for breath. 'But I've no capital at all.'

Arabella brushed that aside. 'I thought about it all last evening after Charley rang me, and I must admit I was thrilled. I've always been fascinated by antiques and pictures, and with your knowledge of the stuff and your administrative ability – well, I don't see why it shouldn't work rather well, do you? I decided to sleep on the matter and let the cold light of day do its work, but d'you know, I woke up even more set on it. A partnership. How about your coming round this evening after dinner for coffee and a drink or two? We could mull it over. You will? Good. See you at about nine. 'Bye.'

Louise put the telephone down, her skin prickling with growing excitement, and turned to face Simon. 'I think you'd better drive me to the station yourself this morning so we can talk. Charley came up with an idea on the train last night that I thought was pretty good, but as it needed a great deal of capital investment, I dismissed it as pie-in-the-sky Charley-talk, despite his contention that he could find me a backer. Now it seems he has and we'd better discuss it as we go so that you, too, can mull it over – with your accountant's mind, my darling.'

The following morning as she drove off towards the train she found that the excitement of Charley's richly painted ideas and Arabella's enthusiasm, together with the sunshine and the scents of the autumn morning, sparkling and fragrant and fresh, made her feel as though she were dancing to the sound of violins.

The wine that she had drunk the night before, instead of making her feel sleepy and dull, had left her with a sense of amazing clarity, a stimulus not only to her senses but to her thoughts. She drove along the valley with the car window half-open and the passing trees held great strength, the bird-song had an almost unearthly beauty, and the wind caressed her cheek. All contributed to confirm that providence had her in its grasp, that she could create in her life a changed and richer pattern and become a new achieving woman, one who could combine children and a career successfully and on her own terms. She and Arabella Manningford would form an excellent partnership; their strengths and shortcomings would complement each other; they would compete with the best in the land. There would be no commuting, no awful Aylmer, no testy curators, no argumentative workmen. The stresses she had been subjected to would be eliminated and her days would become more complete and content than it would be possible to imagine. Looking at the flaming colours of the beech trees, the fields of stubble and the rising line of the downs, she felt that she could apprehend God.

Chapter 19

As October approached November, Maggie, unable to sink into the condition of blissful contentment normal to her when in a pregnant state, found herself instead battling with layers of unease. Jack, normally the most predictable of men, had become suddenly unaccountable, one day almost rabid with jealousy of Charley or any other man who happened to talk and laugh with her, the next abnormally helpful and affectionate, even perceptive enough to replace blown light bulbs, oil the groaning front door, or take the boys kite-flying, acts previously never performed without the endless reminders that he called nagging. Never having had cause to wonder before, she pondered what was in his mind. Charley, too, and more worryingly, was being erratic. To be wayward was natural to him, but this was not the normal eccentric Charley, this was a driven man. The tribulations and calamities that had struck his publishing firm from time to time now appeared to have been eliminated: at least they were no longer mentioned. He informed her instead that Icarus Publishing had a backer, a woman, wealthy and deeply admiring of what they had achieved, who would enable Charley and his partner to break into new areas, to grow and compete at ever high levels. But since Maggie had so stupidly let out to him that she was pregnant, the light-hearted affair she thought she was running so cleverly had on his side turned into a runaway passion. He desired her wholly for himself, he wanted his child: she must leave Jack immediately and bring the boys with her to live in The Old Barn.

He was enamoured of a picture of himself with a ready

made family and more to come. They would have dogs and ponies and a parrot in the Victorian bird cage. He would be the perfect stepfather and teach her sons to fish and shoot and play cricket; he dismissed the very idea of any difficulties. The boys had told him that he was more fun than their father, and now, with his firm poised for success, he could take on the fantastic trio as his responsibilities, pay for education, for sports training, for innumerable holidays abroad and school trips. The world was his oyster and he would make it theirs also. Maggie was terrified that his insistence on realising this alluring dream would be the force that would wreck her own plans. She had intended to brush Charley off once her own need was fulfilled, sure that he would shrug in his normal good-natured way and disappear to chase some new young Melody, but Charley had deep needs that drove him as ruthlessly as ever Maggie's had. His fantasies were all consuming, nothing would persuade him to abandon them; pushing him from the door when he turned up, terrifyingly, at dinner time, hanging up when he telephoned at midnight, repeating innumerable times when he caught up with her in the village: 'No, Charley, no!' served only to ratchet up his enthusiasm. The consumption of nervous energy necessary to deal with him left her exhausted and bad-tempered with Toby and Eddie, which in turn meant that they whined and squabbled under her feet, competing for the attention she was too drained to give, yet again infuriating Jack.

When she turned to Louise for sympathy she found none.

'You were playing with fire. Why start in the first place? Oh, no, sorry, stupid question. Maggie's special needs.'

Maggie expostulated: 'Most men take lovers for recreational purposes and keep it on that level – I thought with Charley I'd be safe from involvement.'

'You did it for procreational purposes and now you are involved. Work it out for yourself, but do it quickly and cleanly before you hurt poor old Jack worse than he's been hurt already.'

'Jack hurt? How's he hurt? He doesn't know anything. But he wouldn't give me my baby. That hurt. I've a right to control my own life and my choices. And I have.' Her plump body heaved with indignation; she burst out: 'Don't turn self-righteous on me just because you haven't the courage of your own convictions. I've come to know your Simon better since you moved to Abbotsbridge. He's patronising and demanding and you give in to him all the time – moving to Hampshire, gardening, taking on that cat, having a baby when *he* chooses, not you. Now you're planning to leave your job – your real career – because it's what he's subtly manoeuvred you into seeing as necessary. Oh, sure, he's kind and helpful on the surface, but in essence he's a spoilt brat. Why don't you take a stand?'

'If I do give up working for the Holbrooke Collection it will be on my own decision,' Louise pointed out, taken aback by Maggie's attack. 'It has nothing to do with Simon.'

'Rot. In advancing his own career he'd made your previous way of life impossible. Under his charm there's an inner core of resistance. He never reaches a compromise. Don't just blame Aylmer Littlejohn for your predicament – you say he's a woman-hater, but aren't all men at heart? Look at Hubert Hamilton, look at James Manningford, at Harry Coleby, or Jack or Simon. Most of all at Simon. Which of them has made sacrifices for his wife's sake? Real sacrifices, I mean, not just cooking the occasional casserole or agreeing to their wives doing a little unpaid work for the local community?'

Louise was sitting on a stool amid the usual clutter of Maggie's kitchen. It was always simpler for her to visit Maggie than the other way about because of the small boys. She pushed away a crumpled half-deflated balloon, the remains of a bread roll, a Thomas the Tank Engine comic and a half-eaten pear from before her on the table and planted her elbows there instead, clasping both hands round a cup of Maggie's herbal tea. She said mildly: 'You're muddling conscious manipulation with normal selfishness and the desire for an easy life – characteristics of both sexes, incidentally.'

An infuriating retort. But true. Maggie grinned and shrugged, the momentary burst of annoyance with Louise for being so weak dying in her. She had been proud of having a friend who lectured at the Holbrooke Collection, pleased that

236

Jack admired her too; he did not favour all her acquaintance as he did Louise. Having no desire to copy her achievements, Maggie had felt no jealousy, only respect. Now she felt let down. To her exasperation Jack even admired Louise for her projected change of course, pronouncing it sensible; he wished his own wife could have a similar offer to work with a woman of position and attainments like Arabella Manningford. Maggie looked through the window at her autumn garden, at her sons fighting like puppies on the damp grass, at the apple trees under which she had put her babies in their prams to sleep, where once Felicity had cooed at the fluttering leaves above. When spring came with all its delicate greens and whites there would be another baby there. Could anything be more important?

Louise prodded: 'If you think so little of men then why get married? And why Jack?'

Maggie snorted. 'Apart from babies I married Jack precisely because he was so four-square stolid and solid. I didn't want the messy divorce my parents had that left me and my brother feeling lonely and rejected. Mark went with Dad, I stayed with my mother, and the levels of guilt and resentment between us all was terrifying. Perhaps I was the victim of my past, but I wanted safety. In the end I got too much – I was suffocated by it.'

'But now you want it back again?'

'Oh yes. Every creature wants security when it's nesting!'

The opening was irresistible. 'A cuckoo's egg?' Louise jibed.

'Oh God, shut up, will you? Here, let me pour you some more of my special tea. Good for both our eggs!'

Hell, she refused to be pushed into guilt feelings for what she had done. Being with Charley had been great, a fun time, a time out of life, and now she was having her baby and that was great too. She kept a closed mind about who the father was: it was Jack's to bring up – it was his.

Toby came running in howling, flung himself at his mother and buried his head in her shoulder. Eddie followed more slowly, looking apprehensive.

'He hit me!' Toby sobbed, lashing out with his foot as his brother drew near.

There was a red mark on his cheek and Eddie looked undeniably guilty. Both were muddy and the top button had been ripped from Eddie's shirt. Maggie looked at them with disfavour. They had been aggressive and male and horrible all morning, playing man-eating dinosaurs, roaring and yelling and squabbling. She had bundled them up in old clothes and pushed them outside to work off their excess energy and the result was this.

'Did you?' she asked Eddie.

'He bit me!' Eddie said anxiously. His thick socks were concertinaed round his ankles. He indicated a faint mark on a calf that might have been toothmarks.

'I was a tyrannosaurus,' Toby protested, smearing mud across his cheek as he knuckled his eyes. 'He was only an iguanodon, so I had to eat him. I was only pretending. He's a baby.'

'You're the baby,' Eddie retorted. 'You cried 'cause I shoved you off. I never hit him, Mummy, I never did!'

'You're both horrible noisy monsters,' Maggie adjudicated firmly. She got up to find a flannel at the sink. This she wetted with a jet of cold water from the tap, then held each of them in turn to rub briskly and without sympathy over faces, hands, knees and calves. 'Ow!' they shrieked. 'That's cold!'

'Cool you off,' Maggie said, mopping at mud stains on little jackets and trousers.

Louise stood, drained her tea which tasted more of wet straw than the products of the herb garden, and said she must go.

'Then we'll walk you home,' Maggie said. 'Down by the river, I think, don't you? Let the boys rush about and rid themselves of some of their excess energy. Wellies, Toby, Eddie. Fast!'

The leaves of the gnarled old willow that wept over the river were curled and yellow and the trees in the nearby spinneys had changed colour too, groups of trees standing out more clearly than in summer, every species with its own colour, gold or coppery orange, and every shade of brown from raw sienna to burnt umber, only a few still lingering in the dusty

238

dark green of late summer. Small stirrings of breeze fluttered their leaves, breaking them here and there from the branches to come spiralling down through the broken sunlight beneath. 'A leaf caught before it touches earth brings a month of luck and mirth!' Maggie called, and the two small boys darted around and around, hands outstretched, but just as they thought to grasp them the leaves twisted and fluttered aside, causing squeals of excitement and frustration.

'Got one – oh no, it's gone – naughty leaf . . . Oh, I've caught it! It nearly hit the ground, but I caught it, Mummy. Look Louise, I caught it!'

'Well done, Toby! Put it in your pocket for safety and catch another.'

'I've got three!' Eddie boasted, hurling himself sideways over the tussocky grass as a golden beauty flipped tantalisingly away from him.

Caught up in the challenge, Maggie and Louise joined in, laughing and panting and colliding over the elusive leaves, giving their spoils to the two boys. 'There, now you've both won yourselves luck till May!'

There was a wonderful sweetness in the breeze. As Louise breathed she felt it turn inside her into happiness that swelled and blossomed in her chest. She wanted to run and kick like the boys; she wanted to dance. Over the last two or three weeks she had hesitated to commit herself to Arabella Manningford, testing Charley's ideas against tough realities, looking at prices, checking figures, talking to dealers she knew through the Holbrooke, careful always to give nothing away. Arabella Manningford had understood, had not pushed her. 'It's easy for me,' she said, 'provided that I accept the rôle laid down for me. I'm not faced with all your choices, not since I made the original choice to marry James. But you, at a crossroads, how do you choose one direction rather than another?'

Now, without conscious thought, but as if in receipt of some strange revelation, Louise knew that she would leave the Holbrooke Collection and go into partnership with Arabella. Walking through the autumn morning sunshine, watching the small boys in the shallows of the river stamp their boots to send fountains of gleaming droplets up through the pellucid air, she felt an astonishing sense of freedom. Her future, wide and expansive, paraded before her. She and Arabella would work excellently together; their minds moved on similar lines, their tastes coincided. She saw in vision the interior of Abbotsbridge House, the great hall, the drawing-room, the library, the dining-room, the way Arabella had used wall coverings, curtains and upholstery fabrics in soft yet happy colours that seemed to suggest sunshine on the most bleak days, while even to Louise's eyes, accustomed to the magnificent pieces displayed at the Holbrooke Collection, the furniture was something special. Each time she went to the house she was awestruck afresh at seeing cabinets and tables and chairs of such quality looking natural and right in a private setting, a startling contrast with the museum background in which she saw them daily. Arabella's knowledge, while not so detailed as Louise's, was extensive: she had lived all her life among things of beauty and value and she had an instinctive feeling for the good and the great. She was sharp-witted too, and crisp of decision. She would never work in the shop, she said, but she would thoroughly enjoy the interest of the business and would find it stimulating to search for pieces to sell, to attend auctions, to go to country house sales, to bid at Sotheby's. They would never grow rich on the proceeds of their work, they had agreed, not in the current climate, but the rewards should be adequate to keep them happily in business.

As she strolled along the meadow towards Walnut Tree Cottage Louise began thinking aloud about the nanny problem. At least, she told Maggie, the antique shop idea had the bonus of requiring a less expensive nanny, for she would be able to give a great deal more time to her baby. The difficulties of finding the right person, however, still filled her with gloom. How would she know whether an applicant would fit in with her and Simon, or drive them mad? How would they know if she would carry out their instructions implicitly regarding the handling and upbringing of their precious child, or whether she would go her own way regardless? They fretted; the whole area was a minefield, they told each other. The rector and Doctor Jane had their au pair Selma underfoot. No one, knowing them and having met Selma,

240

could imagine they found themselves soulmates. And Nancy Chubb gave her customers darkling looks as she hinted at terrible goings-on between the village lads and Selma, and added goodness knew what the children mightn't pick up from a young madam like her. Maggie and Louise were laughing over Nancy's wilder fancies when Maggie suddenly stopped dead and turned to stare at Louise.

'I've just had the most fantastic idea,' she exclaimed.

'What?'

'Boys, out of the river, please! You're getting soaked and the river gets deep there. No, now! Thank you. Lou, this antiques scheme – your hours will be entirely different. With a manager as your linchpin you could work part-time even.' She drew a deep breath. 'Why not use me as your child-minder? Bring the baby to me every day.'

Silence. A smile spreading. 'Would Jack agree?'

'Why not? He's been talking gloomily about the hellish expenses of our growing family. I could contribute!'

'Two babies? Wouldn't that be too much?'

'No. No worse than twins. Remember what an experienced mum I am. And you'd be mainly at home for the first few months, I take it.'

'It would solve a lot of problems,' Louise said fervently.

'All round! I'd charge you the going rate per hour, whatever that is. And I'd love it.'

They stared at each other in delight. Sheer genius, they agreed.

They parted at the little wicket gate to Louise's garden.

'Don't forget,' Maggie called as she turned to walk back with the boys, 'Bonfire Night next Saturday with all the annual rites. All our friends come. We burn our autumn leaves and prunings in a great fire down beyond the apple trees and set off every firework known to man. It's sensational. Then we go indoors to hot punch and baked potatoes and venison sausages and yummy things like that. See you then – and tell Simon about my offer.'

'Of course, but you must consult the boys as well as Jack.'

'I shall.'

'What? What? What?' The boys tugged at their mother's

241

arm and she towed them away, half-running, looking unexpectedly happy and released.

Louise watched half-abstractedly. 'Babies,' she thought. 'Babies, babies, babies.'

She turned to lean on the gate, looking at her garden. On the lawn was a lone and lovely tree whose leaves had turned a soft yellow and dropped beneath it to lie in a pool, like a still reflection. A Japanese maple. She had never seen anything so beautiful. She stood staring, wishing she could paint it. Then her eyes moved on towards the blue-flowered hibiscus at the back of the long border and the burning carmine red leaves of the vitis coignetiae on the cottage wall. It was all immaculately kept, hardly a leaf or a twig or a blade of grass out of place. Yet it looked somehow wrong beside the untidy and colourful riot of leaves and berries and dying goosegrass and Old Man's Beard that she had walked through by the river. It looked too ordered, too exact. She saw the figure of Simon walking round from the cottage, a rake in his hand.

She unlatched the gate and called to him breathlessly, 'Don't touch the maple leaves, please don't.'

He was smiling as he came across the lawn: 'I wasn't going to. Aren't they splendid?'

He dropped the rake and put his arms around her, smoothing her dark hair where the slight breeze had ruffled it and dropping a kiss on top of her head. She leaned against him and told him that she had finally come to a decision about the antiques gallery proposal. 'I shall do it,' she said, and then she told him of Maggie's unexpected suggestion.

They stood together talking and looking about them. 'It'll all work out just as we want,' Simon said. He indicated the yellow leaves. 'You missed these in the week by coming back at dusk from the train. Now you won't have to miss things. You're sure you won't mind leaving the Holbrooke Collection, losing your London days?'

She shook her head. 'There'll be so much more we can do together, so many more hours to do it in,' she said. 'And no hovering nanny about.' She thought of gardening, and of evening walks; she thought of the sofa and Vaughan William's 'Lark Ascending', and began to laugh softly: 'It'll be fun.'

'Yes,' he said, and he laughed too, as if he knew what was in her head. 'Us.'

'Us,' she agreed. It was their significant word.

Louise had wanted to tell Maggie of the discovery she and Simon had made over these autumn weeks, that being two people coupled together was not the same as being a couple. In unity you desired what benefitted the whole, that special being referred to as us. It demanded responsibility, it meant losing a part of yourself to create something new, something greater than its parts – and soon those parts would be three. It was a unity she had resisted for years, but in the last weeks succumbed to and found sweet. But she had not dared tell Maggie: she had had a feeling that Maggie would scoff and speak of copping out to preserve the peace, that she would cry as she had before: 'It's a matter of strength. There's a power balance in every relationship – why do women choose always to be the weak one?' She did not want her contentment marred.

'I'll see you at your party on Saturday,' Charley told Maggie over the telephone.

'No!' she hissed. 'No, you can't come.' She pushed the bedroom door shut with her foot, prayed Jack wouldn't pick up the telephone downstairs to discover who was telephoning this late. Half-past eleven. Ridiculous. Dangerous. She'd had to sprint half-naked from the bathroom to reach the telephone first and any second Jack might come up. 'No!'

'Why not?' Charley was saying. 'I like fireworks, I'm good with them. Learnt all about them in chemistry lessons. The boys'll have a great time with me there. Not like old Jack, pontificating about danger, chuntering on about history, turning it into a school lesson.'

'He won't and you're not to come. Seriously, no!' The time when she'd had loyalty and her own needs and Jack's short-comings all muddled up was over. Charley was laughing. Damn him, why couldn't he understand?

'I'm bringing old Brozie. I'll be good, I promise.'

'No, I don't want Jack upset. He suspects there's been something between us and I've barely managed to calm him down. Seeing you leering after me could undermine the last of his confidence.'

'He'll have to know soon. You're carrying my child and I'm not having him bringing up my child. You're going to leave him and live with me. You are – you know you are! We're made for each other. You can choose your own time to tell him, but do it soon, or I shall.'

'No!' She dropped the receiver as though it were a threatening animal she had grasped by mistake. She was frightened now, deeply frightened. Everything that she had ever striven for was under threat: her dull but always so reassuringly secure marriage, her children's planned and safe futures. The all-consuming desire to have another child had whirled her into dubious channels of lying, conniving and cheating; it had dominated her life to the exclusion of all prudence. She looked back in shock at her own ungoverned passion, her obsession. Now Charley was in the grip of a similar obsession, refusing to recognise impediments to his plans, refusing to admit that she had no similar wild love for him: he had built his dream castles in the air, and she must share them. If she couldn't get him under control shortly there would be an explosion of fireworks far more deadly than any of bonfire night's. She felt sick at the thought of the damage he could do to all their lives. It was not regrets that troubled her, but a deep desire for the peace and security she had threatened in her desperation and a sudden wrenching understanding of Jack's pain and fear. Poor Jack, poor miserable sod, she would make it up to him.

But oh God, how was she to deal with Charley?

By two o'clock on Saturday Brozie was concerned at Charley's lateness for lunch. He'd said he must work all morning with Tony. It was not the first time he had been late, sometimes spectacularly late, for meals, but normally he telephoned to tell her what incredible drama delayed him. Once he said a stag had leapt a hedge to land on his car and break a leg, another time he had rescued a woman whose car had burst into flames, getting his name in the papers for courage. She dialled his car phone number, tried his office and his house, no luck. She pondered nasty possibilities, then scolded herself for folly. Charley always turned up.

She knew him well enough now to cook meals that would keep; casseroles were her standby; they, like her, would wait without fuss. But she would fuss this time, it was too bad. She ate the spiced beef without tasting it and put Charley's portion back in the oven. Three o'clock.

Each time a car passed the house she thought, that's him, it must be. But it never was. No sight of the red car, no sound of his deep voice, only her robin fluttering on and off the windowsill, chirruping loudly. Goodness, his lunch was late too, poor little soul. She ran into the icy garden to toss him crumbs, came back comforted by the glimpse of her newly transformed house, all parchment and white outside, so pretty in the frost, while within it was all new warm carpets and curtains. Dear Charley, he'd helped her choose, as excited as she.

At four o'clock she scraped the dried out beef into the bin; at six she went to get changed for Maggie's Guy Fawkes party. Warm clothing was essential: knitted woolly knickers underneath like her mother used to wear – no one would know! – and a thermal vest, and on top her warm coat, a thick scarf, her green tweed hat and thick socks to go in her wellies. Properly cosy to enjoy herself; she had never been to a bonfire party before. She would leave a note for Charley secured to her letterbox. She did hope he would turn up at the Eastons' and join the fun. Goodness, she had such fun herself nowadays: new friends in the village, parties, Icarus Publishing, Charley joining her for supper most evenings, always so lively. And people who once hardly noticed her now stopped to talk over the hedge about her garden or to praise the church flowers. Was it her hats that had brought her out of the shadows, her new friends, or the absence of Hubert's glowering presence? No matter, it was delightful to be a somebody, no longer a nobody. She poured herself a tot of whisky, added hot water, lemon and honey; a little treat, just the thing for a cold evening and to stop her worrying about Charley. She told herself perhaps he'd bumped into old friends, forgotten his lunch with her. She wouldn't scold, so long as he was all right; so good he was to her.

At the Eastons' no one knew anything of Charley's where-abouts; nor did they seem worried for him. 'It's just that he's never let me down before, late, yes, but not appearing, never. He values his stomach too highly,' she told them, trying weakly to joke.

Jack Easton looked at Maggie and said nastily: 'Maybe he's found a new girlfriend.'

'He probably went to the races,' Simon Fennell said quickly.

'To waste his money on wild bets,' Jack concluded. He looked glum, the flesh on his face looked old and grey and his shoulders slumped as though he were tired to his bones.

'Come on, children,' Maggie ordered. 'Let's go out in the garden and light the bonfire, shall we?'

There were a dozen children; Brozie saw the Eastons' boys and the rector's two jostling by the back door, bouncing on the balls of their feet, anxious for the excitement to start. She smiled at them.

'I've brought lots of sparklers,' she said. 'Why don't we light them, then you can all take one in each hand to light the path?'

The small ones were rotund with extra clothes and scarves; the grass crunched beneath their feet as they made their way to the very bottom of the garden, squealing with a fear of the dark that was half real, half pretend, their breath smoking in the light of the sparklers that danced in the air like fireflies. There was an almost full moon and the sky was frosted over with stars. Brozie thought she had never seen so many. Beneath them the garden was black and white, shadowy and mysterious; there was a scent of cold and autumn, woodsmoke and compost heaps.

The bonfire was started and slow to catch at first, then with a whoosh it burst into flames, sending its own sparks, golden and wandering, wafting upwards. Brozie put her head back to watch them, thinking how magnificent the sight above her was, wondering about space and infinity, about time and God. Where were the dead in all this empti-ness, were their souls up in the heavens as she'd believed as a girl? Was Hubert up among the stars? Perhaps he was lost in a black hole somewhere. Certainly he was not

246

haunting her here on earth; she had nothing but a sense of total absence.

The first firework went up, a rain of colour lighting the garden, showing people's pale upturned faces, the Fennells with their arms round each other, Doctor Jane holding her small and amazed daughter, Maggie making sure her boys stood well back. The children jumped and murmured and laughed. Where was Charley, why wasn't he here to enjoy it with her, to laugh and joke and clown?

More fireworks, some singly, some together, bursting spectacularly and loudly overhead. Then came the rockets, soaring, vicious and splendid. Brozie covered her ears against the bangs. In the dark a small boy trod on her toe. 'Sorry!' he said. 'I didn't mean it.' A rocket's burst showed her Toby, his hands over his ears also, stepping backwards. She caught him by the shoulders, held him still beside her. He leaned against her leg and confided: 'The bangs are too loud. I'm not frightened though. Not really.'

She patted his shoulder. 'I don't like bangs.' It was strangely warming to have the little boy so close to her, needing the reassurance of her size and her age. She stood very still and oohed and aahed with him at Roman candles and Catharine wheels, his hand in hers.

Afterwards they all went indoors and drank the hot drinks and ate the warming food with their fingers and sighed with relief as they thawed.

The various guests were saying what a magnificent display it had been and struggling to sort out woolly hats and gloves in the hall when the rector arrived to collect his children and his wife. He stood blinking at the noise, and looking tired and somehow shocked.

'What is it?' his wife asked quickly.

'A tragedy.'

Jane pulled him into the sitting-room, sent out Toby and Eddie to help her Flora find her gloves, pushed the door to behind them and said: 'What? Who?'

The rector unwound his scarf and held the ends with both hands. 'Charley St George,' he told her. 'He's dead.'

247

Chapter 20

Beyond the door the children's voices chattered on.

'When?' Brozie said in a voice that was almost a howl. 'How?'

Maggie moved to stand beside her; her hand grasped Brozie's forearm, her eyes were very wide.

'It was early this morning, in Basingstoke. A toddler darted into the road in front of a bus. Charley saw and ran to hurl him out of the way . . . The bus hit him instead.'

'Oh my God!' Simon said.

'Sit down, Brozie,' Doctor Jane told her.

'I don't want to sit down,' she cried out. 'I want to know.'

'He died instantly,' Thomas said.

'How do you know?'

'I heard it on Solent Radio an hour ago. I rang the police. When I told them who I was they gave me the details. His family has been told.' His voice was quiet and gentle. 'There's no doubt, Brozie, he wouldn't have known a thing.'

'Except that he'd saved the child. He'd have known that, wouldn't he?' her voice implored them. 'His last thought. He was such a kind man.' Tears welled in her eyes and began to dampen her face. She fished a handkerchief from a sleeve and blotted them. 'Sorry,' she said.

'You'd better have a cup of tea,' Jane said. 'And there are others too who could probably do with it.'

'I'll put the kettle on,' Maggie said. She looked stunned and very white.

'Not for me,' Brozie said. 'If there's some wine left I'd rather have that. It seems more suitable for Charley. He never drank tea.' She wrenched her face into a grimace of a smile and Maggie nodded back.

'You're right. Wine it is. Jack?'

Jack, whose eyes had been focussed on his wife all this time, now jumped. 'Oh, yes. Wine. Of course.'

'Then we must say goodbye to our guests.' Her voice rebuked him. She opened the door to the hall and the sounds of the children's chattering voices, high-pitched still from the excitement of the fireworks, and the grown-ups' deeper conversations over their heads, sounded out of place, indecent almost. She flinched. But they did not know. She breathed deeply, lifted her head and went among them.

'Have your gloves been found yet, Flora? Oh, good. Put them on, sweetheart. And you've got your boots, Alex? Let's put them on your feet, shall we? And Lucian too. You're going now. Yes, see you at the playgroup on Monday. Jane, goodnight, and will you leave Thomas with us? Yes? Thank you. It's very good of you both to want to help. Yes, indeed, he can take Brozie home when she's ready and see she's all right.'

When the last feet had scrunched away over the gravelled drive, the last car swung out into the road, Maggie stood for a moment staring up into the night sky, at the moon hanging overhead, at the stars blinking as emotion pricked behind her eyes. There was a feeling of immensity, of eternity. Where was Charley now? Was he part of that immensity, or was all of him that had ever been encompassed by the body still shrouded in some Basingstoke hospital mortuary? Who could tell? Who would ever know? She wanted to stay in the quiet porch, thinking. Sadness pressed down upon her, sadness mingled with an almost unacknowledged relief, yet a depth of sadness that she dared not reveal in any way other than through the customary murmurs of shock and distress at the death of a man not yet thirty. Dear Charley, naughty Charley, dangerous Charley.

'I waited for him,' Brozie said in an amazed voice. 'I waited lunch for him. For hours and hours I waited. But I wouldn't let myself worry, I told myself not to be silly. He was often late . . . time didn't seem to mean the same to him as it did to other people. He always turned up in the end. But this time he was dead. It's unbelievable.'

249

She looked at the others, the tears flowing slowly, steadily, from her reddened eyes. She had not sobbed once, she retained her odd dignity under the green tweed hat. Only the tears would not stop.

She sipped her wine. She lifted her head. She said: 'He was like a nephew to me. I hadn't had any family for a long time. And then Charley came and he cared what happened to me. I thought of him as my nephew.'

The rector looked at her with his gentle look and remarked that while Charley had by no means been a regular attender at church he had been a wonderful support. 'He was a lover of the old and the traditional and that was why he spent time raising money for our church timbers fund. Once we had received what grants we could – and the Lord knows those were small enough – from the big charities like English Heritage, the majority of us could think only in small ways, of church fêtes and jumble sales, ways that Charley poured scorn on as pathetic. He thought big; he did what none of us had the courage to do, he went straight to the really rich – and he didn't ask so much as dare them not to give. He could make ridding a mediaeval church roof of death watch beetle sound not only the most worthy, but the most exciting cause ever supported. He could make the church sound very special indeed in terms of our architectural and historical inheritance.' He smiled reminiscently. 'He was a master of hyperbole, a genius of salesmanship. He raised all that we still needed.'

A murmur of approval and sympathy came from round him.

'But what about his businesses?' Brozie exclaimed. 'What's to become of them? Will his partner take over everything?'

Jack turned his tired face towards her. Even for a bonfire celebration he was wearing a tie and now that this terrible news had come to them his formality looked right: solid, traditional, undeviating. 'It will depend whether he had thought to make a will, or whether there is a partnership agreement. Knowing Charley, I doubt whether either will exist.'

Brozie took no notice of this last remark. 'I couldn't work with that partner of his. Not Tony, not alone. He's self-satisfied, he's lazy, he's arrogant and he's horrid.'

The room was quiet. For seconds nothing could be heard but the crackling of the log fire. Eyes looked at her in stupefaction.

She said defensively: 'I've invested in the publishing side. It means a lot to me.'

'Oh my God!' Jack said, his voice appalled. 'Whatever did you do that for?'

She took his exclamation literally, explaining: 'I had money from Hubert and I knew Charley was having cashflow problems with the publishing business so I suggested I should help him. He was . . . it was under-funded, you see. He was tremendously pleased.'

'You mean you really have invested?' Jack insisted. 'You've paid out money?'

'Yes,' she said proudly. Her eyes were dry now. 'We were planning to work together. He welcomed my offer.'

'But his businesses are in trouble. Charley was in trouble.'

'I know. He didn't hide it. He explained it to me.'

Jack shook his head and groaned. 'Did he also tell you he was bankrupt? That the business was on the verge of liquidation?'

A row of shocked faces stared at him.

'It's not true!' Brozie exclaimed, a hand going to her mouth.

'He went bankrupt at the end of June. June the twenty-third, to be exact. In the sum of eighty-one thousand pounds.'

'Oh, shut up, you ghoul! How the hell do you know anyway?' Maggie snarled.

'I . . .' He looked at her and looked away. He sighed. 'I made it my business to find out. I spoke to one or two of my Round Table acquaintances. Things were pointing in a certain direction. I rang the County Court. It's public information for those who wish to know.'

'Eighty-one thousand pounds,' Louise murmured. 'How on earth . . .?'

'Nothing too reprehensible,' Jack admitted. 'Essentially it was his property development in Southampton that let him down. Backed by an old school friend – an accountant, would you believe it? – he bought at the wrong time and the

251

wrong price and borrowed at ludicrous rates. Charley had grandiose ideas, believed he could make enormous profits. But as anyone like Simon or me can tell you there's a glut of office accommodation around at the present time. So . . . disaster.' He shrugged. 'When he ran into trouble and the bank wouldn't back him any longer, he tried to sell, but half-finished as it was the price had to be dropped heavily. I'm told it only sold very recently. Whatever the development fetched will have paid off something of his bankruptcy debts, that's all.'

'Oh, poor Charley,' Brozie breathed. 'Poor poor Charley. He must have been so worried. Why ever didn't he tell me?'

Jack's eyes were cynical but his voice was gentle as he replied: 'Someone like him would probably dismiss bankruptcy as a mere temporary setback. Only three years to wait before he could have a bank account once more, whether the bankruptcy was discharged or not. And he was such a wild optimist that he'd have been certain your investment would put Icarus Publishing back on its feet again, whatever the evidence to the contrary, whatever its debts. To tell you might have stopped you.'

'He'd never have deceived me on purpose, never!' Brozie declared passionately, glaring at him. 'He was my friend. Once I'd put my money in then the whole business was turned round and all the invoices met. We published several books this month, and they were good. Charley said it was all systems go.' She rushed on, scarlet-faced, her bony fists clenched. 'I've been told everything. I've seen their accounts and spoken to their accountant – nothing was put in my way, I was given every facility. I know.'

Jack, apparently feeling that he had gone a little too far, said nothing.

Goaded, Brozie flew at him again: 'Your informants are out of date, Jack, that's what it is. Icarus Publishing's on a secure footing now. You're libelling Charley. Take care what you say.'

The rector stirred. 'We cannot discuss this to any benefit until we know a great deal more of the facts,' he said. 'I must confess that I had no idea he had any financial problems. I knew him only as a person concerned for my church, a very attractive person, full of energy and determination and unusually generous with his time. As far as the PCC was concerned he was highly successful and we have nothing but praise for him. *De mortuis nil nisi bonum.* I had far rather we dwelt on the positive side and mourned a man who was our friend and gave a great deal to us in the village.'

The stupefied group in the room gave a murmur of agreement and fell silent. There was a moment's constraint while people glanced at each other only to avert their eyes. Louise thought how hopelessly tactless Jack had been with Brozie, suffering from shock as she was. No wonder Maggie became exasperated with him, no wonder Brozie had shouted. Then abruptly her thoughts swerved in the opposite direction: his lack of sensitivity, his indiscretion, were a hardly surprising reaction to the weeks of doubts and unhappiness Maggie had put him through with Charley. Jack was not the sort to advertise his misery to his neighbours, to tear his hair and rend his garments: he suffered in silence. Was it really so reprehensible to have vented his dislike and his suspicions of Charley's behaviour by making any normal solicitor's enquiries into his rival's probity? A wave of sympathy for poor kindly, well-intentioned, heavy-footed Jack swept through her. Whatever he did, she thought, he was a loser, a harbinger of ill-tidings, a man of gloom and doom. How random and ill-natured fate could be. She had wanted to give Brozie a hug of sympathy and comfort in her loss of the young man who had brought gaiety into her life, now she wanted to hug and comfort Jack; he had suffered his own loss.

'Cerberus!' Brozie exclaimed, her voice shaking. 'What became of Cerberus? He would have been with Charley at the time! Oh, poor boy, poor boy!'

'I have no information about the dog,' Thomas said, pushing back the thatch of his white hair and looking with worried blue eyes at Brozie. 'It may be that Charley's partner has taken care of him, or possibly his parents.'

'I want him,' Brozie declared, rising to her feet in her distraction. 'He wouldn't want to be with Tony, that man isn't the sort to care for a dog properly. Cerberus likes me, he should stay with me. I must ring the police straight away and find out what happened to him. Jack, can I please use your ...'

253

Thomas stood too, putting out his arm to stop her. He said with a kindly firmness: 'There'll be no one left who was on duty then to give you information. Wait till the morning and I shall find out and tell you. Now, I must get back to the rectory and I'll run you home as I go. Where are your coat and hat?' His words brooked no discussion; he put his hand under her elbow and ushered her into the hall.

A series of thuds followed by a crash and a shriek overhead led Maggie to say distractedly: 'It sounds as if the boys are re-enacting the Guy Fawkes incidents. I'd better shoo them off to bed before explosions start. Jack, look after Brozie and the rector and see them out, will you?'

As they departed Louise gave Simon a comprehensive up and down stare and said accusingly: 'You are pregnant with disaster, I know it. You have on that smug accountant's *I could see it all coming* look.'

He gave a short laugh and denied it. 'Nothing so clever. Only that everything is falling into place. Pure hindsight. The way Charley radiated happiness and confidence put me off his track. Can't you see it though, Louise? The deals he rushed around clinching? Those vast wads of notes he carried? The bank would have confiscated his cheque book and his credit cards well in advance of any bankruptcy hearing – his pocket had to be his bank. And he needed extra money. In folding notes.'

There were sounds of goodnights being called and the front door closing. Jack came back into the room and dropped heavily down on the sofa. He pressed his hands against his face, then lifted his head to look at Louise and Simon. 'Folding notes?' he said. 'His salary would have had to be paid in notes – bankrupts are allowed to keep a certain level of earnings. But if Icarus Publishing was in deep trouble – and that's my information – well, he'll not have got much from that source. Besides, a gossiping woman from Andover I met at Charley's party gave me to understand that the pattern had been going on for some time.'

'But where did those hoards of notes come from?' Louise asked.

'The horses most of all,' Simon guessed.

Louise chuckled suddenly. 'His mad system of increasing his bets by geometric progression. Melody said he'd make big winnings and take her out to dinner.'

'A great system when it works,' Simon said, exchanging wry glances with Jack, 'but disaster when it doesn't.'

'And when it worked he spent it – and when it didn't he laid low,' Jack said sardonically. 'He could keep going remarkably well on people's goodwill, you know. Friends fed him, he'll have taken all his petrol costs from his firm, even his fishing was free.' His voice was bitter.

'You kept your knowledge very quiet,' Louise said.

Jack shook his head. 'Much of it came in the last couple of days – and bonfire parties aren't normally the place for such revelations.'

'No,' Louise agreed, thinking, And you'd better keep quiet now.

Maggie came back into the room. Jack rose to pour her a drink but she refused it. 'No,' she said, not looking at him. 'Not good for me.' She looked very white and strained; even the skin of her face seemed tight. 'You can make me a cup of camomile tea instead.'

Jack nodded and went out silently.

'Poor Charley,' Maggie said. 'Poor poor Charley. Gone, just like that. Finished. Eternally. His poor parents.' She stared into the fire in silence for a minute, then she added: 'And that poor miserable sod of a bus driver. What must he feel like? But as for the mother of that child, I hope she's squirming. I hope he haunts her for ever. Why in hell's name didn't she keep hold of her child?'

'Don't dwell on it, Maggie, please,' Louise said.

'How can I not?'

'Try not.'

When Jack came back carrying a mug of tea Maggie clasped it in both her hands and continued staring at the now dying fire.

'We must go,' Simon said, 'And let you both go to bed. I think it's what Maggie needs. I'm sorry that the evening had to end so badly, Jack, but your fireworks were excellent. Maggie,' he stooped and kissed her cheek, 'take care of yourself and your infant. Goodnight.'

255

'Goodnight,' Louise echoed him, crouching beside Maggie to give her a hug.

Maggie looked up, abruptly, angrily. 'Death,' she said. 'I don't understand it. You believe it's for the old, something gentle at the very end when life's spent. But that's an illusion, it isn't. It's there, near you, all the time, waiting to blast you, waiting to blast the people you love. Life is so fragile, such a thin, thin thread between everything and nothing. Cut off, that's what they say, isn't it? Cut off in their prime. But why some people and not others? There's no reason to death, no sense. Why Felicity? Why Charley? It's so vicious, it's so random, it's so unfair.' Quietly she began to sob.

'You'd better go,' Jack told Louise and Simon as they hovered in doubt and concern. 'I'll take care of this. It is something I've dealt with before.'

'He was a nice man, Charley St George,' Nancy Chubb said, hanging broodingly over her checkout point in the village shop, 'a very nice man, I daresay, but he owed me money. There's no getting away from that. He promised he'd pay this week but now Mr Easton tells me we're not likely to see any of it. Said his firm went bust just three days after he died. Day before yesterday it was. Couldn't do without him selling, or something.'

She rang up the items of Louise's shopping with stabbing fingers as if she were totalling the sum of Charley's mendacity. Louise pushed packages into her bag and said without looking at Nancy that she hoped it wasn't too much.

'More than four hundred,' Nancy told her with a kind of obscure triumph. 'That's what comes of letting people run accounts. Got to compete with the supermarkets and superstores somehow, haven't we? So we give our customers special services and this is how they thank us.'

Louise tutted. From the corner of her eye she could see old George lift his head from his *Farmers' Weekly* to stare at Nancy in glee.

'It was his party did the big damage. Said he'd buy everything from us if we'd let him put it on the slate. Made out it would be easier with Mrs Hamilton and Mrs Easton that way, they doing the food for him. First he lost his cheque

256

book, then he said the bank had sent the replacement one to the wrong address . . . I don't know, always something. But then he made a joke of it, and it didn't seem so important.' She sighed gustily. 'Never thought I'd be a sucker.'

'You was soft,' George scoffed. 'You had a thing for him. Soft and quivering as a jelly you was when he came in!'

Nancy jumped and turned to glare at him. Livid, she told him to put her magazine down and go and do something useful. 'Get all the rubbish and car wrecks off that garden of yours, 'stead of hanging around wasting my time. How can we get to win Best Kept Village competition next year with the likes of you wrecking the place?'

'Best Village?' George jeered. 'What you think this is? A soppy suburb, all commuters an' pretty flower faces an' them 'anging baskets? I've 'eard you – I've 'eard women fussing about mud on the road and cowplops! This is the country, a place where there's farming going on, real work, man's work. Mr St George, he understood that, he liked it. Liked my old cars, too. Bought some parts off me, he did once. Paid me, too. Don't you go spreading nasty tales about him, he was a decent man, he wouldn't do no one down.' He flung *The Farmers' Weekly* on the floor and stomped out.

Charley's funeral was held in the village church and he was buried in the churchyard. His father told the rector over the telephone that it was what he would have wanted. He and his wife lived in Eastleigh and their parish church was a dark red brick Victorian Gothic monstrosity that Charley loathed. He had always wanted to live in the village, always loved the River Test, spoken with warmth of their old church; he had been happy in Abbotbridge in these last few months of his life: he should stay there now. Brozie wanted to provide drinks and food for the mourners at her house after the funeral, but Mr George thanked her and refused. The chap at The Bull was prepared to offer hot or any other kind of drink and sandwiches, and they had agreed on that. From what he had heard Mrs Hamilton had done a great deal for Charley, maybe too much; already he and his wife hardly knew how to thank her for her kindnesses.

The village was amused and not over-surprised to learn

that Charley St George was in fact plain Charles George. 'A pity though,' the rector said. 'The name suited him – a swashbuckling sort, he looked as though he could slay dragons.'

'He did,' Doctor Jane said. 'He slew the dragons in your church roof.'

The others gathered round the fire in the big old hearth at The Bull smiled and agreed. It was after the crowded funeral service and most of the mourners had said their goodbyes and slipped away. Just the village contingent and Melody now sat clutching their drinks and staring into the roaring heart of the blaze that had been built to warm them all. There had been a special bleak coldness in the wind that had buffeted and chilled the still figures in the churchyard on that November afternoon; now they sat, flushed and thawed, unwilling to face nature's rude curses outside while the air within quivered with heat and a ruddy comforting light.

'More drinks?' James Manningford suggested. 'Arabella?'

'Whisky,' she replied promptly. 'It's doing me good.'

'Brozie?'

'Oh, how very kind!' she said in a flurry. 'But no, I must get back to poor Cerberus and take him for his walk before it gets dark. He needs reassurance and care. He had a bad time for more than a day wandering Basingstoke, you know, trying to find Charley – it makes me want to cry every time I think of it. Wasn't it good of Charley's parents to let me have him? He's going to be such a companion.' She stood up, looking vaguely for her coat.

'Allow me,' the rector said, retrieving it from a nearby chair and helping her into it. 'I'm sure Cerberus will have a happy home with you. Now, can I run you back?'

'Oh no,' she said, adjusting her best burgundy-coloured hat to a more perky angle. 'No, no, it's really no distance. You stay here and keep warm.' She waved to the others and went out on a chorus of goodbyes that were full of sympathy and goodwill.

'Poor thing,' Simon said, turning back to the fire and accepting another whisky from the landlord's tray. 'She's bearing up remarkably well. Has she really lost a great deal of money, Jack?'

'I suppose strictly I shouldn't say anything, but since she's made no secret of it I will say that she's lost some money Hubert Hamilton left her, but that she won't be destitute.'

'A bit strapped for cash, eh?' James Manningford said.

'She spoke of possibly having a lodger,' Maggie said, sighing.

'But what about The Old Barn?' Simon asked in puzzlement. 'Is there no money to be raised there?'

There was a moment's silence, then Arabella Manningford said: 'But Charley never owned it. It's ours still. We couldn't find a buyer at our price so we let him have it at a reasonable rent. He spoke of being in a position to buy it shortly; we hoped it might work out.'

'Good Lord!'

'He owed us for almost three months, too,' James admitted ruefully.

'Ouch,' Doctor Jane said.

'But what went wrong for the poor man?' Louise wanted to know.

'Vaulting ambition,' Jack said sourly. 'He and that partner of his, Tony Smithson, set up their vanity publishing business with little money and less experience. It's an area that notoriously attracts rogues. Tony Smithson ran the publishing side, Charley rustled up the clients and dealt with the marketing. My informants tell me Charley was brilliant at both, but, and it's a big but, on the finance side he was useless, and he needed expertise, badly needed it, because this fellow Tony was lazy, inefficient and self-satisfied. The clients rolled in and paid their money up-front, and for many months the firm's accounts gave the impression of being in excellent order – at a cursory glance. However, the books were not rolling off the presses at even half the speed they should have been. Mistakes were made, overheads mounted up, the pair of them overpaid themselves and their staff too – they were both given to lavish gestures – and the money steadily evaporated, leaving angry and upset men and women shouting either for their books to be produced tomorrow or for their money back. It was at this point that Charley must have pursuaded Brozie to step in . . .'

'Brozie offered,' Maggie interrupted swiftly. 'And she

didn't go into it blindfold, she checked with the bank manager and with the accountant.'

'The bank manager,' Simon pointed out drily, 'would probably have welcomed her interest with open arms. Icarus Publishing's large overdraft would have aroused the ire of Head Office and someone who might pay off that overdraft and turn the firm round would have seemed a Godsend. He wouldn't have deterred Brozie if he thought there was any hope for the firm. Who were the accountants? Not my lot, I do know that.'

Jack named a well-known local firm, adding: 'They sent a girl called Holly Brooks along.'

'Ooh,' Simon said in a thoughtful drawl. 'That could well explain it. I've met her. Nice girl but naive. No match for Charley's chat and charm and his salesmanship.'

'If either of you is implying that Charley was a con man,' Maggie said coldly, 'that just is not true. Charley believed whole-heartedly in Icarus Publishing – and in everything else he was doing.'

'He did, didn't he?' Louise put in thoughtfully, before Jack or Simon could reply. 'He mentioned setbacks to me once or twice, but in general he was convinced he was going to make his fortune. If he hadn't he would never have been so happy. And he was happy, he was always happy.'

'Permanent happiness,' Doctor Jane said in a detached and clinical voice, 'is a rare thing, but it is a phenomenon doctors do come across in their practices from time to time. It's most clearly seen in people suffering from mania – the other end of the mood spectrum from depression.'

'Charley wasn't manic,' her husband protested. 'Bouncy, yes, talkative and delightfully cheerful, but not manic, surely!'

'I'm not saying that,' Jane returned. 'Let me put it in a different way. One might say that he was one of the chronically happy. To be so is almost a psychiatric disorder in its own right. People in that condition ignore upsetting events in their lives, they often indulge in spending sprees, and they over-estimate their own capacities – and others' too.'

'That sounds like Charley,' Simon said, interested.

'I'm theorising,' Jane admitted.

'You may be on the right track,' James Manningford said abruptly. 'Do please go on.'

'Reality slippage,' Jane said. 'If reality bears an ugly face its existence is dismissed. The most famous sufferer from chronic happiness was Mozart. His refusal ever to contemplate failure was an integral part of his genius. His setbacks – and he had many concerts that were financial disasters – he invariably attributed to outside causes. Fate was for him and he would succeed, and so he blithely pressed on – unlike depressives who believe that fate is against them and that it is their fault. Towards the end of his life, when Mozart had lost four children, he was suffering serious illness and had repeated financial and professional catastrophes, his letters show him as even more optimistic.' She paused for a mouthful or two of hot coffee while her audience murmured 'Strange man!' and 'How extraordinary!' Then she continued: 'People like Charley are few and far between and we find them highly attractive because of their energy and their gaiety – but chronic happiness is a dangerous happiness.'

Silence. A log in the hearth suddenly hissed, blowing off bubbles and blue flames. Another log tumbled forward to lie smoking on the hearth, sending thin white puffs of smoke wavering up towards the ceiling. Jack thrust out a leg to kick it back into position on the red embers.

'You're right about its being a dangerous happiness,' Melody said with emphasis, twisting her long hair round and round with a thin hand. She had spoken little so far and her neighbours swung round in surprise. 'Sometimes living with Charley was lovely, red roses and new clothes for me and gorgeous meals out where he knew everyone, but then when things went wrong he'd get threatening letters about bills and all he'd do would be to say "Bin job!" and chuck them away. Sometimes he'd rush off chasing deals, sometimes he wouldn't bother: "Let them sweat for it!" he'd say, and he'd laugh. But it wasn't a laughing matter when they came after him. A man he bought building materials from for his development, well, the cheque Charley gave him bounced so first he kept phoning and being horrible, then he appeared at the door and wanted to beat him up, but Charley was too big and he told him the doors he'd sold him were rubbish – just take

261

them away. He mocked this man, so then he threatened me. He said he'd break my arms if Charley didn't pay up. He was dangerous. I got out.'

'Oh my God,' someone said.

'I miss him,' Brozie said sadly to Louise and Arabella Manningford. 'I understand now he was careless with other people's money, I know he was naughty, but I'll never believe he meant to do any harm. It was just the way he was. Maggie told me what the doctor said. He wasn't wilful, he just wanted everyone to be happy – like him. Who could be nicer than that? He did make me happy too, just when I was really wondering how I could go on. He changed my life and I miss him so much.'

They were standing talking by the church porch after the Sunday morning service. It was a crisply bright December day and they were hatted and scarved and booted against the chill, but the pale sunshine was pleasant to stand in for a moment, looking down the slope into Abbotsbridge and seeing its houses lying glittering beside the sparkling river, thatched roofs all rimmed with silver and the flint walls and outhouses gleaming with the frost that had come in the night. The grass crunched beneath their feet as they shifted them about to keep warm and their breath smoked.

Louise nodded in understanding. 'We all miss him,' she said. 'He changed my life too, you know.'

'And mine,' Arabella acknowledged.

Brozie blinked. 'How did he change your life, Mrs Manningford?'

'Louise and I are going into partnership to run an antiques business in Winchester. I needed a focus for my energies and with her baby coming Louise wanted to give up her London work and find a new career round here – Charley came up with this brilliant idea.'

Brozie looked at Louise. 'But I thought you were so set on your work with the Holbrooke Collection. You gave us that lovely lecture at the WI. Are you truly going to give all that up?'

'Yes, in a month or so, when our plans have progressed a little further then I shall resign. But I shan't lose touch

262

entirely. I shall still be happy to give lectures on the Collection.'

'You'll miss it,' Brozie said. 'I've always thought it was one of the loveliest places to visit in London.'

'It is, isn't it? But to continue meant seeing little of my husband and baby, and then only at the beginning of the day in a rush and at the end in exhaustion. So it had to be. I find myself regretting it far less than I thought.'

Aylmer Littlejohn's reaction to her pregnancy had been one of shocked animosity. He supposed she would have to have maternity leave and that a temporary replacement would have to be found for her, but had she ever considered the difficulties that would cause for her colleagues? He trusted this would not be a regular occurrence. She knew now how deep a relief it would be to be free of his manoeuvres and manipulations, to be away from his antipathy and from the poor working atmosphere he engendered, not only with her, but with any of his colleagues who were not his admirers and toadies. But not even these would support her when Aylmer played out his nasty games with her – how could they? They were too busy protecting their own backs. Aylmer was more clever, more Machiavellian, than she had realised. Louise had hoped that perhaps sisterly solidarity might persuade Josie to back her, but she saw clearly now, and without bitterness, that she had been foolish to expect her friend to fight on her behalf. Josie was ambitious, she coveted the post of director and was on course to gain it on merit. To attack the current incumbent would appear blatantly self-serving. Considering this and the fact that Josie was only just back at work after her own baby, Louise saw that the most she could expect would be the occasional mild comment: Josie would never jeopardise her own position.

Louise rubbed the backs of her gloved hands against the cold and added: 'Now I shall be able to enjoy family life as well as my sort of work – locally.'

'My sort of work too,' Brozie said. 'My father was an antique dealer and restorer as well as Hubert. When I was young I used to help Father. I loved it; it's always been part of my life.'

'You could be most useful to us then,' Arabella

Manningford said, pouncing. 'What luck. We believe we've found the right premises, we're only waiting for the surveyor's report before having the contract drawn up. Now we have to find a manager, someone thoroughly knowledgeable and sensible, whom we'd like. You may well know of someone, or at any rate have contacts who could put us in touch with the right person.'

Brozie stared at them both for so long, her eyes travelling from face to face, that Louise almost thought she had been struck dumb. Then she licked her lips, cleared her throat uncertainly and said with a slight stammer of eagerness: 'You wouldn't . . . wouldn't consider me . . . me, would you? I know I'm a little old, but I'm not out of touch. Hubert only . . . only retired four years ago and the knowledge doesn't go. Antiques don't get out of date, do they? Accounts are not a problem, and I'm not that out of date with prices – and I always read the trade journals.'

Their eyes fixed upon her hopeful face and stared back.

'It is a possibility,' Arabella Manningford said.

'It could be,' Louise agreed tentatively. 'How about . .?'

'Yes,' Arabella said. 'She could discuss the stuff in the Abbotsbridge House attics with us, see if our views run together. You see, Brozie, there's discarded furniture from the house up there as well as pieces I inherited from my mother. The best I shall keep for my children, the major part is to become the first stock for the shop. How about that?'

Brozie nodded.

'You really feel you want to do this? Think it over.'

'I don't need to. The way things have panned out, well, I definitely could do with some extra income. But above all I need the interest. I've never been on my own before, I've always had someone to look after – recently it was Charley – now I've no one. This would be so right for me.' A thought struck her. 'You wouldn't mind having Cerberus in the shop? He's a good guard dog.'

They laughed. 'Not so long as he kept that muscular ever-wagging tail of his away from the porcelain,' Louise said, stamping her chilling feet on the path.

'Brrr,' Arabella said, clasping her arms about herself. 'I must go before I freeze to the spot. Come to my house tomorrow evening before dinner, Brozie, and you too, Louise, if you can manage it, and we'll talk. That all right? Good. Now, where's James? Oh, look, waiting patiently for me by the car – isn't he an angel? 'Bye!'

Maggie, who had been talking to the rector, left her sons to leap and gambol among the graves and came over to talk to Louise and Brozie.

'What was all the animated conversation about?'

Louise explained with Brozie listening and occasionally interpolating excitedly. Then she turned to Brozie and drew her the word picture Charley had once drawn for her of beautiful galleries in an old building in Winchester, filled with specially lovely pieces of furniture and porcelain, with pictures on the walls in regularly changing exhibitions, the subtle lighting that would make the most of every piece, and told her of the parties they would have to inaugurate each exhibition, drawing the elegant crowds of clients to flock there and look and exclaim and buy. Brozie was entranced, more enthusiastic than ever. She clutched Maggie's arm.

'These were Charley's ideas? He was a genius with ideas. He was, wasn't he? My parents and Hubert would never have thought of such things.' She reiterated, shyly but with determination, that Charley had changed her life, moving her from deep depression to contentment. 'He may have been naughty, even dangerous in his wild optimism, but he made me come alive. Maybe even now he's looking down from Heaven to help me.'

'It could be,' Maggie said, her eyes sympathetic. She had felt her daughter's presence with her at times. 'My life was sad after Felicity's death. He cheered me in a way no one else did. He . . .' She gave Brozie an odd little smile. 'You could say he gave me new life.'

'All of us were changed by him in some way,' Brozie said softly. 'And not for the worse, after all. He couldn't be altogether bad, could he?' And she looked comforted.

Births

FENNELL – On 2nd April 1994, to Louise (née Bennett) and Simon, a son, Alexander Simon.

EASTON – On 19th May 1994 to Margaret (née Dunn) and Jack, twin daughters, Charlotte Felicity and Jacqueline Rosemary, sisters for the boys.